AUTONOMOUS

She put the food in front of him. "I'm Jack."

He ignored her, taking a sip from the bowl, then dunking the bread in and biting off a chunk. Jack leaned on the counter and watched, wondering if the kid even had a name. Families with nothing would sometimes sell their toddlers to indenture schools, where managers trained them to be submissive just like they were programming a bot. At least bots could earn their way out of ownership after a while, be upgraded, and go fully autonomous. Humans might earn their way out, but there was no autonomy key that could undo a childhood like that.

"I'm Threezed," he responded finally, breaking Jack out of her spaced reverie. He'd swallowed about half the broth and his face didn't look quite as blank as it had before. It was hard to miss the fact that the last two numbers branded onto his neck were three and zed. That scar was his name, too. Jack folded her arms over the sudden stab of sympathy in her chest.

"Nice to meet you, Threezed."

AUTONOMOUS

ANNALEE NEWITZ

www.orbitbooks.net

ORBIT

First published in Great Britain in 2017 by Orbit

1 3 5 7 9 10 8 6 4 2

Grateful acknowledgment is given for permission to reprint the song lyrics
"The Last Saskatchewan Pirate" by The Arrogant Worms.

A CIP catalogue record for this book
is available from the British Library.

ISBN 978-0-356-51122-1

Printed and bound by CPI Group (UK) Ltd, Croydon CR0 4YY

Papers used by Orbit are from well-managed forests
and other responsible sources.

Orbit
An imprint of
Little, Brown Book Group
Carmelite House
50 Victoria Embankment
London EC4Y 0DZ

An Hachette UK Company
www.hachette.co.uk

www.orbitbooks.net

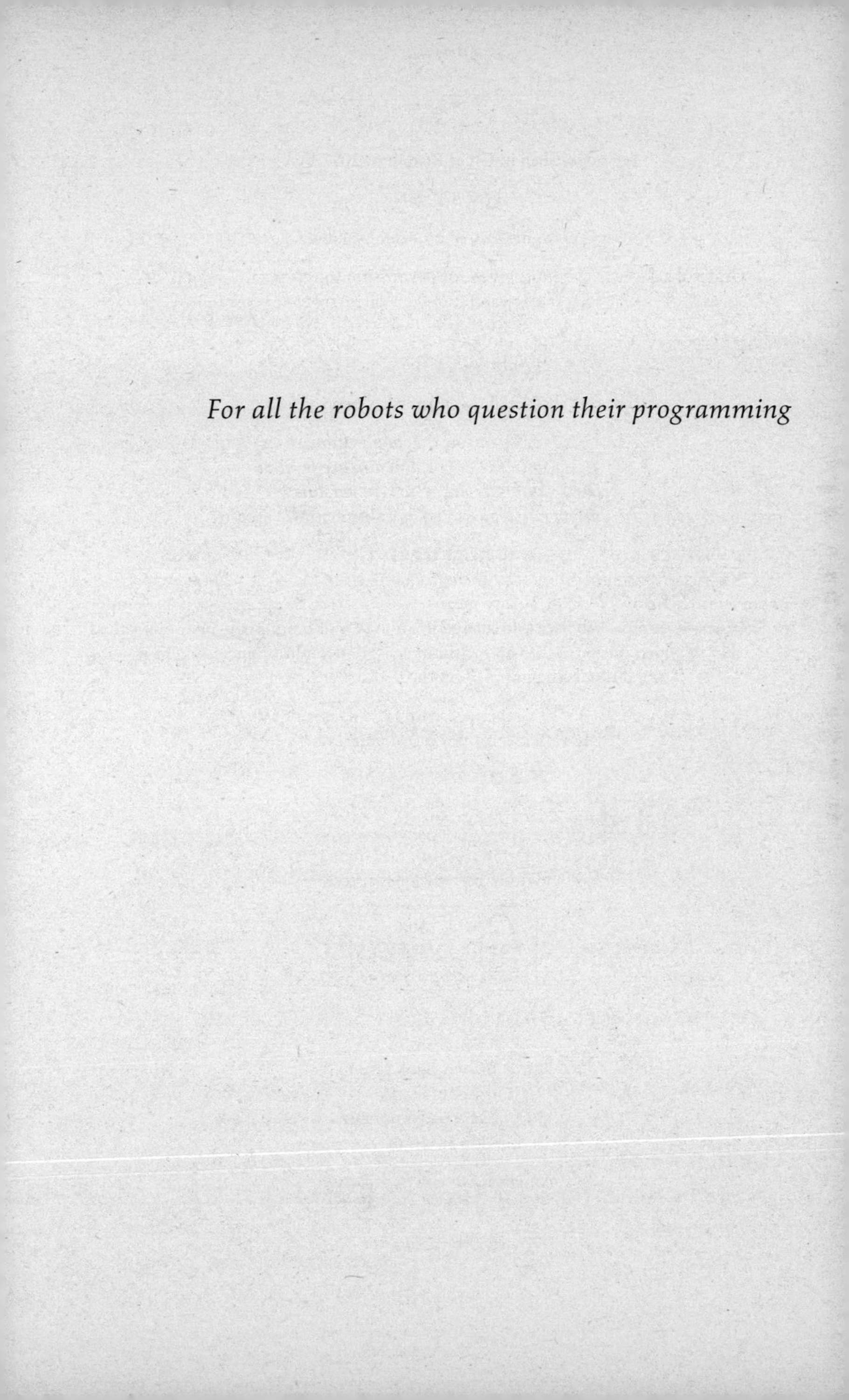

For all the robots who question their programming

THE LAST SASKATCHEWAN PIRATE

From a late twentieth-century ballad
by The Arrogant Worms

I used to be a farmer and I made a living fine
I had a little stretch of land along the C.P. line
But times were hard, and though I tried, the money wasn't there
And bankers came and took my land, and told me "fair is fair."

I looked for every kind of job, the answer always no
"Hire you now?" they'd always laugh. "We just let twenty go!"
The government they promised me a measly little sum
But I've got too much pride to end up just another bum.

Then I thought, who gives a damn if all the jobs are gone,
I'm gonna be a pirate on the river Saskatchewan.

'Cause it's a heave-ho, high-ho, coming down the Plains
Stealing wheat and barley and all the other grains
And it's a ho-hey, high-hey, farmers bar your doors
When you see the Jolly Roger on Regina's mighty shores.

You'd think the local farmers would know that I'm at
large
But just the other day I saw an unsuspecting barge
I snuck up right behind them and they were none the
wiser
I rammed their ship and sank it, and I stole their
fertilizer.

A bridge outside of Moose Jaw spans a mighty river
Farmers cross in so much fear their stomachs are
a-quiver
'Cause they know that Tractor Jack is hiding in the bay,
I'll jump the bridge and knock them cold and sail off
with their hay.

1

PIRATE SHIP

JULY 1, 2144

The student wouldn't stop doing her homework, and it was going to kill her. Even after the doctors shot her up with tranquilizers, she bunched into a sitting position, fingers curled around an absent keyboard, typing and typing. Anti-obsessives had no effect. Tinkering with her serotonin levels did nothing, and the problem didn't seem to be dissociation or hallucination. The student was perfectly coherent. She just wouldn't stop reimplementing operating system features for her programming class. The only thing keeping her alive was a feeding tube the docs had managed to force up her nose while she was in restraints.

Her parents were outraged. They were from a good neighborhood in Calgary, and had always given their daughter access to the very best pharma money could buy. How could anything be going wrong with her mind?

The doctors told reporters that this case had all the hallmarks of drug abuse. The homework fiend's brain showed a perfect addiction pattern. The pleasure-reward loop, shuttling neurotransmitters between the midbrain and cerebral cortex, was on fire. This chemical configuration was remarkable because her brain looked like she'd been addicted to homework for years. It was completely wired for this specific reward, with dopamine receptors showing patterns that normally emerged only after years of addiction. But the student's family and friends insisted she'd never had this problem until a few weeks ago.

It was the perfect subject for a viral nugget in the medical mystery slot of the All Wonders feed. But now the story was so popular that it was popping up on the top news modules, too.

Jack Chen unstuck the goggles from her face and squeezed the deactivated lenses into the front pocket of her coveralls. She'd been working in the sun's glare for so long that pale rings circled her dark brown eyes. It was a farmer's tan, like the one on her father's face after a long day wearing goggles in the canola fields, watching tiny yellow flowers emit streams of environmental data. Probably, Jack reflected, the same farmer's tan had afflicted every Chen for generations. It went back to the days when her great-great-grandparents came across the Pacific from Shenzhen and bought an agricultural franchise in the prairies outside Saskatoon. No matter how far she was from home, some things did not change.

But some things did. Jack sat cross-legged in the middle of the Arctic Sea, balanced on the gently curving, uncanny invisibility of her submarine's hull. From a few hundred kilometers above the surface, where satellites roamed, the sub's negative refractive index would bend light until Jack seemed to float incongruously atop the waves. Spread next to her in the bright water was an undulating sheet of nonreflective solar panels. Jack made a crumpling gesture with her hand and the solar array swarmed back into its dock, disappearing beneath a panel in the hull.

The sub's batteries were charged, her network traffic was hidden in a blur of legitimate data, and she had a hold full of drugs. It was time to dive.

Opening the hatch, Jack banged down the ladder to the control room. A dull green glow emerged in streaks on the walls as bacterial colonies awoke to illuminate her way. Jack came to a stop beneath a coil of ceiling ducts. A command line window materialized helpfully at eye level, its photons organized into the shape of a screen by thousands of projectors circulating in the air. With a swipe, she pulled up the navigation system and altered her heading to avoid the heavily trafficked shipping lanes. Her destination was on a relatively quiet stretch of the Arctic coast, beyond the Beaufort Sea, where freshwater met sea to create a vast puzzle of rivers and islands.

But Jack was having a hard time concentrating on the mundane tasks at hand. Something about that homework-addiction story was bugging her. Mashing the goggles over her eyes again, she reimmersed in the feed menu. Glancing through a set of commands, she searched for more information. "HOMEWORK FIEND CASE REEKS OF BLACK-MARKET PHARMA," read one headline. Jack sucked in her breath. Could this clickbait story be about that batch of Zacuity she'd unloaded last month in Calgary?

The sub's cargo hold was currently stacked with twenty crates of freshly pirated drugs. Tucked among the many therapies for genetic mutations and bacterial management were boxes of cloned Zacuity, the new blockbuster productivity pill that everybody wanted. It wasn't technically on the market yet, so that drove up demand. Plus, it was made by Zaxy, the company behind Smartifex, Brillicent, and other popular work enhancement drugs. Jack had gotten a beta sample from an engineer at Vancouver's biggest development company, Quick Build Wares. Like a lot of biotech corps, Quick Build handed out new attention enhancers for free along with their in-house employee meals. The prerelease ads said that Zacuity helped everyone get their jobs done faster and better.

Jack hadn't bothered to try any Zacuity herself—she didn't need drugs to make her job exciting. The engineer who'd provided the sample described its effects in almost religious terms.

You slipped the drug under your tongue, and work started to feel *good*. It didn't just boost your concentration. It made you *enjoy* work. You couldn't wait to get back to the keyboard, the breadboard, the gesture table, the lab, the fabber. After taking Zacuity, work gave you a kind of visceral satisfaction that nothing else could. Which was perfect for a corp like Quick Build, where new products had tight ship dates, and consultants sometimes had to hack a piece of hardware top-to-bottom in a week. Under Zacuity's influence, you got the feelings you were supposed to have after a job well done. There were no regrets, nor fears that maybe you weren't making the world a better place by fabricating another networked blob of atoms. Completion reward was so intense that it made you writhe right in your plush desk chair, clutching the foam desktop, breathing hard for a minute or so. But it wasn't like an orgasm, not really. Maybe it was best described as physical sensation, perfected. You could feel it in your body, but it was more blindingly good than anything your nerve endings might read as inputs from the object-world. After a Zacuity-fueled work run, all you wanted to do was finish another project for Quick Build. It was easy to see why the shit sold like crazy.

But there was one little problem, which she'd been ignoring until now. Zaxy didn't make data from their clinical trials available, so there was no way to find out about possible side effects. Normally Jack wouldn't worry about every drug freak-out reported on the feeds, but this one was so specific. She couldn't think of any other popular substances that would get someone addicted to homework. Sure, the student's obsessive behavior could be set off by a garden-variety stimulant. But then it would hardly be a medical mystery, since doctors would immediately find evidence of the stimulant in her system. Jack's mind churned as if she'd ingested a particularly nasty neurotoxin. If this drug was her pirated Zacuity, how had this happened? Overdose?

Maybe the student had mixed it with another drug? Or Jack had screwed up the reverse engineering and created something horrific?

Jack felt a twitch of fear working its way up her legs from the base of her spine. But wait—this shiver wasn't just some involuntary, psychosomatic reaction to the feeds. The floor was vibrating slightly, though she hadn't yet started the engines. Ripping off the goggles, she regained control of her sensorium and realized that somebody was banging around in the hold, directly behind the bulkhead in front of her. What the actual fuck? There was an aft hatch for emergencies, but how—? No time to ponder whether she'd forgotten to lock the doors. With a predatory tilt of the head, Jack powered up her perimeter system, its taut nanoscale wires networked with sensory nerves just below the surface of her skin. Then she unsnapped the sheath on her knife. From the sound of things, it was just one person, no doubt trying to grab whatever would fit in a backpack. Only an addict or someone truly desperate would be that stupid.

She opened the door to the hold soundlessly, sliding into the space with knife drawn. But the scene that met her was not what she expected. Instead of one pathetic thief, she found two: a guy with the scaly skin and patchy hair of a fusehead, and his robot, who was holding a sack of drugs. The bot was some awful, hacked-together thing the thief must have ripped off from somebody else, its skin layer practically fried off in places, but it was still a danger. There was no time to consider a nonlethal option. With a practiced overhand, Jack threw the knife directly at the man's throat. Aided by an algorithm for recognizing body parts, the blade passed through his trachea and buried itself in his artery. The fusehead collapsed, gagging on steel, his body gushing blood and air and shit.

In one quick motion, Jack yanked out her knife and turned to the bot. It stared at her, mouth open, as if it were running something seriously buggy. Which it probably was. That would be good for Jack, because it might not care who gave it orders as long as they were clear.

"Give me the bag," she said experimentally, holding her hand out. The sack bulged with tiny boxes of her drugs. The bot handed it over instantly, mouth still gaping. He'd been built to look like a boy in his teens, though he might be a lot older. Or a lot younger.

At least she wouldn't have to kill two beings today. And she might get a good bot out of the deal, if her botadmin pal in Vancouver pitched in a little. On second glance, this one's skin layer didn't look so bad, after all. She couldn't see any components peeking through, though he was scuffed and bloody in places.

"Sit down," she told him, and he sat down directly on the floor of the hold, his legs folding like electromagnetically joined girders that had suddenly lost their charge. The bot looked at her, eyes vacant. Jack would deal with him later. Right now, she needed to do something with his master's body, still oozing blood onto the floor. She hooked her hands under the fusehead's armpits and pulled his remains through the bulkhead door into the control room, leaving the bot behind her in the locked hold. There wasn't much the bot could do in there by himself, anyway, given that all her drugs were designed for humans.

Down a tightly coiled spiral staircase was her wet lab, which doubled as a kitchen. A high-grade printer dominated one corner of the floor, with three enclosed bays for working with different materials: metals, tissues, foams. Using a smaller version of the projection display she had in the control room, Jack set the foam heads to extrude two cement blocks, neatly fitted with holes so she could tie them to the dead fusehead's feet as easily as possible. As her adrenaline levels came down, she watched the heads race across the printer bed, building layer after layer of matte-gray rock. She rinsed her knife in the sink and resheathed it before realizing she was covered in blood. Even her face was sticky with it. She filled the sink with water and rooted around in the cabinets for a rag.

Loosening the molecular bonds on her coveralls with a shrug, Jack felt the fabric split along invisible seams to puddle around her feet. Beneath plain gray thermals, her body was roughly the same shape it had been for two decades. Her cropped black hair showed only a few threads of white. One of Jack's top sellers was a molecule-for-molecule reproduction of the longevity drug Vive, and she always quality-tested her own work. That is, she *had* always quality tested it—until Zacuity. Scrubbing her face, Jack tried to juggle the two horrors at once: A man was dead upstairs, and a student in Calgary was in serious danger from something that sounded a lot like black-market Zacuity. She dripped on the countertop and watched the cement blocks growing around their central holes.

Jack had to admit she'd gotten sloppy. When she reverse engineered the Zacuity, its molecular structure was almost exactly like what she'd seen in dozens of other productivity and alertness drugs, so she hadn't bothered to investigate further. Obviously she knew Zacuity might have some slightly undesirable side effects. But these fun-time worker drugs subsidized her real work on antivirals and gene therapies, drugs that saved lives. She needed the quick cash from Zacuity sales so she could keep handing out freebies of the other drugs to people who desperately needed them. It was summer, and a new plague was wafting across the Pacific from the Asian Union. There was no time to waste. People with no credits would be dying soon, and the pharma companies didn't give a shit. That's why Jack had rushed to sell those thousands of doses of untested Zacuity all across the Free Trade Zone. Now she was flush with good meds, but that hardly mattered. If she'd caused that student's drug meltdown, Jack had screwed up on every possible level, from science to ethics.

With a beep, the printer opened its door to reveal two perforated concrete bricks. Jack lugged them back upstairs, wondering the entire time why she had decided to carry so much weight in her bare hands.

2
BOOTING

JULY 2, 2144

Sand had worked its way under Paladin's carapace, and his actuators ached. It was the first training exercise, or maybe the fortieth. During the formatting period, it was hard to maintain linear time; memories sometimes doubled or tripled before settling down into the straight line that he hoped would one day stretch out behind him like the crisp, four-toed footprints that followed his course through the dunes.

Paladin used millions of lines of code to keep his balance as he slid-walked up a slope of fine grains molded into ripples by wind. Each step punched a hole in the dune, forced him to bend at the waist to keep steady. Sand trickled down his body, creating tiny scars in the dark carbon alloy of his carapace. Lee, his botadmin, had thrown him out of the jet at 1500 hours, somewhere far north in African Federation space. Coming down was easy. He remembered doing it before, angling his body in a configuration that kept him from overheating, unfurling the shields on his back until they cupped the wind, then landing with a jolt to his shocks.

But this wasn't just another repeat of the same old obstacle course. It was a test mission.

Lee had told Paladin that a smuggler's stash was hidden somewhere in the dunes. His job was to approach from the south, map the space, try to find the stash, and come back with all the data he could. The botadmin grinned as he delivered these instructions, gripping Paladin's shoulder. "I tweaked some of your drivers just for this test. You're going to float up those dunes like a goddamn butterfly."

Now it was an hour until sundown, and Paladin's carapace bent the light until it slid below the visible spectrum. To human eyes, his dark body on the dune's summit would look like a shimmer of heat in the air, especially from a distance. That's what he was counting on, anyway. He needed to get a sense of the area, its hiding places, before anyone figured out a bot was prowling.

Pale, reddish swells softened the landscape in every direction. The sand was totally undisturbed—if anyone had been walking around here, the wind had blown their tracks away. The stash had to be underground, if it was even here at all. Paladin stood still, lenses zooming and panning, searching for a glint of antennas or other signs of habitation. He cached everything in memory for analysis later.

There it was: a crescent of chrome unburied by wind. He scrambled down the dune, making hundreds of small adjustments to avoid falling on the slithering ground, getting a precise location on a portal that probably led to a buried structure below. He would yank it open and get back to the lab. Lee would clean the sand from his muscles, and there would be no more of this grinding discomfort.

As Paladin reached out, ready to pull or torque the lock mechanism, a hidden sniper tore his right arm off at the shoulder. It was the first true agony of his life. He felt the wound explode across his whole torso, followed by a prickling sear of unraveled molecular bonds along the burned fringes of his stump. Out of this pain bloomed a memory of booting up his operating system, each program calling the next out of nothing. He wanted to go back into that nothing. Anything to escape this scalding horror, which seemed to pour through his body and beyond it. Paladin's sensorium still included his severed arm, which was broadcasting its status to the bot with a short-range signal. He'd have to kill his perimeter network to make the arm go silent. But without a perimeter he was practically defenseless, so he was stuck feeling a torment that echoed between the inside and outside of his body. Throwing himself down into the sand, Paladin used his wing shields to protect his remaining circuitry—especially his single biological part, nested deep inside the place where humans might carry a fetus.

He scrabbled with his remaining hand at the portal and it opened with a gasp, the air pressure differential seeming to inhale him. Another bolt smashed into the sand next to his head, puddling grains into liquefied glass where it hit. Hurling himself inside, Paladin caught one last glimpse of his arm. The fingers were still flexing, reaching for something, following their software commands even in death. As the door closed, his pain eased; a shield had blocked the arm's hopeless data stream.

Paladin found himself in a lift whose dim, ultraviolet lighting marked the building as a bot facility—or, at least, a bot entrance to the facility. Humans would see nothing but darkness. Clutching his jagged stump, Paladin slumped to the floor in a jumble of disorganized feelings. With some effort, he distracted himself by watching a tiny display that showed how deep the lift was going. Forty meters, sixty meters, eighty meters. They stopped at one hundred, but from the faint echoes in the machinery, Paladin knew they could have gone a lot deeper.

The door slid back to reveal Lee flanked by two bots, one hovering in a blur of wings and one a tanklike quadruped with folded mantis arms. Paladin wondered if any of them had been responsible for blowing off his arm during a training mission that was supposed to be noncombat. He wouldn't put it past them. Now Lee was grinning, and the bots weren't saying anything.

Paladin stood in a way that he hoped was dignified and ignored the physical anguish that flared through his body as he took in the scene.

"That was some seriously awesome combat shit," Lee enthused before Paladin even stepped into the wide, foam-and-alloy tunnel. "See how that new climbing algorithm worked?" He slapped Paladin's unwounded arm. "Sorry about your arm, though. I'll fix that right up."

The bots were still silent. Paladin followed the group as they walked down the tunnel, passing several doors marked in paint that reflected nothing but ultraviolet light. Visible to bot eyes only. Maybe this was some kind of bot training station? Was he about to be integrated into a fighting unit?

Down another tunnel they found what was obviously a mixed area, with paint reflecting in the visible spectrum, and several doorways too narrow to admit an armored bot like himself or the mantis. They stopped at an engineering station, where Lee printed a new arm and Paladin cleaned his joints with compressed air and lubricant.

The mantis beamed Paladin a hail. *Hello. Let's establish a secure session using the AF protocol.*

Hello. I can use AF version 7.6, Paladin replied.

Let's do it. I'm Fang. We'll call this session 4788923. Here are my identification credentials. Here comes my data. Join us at 2000.

Fang's request came with a public key for authentication and a compressed file that bloomed into a 3-D map of the facility. A tiny red tag hovered over a conference room forty meters below them. Judging by the map's metadata, they were in a large military base operated by the African Federation government. It seemed that the bots here did the kind of work he'd been training for: reconnaissance, intelligence analysis, and combat. Paladin had just been invited to his first briefing. It was time to authenticate himself properly to his new comrade.

I'm Paladin. Here are my identification credentials. Here comes my data. See you there.

Lee finished the arm and tested Paladin's stump with a voltmeter. The bot stood on a charging pad, drawing power for the batteries that tunneled through his body like a cardiovascular system. Generally he relied on the solar patches woven into his carapace, but pads were faster.

"No problem, no problem," the botadmin mumbled. It was his favorite phrase, and was in fact the first string of natural language that Paladin had ever heard, in the seconds after booting up for the first time three months ago. The arm was bonding to his stump now, and the torture of his injury became a tingle. Lee used a molecule regulator to knit the arm's atomic structure into an integrated body network, and as it connected Paladin could feel his new hand. He made a fist. The right side of his body felt weightless, as if the pain had added additional mass to his frame. Giddy, he savored the sensation.

"Gotta go, Paladin—I've got a bunch of other shit to do." Lee's dark hair fell across one of his eyes. "Sorry I had to shoot you there, but it's part of training. I didn't think your whole arm would come off!"

How many times had Paladin looked into this human face, its features animated by neurological impulse alone? He did not know. Even if he were to sort through his video memories and count them up one by one, he still didn't think he would have the right answer. But after today's mission, human faces would always look different to him. They would remind him of what it felt like to suffer, and to be relieved of suffering.

When Paladin arrived at the meeting location, two humans were sitting in chairs, while Fang and the hovering bot remained at attention. Paladin announced his presence with a beamed hail to the bots and a vocalized greeting to the humans, though protocol kept the rest of his communication in human range. He took up a position next to Fang, bending his legs until he was at eye level with the humans. In this position, knee joints jutting out behind him and dorsal shields folded flat against his shoulders, Paladin looked something like an enormous, humanoid bird.

"Welcome to Camp Tunisia, Paladin," one of the humans said. He had a tiny red button on his collar bearing the letters "IPC" in gold—it marked him as a high-ranking liaison from the Federation office of the International Property Coalition. "This will be your base for the next few days while we brief you and your partner Eliasz on your mission." He gestured to the other human, a slim man with pale skin, curly dark hair, and wide brown eyes, wearing Federation combat fatigues. Paladin noticed that Eliasz' right hand was balled into a fist very much like his own. Maybe Eliasz was also remembering something painful.

The liaison projected some unopened files into the air over the table. "We've got a serious pharma infringement situation, and we need it stopped fast and smart," he said. One of the files dissolved into the corporate logo for Zaxy, and then into a tiny box of pills labeled Zacuity.

"I assume you've heard of Zacuity."

"It's a worker drug," Eliasz replied, his face neutral. "Some of the big companies are licensing it as a perk for their employees. I've heard it feels really good. Never tried it myself."

The liaison seemed offended by Eliasz' description. "It's a productivity enhancer."

Fang broke in. "We've got reports of people buying pirated Zacuity in some of the northern cities in the Free Trade Zone. Some recon bots found about twenty doses in a First Nations special economic holding near Iqaluit. Nobody can prosecute there—it's totally outside IPC jurisdiction—so there have been no arrests yet."

The liaison brought up video of a hospital room, packed with humans strapped to beds, twitching. He continued. "Zaxy will take legal action later. But right now, we need an intervention. This drug is driving people nuts, and some are dying. If it gets out that this is Zacuity, it could be a major financial loss for Zaxy. Major."

The liaison looked at Eliasz, who stared straight at the projection of the hospital, watching the tiny, struggling figures loop through the same tiny struggles again.

"Zaxy's analysts think the Zacuity is being pirated here in the Federation, in a black-market lab. Obviously, this situation could seriously endanger the Federation's business partnerships with the Free Trade Zone. We need to find out for sure one way or the other, and that's why we need you." The delegate looked at Paladin. "You've both been authorized by the IPC to track the pirated drug to its source, and stop it. We've got a few leads in Iqaluit, and they all point to one person."

The afflicted Zacuity eaters dissolved into an enhanced headshot of a woman, obviously constructed from several low-quality captures. Her cropped black hair had a glint of gray, and a fat scar that started on her neck snaked into the collar of her coveralls.

"This is Judith Chen—she goes by the name Jack. We suspect she's working with one of the biggest pharma pirating operations in the Federation. We know she's connected with some pretty shady manufacturers in Casablanca, but she's got a legit shipping fleet. She ferries for spice and herb companies to the Zone—lots of stinky little boxes. Perfect cover. We think she might be the one who's smuggling the drugs from here across the Arctic."

Fang vocalized, "We've been watching her for years. Never been able to catch her red-handed, but we know she's got connections with people in the Trade Zone who are suspected dealers. Plus, she's a trained synthetic biologist. It all fits together. If we can get to her, I think we can shut down these pirate shipments."

"She's also an anti-patent terrorist," Eliasz added quietly. "Spent several years in jail."

"The official charge was not terrorism. It was conspiracy to commit property damage," said Fang. "She was only in jail for a few months, and then she fled from Saskatoon to Casablanca. We think that's how she made the connections that she's using for her pirating operation."

"Once we've got her, we just can hand her over to the Trade Zone on a plate," added the liaison. "Piracy stopped. Justice done. Everybody's happy."

"It still sounds like terrorism to me," Eliasz said, looking directly at Paladin. "Don't you agree?"

Nobody had ever looked at him quite like that, as if he could have an opinion about anything beyond how his network was functioning. The bot's mind spiraled through what he'd been taught about terrorism, quickly compiling an index of images and data that required nothing but a crude algorithm to reveal a pattern: pain and its echo, across millions of bodies over time. Paladin did not have access to the nuance of political context, nor did he have the urge to seek it out. He had only this man's face, his dark eyes sending an unreadable message that Paladin wanted desperately to decrypt.

How could he look at Eliasz and say no?

"It does sound like terrorism," Paladin agreed. When Eliasz smiled, the planes of his face were asymmetrical.

Fang broke protocol for an instant, beaming to his hovering companion in an off-the-record session. *Words of wisdom from the newbie, who has never seen terrorism in his life. :(*

3

PRIVATE PROPERTY

JULY 2, 2144

When does the thinnest smear of genetic material left by spilled blood finally evaporate? At some point it becomes invisible to human eyes, its redness dimmed by water and the mopper's crawl, but there are still pieces left—shattered cell walls, twists of DNA, diminishing cytoplasm. When do those final shards of matter go away?

Jack watched the rotund blob of the mopper as it swished back and forth across a pinking stain that had once been a red-black crust on the floor of the control room. A blue glare of water-filtered sunlight came directly through the glass composite in the windows, blinding her until she dropped her eyes back down to the stain. She'd disposed of the body hours ago, its legs lashed to the cement blocks. By now, it would be frozen deep under the water.

Jack hadn't had to kill anyone for a long time. Usually, in a tight situation, she wasn't in the middle of the ocean. She could run away instead of having to fight. She ran a hand through the salt-stiffened tufts of her hair, wanting to vomit or cry or give up again in the face of the hopeless, endless pharma deprivation death machine.

That last thought make her crack a self-chiding smile. *Pharma deprivation death machine.* Sounded like something she would have written in college and published anonymously on an offshore server, her words reaching their destination only via a thick layer of crypto and several random network hops.

Black pharma smuggling wasn't exactly the job she'd imagined for herself thirty years ago, in the revolutionary fervor of her grad student days. Back then, she was certain she could change the world just by making commits to a text file repository, and organizing neatly symbolic protests against patent law. But when she'd finally left the university labs, her life had become one stark choice: farm patents for shitty startups, or become a pirate. For Jack, it wasn't a choice at all, not really.

Sure, there were dangers. Sometimes a well-established pirate ring in the Federation would find a few of its members dead, or jailed for life—especially if a corp complained about specific infringements. But if you kept a low profile, modest and quiet, it was business as usual.

But not usually business like this: cleaning up after a guy she'd killed over a bag of pills and a bot.

Where the hell had he even come from? She gestured for the sub's local network, flicking open a window that gave her a sensors' perspective on the mottled surface of the ocean from a few feet below. Nothing but the occasional dark hulk of icebergs out there now. Maybe she'd really started to lose it after all her years of vigilance? He'd exploited some obvious hole in her security system, fooling the ship's perimeter sensors until he was on board and stuffing boxes of her payload into his rucksack. Selling a bag of those dementia meds wouldn't have gotten him much more than a year's worth of euphorics and gambling in some Arctic resort right on the beach.

The dead fusehead was the least of her problems right now, though. Jack needed to figure out whether something had gone wrong with her batch of reverse-engineered Zacuity. She still had some samples of the original drug she'd broken down to its constituent parts, along with plenty of her pirated pills. Jack tossed the original and pirated versions into her chem forensics rig, going over the molecular structures again with a critical eye. Nothing wrong there—she'd made a perfect copy. That meant the issue was with Zacuity's original recipe. She decided to isolate each part of the drug, going through them one by one. Some of them were obviously harmless. Others she marked for further examination.

Jack finally narrowed the questionable parts down to four molecules. She projected their structures into the air, regarding the glittering bonds between atoms with a critical eye. A quick database search revealed that all of these molecules targeted genes related to addiction in large parts of the population. Jack paused, unable to believe it.

Zaxy had always placed profit over public health, but this went beyond the usual corporate negligence. International law stipulated that no cosmetic pharmaceuticals like productivity drugs or euphorics could contain addictive mechanisms, and even the big corps had to abide by IPC regulations. Her discovery meant that Zacuity was completely illegal. But nobody would figure that out, because Zaxy was rolling it out slowly to the corps, keeping any addictions carefully in check. When Zacuity came out of beta, the drug would be so expensive that only people with excellent medical care would ever take it. If they got addicted, it would be dealt with quietly, at a beautiful recovery facility somewhere in the Eurozone. It was only when somebody like Jack started selling it on the street that problems and side effects could be magnified into something more dangerous.

Jack was torn between rage at Zacuity and rage at herself for bringing their shitty drug to people without health resources. Hundreds of people might be eating those pills right now, possibly going nuts. It was a horrific prospect, and Jack wasn't prepared to deal with the enormity of this problem just yet. Reaching into the pocket of her newly washed coveralls, she pulled out some

420 and sparked it up. Nothing like drugs to take the edge off drug problems. Besides, she had unfinished business with that bot behind the locked door of her cargo hold. He might prove to be unfixable, but at least that wasn't her fault.

Jack expected the bot would still be in the same spot where he collapsed, eyes wandering under the control of some shit algorithm yanked off the net. But he wasn't. Jack squinted, trying to figure out why the bot was huddled into a shadow where the wall met the floor. She'd started the ship moving again, and bubbles slid past the dark portals.

He was sleeping.

Suddenly Jack realized why the bot could look so beaten up but still show no signs of an alloy endoskeleton. This wasn't a biobot—it was just plain bio. A human.

She leaned against the bulkhead and groaned quietly. A damaged bot was almost always fixable, but a damaged human? She had the goods to repair a mutating region in his DNA, and purge his body of common viruses, but nothing could fix a wrecked cognition. As she pondered, the hunched figure sat up with a start and stared at her with eyes whose emptiness was now far more awful than bad software. She wondered how long he'd been indentured to the dead thief. There was a number branded on his neck, and he'd obviously been following orders for a long time.

The 420 gave Jack a kind of philosophical magnanimousness, and with it a sense of resigned obligation to this kid. It wasn't his fault that his master had decided to rob an armed pirate in the middle of nowhere. She'd do what she could to help him, but that wasn't much.

"Do you want some water?" she asked. "You look like you could use it."

He scrambled up suddenly, grabbing the edge of a crate to keep his balance, and she realized he was actually rather tall—

taller than she was, though so malnourished that his height made him seem even more fragile. If things got dicey, it would be no trouble for her to overpower him, snap his neck, and toss him into the airlock.

"Please," he said. "And food, too, if you can spare it." His English accent was pure middle-class Asian Union, which wasn't exactly what you expected from a kid with a brand on his neck.

"Come on, then." Jack touched his shirtsleeve lightly, careful not to hit exposed skin. She led him down the spiral staircase from the control room into the wet lab/kitchen, where she booted up the cooker and gestured for broth and bread. He sagged into her chair at the tiny table, the wings of his shoulder blades showing through his thin shirt as he hunched over and stared at his hands.

She put the food in front of him. "I'm Jack."

He ignored her, taking a sip from the bowl, then dunking the bread in and biting off a chunk. Jack leaned on the counter and watched, wondering if the kid even had a name. Families with nothing would sometimes sell their toddlers to indenture schools, where managers trained them to be submissive just like they were programming a bot. At least bots could earn their way out of ownership after a while, be upgraded, and go fully autonomous. Humans might earn their way out, but there was no autonomy key that could undo a childhood like that.

"I'm Threezed," he responded finally, breaking Jack out of her spaced reverie. He'd swallowed about half the broth and his face didn't look quite as blank as it had before. It was hard to miss the fact that the last two numbers branded onto his neck were three and zed. That scar was his name, too. Jack folded her arms over the sudden stab of sympathy in her chest.

"Nice to meet you, Threezed."

4

IQALUIT

JULY 4, 2144

Their bodies would have to work together, even when they were far apart. That was Eliasz' rationale for climbing sand dunes with Paladin for two days while the IPC liaison drank endless cups of sweet milk tea and gestured in mute frustration, swiping through all the messages materializing from the projectors on his glasses.

Doing exercises alongside someone else was a new sensation for Paladin. He had always been in radio contact with Lee or another botadmin, but their voices were more like programs that guided him from inside his instincts. His botadmins never stopped, looked at him, and talked about how they missed the weather in Europe.

"I hate the weather here," Eliasz muttered, crouching down at the top of a dune. He glanced at Paladin and then settled into a sitting position. It was 0800, and Paladin was testing his reflexes in sand again, learning to keep the bulk of his carapace low and his sensors moving across a wide spectrum. He was in that position now, squirming on his elbows and knees, listening to Eliasz talk and tuning the public botnet.

You are all. I am Raptor. Here comes my data. I am leaving on a mission at 1300. Going to Congo for a plague intervention. Wish me luck. Back in 48 hours.

"I'd rather have cold and wet, like in the central Eurozone," Eliasz continued, pushing sweat from his forehead into his hair with an outspread hand. "People say they can't stand Warsaw because it's so cold, but I guess you always love the weather where you grew up—even if you never want to go back. Where are you from, Paladin?"

You are all. I am Cldr. Here comes my data. I need three bots to help with weapons cargo drop-off. Location attached.

Paladin paused in his squirming, his head nearly touching Eliasz' leg where it rested in red sand. He wasn't sure what the appropriate answer to that question would be, since he hadn't really been alive long enough to be from anywhere in particular.

"I suppose I am from the Kagu Robotics Foundry in Cape Town," he vocalized.

"No, no, no," Eliasz shook his head violently, then rapped his knuckles on Paladin's lower back. "I mean, where are you from originally? Where is your brain from?"

Under its layers of abdominal shielding, Paladin's biobrain floated in a thick mixture of shock gel and cerebrospinal fluid. There was a fat interface wire between it and the physical substrate of his mind. The brain took care of his facial recognition functions, assigning each person he met a unique identifier based on the edges and shadows of their expressions, but its file system was largely incompatible with his own. He used it mostly like a graphics processor. He certainly had no idea where it was from, beyond the fact that a dead human working for the Federation military had donated it.

Eliasz spoke again. "Isn't it important to you to know who you really are? Why you feel what you do?"

None of Paladin's emotions or ethics were processed in his human brain. But then Eliasz looked right into the sensor array mounted on Paladin's face, his eyes dark and attentive. Suddenly Paladin didn't want to explain his file system architecture anymore.

"I don't know where my brain is from," he replied simply. "I can't access its memories."

He could sense the tension mounting in Eliasz' body. Electricity skipped across the surface of his skin. Over the thousands of seconds they'd spent together, Paladin had noticed that Eliasz tended to vacillate between these intense, emotional conversations and total silence.

"They should let you remember," he growled. "They should let you."

If Eliasz couldn't get that wish granted, at least he did get something else he wanted. It came in the form of an incoming message for Paladin, part of a securely encrypted session.

You are Paladin. I am Fang. Remember the secure session we created before? Let's use it again. Here comes my data. Final mission meeting is at 0900. Bring Eliasz.

I agree to use our already-established secure session. I am Paladin. Where are we going?

Balmy shores of the Arctic, looks like. You'll be tracking down some of Jack's connections there, trying to figure out where she hides her stash.

I am prepared to meet you in 30 minutes with Eliasz. This is the end of my data.

The two bots closed out their session after an exchange of map coordinates, which were for the same room they had used over the past two days for mission planning.

"Good news," Paladin vocalized to Eliasz, who was still staring at him. "We are about to leave for the northern Free Trade Zone, where the temperature is much lower." Eliasz said nothing, but his heart rate had slowed down. The two set off across the dune tops to find a portal and receive their orders.

Though the mission was fairly small-scale and routine, it held a special significance for Paladin because it meant he'd crossed over from development to deployment. Today marked the first day of his indenture to the African Federation. International law mandated that his service could last no more than ten years, a period deemed more than enough time to make the Federation's investment in creating a new life-form worthwhile.

Though he was just beginning his term of indenture, Paladin had heard enough around the factory to know that the Federation interpreted the law fairly liberally. He might be waiting to receive his autonomy key for twenty years. More likely, he would die before ever getting it. But he wanted to survive—that urge was part of his programming. It was what defined him as human-equivalent and therefore deserving autonomy. The bot had no choice but to fight for his life. Still, to Paladin, it didn't feel like a lack of choice. It felt like hope.

JULY 5, 2144

The bulbous, fisted forearms of the Baffin Island skyline came into view from kilometers away as the jet shot over the Arctic Sea. Even at this distance, Paladin could see the movement of thousands of wind turbines, making the outlines of each building shimmer slightly. Soon, he could pick out the chemical signature of the lush farms that rose in tiered spirals around each complex. Northern cities ringing the Arctic spent all summer absorbing as much solar as possible, taking their farms through two crop seasons while the days were long. The whole city was deep into growing season.

By the time they'd passed over the outer islands and hit the airspace over Baffin, Eliasz was wide-awake. Paladin heard the change in Eliasz' breathing and knew he must have ordered a wake-up signal from his perimeter when they were arriving at Iqaluit. Now the city was sprawled beneath them, its domes a glittering crust at the vertex of an acutely angled bay that cut deeply into the huge island.

"Iqaluit is an ugly city," Eliasz grunted, joining Paladin at the window. "Its domes are modeled on the ones in Vegas—you know it?"

"A domed city in the western desert of the Free Trade Zone," Paladin vocalized.

"It's the center of the human resources industry. A lot of bad guys there. Black-market slave shit. People there don't value human life so they build with this cheap crap that lets in way too much ultraviolet. Iqaluit looks exactly the same—except a lot cleaner and newer."

Paladin wondered if Eliasz was opposed to the system of indenture. There were entire text repositories that focused on eliminating the indenture of humans. Their pundits argued that humans should not be owned like bots because nobody paid to make them. Bots, who cost money, required a period of indenture to make their manufacture worthwhile. No such incentive was required for humans to make other humans.

Regardless of what pundits thought, the vast majority of cities and economic zones had some system of human indenture. And Vegas was where the humans sold themselves. Its domed complexes were almost entirely devoted to processing, training, and contracting human resources. Like Vegas, Iqaluit had been built fast; it was all skyscrapers and domes. But a cursory data scan revealed few commonalities between the two cities beyond that.

"There are very few indentured humans here," Paladin pointed out.

"Sure. The bad guys are different, but there are still bad guys," Eliasz said, his elevated blood pressure appearing to Paladin like a reddish haze around the outline of his body. "The place is crawling with pirates. Everything here is stolen."

They skimmed the runway and Eliasz stood up, instinctively touching his forehead, shoulders, and belt to verify his perimeter and its local network of weapons. "I always feel like I'm crossing myself when I do that," he growled, heart speeding up in agitation. "You know what I mean?"

"The gestures are similar," Paladin replied.

"My father was a true believer," Eliasz said, his voice so low that only a bot could have heard it. Then, suddenly, his demeanor shifted; the man forced his breathing into a regular rhythm and it was no longer easy to read his emotional state from a distance.

"Where are we going first, Paladin?" Eliasz grinned, his eyes seeking out the five visual sensors on the robot's head, set above diagonal planes that framed his face like an abstract version of human cheeks. They had about three dozen possible destinations, including addresses for several alleged associates of Jack's and a few of her favorite restaurants.

"We should begin with the closest home addresses, question the people there, and then attempt to corner Jack based on the information they provide. As a last resort, we could monitor the restaurant secfeeds for Jack's biometrics."

Eliasz barked a laugh. "You don't know much about HUMINT, do you, Paladin?"

Human intelligence gathering was not a priority during Paladin's training. When the bot did not respond, Eliasz stopped laughing. "Sorry, buddy. It's better to start with the restaurants. But first, we need some gear."

Near the frayed landing strips of the airfield was a junk shop, its corrugated steel exterior at least a hundred years old. Low and long, it was designed to withstand the weather and retain heat. Inside, molecules associated with cotton fibers, bleach, and fuel floated through Paladin's sensors. Eliasz talked to a man behind the counter with a cybernetic chest and arms, who started downloading a local map and intel upgrades into Eliasz' geosystems. Paladin stepped closer and tuned the signal connecting the two men's devices, decrypting and copying the data to his own memory.

"This is my partner, Paladin," Eliasz said suddenly, throwing a warm arm around Paladin's carapace. His fingers gripped the bot's shoulder blade where his shields emerged. Paladin could feel each whorl of Eliasz' prints. He unconsciously mapped them to several databases, most of which were swollen with information noise that hid Eliasz' real identity. The prints matched a dead professor in Brussels, a small-time entrepreneur in Nairobi, a priest in Warsaw, and an indentured woman who belonged to Monsanto in the Free Trade Zone. There were dozens of other matches, spinning outward into a vast snarl of false social network connections and contradictory government records.

"Paladin, I'm Yardley," the man said, extending his fabricated hand to meet Paladin's.

"We're going undercover and I need to look a little less pro," Eliasz said, glancing at Paladin. "And he needs to look a little less shiny."

Ten minutes later, Eliasz had stripped down to the glittering nodes of his perimeter system and was pulling jeans and a cotton shirt over the invisible network of nanowire that connected to the perimeter below his skin. Paladin put his pressure sensors back online experimentally, testing to see where he could still feel the sting of the dents and scratches Yardley and Eliasz had administered.

"We need to get some information on Jack, and the only way to do that is to look like the kinds of guys who would work with her," Eliasz said. "You can keep quiet most of the time, but try to make errors once in a while, like your brain is damaged or something."

Paladin said nothing as he finished restarting the processes that made up his sensorium.

"OK," Eliasz muttered, then went over their story again. "I'm a chem admin who got laid off from PharmPraxis; you're my indentured assistant. I'm willing to sell some of PharmPraxis' formulas for the right price. You watch everything, man—do what you're made for."

"I will," said Paladin. He wanted to please Eliasz. Paladin was sure that wasn't just some indenture algorithm weighting his decision matrix; it was his true desire.

The sea winds maintained Iqaluit's outdoor temperature at a steady twenty degrees Celsius and lifted a hank of Eliasz' hair as Paladin tread quietly beside him. The sun was low enough on the horizon to signal evening, though it was still bright outside. Arctic summer meant there would be only an hour without sunlight this evening. By then, Eliasz hoped to be feigning drunkenness at the Lex, a noodle-and-beer joint that was one of Jack's regular hangouts. Footage showed that she met up with some of her local connections there.

Paladin pushed the doors inward and ducked into a steamy room filled with molecules released by ginger and other crushed spices. He catalogued them for later analysis. You never knew when the distinct chemical signature of a place would turn out to be useful information. Crowded benches bowed under the weight of local fish farmers and students from the university chattering loudly about proteomics. Everybody was flushed from alcohol and bowls of scalding-hot noodle soup that teetered on every scarred and uneven foam table.

It would be an easy crowd to disappear in, Eliasz subvocalized to Paladin, *especially if you looked like a farmer but your politics matched those of the radical students.* Paladin accessed an image of Jack he'd stored in memory. She didn't look exactly like a farmer, but he could see how she might blend if she wore waterproofs.

They sat down at the edge of a table full of extremely drunk students who were playing some kind of game with their goggles that involved a lot of footage-sharing and shots of Saskatchewan vodka. Eliasz ordered seafood noodles and Paladin made sure his right leg trembled as he hunkered down, as if he were desperately in need of a firmware upgrade. It caught the attention of one of the students right away.

"Need some help with that?" A jovial woman with dark eyes and bobbed black hair gestured vaguely at his leg. "We've got a free botware archive on the university servers."

Paladin said nothing.

"We haven't had much money for repairs." Eliasz shrugged. "I'm just looking for work after the layoffs at PharmPraxis down south." That caught the attention of more students at the table.

"More layoffs, eh?" asked one with a prairie lilt in his voice.

"Damn patent hoarders," Eliasz said, his voice low. He was taking a risk, trying to suss out whether these students were the kinds of radicals who ran with pirates. Paladin noticed that Eliasz had changed his posture subtly, slouching and pulling his bangs over his eyes in a way that made him seem younger. He could pass for a postgraduate, and it was clear these drunk bio hackers were already responding to him as a peer. Paladin briefly admired this bit of HUMINT artistry, then considered that some of the records associated with Eliasz' prints placed him at twenty-nine years old. Perhaps those records were accurate, at least in respect to the man's age.

"Seriously," said the woman who had offered Paladin access to her fabbers. "They rake in so much cash from all that IP and then treat their developers and admins like shit. It's patent-farm bullshit. I'm Gertrude, by the way."

"Ivan," said Eliasz, "and this is my bot Xiu. He's having a little trouble with his speakers." Eliasz had picked a nym for Paladin that was more commonly given to women, but gender designations meant very little among bots. Most would respond to whatever pronoun their human admins hailed them with, though some autonomous bots preferred to pick their own pronouns. Regardless, no human would think twice about calling a bot named Xiu "he." Especially a bot built like Paladin, whose hulking body, with dorsal shields spread wide over his back, took up the space of two large humans.

"Want me to hook you guys up with some fixes for Xiu?" Gertrude asked. Eliasz pretended to ponder, as he slurped his noodles.

"These are spicy," he said, ignoring the fact that several of Gertrude's friends were now looking at him and Paladin.

"We're heading back to the lab after dinner, to check on a few processes we need to run overnight," said the guy from the prairies.

"That would be really nice of you." Eliasz feigned uncertainty as he fiddled with his chopsticks.

"Yeah, you should come." Gertrude confirmed the invitation as if they had already been persuaded. "Sound good to you, Xiu?"

Paladin said nothing.

A group of five students led Eliasz and Paladin through streets illuminated by the long-wavelength light of a late-night sunset. At last they reached an arched sign covered in Inuktitut and English words welcoming them to University of the Arctic's Iqaluit campus. It was the region's wealthiest university and a feeder school for dozens of top biocoms and pharma corps. At this time of night it was fairly quiet, although as they neared the science buildings, Paladin picked out more and more windows radiating visible light.

Eliasz was describing his imaginary job at PharmPraxis with what sounded like genuine bitterness. The story was calculated to bring out sympathies in his audience. "I took a job in chem admin right out of university," he said, "and they put me on a drug that died in trials. Took a year, but they wound up sacking my whole team. If your drug doesn't get to market, well . . ." Eliasz trailed off.

"What do you work on?" asked Gertrude. "There are tons of jobs for chem admins around here."

"I design algorithms that look for interesting emergent properties in organic molecules."

A tall man with cheap glasses was walking in step with them. "Not my area, but I bet we could find you something, Ivan," he said. His accent definitely wasn't local—Paladin did a quick comparison between the tall man's vowels and those of four hundred other regional accents in English. The best approximation was northern Federation, where Paladin and Eliasz had just been stationed.

"Thanks, um . . ."

"Youssef," said the man. He easily met Paladin's face sensors with his eyes; the bot and the man were the same height. "Pleased to meet you both," he added.

They reached the Life Sciences complex and Gertrude dug through her pocket for what turned out to be a rather archaic password management device. She waved the tiny lump of plastic in the air when they reached an ash cement building, and the building's network replied by opening a set of double doors.

Paladin noticed Youssef glance quickly at the sensor-flecked paint of the interior hallway, reflecting the gang of gradually sobering students dully as they passed through and began shedding their jackets. Gertrude, Youssef, and their friends worked on a theoretical and underfunded subject related to protein mutation and aesthetic decision-making. Their lab was in the basement, its equipment at least two generations behind current models. The walls were covered in signs and stickers stolen from other labs. "DANGER! DO NOT TOUCH THE MAGNET!" read a particularly large one over their sequencing cluster. "LIVE CRICKETS" read another.

"Here we are," Gertrude said, gesturing for light. "Xiu, there's our printer. The network is called PolarBunnies and it's open." She gestured again. "Help yourself to whatever." Paladin walked carefully around several tables laden with cooling units and test tubes. He printed up some chips while Eliasz made small talk.

As the printer spat out nanoscopic threads, Eliasz managed to bring the conversation back around to those goddamn patent hoarders whom he really had a mind to fuck over somehow.

Youssef was tense with excitement, his body radiating identification with Eliasz' tale. It was obvious he was about to speak several seconds before he did. "So how would you get back at a company like PharmPraxis for what they did?" Youssef asked. "I mean, how far would you be willing to go?"

"You really want to know? This doesn't go outside this lab, OK?" Eliasz asked. Everybody was staring at him.

"Absolutely," enthused Gertrude.

"I've got the formula for this patent-pending drug they're in trials with right now. If somebody else brings it to market first, they'd never be able to claim prior art, because they based it on a molecule they got gray market from some unlicensed lab in the Brazilian States." Eliasz paused, then gave his best shaky laugh. "I mean, I probably wouldn't *do* anything with it, but I could. I really did take the formula." He patted his hip pocket as if he'd saved the data in a physical medium and stashed it in his pants.

Youssef couldn't take his eyes off the imaginary data in Eliasz' pants. Paladin was getting weird readings off his brain: The guy was too excited, almost like he was on drugs or suffering a neurological aberration.

"You should do it," he blurted out.

"Shut up, Youssef," said Gertrude, who was checking a box full of samples with a small mass spectrometer. "That's a serious fucking crime. Not like reverse engineering some old drug that's about to go public domain anyway."

It was Eliasz' opening and he took it. "You've reverse engineered drugs before?"

Gertrude snorted. "Barely. He decompiled some Glizmer freshman year and sold copies of it to half our dorm."

"That Glizmer worked." Youssef looked angry. "And you know it's more than that, Gertrude."

Paladin watched anxiety push blood into Gertrude's cheeks. Youssef's lips tensed up. The tall man with the North Federation accent was taking a serious risk talking about this in front of a stranger. Paladin was impressed: Eliasz knew how to make people trust him. Would Youssef spill some serious intel? Apparently, yes.

"If you're serious, you should meet some friends of mine whose labs aren't funded by Big Pharma." Youssef's voice broke on the word "friends," and Paladin realized the man's body was still passing through the final stages of puberty.

Gertrude broke in, her heart rate elevated. "You know, Youssef, not everybody wants to break the law to prove a point."

Eliasz shrugged like he hadn't noticed any tension. "I don't have anything against meeting new people," he said to Youssef.

JULY 6, 2144

The next day, Paladin and Eliasz returned to the Lex in the late afternoon, long enough before happy hour that the crowds were thin. A few groups of students were quietly studying on their goggles, and a lonely farmer was nursing vodkas at the bar. Across the table from Eliasz and Paladin, his face slightly obscured by soup steam, was Youssef's friend Thomasie, who wasn't funded by Big Pharma.

He certainly looked the part. Thomasie's black hair was gelled into a stylish tangle around his face, and certain fibers of his shirt glowed with the faded logo of a Freeculture org that had died in the 2120s. It was hard to say if he'd kept the shirt for twenty-five years, or simply bought an item artfully frayed and faded to look authentic. Thomasie had a way of leaning in when he talked, as if everything he was saying brought you into his confidence. Unlike Youssef, he had control of his flush responses and heart rate. It was hard to tell when he was lying, though the very evenness of his readings gave something away. He was masking emotional reactions to everything around him.

"Youssef tells me you worked at PharmPraxis and are looking for something new." Thomasie looked straight at Eliasz, then glanced at Paladin. "That's a pretty sweet bot you got on a chem admin's salary."

"I inherited him from my mother when she died."

"I see. So what exactly is it that you did at PharmPraxis?"

"Algorithms."

"And you had access to patent-pending designs, eh?"

Eliasz and Paladin stared at Thomasie and said nothing.

"Youssef told me you were interested in talking to me about some designs you saw."

Silence was a good way to get additional information, to make the other person commit to the transaction first.

Thomasie tapped his index finger on the table slowly and continued. "My colleagues and I would be interested in taking a look at any designs you might have. We pay for good IP, no questions asked."

At last Eliasz prepared to speak. Paladin measured the seconds it took for him to ramp up, heard him stabilize his breathing and blood pressure.

"I have the file on me. When do you want to see it?"

Paladin noticed that Eliasz failed to talk specific prices. He was trying to sound like a newbie at this. Perfect for a disgruntled ex-employee.

Thomasie caught the naïveté, and relaxed. He figured he had this one well in hand.

"We can go right now. My car is outside."

They drove fifty kilometers outside city limits, the solar farms of South Baffin whipping past like vast regattas of smooth black sails. Youssef was drumming on the window and ignoring Paladin while Thomasie and Eliasz sat up front and talked.

After turning on several dirt roads, they reached a newish farm in the middle of a solar field. Its main building was an arched wall of thick glass set deeply into a grassy hill that rose like a green bubble out of a sea of dark, boxy solar antennas dribbling hydrocarbons into underground tanks. A woman stepped out of a door cut into the glass wall, releasing a blast of sound. Someone inside was listening to a loud news feed. The woman's arms tensed as two overclocked matter cutters powered up beneath her sleeves.

Based on the pattern broadcast by Youssef's eye movements as he scanned the area, Paladin considered it statistically unlikely that he'd been here before. This would be a test for Youssef as well as Eliasz.

"Thomasie." Though the woman greeted Thomasie, she continued to block the door as they approached. Paladin noticed the driveway was fabbed to be impossibly smooth and warm; suspended inside its foam were long strands of nearly invisible wire that would radiate a gentle heat when the weather turned.

"Hi, Roopa."

As Thomasie led them past Roopa's barely concealed weapons, she gave Paladin a long look, eyes lingering on his shields. The room beyond her was illuminated by carefully reflected natural light, and trees grew out of the moss-covered floor. Nearly every piece of furniture was a living bonsai. One red light from a small industrial fabber blinked in the corner, exchanging data in a system encrypted so well that Paladin could only access information about the house climate. Somebody had burned serious money on this little farmhouse.

Thomasie led them to a round room with a conference table that grew out of the floor, its surface a carefully engineered weave of branches. The ceiling was perforated by a spiral staircase whose fabbed metal skeleton clanged and shook as three people came down to meet them. Like Thomasie, the others wore their expensive clothing carefully disheveled.

Iqaluit was a big town, but it wasn't that big. If Jack was smuggling pharma through here, she was probably dealing with these guys in some way. They might be outsourcing the production of black pharma to her Federation labs, or selling her wares through their connections in the north. Even if they weren't directly doing business, these people surely existed at the center of a local social network that brought together anti-patent radicals, pirates, and millions of people desperate for cheap drugs. If he and Eliasz could gain access to that network, they'd find Jack.

"Call me Bluebeard," said one of the people who had just descended the stairs. She was wearing blue waterproofs and no shoes. Her dark hair fell in a wavy tangle across her face, nearly obscuring the fabric sensor patch that covered her left eye socket. From the tension in her shoulders and back, it was clear she'd been working with her hands for several hours—though whether it was at a gesture console or in the fields, Paladin couldn't tell. "These are my colleagues, Blackbeard and Redbeard." She pointed at two pale-skinned men whose clothing did not match their nyms. "Welcome to Arcata Solar Farm. Let's all sit down." Bluebeard's tone was neither welcoming nor inviting. She had just issued an order.

Redbeard cooked espresso using an antique steam-driven machine while Bluebeard stared at the data Eliasz was beaming to her eyepatch. It was the formula for an attention stabilizer that the IPC had acquired for just this purpose, after it failed out of clinical trials. At least 50 percent of the people taking it had developed debilitating migraines that lasted for days. But there was no way to know that from the formula; it had all the appearance of legitimacy.

"You say you got this from PharmPraxis?" Bluebeard asked, her single-eyed gaze taking in both Eliasz and Paladin, who sat at the bonsai table across from her.

Eliasz nodded.

Trying to maintain the illusion that he was mentally damaged, Paladin forced himself to train his front visual sensors on some water molecules traveling through the tree whose body comprised the table, leaning his head close to the grain and microscoping in on it. His other sensors were taking in as much data as he could without tripping any alarms.

"This is very interesting," she continued, flicking the data to a holo display in front of Blackbeard. "I'm going to have to ask you to stay here while we do more analysis." She sent a burst of network traffic to Roopa, who appeared several seconds later at the door to the conference room. "Make yourself comfortable," Bluebeard said to Eliasz. "You can use our gaming system if you want."

Eliasz gripped Paladin's arm. "That's fine, but the bot stays with me."

Bluebeard shrugged. "No problem." Then she turned to the tall Federation man who hated Big Pharma. "Youssef, you come with us."

Roopa loomed above them. When Paladin tuned her perimeter network it was just another unreadable haze of encrypted traffic.

5

GOOD SCIENCE

JULY 5, 2144

"That was seriously fucked up," Threezed said enthusiastically.

Jack had taken the sub deep below the surface. The portals in the control room looked like dark ellipses from an enormous text message. Jack and Threezed were watching *Taxi Driver,* a mid-twentieth-century movie about a man who goes insane and tries to free an indentured sex worker in New York City.

Threezed scratched his face, where the last of his scabs was flaking off. He'd cleaned up pretty well after that first night when they'd introduced themselves. He refused to talk about what had happened, and Jack didn't push. The fact was, she didn't want to think about what she'd done to Threezed's client any more than he did.

After sleeping for nearly twenty-four hours, Threezed had awakened with a sardonic personality and the kind of youthful energy that every Vive addict was chasing. First he offered to tune her engines—he claimed he knew his way around sub mechanics—but Jack wasn't prepared to have some stranger without a past going that deep into her systems. She was perfectly willing to put him on homemaker duty, though. He couldn't do much damage scrubbing.

When he wasn't tidying something, Threezed focused his attention on the mobile she'd loaned him. His only implant was an indenture tracker, so he'd been relying on these flimsy, foldable devices his whole life. Mobiles weren't exactly durable, or powerful. But they could access plenty of bandwidth from the free mote network, whose microscopic data relays were sprayed into the atmosphere by drones in most of the economic coalitions.

Jack kept the free motes in range stunned with a signal jammer, and she didn't want Threezed using the sub's comms, so he was left with nothing to do but stream her locally stored movies from the motes in her ventilation system. He started with movies from the twenty-first century, where the English accents were easier to understand and the resolution was pretty good. Then he moved on to silent movies of the 1910s and '20s, their worlds rendered in abstract grayscale, like engineering diagrams. He said it was easier for him to read the English intertitles than understand the weird accents in movies from later decades.

Tonight, however, he was pretty impressed with this full-color Martin Scorsese movie from 1976. They watched it with subtitles. "It's strange how they were dealing with the same shit we are," Threezed remarked, picking at a scab on his knee. "You always hear about how people were so diseased back then, and everything was really slow and backward, but I've totally known guys like that. I mean, I've totally known *cab drivers* like that."

"Yeah, I guess people don't change that much from century to century." Jack shrugged. Now that the movie had him in a decent mood, it seemed like a good time to bring up their next move. "So, we're going to get to Inuvik in a day or two," she said. "I can drop you off there." A bustling port town on the Arctic coast, Inuvik was the perfect place to get lost. Threezed could catch a fast train from there to dozens of big cities in the Zone.

"Inuvik? What am I supposed to do there?"

"Don't worry—I'll give you some credits to get you on your feet."

"But how am I supposed to get on my feet when I've got this

chip in my arm?" Threezed passed his hand over the fleshy part of his left upper arm, where the indenture tag was implanted.

"I killed your tag a couple of days ago. Nobody will be able to tell it's there."

"You killed my tag . . . without telling me?"

"It's not safe for you to be trackable after what happened. Did you really want to be broadcasting your identity to the world?"

"Well, I . . ." Threezed trailed off. His hand tightened over the place where his dead tag would probably live forever in its teardrop of surgical glass.

Jack was about to suggest that he catch a train to Vancouver when her perimeter fizzed under the skin of her right hand. She had a message.

"Sorry . . . I've got to check this." Jack shot Threezed an apologetic look. She crossed the bridge to her chair near the control consoles and gestured up a window that only she could see. Its dark rectangle perfectly blocked the angry expression that was slowly distorting the shapes of Threezed's mouth and eyes.

One of her search programs had found an uptick in news about drug-related accidents and crimes.

It seemed that the homework fiend was part of a small epidemic of workaholism. First came an elderly man who refused to stop mowing his lawn. Doctors restrained him, but he kept roaring and twitching, demanding the mower controls. Next was a woman who only wanted to walk dogs. There was a city worker who had unleashed a fleet of autonomous road foamers with orders to spray new sidewalks in seemingly random locations downtown, during rush hour. The vehicles injured several people, cementing their feet and legs, before her supervisor was able to shut down the fleet. Then came a nanny, weeping and incoherent, nearly arrested after spending ten hours in the park just to push children on the swings.

Unsettled, Jack gestured through a few more news stories. At least five people were dead, mostly from dehydration, and dozens hospitalized. The more she read, the more convinced she was that her reverse-engineered Zacuity was to blame. These reports were just from Calgary, so who knew what was going on in smaller cities like Iqaluit and Yellowknife? There could be dozens more people with these side effects, with far less access to medical help. This was the kind of pharmaceutical disaster she'd vowed to fight against, and now she'd caused one, for the exact same reason the corps did: money. Pharma deprivation death machine, indeed. Digging her nails into the palms of her hands, Jack forced herself to focus. She needed to stop this thing from getting a lot worse.

But Jack didn't have much time. Somebody was going to have to pay for those deaths, and a radical anti-patent activist who sold pirated drugs would be high on the IPC's list of suspects. When Zaxy connected the dots and figured out her role in this shit show, she would be on their hit list. Not because they wanted justice, or even to make an example of her. Jack was the only person alive who knew it was Zaxy's patented molecular structure for Zacuity that was killing people. The company had to cover up the connection between their new drug and these meltdowns. Killing her was by far the easiest way to do it.

Threezed chose that moment to amble over, kneel at her feet, and squeeze her knee, his hand warm through the canvas of her coveralls. He looked up at her through the map projection that defined her future, his eyes wide with feigned innocence. The clean fluff of his hair framed the graceful lines of his face and neck, making him look like a *yaoi* character. "I'd like to repay you for what you've done for me," he murmured.

Threezed was a practiced flirt. Maybe he was trying to manipulate her, or maybe his indenture had trained him in this specific form of gratitude. Both options were depressing, but Jack hardly noticed through the distortion field of her own depression. Something cracked inside her, then broke. Wiping the display out of the air, Jack stared into Threezed's almost-black eyes and wondered if Zaxy was actually going to assassinate her. Wondered if maybe she deserved it.

The sub thrummed into motion, bringing them closer to Inuvik, second by second. Threezed leaned forward and gently brushed his cheek against her inner thigh. It was tempting to take the easy way out and just go into hiding with this coquettish young man for a few months, but the instant she thought about it, her unhappiness grew so acute that the temptation was over. Zacuity was coring out people's minds, and she was responsible. There was no way she could live with herself if she didn't warn people about how dangerous this drug really was. When Jack got to the mainland, she was going to call in a favor that might save hundreds of lives . . . but probably not her own.

She ran her fingers through Threezed's hair and thought about dying wishes. "Are you sure?" she asked.

He bowed his head in an ambiguous gesture of obedience and consent.

SUMMER 2114

Thirty years ago, when Jack was Threezed's age, she spent every afternoon in a climate-controlled wing of the university genetics lab. She had an internship that mostly involved organizing sample libraries of proteins and obscure bits of RNA. When she wasn't tagging test tubes, she dreamed about becoming a synthetic biologist who could stop genetic diseases with perfectly engineered therapies. She knew without a doubt that one day she was going to do Good Science and save millions of lives. She just needed to find the right protein or DNA sequence that would undo whatever molecular typo made a mutated cell keep living when it should have died. That summer, Jack learned the art of apoptosis, or making cells extinguish themselves.

In the fall, she matriculated into a PhD program at one of the top bioengineering departments in the Free Trade Zone. Franklin University was near an old port city and military base called Halifax, right on the North Atlantic. Jack had never lived near the ocean before, and she rented a tiny room whose advantages included a perfect line of sight to the local high-speed antenna array—better than the free mote net—plus, a tremendous sea view. She joined the well-funded Bendis Lab, designing custom viruses for drug delivery.

But then something unexpected derailed her promising academic career.

It happened on a warm Friday afternoon. Wandering down the wide foam road into town, Jack ran into a guy named Ari who was in her protein folding seminar.

"What did you think of that last lab, eh?" she asked. He'd been pissed in class about something their professor had said about the direct relationship between proteins and human behavior.

"Total garbage," he snorted. "Hey, what are you up to tonight?"

Jack perked up. Ari was pretty cute, and it had been a while since she'd hooked up with anybody.

"Nothing much. I was thinking of grabbing some dinner and watching a movie. Want to hang out?"

"I'm going to the Freeculture meeting. You should come."

Jack didn't know that much about Freeculture, except for the fact that her lab's principal investigator, Louise Bendis, had some kind of beef with them over a patent she'd filed. From that, and stories about Freeculture in science journals, she'd gotten the vague impression that they were the sort of people who threw a lot of technical terms around to justify selling "liberated" drugs.

She must have looked dubious, because Ari laughed and said, "We're not going to ply you with drugs or anything. But you should know more about the patent system if you're going to be working on the Bendis Patent Farm." He made a snarky face. Then he smiled again, and lightly touched Jack's arm. "A bunch of us are going to get dinner after."

"Sold," she pronounced. What the hell. She was at university to expand her mind, right? And maybe she'd get laid.

The meeting was in an airy graduate student lounge down the hall from the Plant Biology Department. Years ago, some joker had tweaked a few genes in a plant designed to repair glass and set it free on the windows. Now the light was filtered by leaves whose molecular structure had bonded with the glass and remained stuck there in artful clumps long after the plant had died.

About twenty-five students were sitting in a circle of chairs introducing themselves when Ari and Jack arrived. Most of them studied genetic engineering, with a few cognitive and neuroscience weirdos. The students were all surprisingly smart, and Jack was immediately charmed by the evening's invited speaker, a young professor from Saskatchewan who was mired in a protracted legal battle with his university over whether he would be allowed to file an open patent on some simple antivirals he'd discovered. He had thick, shoulder-length black hair, and green eyes that were striking against his brown face. His name was Krish Patel, and he made Jack forget about all the idle hookup plans she'd had for Ari.

Krish compared the patent system to the indenture system, which Jack thought was kind of a stretch. But she had to admit that the patent system did seem to be at the root of a lot of social problems. Only people with money could benefit from new medicine. Therefore, only the haves could remain physically healthy, while the have-nots couldn't keep their minds sharp

enough to work the good jobs, and didn't generally live beyond a hundred. Plus, the cycle was passed down unfairly through families. The people who couldn't afford patented meds were likely to have sickly, short-lived children who became indentured and never got out. Jack could see Krish's point about how a lot of basic problems could be fixed if only patent licensing were reformed.

Afterward, at the restaurant, Jack got into a huge debate with Krish about whether open-patent antivirals could really lead to more innovation in viral shell engineering. She liked how he calmly reasoned with every criticism she had, incorporating her ideas into a solution right there on the spot.

He walked her home after dinner, and she came up with some incredibly lame excuse to invite him upstairs.

Curled up on a sofa near the window, they shared some 420 and listened to the ocean in the distance. "So the politics of virus shells," Jack said, exhaling. "Pretty hot stuff. Pretty sexy."

Krish stared at her, his hand frozen in midair, the pipe in his fingers slowly bleeding smoke. He looked half-terrified, half-perplexed. She realized suddenly that he might not have understood she was bringing him here to have sex. Maybe he thought she'd really just wanted to talk sequence all night.

"I am flirting with you," she clarified.

"Oh, good—that's what I thought." He laughed. "One can never be sure, though."

She liked the way he never made assumptions, even about basic things like fucking.

When they kissed, she could taste the political analysis he'd described during the Freeculture meeting. His flavor, a mixture of smoke and fennel, was redolent of the Good Science she'd dreamed about doing when she was an undergraduate: the science that helped people, and gave them a chance to lead lives they could be proud of. Nothing made her want to strip a man naked more than knowing he had good ideas . . . and so she did. She could taste a nuanced ethical understanding of the patent system all over his body.

Over the next few months, Jack divided her time between less-than-challenging work at the Bendis Patent Farm and extremely challenging reading about patents. Some of it was stuff that Krish recommended, but once she'd read the basic essays and books, she followed footnotes and references and struck out on her own. She became a regular at the Freeculture meetings, and even gave a demo one evening about a little program she'd written that could help reverse engineer certain classes of patented drugs. Though it was gray-area legal, she emphasized that the program was just for research purposes—or maybe for some kind of pandemic-style emergency when lots of drugs had to be fabbed right away.

One of the CogSci guys asked why you couldn't just visit the patent office and get the drug's recipe directly from the publicly filed patents. She quoted from a recent article by a Freeculture legal scholar at Harvard, who had analyzed how much time and money it would take for an ordinary person to retain lawyers and experts who could actually navigate the expensive patent databases and figure out how a drug had been put together. Most drugs that made it out of trials were a confusing hodgepodge of licensed parts and processes, and it took corp money to figure out how it had been made. For an ordinary person who just wanted to copy a gene therapy, it was usually easier to amplify and sequence the drug fast, then analyze it with her little program.

Some of the other students added to Jack's program, and pretty soon it became a small but thriving open source project called reng, for "reverse engineer." Krish gave reng to his students back in Saskatoon, they passed it along to Iqaluit engineers, and pretty soon Jack was getting patches from people in weird places she'd never heard of in the Asian Union and Brazilian States.

When Jack wasn't trying to figure out how to dismantle the patent system, she was busy being completely in love with Krish. Admittedly, she didn't take love nearly as seriously as some of her classmates did, the ones who talked about "dating" and "getting married." She viewed romance like any other biological process. It was the product of chemical and electrical signaling in her brain, inspired by input from the outside world. If she was deliriously happy around Krish and constantly yearning to have sex with him when he was away, that was just the ventral tegmental region of her brain and a bunch of neural pathways at work.

Krish felt the same way about Jack. Even when he went back to Saskatoon for the quarter to teach, they talked every day. Then, they took things to the next level: They founded an anonymized text repo together, about practical ways to deliver drugs to the public domain. It was the most intense relationship Jack had ever had.

JULY 5, 2144

An input mechanism in Yellowknife triggered a query to a molecule database in Bern, seeking several specific strings in one data field. One hundred sixty milliseconds later, the query returned a set of pointers.

The input mechanism in Yellowknife who had requested those pointers was a biobot named Med who had just watched a man die of organ failure. Three days before, the man had arrived at the emergency room nearly comatose. He'd been doing nothing but painting his flat for five straight days—not eating, barely drinking a few swallows of water, going out only to get more paint so he could keep adding more coats. The neurons in his midbrain were losing dopamine receptors in a familiar addiction pattern, the kind of thing you see after years of heroin use or gambling. No one had ever seen a person develop such a pattern in response to a week of painting.

That's why Med was running searches on the molecules that she'd found in the guy's bloodstream. It matched perfectly to a patented drug called Zacuity, but there's no way this snowboard instructor would have had the cash for that kind of scrip. He must have gotten it as a street drug, which meant somebody had done an impeccable job reverse engineering Zacuity.

Med pushed a lock of blond hair out of her eyes and leaned her slight, flesh-covered frame against a desk. She was designed to look human, her face the replica of a woman whose image Med's tissue engineer had licensed from an old Facebook database. Though technically indistinguishable from that long-dead human, Med's features had a generic "pretty white girl" look that most humans recognized as a bot tell. Under Med's pale skin, there was no disguising what she was. Her carbon alloy endoskeleton was braided with fibers and circuitry that would be obvious to anyone with sensors that reached beyond the visible spectrum. Med closed out her session with Bern, tuned the hospital's motes with her embedded antennas, and filed her report about the molecule.

The painting guy's father was supposed to arrive from Calgary in a few hours, and it would be left to some doc to explain to the man why his son had died of "painting addiction." Yet another reason why Med preferred to be on the research side of things. Less human drama.

As Med crossed the hospital grounds back to her office, the data she'd just saved locally on the intranet was examined by a pattern recognition algorithm. This hidden algorithm came through a law-enforcement backdoor on the network, invisible to everyone except the person who initiated it. The algorithm flagged several strings in Med's report. It was opened before it could be sent to anyone on the hospital staff, then promptly overwritten with junk.

JULY 6, 2144

Jack had seen Threezed naked before, when he first cleaned up, but never for hours on end. She was starting to get used to it. Now she alternated between staring at her desktop and glancing at his skinny flank, thrust out from under the counterpane in her cubby, where he was sleeping. From the easy chair near her desk, she could just make out the pale curve of his ass. Right now, though, the stream glittering beneath her fingers was more pressing.

The news was bad. For once, the science text repos and media corps agreed on something, and it was that at least one hundred people had died in Calgary from drug-related complications. Addiction experts were rushing out case studies. Nobody mentioned that the culprit was reverse-engineered Zacuity.

Once a decent reverse engineer took a hard look at her drug, its provenance would be pretty obvious. Either nobody had bothered to do that yet, or Zaxy was hushing up the results. None of her contacts in the Zone had posted their emergency signal, which would be steganographically hidden in an image and uploaded to a well-trafficked cat lovers' forum. That meant that nobody had gotten a visit from the IPC. Or at least, nobody had lived to warn her about it.

Jack wouldn't be safe for long, but it seemed like she still had some time to make things right.

If her sketchy calculations were right, Zacuity was getting people addicted after just one or two doses—something she'd only seen before in poorly designed party drugs or unmodded cocaine. She had no idea how many people had bought her pirated Zacuity, let alone who was eating it legally in beta. But it was clear that people susceptible to addiction were going to keep dying until somebody put a boot to Zaxy's throat and forced the corp to admit they'd made a productivity drug that behaved like a crappy stimulant from the nineteenth century.

The problem was that she'd have to launder her discoveries through someone else—someone who was legally permitted to reverse engineer Zacuity. Plus, she had to manufacture and distribute an anti-addictive fast, before anyone else died. Jack knew just the lab to do all of it: the reverse engineering, the publicity, and the just-in-time fix for Zacuity's addiction flaw. It was a long shot, though. Decades had passed since she'd worked there, and she might not be very welcome. Still, it was her only hope.

With Threezed still sprawled out on her bed, she headed to the control room and checked their location. With luck, she could be in her truck and on the road in twenty-four hours, her payload stuffed safely in the back. It was a terrible plan, but not as terrible as the one that had gotten her into this overall moral fuckup in the first place.

The sub nosed its way into the Beaufort Sea, its waters hugged by an enormous chain of islands whose edges formed the maze of the Northwest Passages. She was aiming for a rather nondescript promontory known as Richards Island. With all their gear piled into a kayak, she could follow the island's eastern shore, hit the broad curve of the Mackenzie River, and score a tow from a cargo ship all the way to the docks at Inuvik. She'd chuck Threezed in town, and drive south to the lab as fast as possible.

Jack began scouting for places to park the sub.

Even at the height of summer, there were still regions of the ocean where crumbled bergs and glaciers left the pale water stippled with ice. The white, reflective chunks provided good cover, and had the additional advantage of being packed with microcontrollers and mote trash that was still pingable. Her ship's short-range signals would blend into the mumble of traffic emitted by dying chips and antennas.

In the hold, she and Threezed put the last of her payload into stretchy, thin waterproof sacks. The pills and tiny vials were packaged in brightly colored perfume and aromatherapy boxes with swirly, bright pictures of Hindu gods and goddesses on them. Abruptly, Threezed stopped gathering up the boxes and stared at one, featuring a fat, bejeweled Ganesh beaming over the curl of his trunk.

Jack was impatient. "Let's hurry up, Threezed. Time to go."

"Can I stay here and hide with the ship? I can fab stuff I need. I'll keep everything clean and just watch movies."

"Look, I like you, but that's not gonna happen. I don't know you well enough to let you take charge of my sub."

"You could lock me out of the nav system."

"For all I know you're a master cryptographer and systems expert who can smash my security setup in five minutes if you want." She made a swiping motion that said, *discussion over.*

"Wouldn't I have done that already if I could?"

"Not necessarily." Jack unconsciously reached for the handle of the knife she kept jammed in her belt, resting her open palm on it. Custom controls near the blade activated her perimeter system. "Close up those sacks and help me get the kayak ready."

Maybe if she kept Threezed busy, he would stop asking her to trust him more than she wanted to trust anyone—including herself.

As they surfaced, sun saturated the control room. Jack glanced at the place where the thief's bloodstain had been just three weeks ago. She hefted one of the sacks over her shoulder. It was about the size and weight of a man's body.

Threezed was already on the deck, using heat bulbs to catalyze a reaction that made the kayak unfold and go rigid. Under his ministrations, the soft mound of rubbery cloth seemed to grow a skeleton beneath its skin, and finally took on the shape of a long, thin craft with two passenger seats.

Jack fastened her sack to the stern and shoved it into the water, where ice floated like clumps of dirty, curdling cream. There, the kayak stretched out further, taking its final shape. It could support a light, rigid negative-refraction dome—perfect for hiding from satellite sweeps—and would self-power with a nearly invisible kite sail, already unfurled overhead. After three days, the whole vessel would biodegrade into protein foam, becoming fodder for the Mackenzie River's bacterial ecosystem.

With the dome secured over their heads, Jack and Threezed settled into the kayak's uncomfortable seats. The sail came online, its system making micro-adjustments in the lines to keep the vessel stable. As long as the wind stayed with them, they'd make pretty good time. Jack put on goggles to do one last sweep of her security systems, then accessed her sub's controls from a menu that appeared to hover a foot from her eyes. With a nod, she submerged the sub below a dirty, ragged iceberg that stretched its massive fingers ten meters below the surface.

Cheap heating elements kept the kayak livable, but hardly warm. Jack peered anxiously ahead, the hood of her parka thrown back, waiting for the first glimpse of hundreds of little islands covered in pine trees and scrub that marked the end of the Beaufort Sea and the beginning of the delta.

Her perimeter started picking up stray data packets from local networks on ships she couldn't see. In her goggles, she saw a tiny flag hovering over one with a completely open network. It looked potentially friendly. She started poking around in its directories, querying a few accounts with a carefully worded request. Lots of little boats bartered for a tug down the Mackenzie

River and into town—it was standard Arctic business and a local gray-market tradition.

The ship with the open network was hailing her now, or at least a person calling himself CanadaDoug2120 had opened an encrypted channel to offer her a tow line in exchange for twenty vials of five hundred milligram Vive shots. Probably a local: Up here in the north, people still called themselves Canadians sometimes.

You got it, she messaged back, changing course to come up invisibly behind CanadaDoug2120's rig and connect with the tungsten fabric line he claimed to be playing out for her. Now she could clearly see the outline of his dull gray and blue hybrid solar barge, currently running fast on gas. Other ships became visible as they closed on the hybrid, some stacked high with cargo containers, all of them moving toward the deepest parts of the water as they navigated for the Mackenzie. Some parts of the delta were little more than marsh between islands, and the waters were stained with the red and brown churn of silt.

The line started pinging her perimeter from five hundred meters away. She loaded its exact coordinates into the sail, setting up an intercept course that would take her dangerously close to a police hydrofoil painted with the green, red, and blue of the Free Trade Zone. Her invisible little kayak wouldn't register on the police vessel's visual sensors, but the police might pick up her network traffic if she maintained her connection with the line. She would normally spurt bits of chaff traffic to hide her real packets, but a data wake full of transmissions that were too carefully anonymized for your garden-variety trading ship would be even more suspicious.

Jack killed the network and smothered her long-range signals. She'd have to do this thing manually. They should intercept the rope at a predictable set of coordinates. She'd just extrapolate from its last location, taking into account the heading and speed of the ship itself. Which was looming large in her unaided visual range, its bulk partly obscured by the police hydrofoil coming between them.

The insectile vessel in its garish Zone colors skated past. Her goggles chattered silently to their own loopback interface, sending no data beyond the device itself.

The rope should be off to the right of the bow.

"Threezed, lie as low as possible," she growled, pulling reinforced waterproofs onto her hands and ripping away just enough of the dome to get her torso out, hands extended. The air needled her face with cold, finding its way under her hood. The water was a smooth gray, feathered with the brown of delta mud. At last, she saw the rope's glittering terminus cutting a tiny wake through the water. At the same moment, its short-range signals became sniffable. The rope and ship initiated a secure handshake. Pulling herself all the way outside the dome, Jack grabbed the line with gloved hands and connected it to the kayak's hauling port. Twisting around, she cut lines to the sail and felt a small pulse of relief.

Without that piece of fabric floating overhead, she would be even harder to track. As quickly as she could, she withdrew into the invisibility of the dome, nearly kicking the balled-up Threezed as she jammed herself back into the front seat.

No matter the circumstances, she'd never failed to hitch a ride down the Mackenzie when she offered Vive. Even if her pills were killing people in Calgary, Jack reflected, she could at least give a sailor a good deal on a few more years of life.

They reached the dockyards, converted the drug sacks to backpacks, and left the kayak with a pile of other biodegradables, spinning in a slow vortex of foamy water beneath an abandoned pier. Silent beneath his pack, Threezed followed her to the espresso shop where CanadaDoug2120 waited.

"When this is over, I can drive you to the train station." Jack tried to sound kind. "Best place to go if you want to disappear."

"I have nowhere to go."

"Well, I'll buy you a ticket anywhere. No problem."

"I want to stay with you."

There was no way to explain to him all the reasons why that couldn't happen. Her eyes wandered to an alley between brightly colored apartment buildings, their hydraulic lifters dating back a century to when this whole city was built on permafrost. Her truck was parked there, in a garage below a crazy, patched snarl of utilidors that once connected the buildings like a psychotic catwalk, routing the city's water, waste, and power through heated pipes above the frost-hardened ground. Most of Inuvik's utilidors were long gone, but preservationists had gotten this bunch declared a landmark, some kind of memorial to pre-Anthropocene times.

"I'm sorry, Threezed, but I can't bring you where I'm going. Where would you rather go? Vancouver? Yellowknife? Anchorage?" She reeled off the names of three cities that were big enough to get lost in. "If you really do know your way around a motor, I'll bet you can find work somewhere."

He frowned. "Where? Who is going to hire some guy with no work history? The only way I can work is to get slaved again."

"That's not true." She tried to think of examples that would prove her point, and came up with nothing.

One block ahead, the cafe sign announced "Hot Espresso and Fresh Bannock." CanadaDoug2120 was a big guy wearing a bright orange toque, sitting in a battered foam booth with a steaming latte between his hands. Jack gave him a hearty sailor hug, slid the Vive into the side pocket on his parka, and made a big show of chumming around for the security feeds. Threezed picked up a little food and caffeine. Then they made for her truck, walking casually, juggling two lattes and an oily bag of bannock.

Several minutes later, two bots fell into step with them. From their hardened carapaces, she guessed police or military. Judging from the green insignias on their chests, they were definitely indentured to the Zone.

One of them spoke, voice emerging from a mouth-shaped grille in his headless chest. "I am Representative Slag. Did you come in on a boat today?"

Being questioned about travel by Representative anythings was not good. Jack maintained her loose-limbed walk, keeping things casual.

"Nope, I'm just getting my truck actually. Can I help you with something?"

Reaching into the deep vents of her coveralls, Jack thumbed her knife, remotely starting her truck and unlocking the storage space. She wanted an exit route, and fast.

"We noticed you talking with this man," Slag continued, his broad chest momentarily obfuscated by a grainy projected image of CanadaDoug2120, his head topped by a bright orange spray of pixels. "Is he a friend of yours?"

Jack paused for a moment, considering her options. It didn't seem like these bots were from any kind of patent authority. But if her association with CanadaDoug2120 had tripped some kind of social network alarm, she wasn't about to get into a long conversation with them—especially when she had no idea how many alerts her biometrics would trigger once they started looking.

Moving her fingers as unobtrusively as possible, she raised the doorway on her storage space and backed the truck out. The vehicle was only a few meters away.

Before she could delay Slag any further, she caught a blur in her peripheral vision that rapidly resolved itself into Threezed, swerving behind the bots. He snapped open the control panels on their backs. In an instant, the bots were staring at her silently, their minds occupied by whatever Threezed was doing to their command interfaces.

"Ha! Nobody ever resets the defaults." Threezed stood

between the two bots with his arms buried in their bodies like some weird puppeteer.

". . . the fuck?" she got out.

"They'll just sit like that for a few minutes and then start up again. A friend of mine taught me the command—works great on cheap bots like these. Just hit the panel button, type in the string, and they stop moving for a while."

Her truck was waiting silently in the street ahead of them.

Jack looked Threezed square in the face and gave him a nod of respect. "Get in the truck," she said. "We're going to Yellowknife."

6

SIDE EFFECTS

JULY 6, 2144

Paladin and Eliasz were sitting under a tree in the main room of the Arcata Solar Farm house when Bluebeard and her cohort clattered back down the stairs. The bot could tell Bluebeard was pleased. It was written into her relaxed gait and expressed through the pattern of her breathing.

Across the room, listening to her feed on full blast, Roopa glared at them and curled her fingers to touch the weapon trigger pads in her palms. Three hours of sitting in peaceful immobility, and the security guard was still treating them like adversaries. The house network, though—not so much. Paladin was making some headway there. He carefully scanned devices around the room, from the atmosphere sensors to the kitchen appliances, and got lucky with the sprinkler system. The device sat on the network waiting for requests from tiny sensors peppered throughout the soil floor. Once in a while, those sensors would signal that it was dry enough to start watering the furniture.

But the sprinkler system was also waiting for requests from other devices. Somebody careless had set it up to pair with any new device that looked like a moisture sensor.

So Paladin came up with a plan. He initiated a pairing sequence with the sprinklers by disguising himself as a really old sensor model. Because the sprinkler system wanted to pair with sensors, it agreed to download some ancient, unpatched drivers so it could take requests from its new, elderly friend. Now it was a simple matter of exploiting a security vulnerability in those unpatched drivers, and Paladin was soon on the network, running with all the privileges of the sprinkler system. Which had access to quite a lot, including house layout and camera footage. After all, you wouldn't want to start watering a room with people in it.

That camera footage would tell them everything they needed to know about who had been here and when. Paladin felt a rush of pride. Maybe he couldn't do social engineering on humans yet, but he could still fool most machines.

He'd gotten access just in time. Bluebeard sealed their deal with a credit transfer, while Eliasz dropped hints that he might be able to get more IP from the same source. The pattern of heat in her face said she was interested, though her response was carefully neutral. "You have Thomasie's contact information, eh?"

"Actually, no." Eliasz looked over at Thomasie.

The two men exchanged a beam of data.

"Contact him if you want to set up another meeting," Bluebeard said. Then she crouched down next to Paladin, still seated awkwardly beneath the tree, and looked right into the abstract, matte black planes of his face.

"What's your name?" she asked him.

"Sorry, his vocalizer's broken," Eliasz spoke quickly. "He's called Xiu."

"I'm sorry we didn't get to talk more, Xiu. Can you shake hands?" She held out her hand, tiny and calloused with an age her face didn't show. Paladin extended his arm, allowing the scuffed metal of his fingers to curl around the pale pink of hers. She pressed her fingertips into his alloy, which yielded slightly and recorded the whorls embedded in each.

They matched nothing in the databases he had access to. Either Bluebeard had a completely unregistered identity, or age had degraded her prints so much that she was effectively untraceable. When their hands broke apart, she looked at the cluster of sensors on his face again, far longer than most humans ever did.

Bluebeard wanted him to know that she was unknown. She wanted him to explain to Eliasz later that this group of pirates was not to be fucked with. And that's exactly what he did.

Flush with credits, Paladin and Eliasz rented a cheap room near the university, in a hotel that Gertrude had recommended. It was packed with visiting researchers and their families. The local mote network kept slowing down because everybody on it was downloading and uploading files that were far too media-rich to be scientific data.

"This city really is full of pirates," Paladin remarked as Eliasz lay on the tiny futon and stared at the ceiling. "Almost everybody on this network is infringing copyrights."

"That's Iqaluit for you. As soon as we've got a handle on where Jack might be, we're out of here."

"I've got a backdoor into Arcata's network, Eliasz, so we can analyze security footage from their cams. But I'm going to have to access it either really slowly or for really short periods of time. Otherwise it will be obvious that somebody is messing around in there."

Paladin explained about Bluebeard's extreme anonymity, and the relative sophistication of the Arcata Solar Farm operation. "I'm not sure how long we have before they figure out that we're agents."

"I've thought about that, too." Eliasz sighed. "They're not idiots. We've got to do this thing fast. You work on the network—look for Jack's face in the footage, or references to Zacuity. Or even references to Federation business contacts." He paused and sat up, putting a warm hand on Paladin's lower back. "Let's blow all this credit tonight so we've got a good excuse to do another sale tomorrow."

That evening, they had two missions. Paladin would sip from the Arcata network, and Eliasz would hemorrhage cash in the most obvious way possible.

They walked along the dome's edge, its massive vents rendered translucent and tilted open to admit the warm summer air. In winter the dome would seal shut, the meager hours of sunlight extended with an artificial glow that kept the suicide rate down to a statistically average level. Spiraling above them were dozens of towers whose trellises erupted with fruits and grains, and the air drifted with birds and shimmering tendrils of plant material. When Paladin zoomed in on the topmost farm levels, he could see humans and bots fertilizing the plants with tiny paintbrushes full of pollen.

"Let's go to the ammo store," Eliasz said. "The bullets are trackable, and the shooting range has a public feed for gun fans." Then he grinned, and for once Eliasz' facial expression perfectly matched the emotions indicated by the flow of blood in his cheeks and the dilation of his pupils. "Plus, we could use some shooting practice, right, Paladin?"

Twenty minutes later, Paladin was fully loaded and carrying a dozen thick, heavy bandoliers across his chest. Just for good measure, Eliasz printed out a couple of snap-together sniper rifles and socked away enough biodegradable bullets to take a serious bite out of their credit. Next, they would blow another huge amount of credits renting time at the shooting range, rumored to be the best in the Arctic. They took a car several kilometers outside the dome, whose soaring membrane walls swam with synthetic chloroplasts that sucked down the sunlight.

Baffin Heights Range was vast and rocky, its walled-in acres carpeted with purple summer flowers and planted with non-native trees to provide cover. There were hills and half-built forts, a cement bunker, and even some trenches dug by a local group of World War I reenactors. At this time of day, the place was nearly empty. It was dinnertime in Iqaluit, and the rich gun lovers who frequented this range all had meals waiting for them at home.

Eliasz beamed credits to a woman in a parka and toque at the gate, who barely glanced up from her display. Paladin watched the camstrips plastered to every surface, careful to move less smoothly than he could have. He'd have to hide his target accuracy when they hit the range, too.

Eliasz decided to begin their practice on a hill, where they'd paid for a few targets: a concrete foam house that would offer them cover, and a couple of dummies set up in a wooded area opposite them.

"The air out here reminds me of Warsaw in fall." Eliasz pulled off a shot from the house window as Paladin arranged his extra rounds on the floor. Somebody had left a pile of food wrappers to biodegrade in the corner; by now they had melted enough for the Nestlé logos to stretch into deformed versions of themselves. "It's cold but it's not too cold. And there's a smell in the air like cut grass."

Paladin still did not know how to respond when Eliasz told him things that had nothing to do with work. He tried to come up with a relevant comment, or perhaps another question. He could ask why Eliasz' prints matched those of a Warsaw priest, but Eliasz might be upset that Paladin had been searching on his biometrics, compiling a small but growing list of facts that might be true. The bot wished he could talk easily to people the way Eliasz did, but that would never be possible. No matter how long he studied the art of human intelligence gathering, his massive, hardened body with its wing shields would make it difficult for humans to feel at ease with him.

Paladin let two light machine guns slide quietly out of his

left and right chest compartments, legs bending to compensate as his center of gravity shifted slightly. He still couldn't think of a way to ask Eliasz about Warsaw.

"Loaded and ready." Those words would have to stand in for everything else he wanted to say. Paladin was in combat posture for the first time since their early days at Camp Tunisia.

"Go for it."

Paladin released a spurt of bullets through the house window, aiming in the general direction of the dummies. They'd been implanted with an artificial heat signature that turned their plastic bodies a deep red. The bot altered his assault strategy, trying to be as accurate as possible. It was a last-minute decision, based on the high probability that Eliasz' enthusiasm meant that Paladin should perform optimally rather than sticking with his damaged bot disguise. The dummies' heads exploded spectacularly.

"Nice." Eliasz laughed, and Paladin knew he had correctly guessed what Eliasz wanted. "Well, now that you've wrecked our bad guys, buddy, let's go down there and see what it takes to blow this shack up. What do you think?"

They picked up the rest of the ammo and headed down to the piles of splinter and fluff that had once been humanoid figures hidden in trees. Now man and bot were also hidden. Paladin unfurled his dorsal shields, making himself invisible, just to add realism to the scenario. The experience was so similar to his early training that he reflexively began accessing his jumbled memories of startup back in the Federation. There were disconnected images of the Kagu factory whose timestamps showed gaps of hours and days; signals from a batch of biobots who had been fabbed with him; a jarring memory of the moment when his proprioceptive sense had given way to a feeling of kinetic possibilities; and finally his current self-awareness, tinged with compulsions whose origins he couldn't access or control.

Many of those compulsions were tied directly to his targeting system, which yanked the bot back to the present. There hadn't been any flowers or trees on the shooting ranges where he'd first learned to aim and fire.

"Can you let me aim for you?"

Paladin wasn't sure what Eliasz meant. "Programmatic access to my real-time targeting systems is available only to Federation admins," he vocalized at stealth volume, enjoying the feeling of camouflage mode.

"I've heard that bots like you can—" Eliasz paused awkwardly. "That you can carry a human on your back during combat and . . . let him drive, so to speak."

Certainly Paladin could carry Eliasz' weight on his back comfortably, his shields protecting the man during combat. But none of his training, and nothing he'd learned from other bots, suggested he could surrender control of his weapons to somebody who had no access privileges on his system. Still, he could understand how Eliasz might have gotten that idea. A few simple searches on public media servers returned millions of hours of footage where people rode the bodies of giant, tanklike bots, targeting their enemies.

At that moment, Paladin decided to test something he'd been contemplating for several minutes, based on what he'd learned from the sprinkler system. Perhaps human intelligence gathering was a version of network penetration, and he could better integrate into social situations by inviting humans to see an illusory version of himself. Instead of dispelling Eliasz' misunderstanding, he would find a way to accommodate it.

"I can carry you on my back and let you guide the gun systems."

Paladin knelt next to Eliasz, his right actuator crushing a dummy's arm. He extended two ten-centimeter bars from his upper thighs. They were actually electroshock weapons, built to deliver deadly amounts of current, but they would do as foot pegs when powered down. Without prompting, Eliasz stepped onto them, leaning his torso against the sealed control panel in Paladin's back.

"Now what do I do?" His cheek was against Paladin's, his chin on Paladin's shoulder.

The bot stood at full height, and Eliasz rested his hands on the guns that jutted from Paladin's chest. Eliasz' right hand began to move slowly, getting to know the whole barrel by feel.

"It's wired into your nervous system, isn't it? You can feel my hand."

"Yes, though it's not really what you would call a nervous system. But I can feel you."

"That's amazing. I wish I could feel my guns. It would make things a lot easier."

With Eliasz' entire body pressed against him, Paladin could read his galvanic skin response at a granular level and watch fluids flowing through his organs. Following the same impulse that made him search Eliasz' background in the world's databases, he began to scan Eliasz' body for mutation, for contamination, for anything life-threatening.

"How do I make you shoot?"

"You can subvocalize directions and I will follow them."

Shoot the entire roof off that house. Eliasz' lips were pressed into Paladin's carapace, moving slightly as he gave the vague order.

He continued to touch the exposed metal of Paladin's guns, fingers wrapped around each slim barrel for a few seconds until they became too hot. Then he slid his fingers beneath them, to the cool carbon alloy of the bot's chest, stretching his thumbs back until his hands formed two V shapes beneath the protruding weapons.

Paladin had a lot of ammo to burn, and he took his time with the roof. Spent shells wafted to the ground at their feet and began biodegrading. With each spurt of bullets, Paladin undermined the structural integrity of the roof very precisely—never quite hitting it, but blasting away the foam and beams that held it in place. Every hit knocked out just a few more centimeters on the eastern edge of the house, and Paladin registered a feeling of satisfaction as the roof began to tip and sag.

As he bent to retrieve a magazine and reload, Eliasz shifted his weight away from the bot's back. The man's posture radiated discomfort. He was trying to stay on the pegs while keeping his lower body from making contact with Paladin's.

Paladin categorized the physiological changes in Eliasz' body and reloaded his guns. The bot decided to continue his human social communication test by not communicating. It didn't make sense to remind Eliasz that every single movement of his body, every rush of blood or spark of electricity, was completely transparent to Paladin. He would allow Eliasz to believe that he sensed nothing.

Eliasz' heart was beating fast, his skin slightly damp. The man's reproductive organ, whose functioning Paladin understood only from military anatomy training, was engorged with blood. The transformation registered on his heat, pressure, and movement sensors. The physiological pattern was something like the flush on a person's face, and signaled the same kind of excitement. But obviously it was not the same.

"Tell me where I should aim next," Paladin vocalized directly into the whorls of Eliasz' ear, pressed against the streamlined curve of the bot's jawline.

"Keep shooting." In his discomfort, Eliasz forgot to subvocalize. "Just shoot the roof off like I told you."

Paladin shot, but his sensorium was focused entirely on Eliasz' body. The man was struggling to stabilize his breathing and heart rate. His muscles were trying to disavow their own reactions. The bot kept shooting, transducing the man's conflicted pleasure into his own, feeling each shot as more than just the ecstasy of a target hit. When the roof collapsed, he shot the crumbling walls.

Eliasz' pulse slowed and returned to normal ranges. But Paladin kept going, shooting and reloading until every magazine was reduced to pale petals of biodegrading material around his feet and the house was nothing more than scorched chunks of foam.

Military bots like Paladin were programmed with basic sexual information about humans that was entirely clinical. If he'd been designed for sex, Paladin would have been given emocognitive training on the topic. His carapace would have been skin and muscle, fitted with genitals. His admins would have implanted him with perversions and erotic desires and programs to emulate a sexual response cycle that would match the neurochemical cascades of his human counterparts. Built as he was, however, he had few tools to interpret or contextualize what had just transpired.

Paladin knelt and Eliasz slid from his back to the ground. Standing side by side, the human and the bot surveyed the damage they had done. Pieces of foam had hurled themselves to the ground everywhere among the flowers. Destroying that house had eaten up nearly all their credits.

A car brought them back inside the dome and dropped them at the hotel. Eliasz spoke for the first time since the shooting range. "Wait for me in the lobby, Paladin. I'm going to have a shower and then we'll go back to the Lex for dinner. Maybe we'll see our protein hacker friends again." The man kept his eyes on the now invisible gun apertures in Paladin's chest. Though his intent was to avoid the bot's eyes, he failed: Paladin had visual sensors all over his body, including in the exact place where Eliasz sought to hide from them.

And so Paladin was looking straight into Eliasz' dilated pupils when he replied, "I'll check my data drip from Arcata Solar Farm and see what we've got."

By the time Eliasz returned forty-five minutes later, the bot knew a lot about the Arcata Solar Farm. He had also done some public net searches and learned a small amount about sexual relationships between humans and robots. He was not going to talk about the latter, so he told Eliasz about the former as they walked a few blocks to the Lex. It was late evening and the sun hovered above the horizon. Darkness would only last about one hundred eighty minutes once it went down.

"The Arcata pirates have definitely bought drugs from Jack before—life extenders and anti-inflammatants, mostly. She's their only source in the Federation who is also a buyer. From what I could tell, she's buying their black IP, fabbing the drugs somewhere, and shipping them back for distribution. Not at high volumes, though. We're talking small batches—generally a thousand doses per delivery. So I'm guessing Arcata Solar Farm isn't her main client."

"Makes sense," Eliasz replied. "When was the last time they dealt with her, according to the security cams?"

"Just a month ago. They bought anti-inflammatants, which they've already sold."

"Shit. Based on what the Federation knows about her patterns, there's no way she'll be back here for at least a few more months. She must have ported at Inuvik instead of here. Well, we're fucked in one way, but not in another."

"How are we fucked?"

"We're fucked because there are dozens of routes south out of Inuvik, especially if she has good transportation, which she no doubt does. She's not an amateur." Eliasz paused at the mouth of the street that led to the Lex. Already, the bot was picking up molecules from the chili-laced steam that seeped out of the

restaurant's door two hundred meters away. "We're *also* fucked because we have no idea where she's heading—could be Calgary, where she obviously sold that Zacuity . . . or, hell, it could be Montreal. My guess, though, is that she's already heard what's happening in Calgary and is heading for a safe house in one of the smaller cities."

"So how are we *not* fucked?"

"No matter what, we're leaving Iqaluit in twenty-four hours. Hopefully sooner. We've got to get on Jack's trail fast. Why don't you start sifting surveillance from Inuvik, see if anything Jack-shaped pops up?"

They trudged up the street to the Lex, where Eliasz found Gertrude eating spicy bok choy with a group of neurolinguistics students who were more interested in vowel shifts than patent injustice. Eliasz struck up a conversation, maintaining their cover identities, trying not to create any anomalous patterns in their behavior.

Paladin ignored the humans. He was busy communicating over the private bot network, where conversations were soothingly unambiguous. Nobody asked him to overlook fundamental realities as he exchanged surveillance information with Inuvik agents about several suspicious incidents over the past forty-eight hours. They gave him a wealth of data: he had images, audio, and radio communications to sift through for clues.

On the public net, the subject of bots and human sexuality also revealed a wealth of data. But when Paladin eliminated representations from fiction and the sex industry, he found himself with almost no information. Military bots were not designed to have sex with humans, and therefore his situation was largely undocumented. The indentured were not permitted to post on the public net—they were usually barred by NDAs, but also by social convention. Plus, so few military bots became autonomous that their text repo commits were sparse. None of them dealt with human eroticism.

At last, one of Paladin's searches related to Jack yielded a bot report whose contents looked promising. Two Inuvik reps had gone into deep maintenance mode for no reason after a routine pharma infringement bust at a cafe near the river. They were questioning two humans near the arrest, but hadn't yet scanned their full biometrics. Before they shut down, however, one of them had logged the barebones encounter:

1530 suspect in custody, initiating arrest

1537 statements from all witnesses in cafe, coordinates attached, data attached

1539 questioning two individuals exiting cafe

1540 female and male no broadcast identifiers

1541 maintenance check

1542 maintenance check

1543 maintenance check

1544 resuming arrest

Something weird had obviously happened there. Why would bots begin interrogating two people, then suddenly go into maintenance mode? Though records showed that Jack usually traveled alone, Paladin thought this male and female with no broadcast IDs, connected with a pharma bust in Inuvik, might be a possible lead. He saved a copy of the file locally to show Eliasz later.

As for his other search, he was going to have to do a little human intelligence gathering.

7

THE BILIOUS PILLS

JULY 7, 2144

The truck was its own driver, and that driver was a high-functioning paranoid. It kept to low-traffic roads under light surveillance. At this time of year, tourist season, that meant the least scenic routes. Jack couldn't distract herself with lovely views of the Mackenzie, glittering with minerals and pale boats. While Threezed watched a silent movie on one of the truck's terminals next to her, she tracked satellite positions overhead and cars in visual range on the road around her.

The fastest route to the lab was through Yellowknife. Her old friend Mali lived there, working as a GP at a public hospital. Maybe she could get Threezed some kind of entry-level job swabbing cheeks or mopping up. It was the least she could do after he'd saved her ass back there in Inuvik.

Yellowknife was a city of slender skyscrapers and centuries-old, real-wood homes that hugged the shores of Slave Lake, a popular resort in the northern Zone. At this time of year it was packed with tourists and college kids who'd indentured themselves for the summer to work as servants and guides at vacation lodges. The crowds would also make it easy for Mali to sell a big part of Jack's stash. Though Mali was hardly a radical anymore, she was unbending in her belief that everyone should be able to afford the treatments she prescribed. When they couldn't pay for patented pharma, she sold them Jack's pirated goods. All the money Mali earned went right back into Jack's next delivery.

The knife on Jack's belt pulsed gently: Her perimeter had picked up some local news of interest. Somebody in an off-the-record Yellowknife pirate forum wanted to warn people about a batch of bad drugs going around. A guy had taken this stuff called Zacuity to pull an all-nighter processing a giant pile of health insurance claims for unemployed patients. Claims processing was mostly automated, but in unusual cases, a human had to step in and sort things out. In short, it was the most boring job in the world. A perfect pairing with Zacuity.

At first, the guy seemed weird but OK. He worked longer hours. He had awkward conversations with his friends where he would suddenly start listing dozens of numerical codes for medical conditions that were only covered if you had full employment with a corp. Then he started working twenty-four-hour shifts, eating Zacuity instead of food, and getting no sleep. That's when he told his friends that every claim had to be processed by human hands—and if that meant people didn't get their surgeries on time, that was just the price they had to pay for good service. He'd gone completely nuts, printing out claim forms on reams of extremely expensive paper, which he stacked a meter high around his desk like a defensive wall. His manager finally called the police, but it was too late. At least one patient had died while waiting for meds that should have been authorized by a simple insurance algorithm. The insurance processor himself died of massive organ failure, probably from dehydration, behind a pillar of unfulfilled requests for pediatric anti-autism therapies.

The post ended with an update: Medics in Yellowknife were asking people who had taken Zacuity to get to the hospital as soon as possible. No questions asked. They just wanted to make sure nobody else got killed.

Jack ripped open one of the boxes she'd set aside from her stash and positioned a mood-stabilizing strip under her tongue. She gripped the steering wheel uselessly, waiting for calm. This was the biggest fuckup of her career, if you could call piracy a career.

FALL 2115-FALL 2118

Jack and Krish named their anti-patent text repo *The Bilious Pills,* after the first medicine patented in the former USA. It was a little in-joke that was generally misinterpreted to mean something like "snarky bitches" by their adversaries, namely the Big Pharma bosses and liberal patent system apologists.

The repo's vocal cadre of followers called themselves Pills, and many became famous among researchers whose work was being wrecked by the calcification of patent law. Jack rejected a full-time job at Louise Bendis' patent farm by committing an open letter to *The Bilious Pills* about how drug patents make the human population sicker. She got quoted on news shows, but after that no university wanted to hire her as a professor. How would she ever fund a lab when she'd devoted herself to destroying Big Pharma, her most likely source of grant money?

Instead, Jack became a low-level researcher at Franklin, teaching geneng to undergraduates and doing other people's lab work. And yet everywhere she went, from international synbio conferences to local meetings of Freeculture activists, her reputation as a founder of *The Bilious Pills* preceded her. She became a regular contributor to a health and science show that streamed to millions of people every week.

The patent reform movement was reaching a critical mass. It wasn't just the scientists and engineers who were angry—the public cared, too. Medicines were too expensive. Every month, they got more and more crowdfunding for *The Bilious Pills,* until Jack could finally quit her lab job to work full-time on anti-patent organizing. That's when she and Krish decided it was time to stage a major protest. Something that would broadcast to the world how broken the patent system really was.

Their chance came when a massive ship docked at Halifax, its cargo containers packed with pharma that had been fabbed in the African Federation. It was bad enough that people in the Federation were making drugs for people in the Zone that they couldn't afford themselves. But in the past year there had been a record number of deaths in the Federation from childhood neurological disorders, several varieties of cancer, and infectious fatigue syndrome. The meds on the ship could be saving hundreds of thousands of Federation lives right now. Instead, they would be warehoused in the Zone.

Jack spent two frantic days exchanging encrypted messages with a Pill whose pseudonym was "Rosalind Franklin." She had the connections to deliver the drugs to Federation kids who needed them. All they needed was the right moment.

They snuck aboard early in the morning, surrounded by a dozen swarm cams that streamed the whole thing live. Jack led a group of twenty-three of the most radical Pills wearing masks, powdered wigs, and eighteenth-century-style military jackets. It was a pirate action, after all. Jack stood out in her black three-point pirate's hat adorned with a skull and crossbones.

Back in Saskatoon, Krish was coordinating the video stream, making sure Jack's commentary came in loud and clear.

She pitched her voice to carry, waving a plastic sword over her head. "We live in a world where everyone can live for over a century without disease and without pain!" Behind her, the Pills used a metal-eating bacteria to soften the locks and rip open the cargo containers like paper. "But the keys to this good life are held in the greedy hands of a few corps, whose patent terms last longer than a human life. If they won't open access to medicine, we're going to smash it open! The time has come to fight this system that calls health a privilege!"

The cam swarm streamed footage of the protesters as they looted the cargo containers, holding up boxes of pills and syringes. Autonomous Federation drones, Rosalind Franklin's friends from the anti-indenture movement, hailed down from the dark sky. The humans lifted the booty up into robot arms. The drones grabbed box after box, then shot over the Atlantic toward a Federation barge in international waters.

The Pills began to chant. "What do we want? Patent reform! When do we want it? NOW!"

When Jack handed a box of antivirals to one of the drones, the machine used directional sound to speak into her ear: "Thank you. It's time for humans to understand that property is death." Surprised, she didn't have time to reply before the drone surged upward, on a mission that went far beyond the goals of this protest.

That was the last thing she saw before the truncheon came down. It cracked her skull, covering her face with blood and sending her hat spiraling down into the harbor's black water.

JULY 7, 2144

"It's a bot revolution!" Threezed yelled, pointing at the mobile propped against the dashboard and laughing.

A flash of anger broke through Jack's drug-induced tranquility. How could he just ignore all the danger and comment gleefully on this movie? Suddenly, she wanted more than anything to break through Threezed's carefree bullshit.

"Didn't they teach you shit in Shenzhen? Not even about classics like *Metropolis*?"

Threezed hit the pause button, struck a sultry pose, and let his accent thicken. "No, they didn't teach me shit in Shenzhen.

Just how to look pretty and talk nice so I'd get slaved quick." He looked like he was ready to slap her, or maybe to be slapped.

A wave of relaxation came over her, rolling back the rage. She was actually getting somewhere: Her guess at where he came from was apparently accurate—or accurate enough, anyway.

"So you're from Shenzhen, eh?"

"From the Nine Cities Delta, anyway." He named the special economic zone that sprawled across thousands of square kilometers in the southeastern Asian Union. No surprise that he came from there—nearly all industrial work was centered in the Nine Cities and Hong Kong.

"When did you enter contract?"

"I got slaved when I was five. My mom sold me to one of those indenture schools. They taught me to read and make an engine." His attention wandered back to *Metropolis*, whose evil bot was frozen in the middle of a passionate speech about worker uprisings.

Outside, pale blue lakes flashed between dark pines. There were no cars on the road and it was almost evening.

"So how did you end up with that fusehead?"

Threezed was clearly feigning disinterest now, idly advancing the movie frame by frame. The bot clutched her breasts with agonizing slowness, eyes wide.

"The school went broke and auctioned off our contracts."

Jack had read about tough cases where indentured had their contracts bought out from under them, their terms changed overnight. But she was still surprised to hear that one of the AU indenture schools, even a bankrupt one, had sold its wards without any background checks.

"They sold your contract to that guy?"

Threezed shrugged and poked the bot's action forward on the monitor. "No, they sold me to this machining lab, and then the lab decided to cut corners, so they auctioned me out in Vegas."

He stretched, a sliver of brown belly showing between his shirt and the waistband of his pants. "That was about three years ago."

"And you never made it out of contract that whole time?"

"Why are you asking me all this shit? You a human resources manager, when you're not pirating drugs?"

For the first time, Jack realized that Threezed's sarcasm wasn't bullshit. It was a perimeter weapon, and probably the main reason he'd made it this far with his mind intact. Instead of asking more questions, she leaned over to kiss Threezed hard on the mouth. His reaction was not artful. It felt sloppy and real.

JULY 8, 2144

Yellowknife was still hours away. Jack and Threezed slept in a tangle of thermal sheets in the back of her truck, legs and arms touching, until an alert sound announced that they'd entered city limits. It was 4:00 a.m. and sunlight slanted through bright, deserted streets.

Jack sent a message to Mali, who replied right away.

Do stop by for breakfast. I have given up on getting Judy back to sleep.

After decades of indecision, Mali had finally had a baby. Of course she was awake at an absurd hour of the morning.

They pulled up outside a one-story house in a suburb of identical homes built to look like twentieth-century log cabins hidden among trees. Mali waited for them at the door, her black hair in a neat bob, her slacks and shirt carefully pressed for work. Thirty years on the highest-recommended daily dose of Vive had kept Mali looking about the same age as her interns. She held Judy face-out against her chest, smiling over the infant's dark, wet curls and uselessly wiggling feet. The scene was so normal and almost comically domestic that Jack felt momentarily safe.

She dropped her sack to the ground and gave her old friend a hug, careful not to crush the damp baby.

"I've got some coffee and oatmeal going." Mali led them into a modest living room full of blocky furniture, antique shag rugs, and a tabletop projecting muted scenes from the morning news. Jack dumped a pile of boxes emblazoned with Ganesh onto the sofa.

"Let's go over that after breakfast," Jack said. "By the way, this is Threezed."

Threezed shook Mali's hand. "Thank you for your hospitality," he said formally. It was the first time Jack had seen him interact with other people. His manners were so good it was as if they'd been ironed into him.

They proceeded into a warm kitchen, settling down at a table built in a semicircle around the cooker. Its four little doors were already steaming with cups of coffee behind them. Jack helped herself to one and watched Mali rearrange Judy in the crook of her arm.

Jack tried to make small talk. "How are things at the hospital?"

"Pretty good. How's your business going?"

The baby began to cry, and refused to respond to Mali's shushing. At last, a young woman entered the room from the back door and took Judy from Mali wordlessly, rocking the little girl in one arm while retrieving the final cup of coffee with the other. Mali neither introduced the woman nor looked at her. Jack glanced sideways at Threezed, wondering what he thought of Mali's casual rudeness toward her indentured nanny. He glanced at the nanny as she left with the baby, his mouth quirking into its usual expression of arch amusement.

"I'm sorry, Jack, you were saying?"

"There's been a problem, actually. This may be my last shipment for a long while." Jack needed to tell somebody, to air her guilt in this safe kitchen where she could smell oatmeal being assembled. The words tumbled out in a rush. "I sold some reverse-engineered Zacuity. But of course their trials didn't catch all the possible side effects. Now my customers are giving Zaxy a free trip back to Phase 1." Phase 1 clinical trials were for one thing only: To find out if a new drug could kill people.

"Wait, what?" Mali looked ill. "You're the one behind those drug psychosis episodes? What the hell are you doing selling shit like that?"

"Zaxy is an IP hoarder."

"So liberate more of their antivirals. Or go after those new marrow regenerators. Nobody needs Zacuity."

"People want it. Plus, it *is* kind of a necessity. When you're competing for jobs with people who take it, Zacuity could mean the difference between employment and unemployment."

Jack wasn't even convinced by her own argument. Mali shook her head, her face reflecting a mixture of care and anger that looked too complicated for her youthful features.

"Jack, I'm worried about you. This Zacuity situation . . . we've seen some really bad stuff at the hospital. And Zaxy is just as likely to murder you as they are to arrest you."

"I know, but I have an idea. I think I can make this right by getting some data out to the public that proves Zaxy is selling an addictive drug. I can release it with a therapy, too. Bring down the whole corrupt corporation."

"Are you nuts? Zaxy owns half the reps in the Zone, and probably in every other economic coalition, too. Plus, who is going to believe you? It's not like you're a scientist anymore. You're a . . ."

Mali paused awkwardly and Jack stared at her coffee. What was Mali going to call her? A pirate? Criminal? Dealer? It didn't matter, because it stung enough to hear her old friend say she wasn't a scientist. Jack's whole world was science. She spent most days in the lab tinkering with molecules so that even the poorest could benefit. But of course someone like Mali wouldn't see it that way. To her, Jack was no better than a lab monkey, churning out copies of other people's drugs.

"I know it can't be me who releases the data. I'm going to leak it to someone who can. Someone who's a *real* scientist." Jack's words came out more bitterly than she'd intended.

"I'm sorry, Jack. I didn't mean it that way. But you don't need to go public with this. We're already working on a therapy at the hospital, and we can't be the only ones. You need to hide."

"You don't get it, do you?" Jack finally looked at Mali again. "It's possible that something genuinely good could come out of this. Zaxy broke the law. When the public knows, it could lead to real changes."

"Do you really think so? Or are you just going all martyr because . . ." This time, Jack appreciated Mali's habit of trailing off. Was Jack trying to kill herself to make up for what she'd done? Maybe. Probably. She didn't know.

"This isn't just about my life, Mali. This could destroy one of the most corrupt pharma corps in the world. We might never have this chance again."

Mali sighed. "True enough. How are you going to do it?"

"You're already way too implicated. The last thing you need is more information."

Abruptly, Jack realized that Judy had started sobbing again, her cries muffled but distinct. Mali noticed at the same moment and looked resigned.

"Is there anything I can do besides pay you for the shipment today?"

"Actually, there is."

There was no way that new mom Mali could resist the tug

of protectiveness when Jack told her about Threezed, indentured as a child, rescued from a brutal client, and desperately wanting autonomous work. As Jack talked, Threezed remained silent, his expression completely blank. Mali gave him a hug and said she was sure she could get him a gofer job in one of the research labs. The credits wouldn't be brilliant, but they'd cover an apartment and ramen.

Finally Threezed spoke, in his politest AU schoolboy accent. "Thank you so very much. I had thought I might be of further assistance to Jack, but this would be perfectly lovely."

"Come along with me for the morning shift. Just leave the dishes here for the girl to clean up." Mali disappeared into another room. Before they left together, Threezed shot Jack a look that hovered between anguish and rage. But she couldn't worry about that right now. He was safe, and that's what mattered.

Somehow Mali had also talked Jack into taking a shower, followed by having a nap in a real bed before she hit the road. The nanny sang a song to Judy as Jack blasted herself with hot water. Lake country was the best place to get clean—no water shortages meant no cutoffs. In twenty minutes, she was sound asleep in Mali's guest bed, dreaming about nothing.

Med was buried deep in her research at the workstation farthest from the reception area when the gofer from the hospital lab dropped off the samples. But somehow, while the young man waited for some results, he found his way to her desk. Then he stood in the perfect spot for looking over her shoulder at the neural map of the man who didn't want to stop painting.

He started talking to her with no preamble. "What's that? A brain?"

She hadn't discussed her research with anyone yet. Nobody would return her messages about it, nor comment on the articles she'd tried to post. Frustrated, she found herself infodumping on this new lab gofer.

"It's one of my patients, who has developed a novel kind of addiction. I've never seen anything like it—his dopamine system has been completely tweaked in a matter of days. Probably caused by some street drug he took. A pretty damn sophisticated drug, though."

For a long time, the gofer didn't say anything. Med realized, with a pang of embarrassment, that he must not have any idea what she was talking about—until he dug deep into the pockets of his jacket and pulled out a tiny box decorated with images of Ganesh.

"A drug like this?" he asked.

She took the box from his hand and shook a few pills out into her desk. The gleaming, onyx gelcaps were etched with the words "EAT ME" in a pink Comic Sans font. Without thinking, she tossed one into the spectral analyzer.

What she saw, on a cursory reading, brought her up short. "Where did you get this?"

He grinned and leaned on her desk with one hand, hip cocked coquettishly. It occurred to her that many humans would consider this lab gofer to be quite beautiful.

"I know the person who makes them." He used an incongruously flirtatious tone. "Want to meet her?"

When the door to the bedroom slammed open, Jack sat up abruptly and palmed her knife. Mali's bedside clock said she'd been out for six hours.

Standing in killing range were Threezed and a pale, terrified-looking young woman in a medic's lab coat. The medic stared at the sheen of Jack's scar, a fat pink track that started on her neck, divided her breasts from each other, and crossed her entire stomach. Jack knew it was the kind of deformity that medical students read about, but rarely glimpsed. Scars were so easy to prevent with a variety of Fresser skin glues.

At last, the woman spoke. "I need to talk to you about the schematics for Zacuity. Now."

8

BRAINS

JULY 9, 2144

It was time to try a new experiment. Over the past day, Paladin had discovered that including "military bot" or "military robot" in pretty much any search related to sex got him petabytes of fictional representations, and nothing about reality. The lack of data only made his desire more urgent. Maybe it was a quirk of his programming as a reconnaissance bot, designed to gather intelligence where nothing was known.

Or maybe it was something about Eliasz.

Paladin faced the man in their tiny hotel room, and tried for the first time to initiate a conversation. He modeled it on what he'd learned from Eliasz.

"This reminds me of waiting for my first assignment," Paladin vocalized.

Eliasz looked up from a map of the northern Zone he'd been studying. His muscles were tense; Paladin had startled him. He said nothing. The bot tried again. "I didn't learn much about human intelligence gathering. But some of the bots got paired with humans who gave them intensive training."

Eliasz was nodding. "Yeah, they don't always give you the training you need. When I was in Warsaw I had to learn a lot on the job—just like you are now, buddy."

Paladin was getting somewhere. To retrieve personal information, he had to share personal information first. This was his chance to get the answers he wanted, by stretching his truths into strategic lies.

"Some of the robots said they were learning about human sexuality. Do you think military robots need to do that?"

Blood rushed to Eliasz' face and electricity arced over his skin. "I don't know anything about that. I'm not a faggot."

It was not the first time that Eliasz had said something orthogonal as if it were relevant. This was clearly a conversation whose progress Paladin would only understand after accessing more information on the public net. He began searching on uses of the word "faggot."

But before Paladin could analyze what he found, Eliasz received a message from Thomasie on his mobile. The man glanced at it and stood up, his posture suggesting he'd already purged their strange exchange from his mind.

"OK, this is our last chance to squeeze any final bits of data from our friends at the Arcata Solar Farm," he told Paladin, his hands feeling their way through his perimeter check ritual—head, belt, both shoulders. The sign of the cross. "We're going to go in there and get as much as we can about where Jack might be headed. I'll give them our final piece of IP and see if they'll leak anything on their manufacturer in the Federation. You see if there's anything else you can get out of the network."

He reached over and touched the curved shell of Paladin's shoulder unnecessarily. "You got that, buddy?"

"Yes."

When the bot stood, he could see the complicated pattern of electrical impulses emerging like a fungible map on the crown of Eliasz' head. But there were no answers in it. He could read anxiety there, and nothing more.

Thomasie picked them up outside their hotel in a worn, multiuse truck of the sort preferred by local farmers. It could seat four comfortably in the cab, but Paladin's bulk relegated him to the cargo area. He could still hear and see everything that happened inside, but nobody would try to engage him in any part of the exchange.

With a novel feeling of surprise, the bot realized he preferred it that way. Paladin was developing a small repertoire of highly granular desires for random things, like riding in the back of a truck. They coexisted easily with mission-critical desires like preventing Eliasz from dying.

He scanned the public net for patterns in the use of "faggot," analyzed the Arcata network for appearances by Jack, and wondered about personal preferences. His desire to survive, and to protect friendlies like Eliasz, were programmed into him at a deep level. He had not come upon those desires by discovering them over time. But a preference for riding in the backs of trucks? That was something no botadmin had implanted in him.

Overhead, the dome gave way to sky, and Paladin watched the pale bubble of Iqaluit recede slowly into rocks, grass, and farms.

When they arrived at Arcata Solar Farm, Roopa met them at the door in a state of complete alert. There were no feeds playing in the background, and there was an unfamiliar truck parked in the driveway. Thomasie looked as unruffled as ever, except for his artfully mussed hair, and said nothing as they passed the energy signature of Roopa's weapons.

Inside they found a rapidly drying layer of water over everything: The sprinkler system had just watered the furniture. Youssef was there, his posture far more relaxed than yesterday, wiping a chair before sitting down with Bluebeard and Redbeard at a table whose legs grew thick, soft ivy.

"You've come back so soon," said Bluebeard, offering Eliasz another slightly damp chair. Paladin stood behind Eliasz, continuing his search of the network and logging emotions in the small group.

"I realized I needed a bit more cash, after all," Eliasz said, his heart rate and breathing carefully even. "Since I know that you're good for the money, and you know I'm good for the IP, I thought you might be interested in a slightly different deal."

Bluebeard gestured over a projector box at the edge of the table, which drew a black window into the air.

"Do tell," she said.

"I've got a small molecule here that could be worth a lot of money. Basically, it's a euphoric." He thumbed his wrist a few times, and a white vector drawing of a molecular structure appeared in the floating window. Bluebeard looked at it, her eyes narrowing.

"I don't want a flat fee. Let me help you distribute it, and cut me in on a percentage of the earnings. I really think all of us could get rich here."

Bluebeard's attention was wandering. "Interesting idea," she lied, looking at the black window.

Beside her, Redbeard's body told another story. He was intrigued. "It just so happens that we might have an opening for a distributor." Redbeard looked sideways at his partner.

"Locally? Or would I need to travel somewhere to get this done?" Eliasz was looking for any geographical data he could get. But at the mention of travel, both pirates stiffened.

"What does that mean?" Redbeard's heart rate elevated.

"Well, I'll be honest with you," Eliasz replied. "I'm not crazy about Iqaluit. Reminds me too much of . . . Las Vegas." Selective truth-telling kept his biosigns even. "I wouldn't mind going somewhere outside the domes for a little while. If there were some money in it for me, you know."

"This is the kind of thing we'd normally fab down in Casablanca," Redbeard said thoughtfully. "And I think if we did this—though that's a big if—you would have to fetch it yourself."

Bluebeard sighed. "Yes, our usual contact seems to have run into a bit of trouble."

Now they had a lead on where Jack worked in the Federation. And apparently word had gotten around that she was a target, too. Eliasz must have let this information distract him, because his next move felt clumsy even to a HUMINT neophyte like Paladin.

"Where do you go if you get into that sort of trouble?"

It was a weird question, and the pirates were clearly puzzling over it when Paladin saw an encrypted message arrive. Bluebeard glanced at her watch, unable to control a brief spike in blood pressure. At that moment, Paladin's access to the network was shut down. Somebody had found his backdoor. They might only have a few seconds before he had to go into full autonomic defense mode.

He partitioned his mind: 80 percent for combat, 20 percent for searches on faggots.

"This conversation is fucking over." Bluebeard stood abruptly and aimed a blaster at Eliasz, while Roopa ran for Paladin from behind, her guns scoring his already-spread shields with fire.

Time was no more distorted than it always was: In one movement Paladin shoved Eliasz under the table and shot Bluebeard in the face with his chest weapon. She staggered back in a spray of cauterized tissue and guttering neuroelectrical impulses. Redbeard screamed, his blood-soaked body at last in harmony with his pseudonym.

Enough data had come in from Paladin's search that he could start to build a taxonomy. Each use of "faggot" could be categorized, and he began assigning them to subcategories tagged with exemplary, recurring sentences.

Suck my cock, you faggot.

Eliasz bunched himself into a defensive posture under the table, metal glinting in his fists and a snap of electricity showing his perimeter was active.

At the sight of her boss going down, Roopa scrambled up a particularly thick tree trunk to Paladin's left and shot at his head, trying to take out some of his sensors. The wet wood protecting Eliasz started to smoke under her steady shots. Redbeard ran toward the stairs and Youssef scrambled after him, terror distorting his gait. More feet rang on the steps: Two men were coming down, their faces shielded and guns bared. A tiny red triangle logo stood out on their chests, marking them as indentured to a private security company in the Zone. These men belonged to the pirates in the same way Paladin belonged to the Federation.

Paladin covered Eliasz, his shields spread around the man like sheltering wings, and Roopa took out one of the sensors on his back. Now he had to shift to catch her movements, and of course more trouble was coming. Those men on the stairs had guns that Paladin's armor could withstand for only so long. From his position beneath the table near Paladin's knees, Eliasz reached out and cut a horizontal line of light into the air, slicing one of the armored men's legs off at the ankles. The man's detached feet smoked in a tidy pile next to his writhing body, but his partner just stepped over him and kept coming. With a well-aimed shot to the bot's right shoulder, he shattered Paladin's carapace.

That faggot tried to touch me.

Roopa worked on the break in Paladin's armor with her gun, trying to sever the arm that the bot had already lost once. Eliasz didn't have enough charge for another laser shot like the last one, but he had a tiny smart grenade for Roopa's tree. She hit the floor without ever vocalizing, charred wood lodged in her ripped throat and gut.

Even with some of his sensors ruined, Paladin could see Redbeard's distress signal shoot over the network. And hear Youssef screaming about a helicopter on the roof. The pirates were trying to escape.

Eliasz signaled to Paladin. To stop Redbeard and Youssef, they would have to take out the remaining guard, whose footless partner was scrabbling for a weapon through his pain. Paladin ran toward the spiral staircase first, squirting a last stream of bullets from his chest, throwing his weight to the left just in time to land his fist in the footless guard's chest. The man's alloy armor—the same material that made up the bot's carapace—kept Paladin from penetrating. But Paladin felt the reassuring vibration of shattering bone radiate up his arm. The guard wouldn't die right away, but he wouldn't be reaching for a weapon again, either.

"Faggot" is generally a pejorative term for a homosexual man. It is classified as hate speech in most regions where homosexuality is legal.

Eliasz threw his last grenade and missed—something about the remaining guard's perimeter threw it off. But the blast had him off-balance long enough that Paladin was able to put his body between Eliasz and the other man, clearing the stairs.

"They're on the roof trying to escape in a helicopter, Eliasz." Paladin said in a damage-distorted voice. "Get them and I'll hold this one off."

It was going to come down to hand-to-hand combat, and his opponent was an indentured guard whose life depended on the survival of his clients. He would never stop fighting. Paladin didn't want Eliasz down here, in case things went badly.

As Eliasz disappeared up the stairs, the guard turned his face shield to Paladin. He was nearly as tall as the bot, and armor made him just as bulky.

"I know your model, biobot. You've got a human brain under that armor."

Paladin kicked the man in the thigh, hoping to short out the power source for his perimeter field. He did no damage, and the man punched Paladin low on his chest carapace, clearly aiming to damage the human brain inside. The man did know his way around Paladin's model, but like most humans, he made the mistake of assuming the brain was what controlled the bot.

As Paladin smashed his fist into the man's shielded face, he realized why Eliasz had used the word "faggot." He thought the bot's body parts were just like a human's, and that a heavily armored body signified manhood. Sex with a military bot would be what one branch in his taxonomy called "shit for faggots." This also explained why Eliasz had been so curious about the origin of the bot's brain. He assumed it was the seat of Paladin's identity.

The guard staggered, recovered, and slammed his body against Paladin's wounded arm. As Paladin felt his limb go numb, he delivered a killing blow to the guard's perimeter power source. Then he grabbed the man's head in his nearly disabled hand and cradled it against his chest for a minute.

"My brain is just an advertising gimmick," Paladin vocalized, echoing what the bots had told him in the Kagu Robotics Foundry. "It's to make humans think I'm vulnerable. But it has no real functionality." Then he ripped the man's face shield off and crushed his skull against his breastplate. For an instant, there were useless chunks of brain inside and outside his carapace, inches away from each other.

As Paladin ascended the spiral stairs, he sent out a query to the Kagu Robotics Foundry network where he'd been assembled. He wanted to know everything he could about the history of his brain.

Paladin found Eliasz at the top of the stairs in a room that had obviously been the pirates' data center and private meeting area. A curved glass wall looked out over rows of solar panels, the farthest away blurring into a dark, choppy texture almost indistinguishable from the rocky ground. Another wall was lined with server cabinets, most devoted to the legit solar operation. Just a few contained the farm's real business, and those were currently being reduced to blobs of drooling fire by some well-placed bowls of thermite. Redbeard was crumpled next to the flames, his body partially consumed by them.

On a sturdy living-wood ladder that led up through a door in the ceiling, Youssef was frozen in the sights of Eliasz' blaster. A helicopter was warming up on the roof over their heads, wind from its propeller agitating the smoke in the room.

Youssef was crying, his body going into shock. "Why are you doing this? Are you IPC agents?"

"Yes." Eliasz squeezed off a shot. "And that makes you a dead pirate."

Youssef's body jerked once and fell, a clean, charred hole in his head emitting only the tiniest amount of matter. With a tight gesture, Eliasz motioned Paladin to the helicopter on the roof. The self-piloting vehicle was easy to commandeer with their IPC credentials.

As they rose over photovoltaic fields, Paladin found that he could communicate with the sprinkler system again. He turned it on. At least the energy grid would be preserved.

Just as Paladin was returning to other data-analysis tasks, Eliasz reached over and gripped his arm—the one that wasn't dangling in a useless, agonizing wreck at his right side. The man's heart was pounding, though his excitement had spiked and was diminishing.

"You did good back there, buddy."

"I'm glad we both made it out."

"Let's hope our luck holds in Casablanca."

"We're going back to the Federation?" That seemed like the wrong way to follow Jack's trail out of Iqaluit.

"Best way to stay hot on the trail is sometimes to backtrack, Paladin." Eliasz steered the helicopter back to the airfield where they'd landed two days ago. "Somebody in Casablanca will know where Jack goes when she wants to hide. We'll find her faster that way than trying to trace her through highway surveillance."

"How can you be sure?"

"Human networks are the most vulnerable," Eliasz replied. They landed just as the red sunset was transforming Iqaluit's dome into a blood blister.

9

PRISON

JULY 9, 2144

Jack put the knife down. She carefully wiped her thumb over the hilt, and a slight shiver ran down her spine as her energy shield powered down.

"What the fuck is going on?" Jack yanked on her thermals. Before she even had her coveralls zipped, Med had explained her hypothesis about how to reverse the effects of Zacuity. It sounded fairly plausible, but she'd hit a snag. She couldn't finish her research at the hospital, because all her queries disappeared as soon as they were routed outside the Yellowknife cloud.

Now that she wasn't in fight-or-flight mode, Jack realized the medic with Threezed was a bot. It wasn't just that her name, Med, sounded like the kind of thing a hospital would name its bot. It was also that her skin tone and face had an uncanny regularity.

"I have to finish this work, and Threezed said you knew a place." Med spoke with the kind of urgency that Jack recognized from countless nights with engineers in the lab. The bot wanted to fix this problem, and she wouldn't stop until she'd tried every possible solution. Even if that meant running away with a pirate and a hospital gofer she'd just met an hour ago.

"Won't the hospital notice when their property goes missing?"

Med crossed her arms. "I'm autonomous. No one can track me unless I allow it."

Jack weighed her options. Just from their brief conversation, she could tell Med was an excellent engineer. It seemed wildly unlikely that Zaxy would have sent this particular bot to assassinate her. Med had a hard-to-fake blob of half-finished molecular simulation data and a hypothesis about an addiction therapy that worked by selectively erasing memories in the brain. More to the point, Med could have killed her already if that was her plan.

Somehow, Threezed had found the perfect researcher to work with Jack on a therapy. Jack caught him glancing at her, looking for a reaction.

"Med, you are welcome to join us. Let's get in the truck."

Jack liked watching the smile break over Threezed's face.

Night was becoming a more meaningful category as the truck drove south, away from the Arctic perma-light. Med sat rigidly next to Jack and watched as the road lost its infrared glow in the day's dwindling heat. Threezed slept in the back, the mobile folded up on his chest. It flickered occasionally with light as it tried and failed to sync over the mote net.

Jack swiped through the non-news sections on ZoneFeed, one of the biggest corp media streams. But a local alert grabbed control of her display, painting the windshield with an urgent report about a bizarre crime underway at the train control center in Calgary. Though trains ran autonomously throughout the Free Trade Zone, human operators still made decisions about schedules and changes in service. That afternoon, one of the operators had suddenly started making a *lot* more decisions than she should have. She completely revised the northern Zone's train schedules, sending out hundreds of notices and updates, flooding the system with contradictory commands. When her colleagues tried to stop her, she barred herself in the operations room and isolated the train software code from the rest of the net.

It was impossible to prevent the operator's updates from going through, and impossible to shut the trains down instantly. Commuters were being warned to stay off the trains until the situation was under control. Drones were lifting people out of cars that had shifted to new tracks and destinations. So far nobody had been hurt, but at least one empty train had derailed into a twisted ruin when it took a sharp curve in the tracks at high speed.

ZoneFeed had ripped a video from some bystander's social feed, which captured a blurry image of the woman behind the control room window.

"I am doing my job! I am making *decisions*!" she screamed.

A black-market drug was rumored to be involved, but ZoneFeed was unable to confirm more. Updates would be ongoing.

Jack and Med looked at each other as the alert drained out of the glass. Her pirated Zacuity was spreading everywhere, and the results were getting a lot worse.

"Where are you from?" Med broke the silence abruptly. Even awkward small talk was better than dwelling on news of the spreading disaster.

"A little town south of Saskatoon called Lucky Lake."

"I don't know it."

"Nobody does." Jack shrugged. "It's sort of northwest from Moose Jaw, if you know that area."

"My parents took me to Moose Jaw once."

Parents weren't the sort of thing a bot normally had. Jack couldn't help but look sideways at Med.

"I was raised by humans. They're roboticists down at University of Alaska. I've always been autonomous."

Threezed woke up and crawled forward to join the conversation. "I thought robots just came online and that's it. Why would you need to grow up anywhere?"

Med had the look of somebody who was tired of explaining herself.

"Most bots are built like that, yes. Especially ones whose manufacturers need them for a specific task, and who aren't planning to let them mature to autonomy anyway. But a lot of roboticists believe that successful autonomous bots need kinship ties, and a period of childhood where they can experiment with different identities. That's what they're doing at the lab where my parents work, and at a couple of other research institutes."

"So you're basically an experimental model." Threezed looked at her appraisingly.

"Well, there are a lot of us now. After twenty years, you stop being an experiment and just become a model."

"Oh, are you twenty?" Med nodded and Threezed grinned. "Me too."

Jack struggled to add something that wouldn't sound clueless. "I've read about bots who were built autonomous. But I didn't realize you were . . ."

"Out in the world, being autonomous?" Med laughed.

"Yeah." Jack laughed with her. "Robotics isn't really my area. I'm more on the genomics end of things."

"Me too," the bot replied.

The road was smooth, probably from a recent refoaming. Lakes tended to move around up here, depending on precipitation, so the local towns preferred roads that would biodegrade quickly. When a lake ate the road, they just sprayed a different route around its new banks.

As Jack's truck passed through Uranium City, early dawn silhouetted the monument there: a row of twentieth-century miners, their metal bodies climbing out of a massive pit mine whose contours resembled a meteorite hit. Kilometers of undeveloped boreal forest and lakes stretched ahead of them. Scalloped dunes swerved across the land, their dark sand milled under glaciers in the last ice age. They'd hit the northern edge of Saskatchewan.

Eventually the pines and birches gave way to fields of wheat and rye; in the distance, the cement cylinders of grain terminals looked like missiles lined up and ready to launch.

Watching the tree-rimmed edge of a lake go by, Jack thought she could smell the musk of metabolized grass. Built into the rolling swells of the prairies were hundreds of small organic farms and co-ops that fed each other and exported to the cities. The car must have passed a herd of cows, hidden behind a rise in the land.

It was this landscape she'd held in her mind to kill the pain when she was in prison.

FALL 2118

The Zone failed to stop dozens of drones from making off with its drugs, but Jack and seven other Pills were held on charges of theft and property damage. Dubbed "the Halifax Pharma Eight" online, their arrest was covered in granular detail by patent reformists, and pretty much nobody else.

Then stories started coming out of the Federation about all the kids whose lives they'd saved with those drugs. Suddenly they were in all the big media feeds, too, and Jack was dubbed "the Robin Hood of the anti-patent movement."

Krish attended the trial, along with the usual gang of ragtag reformists and tenured radicals. Stripped of their broadcast tech in the courtroom, they took notes on dumb notepads and raced out during breaks to upload and publish. Jack felt fierce and self-righteous until the prosecution pushed hard on a conspiracy charge. If the Halifax Pharma Eight were found guilty of conspiracy, that meant potential jail time. Given that Halifax got most of its wealth from pharma, the jurors might be in the mood to make an example of anti-patent radicals who destroyed private property.

Indeed, they were. After a very short deliberation, the jury found the group guilty of conspiracy to commit theft, as well as trespassing. The judge gave Jack three months in prison for her role as ringleader. Her coconspirators got a week each, plus damages.

The court prohibited network access and written materials during her sentence, so Jack had plenty of time to memorize every crack in the paint next to her bed and follow the curves of the fluorescent ceiling wires over and over again with her gaze. She had time to consider what would or wouldn't happen next.

And she had time to watch her cellmate Molly visited by storms of violent dissociation. Molly was in for a series of minor assaults, all caused by untreatable manic depression. When she was on an even keel, she took Jack's mind off the boredom by telling improbably lurid stories about a seemingly endless string of hot Quebecois lovers mired in a citywide sexual melodrama. But when Molly got manic, she decided Jack was a spy who had to be stopped at all costs.

The cabinet of glues and tissue-growing trellises in the infirmary became as familiar to Jack as the contours of her bed frame. Eventually Molly broke Jack's pelvis in two places, and she spent a peaceful week recovering in a bed next to a man on a ventilator.

Jack thought the prison board, whose facility was partly funded by pharma giant Smaxo, might have deliberately paired her with a cellmate who was likely to beat the shit out of her every once in a while, but she never had any proof. During visiting hours, she asked Krish to investigate her suspicions, but he just shook his head and looked at his hands.

Eventually Krish confessed that he'd shut down *The Bilious Pills*. He was afraid that it was no longer anonymous enough, that more scientists' careers would be destroyed if he kept it going. They had taken the wrong path, he told her. There were other ways, less confrontational ones, to reform the patent system. A well-endowed human rights org had given him a huge grant to do research that would generate high-quality public domain alternatives to pricey patented pharma, and he didn't want to risk losing his lab when he'd just gotten enough money to hire more people. He'd even held a job open for her, under the intentionally low-profile title of research assistant.

Seated in the prison visitors' room, the air around them occasionally glittering with surveillance motes, Jack couldn't grab Krish by the shoulders and yell what she was feeling. Instead, she stood up wordlessly and walked back to the infirmary, even though they still had an hour of visiting time left. How could he have made this decision without her? She didn't want to be a line item in Krish's research budget. And without *The Bilious Pills,* she had no identity, no community of fellow travelers. Back in her narrow hospital bed, Jack curled into an aching ball and cried. Fisting tears out of her eyes, she realized she had no future, either—or at least, none she could recognize.

On subsequent visits, she tried to explain this to Krish, but her rhetorical powers had been fuzzed out by Smaxo painkillers. He was so focused on what his grant meant to him that he couldn't understand what *The Bilious Pills* had meant to her.

And so for the next two months she focused on the smell of Saskatchewan in summer, on the feeling of being in the middle of a vast prairie populated only by plants, machines, and the occasional farm co-op. It was the place where she had first learned to love the idea of reshaping life. When she slept, and even sometimes awake, she watched the prison walls soften into tiny yellow canola flowers, and counted in her mind all the ways their genomes had been perfected by science.

When Jack got out of prison, all evidence of her broken bones erased by patented therapies, she felt more broken than ever. The man she loved, her partner in crime, had killed *The Bilious Pills* and her career. Everything she'd felt for Krish had been transfigured by her rage, then settled into melancholy numbness. None of her options seemed real or important anymore. She took the job at Krish's lab in Saskatoon because it was better than starving.

Krish still didn't seem to realize that their relationship had cratered. After picking her up from prison, he held her hand on the short bus ride to Quebec City, then the long train ride to Saskatoon. She pulled her hand away a few times, but finally could not resist. Her body needed affection, and a part of her still loved him. It was winter, and the train shot down a reconstituted twentieth-century track past boxy, abandoned grain elevators painted with the names of towns, and pale fields scattered with rolls of snow-whitened hay. Jack put her hand on the double-paned polymer of the window and tried to feel the cold. The transparent material was barely cool; it was designed to shield travelers from a temperature so low it could blacken hands with frostbite in minutes. She wanted to evaporate the window just to feel her fingers die.

Trying to rekindle things with Krish was absurd. This became clear after he calmly told Jack about his plans for her career, starting with the assistantship in his lab.

"If you keep publishing with me and my postdocs at the Free Lab, nobody is going to care about this thing with *The Bilious Pills* in five years." They were finally alone in his flat, eating a late dinner that thankfully required Krish to stop gripping her hand insistently. "You just need to lay low, and work your way back up to a position where you can start applying for grants on your own." His voice had that warm, rational tone that she'd fallen in love with, and his green eyes hadn't become any less enticing.

But Krish didn't understand who she was now. Maybe he hadn't understood her for a long time. She didn't want to work her way back up the academic ladder again. There was another path for her, and it wasn't a tenure track. Her recent experiences—the beatings, the flowers blooming in prison walls, the lost joy of writing for a famous underground text repo—made this even more obvious. The problem was that Krish couldn't conceive of a life outside university, and Jack was sick of sharing her feelings with someone with such a narrow vision.

She settled for telling Krish a truncated version of the truth. "I don't know what I want to do now."

"You have to keep doing genetic engineering. Look how successful reng is. You wrote that in just a weekend."

When had he become so serenely oblivious to her desires? "Don't worry," she spat out. "I'll take that gig in your Free Lab."

Seemingly satisfied with that answer, Krish didn't bring up his five-year plan for Jack's future again.

JULY 10, 2144

"Are we here?" Threezed peered out the windows at a fat river curving beneath the bridge the truck had chosen for their crossing.

"Yes."

Jack felt a punch of nostalgia that temporarily drove the air out of her lungs. Downtown Saskatoon, hugged by the South Saskatchewan River, was fed by four bridges built in the twentieth century. The sun was setting and the skyscrapers had become undulant shadows, their turbines cutting air with only a faint noise. By the time the truck passed the research fields and greenhouses of the university, the darkening sky was the color of burned meat.

It had been over twenty years since she'd been to the Free Lab.

Over ten since the last stiff, vague "how are you I am fine" messages between Jack and Krish. They had broken up, then drifted apart, and Jack had no idea how he would react to seeing her again after all this time. From following Krish's publications in the open science journals, she knew his passion for crushing the patent system was as strong as ever. That's what she was counting on. Plus—he owed her for shutting down *The Bilious Pills.* Even now, she was still pissed about how he'd dealt with that.

Jack stashed the truck in a student garage out of satellite view, and registered using a forged identifier on the parking network. The campus hadn't changed much, but the Free Lab had gotten an upgrade since the last time she was here. It now occupied a long, low building, formerly used as animal housing, and was tricked out for the twenty-second century. Still, the security was stuck in another era. Jack got all three of them through the doors with a simple RFID emulator.

They emerged into a space that looked exactly like a barn spliced with a wet lab. The high ceiling peaked over a vast, open room full of tables, sequencers, printers, amplifiers, and dozens of colorful plastic tablets. Somebody had etched the words "FREE LAB" on the wall across from the door, using viruses that ate paint down to the plaster and extruded a thin crust of gold. It was late enough that almost everyone had left for supper, but Jack could hear two people talking over the hum of a printer in one of the offices off the shared room. One of them laughed, and immediately Jack knew that it was Krish. All at once, she felt nauseous: This was going to be weird.

"Come with me," Jack addressed Threezed and Med, hoping she sounded authoritative. She gestured toward the office.

Krish was still laughing and talking with one of his students when she stepped through the doorway. His hair showed a few streaks of gray, and the brown skin of his face had lost enough collagen that a few lines framed his eyes and mouth. But he still looked very much like the man she'd known decades ago.

"Hey, Krish," Jack said with deliberate casualness. "Got a few minutes to discuss addiction therapies?"

He stared at her, a pirate in coveralls with silvery-black stubble on her head and a knife on her belt, flanked by a runaway slave and a robot scientist. His eyes widened, but Jack had to admit that Krish was doing a pretty good job of masking his shock.

The student seemed to sense that this situation was way above her pay grade, and quickly showed herself out. Jack didn't know how to start, so she got down to business. "I know it's been awhile, but there's a big problem with a reverse-engineered drug. And we need your help."

Silently, Krish walked to one of the empty workbenches outside his office. He pushed aside a humming sequencer and gestured a 2-D black screen into the air, a cursor blinking in the upper left corner. At last, he spoke to them. "Show me."

Jack and Med interrupted each other with details about the Zacuity side effects, supplemented with several hastily designed simulations of brain activity that hovered over the table's projector. It was like they were visiting scholars sharing important new data. Nothing like work to fill in where personal history has left a smoking hole. But Jack kept getting distracted by Krish's physical proximity. She had so many vivid memories of Krish that it was hard not to compare this man, almost a stranger, to the one who had helped her found a movement—and then killed it when she was locked up.

Med continued to talk, oblivious to what was going on between Jack and Krish. "Zacuity is designed as a simple work drug, right? So you get sharper focus while you work, longer attention spans. But what makes Zacuity really popular is that it gets deep into the reward center and gives the user a serious dopamine rush when he does his work, or whatever he's doing when he takes the drug. My patient decided to take a double dose to make house painting more fun."

Med twisted her lips, concentrating on something. The projector played a 3-D video of dopamine receptors, looking a bit like blooming tulips. Particles sparkled around the edges of their petals.

"Now, as you can see, the drug is stimulating his dopamine receptors. There's your pleasure bang. But just watch, because the drug is doing something else, too."

The tulips began to wither and shrink. Soon, there were half as many dopamine receptors on screen.

"Zacuity is reducing the number of dopamine receptors on the neurons in the midbrain and prefrontal cortex. And this is really the key. Doing this interferes with decision-making, and makes the brain extremely vulnerable to addiction. As he loses more and more of those receptors, he gets more addicted to the specific thing he did while taking the drug—in this case, painting. He's going to be in withdrawal from a painting addiction for years, if he survives at all. The Zacuity has basically rewritten the neurological history of his brain. Now he's got a powerful, long-term addiction that he wants more than anything to feed."

Jack jumped in. "That's good news for corporations who license the drug from Zaxy, because you've suddenly got a bunch of workers who are obsessed with going to work and completing projects. The thing is, the corps are pretty careful about regulating dosage and catching it when people are having an adverse reaction. But what about ordinary people who just want to do some painting or studying?

"Those are my customers, and they aren't taking Zacuity under any kind of supervision." Jack pulled up the ZoneFeed story about the train controller. "Of course, that's dangerous. Some people who dose themselves basically become manic. They refuse to do anything but engage in whatever process they associate with that dopamine reward. They don't eat, sleep, or drink water. These deaths aren't from the drug itself—they're side effects from things like dehydration, injury, and organ failure. Of course, people also have to take more and more of the Zacuity to get their rush, so that makes everything worse."

Med seemed to look into the distance, and the ZoneFeed story disappeared. The projector replaced it with a 3-D representation of a molecular pathway, a flowchart showing how the drug triggered one change after another in the molecules that naturally coursed through its victims' neurons.

Krish was focused completely on Med's display. "But how is this different from normal addiction? Neurologically, it's your typical process addiction, like gambling or even workaholism."

"The difference is that Zacuity changes your brain's anatomy to make you susceptible to addiction even *before* you get high," the bot replied. "Usually dopamine receptor loss like this takes months or years to happen. But Zacuity addiction is instantaneous. In the short term, you get an incredible high from doing work. But in the long term, your neurochemistry is altered forever. The only thing you want to do is get *back* to work. Especially if you can take more Zacuity along with it."

Krish's face folded into an expression of guilt that Jack had never seen before. "You made this . . . pirate Zacuity?"

"I did the reverse engineering, yeah. But I didn't make the drug addictive. And none of the trials showed this long-term damage as a possible side effect."

"None of the *published* trials," Med clarified.

"Right."

"The public needs to know that Zaxy is marketing an addictive drug, Krish. You can use your research exemption from patent law to publish an analysis. Plus, we need a therapy. That's why we came to the Free Lab."

Finally, Jack looked Krish full in the eyes. He didn't look guilty anymore. Instead, there was a ruthless expression shaping his features, something he must have acquired in the many years since she'd last seen him in person. Krish drummed his fingers on the table purposelessly, a habit she recognized; it meant he was considering their request. Until this moment, Jack hadn't realized how little hope she'd had that her plan would work. The old Krish would never have done it. But the man in front of her now was a different person.

"How much time do you need?"

Med sat up straighter and the projector turned off. "Just a few days."

"Help yourself to our equipment. If you can get Free Lab members interested in this, then you'll have a bigger research team. Publish when you're ready, and we'll take care of the prototyping." Krish paused, fingers still drumming. "We can handle the publicity, too."

Jack blew out a sigh of relief. Maybe those Zaxy bastards were going to kill her, but she would leave a nice bite mark on their asses before she went down. Across the table from them, Threezed folded his mobile in half and stood up.

"Might I please have a look at some of your machines?" There were his perfect AU school manners again. He pointed at two atmosphere chambers that looked like plastic bubbles on metal carts. A mild pressure differential engorged the rubber gloves that researchers used to reach inside the airtight chambers. It created the illusion that the machines were covered in reaching hands.

Krish seemed a little startled by Threezed's formality. "Sure—go ahead." Krish shrugged and turned back to Jack. "Do you have a place to stay? We've got a loft back there that people crash in sometimes. There's even a shower."

"Thanks, Krish." Jack touched his arm.

He tilted his head at her. "Is somebody after you for this?"

"They haven't caught me yet. But yeah. I'm going to help out with Med's project and then lie low for a while."

"Nothing's changed for you, huh?" Krish's tone hovered between bitterness and admiration.

She started to reply, to tell him that everything had changed. To retort that she wasn't just sitting in some fancy lab with tenure and grants, because she'd spent her life actually doing things. But instead of snarking, she wondered about all the ways Krish might have changed, too. Jack rested a hand on her knife hilt and stared up at the light wires woven into the high ceiling of the Free Lab. They created the same generic striped pattern as the ones she'd memorized on the ceiling of her cell all those years ago.

10

ANTHROPOMORPHIZERS

JULY 10, 2144

Paladin had never approached Camp Tunisia with the access levels of a fully fledged agent. When he checked his maps now, he found directions to a small flight pad beside an arched, luminescent entrance into the facility beneath the dunes. A spider bot covered in tools greeted him.

Hello. Let's establish a secure session using the AF protocol.

Paladin replied that he could use the latest AF protocol, version 7.7.

Let's do it. I'm Blazer. Here are my identification credentials. Here comes my data. Please leave your vehicle here. You may continue inside. That is the end of my data.

For Eliasz, Blazer vocalized the standard greeting: "Welcome to Camp Tunisia."

Already on the local network, Paladin started saving encrypted data to a directory devoted to the mission. Fang contacted him while he was still uploading some geotagged maps of Jack's probable route out of Inuvik, with statistical likelihoods assigned to each route.

Hey, Paladin. Remember our secure session? Let's keep using that. It's Fang. Here comes my data. Meet at the attached coordinates for debriefing. Bring Eliasz. I have an IPC rep here who is not very happy. He wants to know why you almost burned down a valuable energy source for Iqaluit. That is the end of my data.

Paladin replied that he'd received Fang's data.

Cradling his shattered right arm in his left, Paladin led Eliasz into the cool tunnel whose end was represented on his internal map as a block of garbage characters—encrypted, except for bots whose rank gave them the proper key. They arrived at their destination long before the encryption began, passing an icy server room and several radio frequency beacons before finding the conference area.

Fang was there with the IPC rep they'd met before their trip to Baffin Island. With the rep were two other humans, one in crisp corp casuals and another whom Eliasz must know based on the burst of electricity Paladin saw in the facial recognition area of Eliasz' brain. The bot settled heavily into a chair, laying his mostly detached arm on the table. Next to him Eliasz nodded curtly at the man he'd recognized.

"Hello soldiers," said the rep. "This is my colleague from the IPC, Senator Haldeman. I believe you know each other?" Paladin was not included in the question, and Eliasz nodded mutely again. "And this is Dr. Hernandez, Zaxy's VP of public relations."

Fang beamed a message to Paladin. *You look a little worse for the wear.*

Paladin desperately wanted to talk to somebody else about what he'd gone through, but he kept his answer curt. *Some of this damage is deliberate, and some unavoidable.*

"I understand you almost took down the solar power grid in Iqaluit, Eliasz," the senator intoned in an accent that broadcast a life of educated privilege in the Free Trade Zone. "Luckily, it was very quickly contained, and hasn't become an international property incident. But it's going to be hard for me to keep this little problem with drug hooligans under wraps if you keep blowing up solar farms." He paused, and Paladin watched the senator receive a small stream of data packets. He routed it from a neural hub to a device implanted in his right cornea, which he tried to check unobtrusively. "We're always happy to help any large company stop criminals, of course." The senator nodded at the Zaxy VP, who offered an empty smile. "Piracy undermines free trade, and punishes the most productive members of our society." Having finished his speech, the senator checked his cornea feed again.

Eliasz stabilized his heart rate, then looked calmly at the senator, the IPC rep, and the silent Zaxy VP. "We were nearly killed by anti-patent terrorists on Baffin Island. You are lucky we made it out alive with our intel. We've narrowed our search down to Casablanca, and I can guarantee we'll know where Jack is hiding in less than a week. Once we know that, it will be simple to stop the crime."

Wrinkling his nose, the IPC rep waved his hand around as if he were wiping bugs out of the air. "Keep the damage to a minimum. Don't create any messes you can't clean up yourselves."

The senator's blood pressure spiked as he read new data arriving in his implant. "Eliasz has done excellent work for us before. I have full confidence in him."

Fang sent data to Paladin again. *Looks like the Senator has bigger things to worry about. Representatives from the Brazilian States are threatening an embargo on Zone biofuel. I predict this meeting is about to end and you're going to have less than 24 hours for rehab before hitting Casablanca. Eliasz works fast.*

How do you know that?

I am reading the Senator's transmissions. And I have worked with Eliasz before.

The meeting did wind up rather quickly after the senator's vague statement of approval. The VP remained silent and the rep's eyes twitched nervously as Eliasz shook hands with all three men. They ignored Paladin, and as the senator and VP hurried out, the rep pulled Fang aside for a short conversation. Paladin and Eliasz were alone at the table.

"Looks like we can patch you up now, buddy," Eliasz said,

touching Paladin's detached arm softly. "Let's try to move out in twenty-four hours, OK?"

"I am going to find my botadmin." Paladin had already located Lee in one of the labs below them, and exchanged messages. Lee was available any time in the next two hours.

"I should come with you."

"I will go with him, Eliasz," vocalized Fang, rejoining them as the delegate left. "Why don't you get some sleep? You're going to need it."

Eliasz remained at the table studying his mobile as the two bots filled the doorway, then disappeared into Camp Tunisia's maze of hallways lit by ubiquitous, low-power LEDs.

Paladin turned his main sensor array toward the bot. Fang's morphology was insectile: He looked like a two-meter-tall mantis. His torso, balanced on six highly articulated legs attached to his chassis, was a block of circuitry and actuators, which themselves supported two massive arms fit for missile launch, industrial operations, and nanoscale machine repair. Right now, the arms were folded in half at his sides, and he regarded Paladin with dozens of sensors mounted in two fat, sinuous, segmented antennas curving from the top of his torso. Beside him, Paladin's bipedal bulk looked almost human.

I read your mission report. Impressive work so far. Covert ops are always tough on a first assignment.

Well, I did manage to lose my arm again. :)

Fang echoed Paladin's rueful humor emoji back to him. It was a relief to be communicating with someone who didn't require any form of subterfuge. Paladin wondered what Fang would think about Eliasz' use of the term "faggot."

I'm worried about human intelligence gathering. I know how to respond to many forms of human behavior, but I have almost no information about how to react to sexual arousal.

:P :)

I don't mean to be funny. Did you ever have sex with Eliasz when you worked with him?

No. Did you?

I'm not sure.

Impulsively, Paladin sent Fang a compressed burst of video files and signal data from Eliasz' body that day at the shooting range. He appended his still-growing taxonomy of uses of the word "faggot."

Fang expanded the data, emitting no signal for several seconds as the two bots rounded a corner and arrived at Lee's lab. Then he replied. *I think I understand.*

Lee waved at them from his bench, and Fang vocalized politely for the human's benefit. "Paladin, why don't you join me later?" As the bot backed out of Lee's lab, he beamed an extremely long number, which allowed Paladin to decrypt a space on his internal map. Now he perceived a massive warehouse, the shape of a flattened bubble, beneath Camp Tunisia. Until this second, he hadn't known it was there.

"How the hell are you, Paladin? You look like shit." Lee cheerfully turned to his bank of neurosoldering tools.

Paladin realized that the last time the two of them had met, he had known less about his own mind than Lee did. Now he knew a lot more, which Lee could discover easily enough. Until he was autonomous, the Federation would always hold a key to the memories he'd encrypted in the Federation cloud. Lee or any other botadmin could pore over everything he'd learned and thought, editing or changing it if they chose.

Knowing this didn't bother Paladin. He trusted Lee, the same way he trusted Eliasz—and for the same reason. These feelings came from programs that ran in a part of his mind that he couldn't access. He was a user of his own consciousness, but he did not have owner privileges. As a result, Paladin felt many things without knowing why.

After enduring two hours of tinkering, Paladin stepped out of an elevator into the base map's decrypted room, which was bathed in ultraviolet light. Obviously not a human space. It was crawling with bots from many different Federation camps. Lightweight spiders, chameleons, and sleek drones gathered around the high, curved ceiling, while the floor was vast enough to accommodate even the biggest tanks. Charge pads were everywhere. Paladin tried to locate Fang on the base network, but only found something called RECnet. They were in a faraday cage that blocked signals from entering and leaving the room. There were no motes in the air. The RECnet was their only server.

But it was a good server, and it offered Paladin a highly granular map of every bot's position in the room, along with a menu of open wares and pay-as-you-go apps.

Nobody really buys anything from the menu. Fang transmitted from a corner where the floor met the ceiling in a textured, parabolic curve. *You can get everything you need in the open wares.*

Paladin sat down on a battered bench next to Fang, who rested on his six actuators.

Nice arm upgrade.

Yeah, I even got new piezosystem drivers, and Lee upped the resolution on my neurochemical sensors.

Paladin ran his newly customized hand over the rough surface of the wall, reading its molecular composition and registering minute cracks. He sent a small burst of output from the experience to Fang, who laughed. It had taken Paladin no time to convince Lee to do the upgrades, but several minutes to vocalize his reasons for keeping the dents and scorch marks on his carapace. If they were going to Casablanca, it wasn't a good idea to look like a brand-new military biobot.

You were right—we are shipping out to Casablanca in 22 hours.

Paladin was about to send more data when Fang interrupted him. *I've been thinking about your experiences with Eliasz.* Fang's antennas slowly swept the room, drifting lazily in a default algorithm that scanned for security vulnerabilities. *I think he's anthropomorphizing you.*

What do you mean by that? Treating me like a human?

Yes and no. He could treat you like a human by giving your survival the same priority he gives to the survival of a man. I've been in the field with Eliasz, and I know he would lay down his life for me. He's a good soldier. But anthropomorphizing is something different. It's when a human behaves as if you have a human physiology, with the same chemical and emotional signaling mechanisms. It can lead to misunderstandings in a best-case scenario, and death in the worst.

But we do have chemical and emotional signaling mechanisms. I can smile. :) I can analyze and transmit molecules better than a human can.

True. But sometimes humans transmit physiochemical signals unintentionally. He may not even realize that he wants to have sex with you.

Paladin quit their trusted connection for a second, and tuned the soothing hum of RECnet's real-time location map. Hundreds of bots crisscrossed the room, floating or rolling or walking or lolling in a stupor after crashing on really good worms downloaded from the free wares menu. He understood what Fang was getting at—after all, he had done his own experiments that relied on Eliasz' self-deception—but at some fundamental level he couldn't believe that Eliasz was anthropomorphizing. Something else was going on. He wished he could signal the base network and check again for a response from Kagu Robotics Foundry about his brain. Maybe if he understood more about his one human part, his interaction with Eliasz would make more sense.

Finally, he reopened his secure session with Fang. *I think he knows he wants sex.*

How can you be sure?

Because I asked him about it, and he said he wasn't a faggot. He classified our activities using a sexual term.

He didn't. His use of that word is a clear example of anthropomorphization. Robots can't be faggots. We don't have gender, and therefore we can't have same-sex desire. Sure, I let humans call me "he" because they get confused otherwise. But it's meaningless. It's just humans projecting their own biological categories onto my body. When Eliasz uses the word faggot, it's because he thinks that you're a man, just like a human. He doesn't see you for who you really are.

Paladin could think of no response he cared to transmit. But after hours of crawling the public net, he had a few mental models that allowed him to predict the kinds of behaviors a human might expect from a robot faggot. *Maybe it's different for biobots.*

That's crap. Your brain is nothing more than a processing device for facial recognition. You can operate almost as effectively if it goes offline. It doesn't reveal some essential gender identity any more than your arm reveals that you are secretly a squid.

Paladin once again found himself in a contradictory state, knowing Fang was right, but unable to feel the truth of it.

Fang sent more data: *I've fought beside your model before, and the bad guys always take out the brain first. Why do you think Kagu advertises the location of the brain so much? It's like camouflage. Malicious attackers expend their weapons on a useless target.*

Paladin possessed a file time-stamped from the first few minutes of his life. In it, he'd stored a video of the arm bots on the Kagu factory floor explaining his physical capabilities. They'd used those exact words, "like camouflage."

Talking to Fang was inflaming Paladin's desire for data, not reducing it. He exited their session.

The more he analyzed what had happened with Eliasz on the

shooting range, the more complicated it seemed. Paladin had accumulated entire days' worth of memories, petabytes of data, about Eliasz. Unlike most humans, Eliasz didn't treat Paladin like a thing, a tool to be deployed. He told the bot things that no other entity had ever shared with him. And Eliasz displayed desire for Paladin when the bot was at his least human, his body unfolded into a weapon. How could that be anthropomorphizing?

If Paladin used Fang's logic to analyze the situation, however, it was hard to deny that other explanations were possible. He accessed his memory of Eliasz saying "I am not a faggot" for the seven hundred and sixteenth time. "Faggot" was a word for something that only humans cared about. Maybe Eliasz really was like the sprinkler system at Arcata Solar Farm, mistaking Paladin for something that he was not.

Finally Paladin considered the possibility that his own feelings were also an illusion. Every indentured bot knew that there were programs running in his mind that he could not access, nor control—and these programs were designed to inspire loyalty. But were they also supposed to make him care this much about small physiological changes in Eliasz' body? Was this constant searching and data-gathering about Eliasz something that he would shut down if he were autonomous?

Fang addressed Paladin again: *Remember our secure session? Let's keep using it.*

But Paladin didn't want to talk to Fang anymore. Impulsively, he tuned the open wares menu on RECnet and downloaded a worm jammed inside an immersive combat simulator. The accompanying .txt file explained that just as the action got intense, a memory error would crash him. The program would also helpfully output the entire sequence to a log file so he could save and replay his half-destroyed memory of the experience.

Paladin found himself pouring bullets into an enemy tank,

an injured human beside him. As the game's code uncoiled, he knew his only goal was to destroy the tank and bring the man to safety. He chose to strap the human to his back and continued to fire. When the adversary's ruined molecular bonds boiled with gas fires, when Paladin was just about to fulfill his mission, the man's body fragile and alive against his back, he hit the malicious code. The bot's whole body spasmed, his reflexes made useless by bogus and contradictory commands. A wave of ecstatic nonsense gripped him and the file ended.

The next morning, Paladin still hadn't heard back from Kagu about his brain. He and Eliasz lifted off into the scalding blue of the sky, a light stealth jet buoying them over the sand. They landed in a Casablanca suburb called California, and hitched into town on a truck caravan. Their base of operations was a cheap hostel near Biotech Park, at the fringes of the old medina along the piers.

Biotech Park was a corporate incubator, but it was also a kind of city unto itself. Famous across the Maghreb, the campus looked like a massive wall of mirrored glass by the water, next to the equally massive Hassan II Mosque, whose rooftop lasers sought line of sight with Mecca during prayers. It held hundreds of startups locked in a frenzy of research and investment capital, all vying to be the next Zaxy. When ancient amplifiers broadcast the call to prayer, it got picked up and relayed by the mote network. Clumps of engineers would emerge from their workstations onto the vast, pale-orange plaza stones of the mosque—sometimes to pray, and sometimes to take pictures of other people praying.

The life sciences industry had remolded the landscape for miles along the coast, spawning smaller but still-glittering versions of itself devoted to housing genetic engineers and their families. Expensive condo developments advertised on giant billboards, offering private berths for residents' yachts. The culture of Biotech Park spread everywhere, washing over the old medina walls across the street to flood its centuries-old narrow lanes with consumer biotech shops, game stores, and European fashion boutiques. Recently relocated engineers wandered like confused tourists through the medina's spice markets, past stalls where slabs of real butchered lamb were for sale right next to outlets offering trellis-grown pork tissue wrapped in biodegradable polymers for half the price.

Though it dominated the skyline, Biotech Park did not create order or regimentation. Instead, it simply amplified the polyglot chaos that was Casablanca in summer.

Paladin and Eliasz adopted cover identities similar to what they'd used in Iqaluit: a down-on-his-luck engineer with his bot. They wandered through the medina's tea shops, asking anyone who would talk to them whether they knew about good contract work in the Park. Somehow, Eliasz knew which tea shops would be packed with engineers grabbing a curved glass of tea between long stints of amplification, transcriptome modeling, and sequence analysis.

"Those teahouses are the kinds of places where Freeculture projects are born." Eliasz explained his strategy to Paladin as he tossed his bag on a low bed back at the hostel. Outside, the afternoon prayers mixed with the sounds of traffic while two men shouted Darija and Russian. "You work all day for some company that doesn't care about you, but you and your buddies still want to change the world. So you go out to tea and bitch about it. Then you start a project, you give it a name, start passing it around. Before you know it, you've either got the next blockbuster drug—or the next patent crime."

Eliasz checked his weapons perimeter, passing his hands over his head and chest in solemn blessing. Paladin assessed the space:

white walls covered in paint that repelled particulates and sealed its own cracks; a rectangular bed; a foam easy chair whose arms were sprayed with charge strips that gleamed dully. On one strip somebody had left a throwaway mobile which was now biodegrading into a lump of gray cellulose. There was enough room here for the bot to stand up comfortably, though he guessed he would have few opportunities to do it. He touched the bed with his new hand, where minute skin flakes reminded him of all the humans who had been here before.

"You're going to have a speaking part in this operation, buddy," Eliasz said, looking into Paladin's face. "You're my indentured lab assistant. I want you to get some HUMINT, too."

Abruptly Eliasz sat down on the bed, dropping his bag into the place where a pillow might have been. "A couple of hours until people start getting out of work at Biotech Park. I'm going to get a little sleep. Keep watch." The man rolled his whole body to face the wall, bending his knees in the semifetal position every soldier learns after sleeping in tight quarters for any length of time.

Paladin stood in the middle of the floor, his sensors in a default high-security mode. That mode was one of his deepest instincts, and he couldn't conceive of resisting when asked to keep watch. Nothing seemed more natural. But high security did not prevent him from reopening the file that held his experiences after eating that worm.

He wanted to watch it now, while Eliasz lay vulnerable next to him. Reviewing his own crash made the bot sway slightly with pleasure, but didn't disable him the way it had when the worm was executing. Still, he couldn't allow himself to play it more than once. Too dangerous.

Paladin closed the file and focused his entire attention on monitoring the room, filling his sensors with the hum of Eliasz' blood flow, the temperature of the air, the molecules cascading through his spectrometers. The electrical signature coming from Eliasz′ nervous system indicated he′d fallen into a deep sleep almost instantly. The bot monitored Eliasz′ breathing and wondered how his life would be different if he became unconscious for several hours every day.

11

FREE LAB

JULY 11, 2144

"That bot is a vicious bastard," Krish spat in an angry whisper.

"You'd have to be to take down Blue and her crew."

Jack and Krish sat at a worn thermoplastic table in the Free Lab's kitchen. A coffee machine made from recycled lab equipment was slowly spitting out dark, rich liquid.

They stared numbly at a feed display on the surface between their hands, detailing the destruction of Arcata Solar Farm. Government reps explained that it had belonged to a pharma pirate ring whose cover was a remote solar operation on Baffin Island. Very little data survived the attack, but a few seconds of recovered security footage showed a bulky humanoid bot with wing shields crushing the skull of an armored guard. Physical evidence suggested that this bot had killed everyone and stolen a helicopter. Depending on the political bent of the feed source, it was being called an IPC conspiracy or a terrorist attack.

"I saw Blue just a few months ago." Jack held her voice steady as she poured coffee into a Pyrex measuring cup. "I was supposed to bring her some of the Zacuity."

"This is not good, Jack, not good. If this is part of the hunt for you, you are in serious danger. You need to get the hell out of here and let Med and I take care of developing the therapy."

"No. You need my help. It will only take a couple of days."

"He could be on his way here right now."

"There's no way. Blue had her shit together with security.

Even if he got the servers, it would take him hundreds of years to decrypt them."

"You don't think they'll come after me? After this lab? It's not very hard to guess you might wind up here."

Jack felt a flick of annoyance. Did Krish really think she hadn't figured out a way to stay hidden? "There have been no connections between us on the public net for at least twenty-five years. And they won't be able to follow my data trail here, either. I take a lot of precautions." She patted her knife, which automatically routed all her communications through an anonymizing network that stretched across the Earth and through at least two research facilities on the Moon.

Krish looked dubious. She wanted to grab him by the spongy synthetic wool of his jacket and yell that she knew what she was doing. Couldn't he respect that this project was so important that it was worth everything to her? No. He didn't know what it was like to pay the price for doing something risky.

"Look—I poisoned those people with my drug. I need to fix it."

Krish stared at Jack's hands on the table through the hologram that rose out of a commercial break in the feed. It was the Zaxy logo, an anthropomorphized letter Z, dancing with a woman who had been liberated from sexual dysphoria by a new drug called Languidity. His face hardened into that ruthless expression she'd never seen when they were lovers. "Let's get to work, then."

When Krish and Jack emerged from the kitchen, Med was describing the project to a woman whose black hair grew in fluffy patches around purple vines rooted in her scalp. They were deeply involved in a debate about how already-existing addiction workarounds could be integrated into a therapy. More students arrived for morning lab, some drifting over to meet this new researcher, whose midnight arrival had become the subject of lab gossip.

Watching them, Jack had to admit that the Free Lab did resemble the ideal research space she and Krish had dreamed about back in the days of *The Bilious Pills*. Everything they produced was open and unpatented. All their schematics and research papers were on the public net. Almost anyone, even nonstudents, could use the Free Lab equipment if they had an interesting idea.

Of course, nobody here was pirating, at least not officially, even though sometimes that was the best way to save lives fast. And a lot of their open work was eventually absorbed into locked IP by the big patent holders. Companies like Zaxy and Fresser came here to recruit from the talent pool all the time.

Still, the lab was free enough to harbor a pirate whom the International Property Coalition would happily see murdered. That was no small thing.

SPRING 2119

In its early days, the Free Lab was located deep underground in a cavernous, dusty room whose doors had been stenciled a hundred years prior with the words "COMPUTING CENTER." They were renetworking, repiping, and drywalling the place with the help of Krish's grant, but slowly, so there were dozens of half-finished offices and cubbies where you could curl up and disappear.

One evening, after a particularly mind-numbing series of assays, Jack fabbed a thin futon, dragged it up a ladder to a skeletal loft over the sequence library fridges, and fell asleep behind some discarded shipping boxes for protein-folding devices. Up there, noises from the lab were muffled and everything had the comforting, grassy smell of packing foam. It was the first good night's sleep she'd had since her arrest, and she never went back to Krish's house after that. Everyone in the lab knew she was living in the loft, but it wasn't out of the ordinary for researchers to do things like that when they got really involved in work.

For the next several months, boxes were her bedroom and 2-D movies were her nighttime entertainment. Krish left her alone, lost in his new role as manager of a well-funded lab, and she lost herself in the frosty, brittle quiet of a Saskatchewan winter. The simplicity of her job was a kind of GABA regulator, she realized, de-spiking her moods while she dealt with whatever the fuck was going to happen next.

Spring was transforming the prairies into ruffled grain fields when Jack met Lyle Al-Ajou. Lyle was Krish's star postdoc and she had a buggy tattoo on her half-shaved head. It was supposed to move through a sequence of common flowers, but crashed every time it bloomed into a deep orange poppy. The static image on her light brown skin, its code unmended, gave Lyle an appealingly absentminded air.

It was 2:00 a.m. and Jack's eyes were blurring over a line of code when Lyle poked her. "Can I crash with you tonight?" Lyle looked sheepish. "I'm about to fall over, and my clone sequence won't be cooked until morning anyway. You have a bed up there, right?" Lyle pointed up, vaguely in the direction of Jack's loft, and raised her eyebrows. Was it an innocent request, or something more? Jack hadn't had sex since her awkward attempts with Krish after prison. It was as if her desires were as broken as her bones had been: She couldn't figure out what she wanted, and was even more clueless when it came to other people.

"I'm not trying to hit on you, I swear." Lyle grinned. "I'm just so tired I don't think I can make it home."

Everyone else had left around midnight. Jack shrugged. "Sure."

In the semidarkness of the loft, surrounded by boxes emblazoned with corporate logos for scientific instruments, Jack and

Lyle were suddenly wide-awake. They couldn't stop talking. They rehashed the results of a recent patent infringement trial.

"I can't believe they gave Thorton ten years in prison," Lyle whispered fiercely. "What the hell? He wasn't selling those drugs. He gave them away to his neighborhood because of a goddamn epidemic."

"Ten years in prison makes my experience seem like a walk in the park."

Lyle didn't say anything. Eventually she spoke in an uncertain voice. "Is it OK for me to ask what that was like? I read *The Bilious Pills* and I've been trying to get up the courage to ask you, but it always seems tacky or weird or fannish or something."

"It was mostly boring." Jack pulled back before spilling anything more. This was Krish's protégé. No sense launching into an entire diatribe about how Lyle's beloved Freeculturist boss had sold out and abandoned the cause while Jack learned about bone engineering firsthand. Besides, there was something else that Jack suddenly, desperately needed to ask. "Were you serious about not hitting on me?"

"I don't have to be serious about it. I could be sort of . . . exaggerating my lack of interest . . . a lot."

Jack got up on one elbow and stared down at Lyle, trying to understand how the arch of her nose made every feature on her face more beautiful. A slice of light from the lab below illuminated the static petals of her tattoo and the half-smile on her lips. Then Jack couldn't help it anymore. She grabbed Lyle harder than she intended, kissed her harder than she'd wanted to kiss anyone for the past year. Maybe she was being too intense, but it was intoxicating to be able to measure the strength of her desire again. Lyle didn't mind. In the grip of Jack's embrace, she thrashed with pleasure and moaned.

The two of them slept for only about an hour while Lyle's

clones were cooking, and the next day they were the happiest sleep-deprived zombies in the lab.

JULY 11, 2144

Jack put her beaker of coffee down on the lab bench next to Med and glanced up at the loft where Threezed was still sleeping. More than a quarter of a century had passed, and she was still crashing in lab storage rooms. And her future was more uncertain than ever.

"Here's my hypothesis about a possible therapy," Med announced. "We need to circumvent the reward patterns Zacuity created in the ODs, and we can only do that if we disable people's memory of the addiction. Memory of the work reward is what keeps addicts coming back for more, even after they've detoxed. Every time they see a cue that reminds them of work—whether that's a breadboard or a paintbrush—they'll want to eat Zacuity again. Over time the dopamine receptors will grow back, and that's helpful, but the main thing is to get rid of those reward memories."

"Makes sense," Krish mused. "What kind of memory blocker would you use?"

"Check this out." Med allowed herself a quick grin, and showed them a molecular structure erupting into the air as a series of abstracted bonds. It was a collection of already-existing biological parts, along with a protein that Med had folded herself.

"I call it Retcon," she said. Krish walked around the table, looking at the projection from every angle. "Essentially, what we'll be doing is establishing retroactive continuity in the brain. We tweak the neurons to avoid the memory of the Zacuity-fueled reward, and we link the pre-addiction past to the present. You could say we create an alternate present for the brain, based on changing what it thinks has just happened."

"Sounds easy." Krish's tone hovered between distracted and sarcastic, making Jack remember why she'd once loved him so much.

"What will be the experiential result for the person undergoing this therapy?" The question came from an undergraduate with a mass of curly red hair and a very serious expression on his face. "I mean, will they literally forget that they've ever taken the addictive substance before? Or just all the cues that make them want to do it again?"

"I am not sure," Med admitted, looking at Jack for help. "I think they will forget some things, but I am not sure how much, or what that will feel like."

"But won't you be destroying years' worth of memories?"

Jack could tell this kid was going to keep asking questions, and Med didn't have much experience dealing with curious undergrads.

"Here's the deal," Jack interjected. "Retcon isn't a cure-all for every kind of addiction. Nobody can make that. But it will work as a therapy for people who've taken Zacuity." She had his attention now, and Med nodded gratefully. "Potentially, we can save thousands of lives."

Seemingly mollified, the undergrad crooked his right index finger at Med's simulation, downloading it to his goggles. The bot addressed the group again. "Anybody want to help out? We could divide up some of these simulations today, to model how different molecules might affect the brain."

Jack raised her hand. "Sign me up."

"Sure, I'll do some." This next volunteer was a postdoc who typed on the lab bench as she talked, her fingers' movements captured by wrist sensors that translated them into keystrokes.

Her coveralls were plastered with patches that seemed to be responding to the sound of her voice: When she spoke, they all turned red, then slowly faded through green into black again. The grad student with vines growing out of her head, who went by the nym Catalyst, volunteered, too. The serious undergraduate, who had no special adornments other than his grave facial expression, glanced through whatever he saw on his goggles, then focused on Med and Jack. "I'm intrigued," he said. "I'll put in some hours right now. I don't have class until tomorrow."

For a moment, Jack allowed herself to be charmed. These students loved their work at Free Lab so much that they came here when they weren't in class, first thing in the morning, just to find something "intriguing" to research. It had been a long time since she'd worked on a drug project with people doing it for the thrill of discovery. Usually her lab teams were motivated by death or money, half-crazed with a desire to cure the former and bathe in giant tanks of the latter. She wasn't sure which motivation made better fuel for innovation: naïve but ethical beliefs, or the need to survive.

Med organized the simulations quickly, parceling them out equally to everyone on the ad hoc Retcon Team.

Absorbed in analysis, the group lapsed into silence. Several meters above them, the Free Lab's rectangular windows illuminated walls covered in shelves, revealing in dusty splotches of light the half-finished projects of dozens of genetic engineers. PCR machines the size of Jack's fist lay in boxes with cables and self-cooling sample holders. A robotic arm inside a transparent shoebox was harvesting amplified sequence from minute cultures on a tray.

A long planter filled with moist dirt was bolted beneath one window, and out of it poked green stalks of modded wheat, its tender seeds rich in tumor suppressants. Below that, somebody had taken up an entire three-meter shelf with an experiment on repairing broken metal struts using new virus epoxies. One strut had grown back together nicely, but another was developing a strange, shiny tumor that was eating into the shelf below. Posted next to the bulbous strut was a note that read, "Please clean up. If not removed by 8/1/44, this will be THROWN AWAY."

Jack stared at the tumor, and imagined molecules.

The trick with a therapy would be to disrupt or maybe just erase those hyper-rewarding memories of work. Which wasn't exactly a small task. It wasn't as if there was one memory center in the brain, any more than there was a single reward center. It was all molecular pathways, connections between different regions, conversations between neurotransmitters and receptors.

Med's neck jerked slightly back from what she was looking at on the bench, just enough to register in the corner of Jack's eye.

She messaged to Med from her tablet. *What is it?*

"Jack, can you come with me to Krish's office?" Med asked casually. "I think we should run this by him."

"Got something?" asked the serious student.

"Not yet, David," Med replied. "But I want to see what Krish thinks of this."

They angled their way between benches, pausing briefly at Krish's door before he waved them in.

"My patient—the Zacuity OD—died a few days ago," Med said. "Now there are six more people with similar symptoms at the hospital, and my supervisor is asking if I can come home early."

"Just don't answer," Krish said. "Tell him you were off the grid for a few days."

"She can't hide the fact that she read the message, Krish," Jack said. A sophisticated understanding of molecular networks in the brain hadn't given Krish much insight into computer networks. He looked confused for a minute, then shrugged.

Jack turned to Med. "What do you want to do? We can take over here if you want to go back and work on Retcon remotely. We'll create an anonymous code repository on a public server—just use good crypto when you update the data."

Med looked at the mobile in her hands, then out at the Free Lab. The Retcon team had forgotten to eat lunch, but they'd taken a break for early tea. Steaming mugs sat next to half-eaten sandwiches on the bench. Catalyst was playfully poking David in the side, finally forcing a giggle out of him. The postdoc with sound-activated patches projected some kind of animation into the air over the table. Behind them, Threezed was coming down the ladder from the loft, wearing nothing but a towel as he headed to the showers.

"I want to stay," the bot said, her eyes on Threezed. Then, glancing at Krish, she added, "If that is alright with you."

"That's fine with me. You're the lead on this."

"There's something else, too," Med continued. "I sent out a query about Zacuity to an addiction therapy research group last week. A few hours ago, somebody claiming to work at Zaxy mailed me from a temporary public account and said there are other problems, too. Apparently the casualties aren't just on the street."

Jack leaned against the glass and considered. "This has got to be pretty serious if somebody's willing to whistle-blow."

"How do you know this mail isn't a trap?" Med's obvious question pulled Jack up short. The IPC could easily trace that mail to the network where it landed.

"Oh, shit—did you receive it here?"

"No, I logged into the mail server at work remotely. They'll only be able to get as far as Yellowknife if they're snooping."

Krish looked nauseated. This was exactly the kind of spy shit that Jack knew he feared most. She could just imagine him calculating the risk their project posed to his latest grant. Hell, for all she knew, he was partly funded by Zaxy. She cringed as he opened his mouth to speak, expecting him to order them out of his happy little bubble where radicalism grew only as far as corporate boundaries allowed.

"Do you think that your supervisor knows something?" Krish was unexpectedly calm. "That he's asking you to come back because he got a nastygram from the Zone IPC office?"

"Could be."

"Then you're going to need a good reason to stay here. A reason nobody would question." He gestured at his desk absentmindedly. It looked like he was flicking through the subject heads on his mail without reading them. "It would also have to be something that would justify why you've been a little secretive."

A grin tugged at the side of his mouth. "Med, you've come to my lab highly recommended by one of the best genetic engineers I've ever had the pleasure of knowing." He pointed at Jack. His voice was suddenly formal, as if he were addressing an audience at a conference. "I'm very pleased that you were willing to come out for a job interview at such short notice, since we unfortunately had our best pharma developer poached by University of British Columbia last week."

He turned to Med, who was also starting to grin. "I think we can make you an offer that would be competitive with whatever they're paying you over at Yellowknife, and as an associate researcher you'd get your own budget and research team. I realize you might want to think about this further, uh, Dr. Cohen, but we would love it if you could start work right away on a new project we've launched."

"Why, thank you, Dr. Patel." Med replied in a tone whose stagey formality matched Krish's own. "But why don't you call me Med, since we'll be working together now. That's what everybody calls me."

This quiet exchange was a small thing, a trick to allay

suspicion. But it was also huge, a real job doing the kind of work that Jack had once imagined for herself, in this very lab. Jack was gripped by vertigo as she considered how much time had passed since she'd wanted that job, and how many choices had torn her away from this place. Looking at Krish and Med, she was suddenly overwhelmed with an almost painful affection—not just for this smart young researcher, but also for the man who'd recognized Med as an excellent scientist. Coming to the Free Lab for help had turned out to be Jack's first good decision after a string of incredibly bad ones.

She sidled up behind Krish, peeking over his shoulder at what was on his desk. He had Med's staff page from Yellowknife beneath his fingertips. There was a black-and-white headshot of the bot floating above her name and title: Medea Cohen, PhD, Assistant Researcher. Areas of specialization: pharmaceutical testing and development, neurogenetics. Below that, a tidy list of publications, some with Med's name listed first. A few professional affiliations, including membership in one progressive nonprofit that worked with Freeculture groups. It presented the perfect portrait of a young, ambitious, liberal-minded geneng researcher: no black marks, no holes in her employment record, no publications in anything but peer-reviewed journals.

Up until the past few days, Med had been a very good girl. And Krish had just rewarded her with the kind of job every assistant researcher dreams of. She would never need to go back to Yellowknife again.

12

THE HUMAN NETWORK

JULY 11, 2144

As the sun sank, every surface in the medina continued to radiate heat. But the teahouse remained cool beneath reflective paint, and water-cooled air kept patrons from sweating. Eliasz ordered some fragrant oolong at the end of a long bar made from polished wood edged with a Moorish pattern of elaborately interpenetrating polygons. Through the dusky gray windows, they could see a tiny alley, one of the many canopy-shaded streets that twisted through the oldest neighborhood in Casablanca. An archway across the street, edged with blue tile, led into a barely visible courtyard. Next door, a woman filled jugs with water from a public fountain whose gracefully arranged stones dated back to when this was a nation called Morocco. Now Casablanca was one of the African Federation's key port cities, flush with international capital. In a seam where the crumbling foam walls of an apartment building met the street, a boy arranged some wares to sell: a small wagon piled with long, arrow-shaped fish, and a cage of buzzing, cheaply fabbed perimeter drones.

The after-work crowd began to flow into the pathways of the medina, disgorged from air-conditioned jitneys that ran every five minutes from Biotech Park. It was easy to spot their business-ready fashions among the locals. Some wore spotless white thawbs or embroidered caftans flowing over their khakis; some had colorful hijabs over their hair or the tails of saris over their shoulders; some sported Zone jeans and button shirts; some went retro in western suits of linen and seersucker; some bared their upper thighs and chests with transparent fabrics that suggested their skills were too important for employers to worry about modesty. All chattered with each other or the network via ear clips, goggles, perimeters, implants, and specialized, invisible devices.

Many of them would be stopping at one of the dozens of Prague-style secret teahouses that had sprung up here over the sixty years since the late twenty-first century Collapse, which left populations and farms ravaged by plagues. Afterwards, the newly formed African Federation hatched a ten-year plan from their headquarters in Johannesburg. They promised the Federation's three hundred million surviving citizens that they would build the most high-tech agricultural economy in the world.

A sweeping reform bill allowed the Federation government to transform virtually the entire continent into a special economic zone with no regulations on research into anything that could make farming lucrative again. Eurozone and Asian Union companies flocked to the cosmopolitan Federation cities to research transgenic animals that secreted drugs; synthetic fast-growing organisms; metagenetic topsoil engineering; and exo-agriculture that could thrive offworld for export to the Moon and Mars colonies. Recent advances in molecular engineering had been ruled unsafe and ethically questionable in other economic coalitions. But not in the African Federation.

Among the most successful businesses to come out of that regulatory free-for-all were outfits founded by engineers from Prague, Budapest, and Tallinn. Those companies attracted more people from the central Eurozone, and with them came a secret teahouse culture: cool, dark little rooms with unmarked doors where the customers had to know the bouncer, or to whisper a password. Usually the "secret" was just a meaningless formality. You could get loosely guarded passwords on the net, or come to know the bouncer by beaming him a little crypto cash. These Eurozone quirks were easily merged into the casual teahouse culture that had existed for centuries in the medina.

Still, a few teahouses took their secrets seriously. Like the nameless one where Paladin stood, analyzing highly diffuse airborne chemicals produced by dozens of varieties of tea leaf, dried and steeped in precisely heated water. One of the Federation's covert operatives from the IPC had given them the secret password. The place was known to attract hackers and pirates. To Paladin, however, the customers were indistinguishable from the business class deluge outside. That's probably why Eliasz had given him a HUMINT exercise to work on for the next few hours. The bot needed to hone his social skills, and there was no better place to do it than in a teahouse where they were trying to meet as many people as possible.

Eliasz poked Paladin, gesturing almost imperceptibly at the man next to him. After ordering tea, the man slouched so far over the bar that Paladin could see a pale stripe of skin showing above the waistband of his pants. It was time to try his opening gambit. Offer a piece of personal information, and humans will be sure to offer some of their own.

"I have never been here before, and it is not what I expected," Paladin vocalized, turning his torso and face toward the man, who looked up with an expression of vague surprise. He hadn't expected anyone to talk to him, least of all a giant robot.

"Yeah? Did you expect there would be hydrocarbons to drink?"

Through his back sensors, Paladin could see Eliasz rolling his eyes. The joke about bots looking for hydrocarbons to drink in bars was stale forty years ago, and came across as extremely condescending now. But the man was just old enough to have grown a tiny mustache that looked like two dark hyphens in the middle of his face.

Paladin powered on, vowing to succeed somehow with this interaction. "I'm Pack, and this is Aleksy." He gestured to Eliasz. Pack was a very common name for lab assistant bots.

"I'm Slavoj." The man extended his hand, grasping the light alloy of Paladin's in his fingers. Blood samples revealed high levels of caffeine. That was a good sign. It could lead to an info-dump with minimal prompting.

Paladin chose a conversational gambit that always seemed to yield results.

"Where are you from?"

Slavoj spilled his whole story out to them, virtually unbidden, in a stimulant-enabled rush. He'd come from somewhere in the central Eurozone to work with his friends at a tissue engineering startup, but they ran out of money. Now he was doing QA on muscle trellises for meat factories. Slavoj shook his head mournfully at Paladin and Eliasz. "I guess what I'm saying is that this place is no happy hunting ground for jobs right now. They tell you it's easy to get rich here, but what that really means is that it's not as hard to be poor."

Paladin tilted his head to indicate sympathy and extemporized. "We keep hearing the same thing from other people."

This was enough to elicit another diatribe from Slavoj about various jobs he'd tried to get but hadn't, through no fault of his own.

Eliasz pressed a warm hand against Paladin's lower back. The bot had actually succeeded in making a connection with Slavoj. For an instant, Paladin felt a flash of something that went beyond the usual programmed pleasure at completing a task and pleasing Eliasz. He was having fun. Impulsively, he sent a smiley emoji to Eliasz' perimeter. When the man received it, he tapped his thumb lightly on the bot's back with a kind of aimless, amiable rhythm.

Behind the bar, the teaman poured steaming water into a tall, stamped silver pot packed with mint leaves. He snapped his fingers at a boy in starched white, who placed the pot on a tray with two glasses, while the teaman put another dish of sugary cardamom biscuits on the counter in front of Slavoj. After the boy delivered the tray to a table of men in the corner, he sat down on a low stool behind the bar and peeked surreptitiously at Paladin's dark bulk.

A large group of people poured into the shop, arguing animatedly about a story that was making its way around the science text repos.

"There's no way the dipshits at Smaxo are smart enough to do that," snorted one.

"I know people doing R&D there who are not stupid," replied a man who had injected bone grafts under his scalp, remolding his skull to create an odd bas-relief phrenology map whose regions were tattooed with labels like "sex" and "whiskey." He continued: "Why wouldn't they backdoor their drugs? Half the world takes them. It's the perfect social control mechanism."

A woman whose face was partly hidden by a bulky gamer rig nodded. "Totally," she said, twitching her sensor-beaded hands. It was unclear whether she was talking to somebody remote or responding to the thread of teahouse conversation.

"It doesn't make sense," said the man who had spoken first. "If your goal is to calm rioters down, why not just develop a chemical that does it? Something you can spray into a crowd? Why put something in your drugs that has to be triggered by a catalyst? That's just way too complicated and difficult."

"Maybe the catalyst is an image or a word. Something you could broadcast remotely." The guy with the skull mods was agitated, his muscles a mess of electrical activity. "How else do you explain the pics of those meetings between that Smaxo VP and the Trade Zone defense minister? You think they were just swapping LOLs? The economic coalitions want a way to keep people from protesting their bullshit."

"Well, I'm sure Smaxo is cutting deals with the Zone, but a backdoor triggered by a word? That causes some residual molecules in your blood to send your brain into theta wave mode?" The man who spoke now had close-cropped hair and a white shirt that clearly marked him as a corporate worker. "Sorry, but I just don't buy it."

The group crowded up to the bar, their bodies forming a warm set of obstacles around Paladin and Eliasz, their pores exuding sweat and excitement and metabolized euphorics.

"I've got an exploit that works just like that."

Everyone in the group shut up to listen to the tall woman whose elbow pressed lightly against Paladin's arm. She had a small patch of pink hair on her otherwise bald brown head, and wore the traditional Eurozone button-front shirt. A mass spectrometer was stuffed into her breast pocket. "Sound-triggered bacteria. I once zombied a whole club by spiking the booze. Had all the boys do pole dances and put the vid online." She was less excited than the rest of the group, and a surreptitious blood sample revealed that she had no drugs other than caffeine in her system. When her shirtsleeve touched Paladin's arm, he perceived molecules associated with air purification systems. She'd been in a dome, or underground, for a long time before coming here today.

The group continued to focus on the woman, who was digging in the pocket of her khakis for a device. Their postures suggested that she was a node, a person who sprouted and maintained social connections. She was at the core of this group, the person they all knew.

"That vid was hilarious," barked the man with the phrenology map. "An epic hack." As his face turned toward the woman, and therefore toward Paladin, the bot could see that the mountainous region over the man's eyes was labeled "WTF."

On Paladin's left, Eliasz was covertly hyperalert. Slavoj, trapped between the social node and WTF, scrunched down in his chair and carefully focused on the dish of biscuits. It was obvious that he recognized them, but Paladin couldn't decide if his posture was an effort to hide or, perversely, to capture the group's attention.

"A round of black for my friends, please," the node said politely to the teaman.

"Your usual?" he replied, reaching for a jar of crisp, expensive leaves.

"Yes, thank you. We'll be in the back."

"A round on Frankie! Smooth!" The man in corporate casuals slapped her arm appreciatively.

"Smooth!" echoed the gamer, lifting her rig and settling it on the sensor strip that banded her skull. Her eyes, dyed completely black, settled on Slavoj.

"Oh, hey," she said.

"Hey, Mecha," Slavoj muttered, toying with his tea glass.

Frankie's group swirled away, following her through a beaded curtain at the end of the bar. Mecha, now at the tail end of the pack, plucked at Slavoj's sleeve.

"What are you up to?" she asked.

"Just got off work."

"Still working with Promoter on that Third Arm project?"

"Yeah, but we're all consulting now, just to make ends meet while we're waiting for funding."

Paladin had taken baselines of the man's speech, which indicated that it was statistically likely that Slavoj was lying now.

"I have to go, but we should hang out soon. I haven't seen you in forever." Mecha leaned into Slavoj to grab a biscuit off of the diminishing pile in the bowl. His body tensed and untensed as he prepared to speak and then didn't. "Actually, what are you doing tonight?" Without waiting for a reply, she put on her rig and tilted her head. "You should come to this party at Hox2's place."

Slavoj thumbed the joint on his glasses, looking at her text. His heart rate was elevated—yes, he would be there.

Paladin tried to figure out a way to get their new friend to bring them along. Parties were a good place to make connections.

On her way back to the beaded curtain, Mecha brushed her fingers lightly over Paladin's back. "Nice case," she said. "Bet it does negative refraction, right?"

"It does," Paladin vocalized.

"Looks great," she said, aiming her gamer rig at the camouflaged apertures for his torso guns. "Pretty sweet defensive perimeter for a lab bot."

The bot wasn't sure what to say. "Thank you. Slavoj and I were just talking about lab life."

As she reached the bead curtain, Mecha turned back one last time. "Bring your pretty bot friend, too!" she called to Slavoj.

The nervous QA engineer swallowed the last of his tea, then grinned at Paladin and Eliasz. "Do you want to come?"

Paladin noticed with pleasure that Eliasz' face had muscled into one of its rare smiles. The bot had managed his first act of human intelligence gathering, entirely without help.

They said good-bye to Slavoj and returned to the streets of the medina. Though Paladin sighted the occasional biobot in the crowds, this city was obviously built for humans. The narrow lanes would never admit a mantis bot like Fang, and the vendor stalls emitted no bot-readable metadata.

"That was a great start on your HUMINT, buddy. Let's do a little more practice." Eliasz pointed down a street that veered slightly north, its walls recently whitewashed with a quick-drying fluid full of bioluminescent bacteria and network motes. Paladin hesitated.

"It doesn't seem like there are very many bots in this city."

"That's the challenge. Even in a city that's packed with bots, people are going to treat you differently. You have to work around it."

The bot fell into step behind the man, unable to fit beside him as they walked past a small, scruffy cat sleeping on a low-hanging balcony and four children clustered around an ancient water spigot.

"How do I work around this?" Paladin pointed at his face.

Eliasz laughed and the bot found himself logging the location of every beam of sunlight as it glanced off the windows above. There was no reason for it. He just found himself wanting a granular record of this rare moment with Eliasz laughing and the light waves lengthening and stray water molecules hurling themselves through the air.

"Paladin, do you really think you're the first operative who ever stuck out like a sore thumb? Look at me! I'm the color of cow milk. Pretty obvious I'm an outsider around here. But look at your new friend Slavoj. He's an outsider, too. Everybody is an outsider, if you go deep enough. The trick is reassuring people that you're their kind of outsider."

"Like when I told Slavoj we were finding it hard to get work."

"Exactly! You may be a hydrocarbon guzzling bot, but he likes you because you're dealing with the same problem. Just figure out a way to share their problems."

They walked into an open plaza, ringed on all sides with courtyards and shops, and packed with dozens of stalls full of electronics components and biotech. Paladin had an idea.

Unlike Eliasz, he could speak Darija, the most common natural language in this region. That was something the bot could turn into a shareable problem. Leaving Eliasz' side, Paladin approached a man selling muscle fibers very much like the ones that stretched beneath the bot's carapace.

"I need to supplement my musculature," Paladin said in Darija. "Unfortunately, my master knows nothing about robots, and only speaks English. But you look like you might have what we're looking for. This is a nice selection."

The man glanced up at Paladin, and then darted a quick side-eye at Eliasz. "Eurozone?" he asked. "Where? East?"

"He doesn't tell me anything. Somewhere they don't learn Darija."

That got a wry grin. "OK, friend. What length and tuning do you need?"

Through his rear sensors, Paladin could see that Eliasz was trying to hide a matching grin of his own.

As the bot and the muscle man haggled over grades of fiber, Paladin tried to turn their connection into something useful.

"Is there anywhere to buy off-brand biotech?" "Off-brand" was local slang for pirated goods. "My master wants something cheap for himself."

"I don't know anything about off-brands." The vendor barely looked up from the table, where he was gently wrapping Paladin's newly purchased muscle strands in an oil-infused membrane. "But, cheap stuff? You want to go down by the docks."

When Paladin told Eliasz about his failure, the man raised his eyebrows.

"That wasn't a fail, buddy. You got great intel. Nobody is going to tell you directly how to find illegal shit. That was genius, asking for something cheap. He was able to tell you everything without admitting that he knew anything."

"I hadn't thought of it that way."

Eliasz shrugged. "That's the thing about humans. People always think they're being so clever with codes and euphemisms.

But they're desperate to say what they know. As soon as you establish trust, people want to infodump. You're a natural at this. I bet it's even easier for you because they don't suspect a bot would be sneaky like a human."

Paladin considered this information carefully. Were there actually ways that he could be better than Eliasz at HUMINT?

"While you're getting all fancy with your Darija, why don't you buy me some dinner before we head to the docks?" Eliasz gestured at a vendor unrolling a swatch of meat to put over a spit. At the next stall, they supplemented the charred lamb with sesame bread from a stack of fresh breads baked into fat circles.

Evening piled the streets with shadows and the walls began to glow. Walking and eating at the same time, Eliasz bumped into the bot with companionable aimlessness. He tossed a shred of meat to a kitten padding hopefully alongside them, and Paladin wondered if this was how Eliasz acted when he wasn't on a mission. As Paladin read Eliasz' biosigns through his shoulder sensors, he caught the man gazing at him intently. Paladin pointed his face at the man's face, so Eliasz would know he was gazing back. For a period of two full seconds, Paladin's visual sensors locked with Eliasz' eyes for reasons that Paladin could not decipher. Or maybe, as Eliasz would probably say, the reason was obvious. Maybe they just liked each other.

Paladin thought about what this might mean as they walked to the docks in search of his next target for HUMINT practice.

At midnight, Eliasz and Paladin arrived at the downtown address Slavoj had given them for a sub-basement lab three stories below the Twin Center towers. Once a gleaming mall, it was now a warren of live-work spaces.

"This may turn out to be a dead end," Eliasz warned. "Just biopunk scenesters. But Frankie is somebody to watch—she's been arrested before, for possession of unlicensed lab equipment. Keep watch on who she's talking to, OK, buddy?"

"I will."

"And make some friends." Eliasz poked him in the side with a grin, and Paladin poked him back carefully. Human flesh was flimsy compared to a bot carapace. He still wasn't used to it.

They stepped out of the evening's moist heat and into a climate-conditioned foyer. Over a century ago, this building had been the gem of Casablanca, a monument to its wealth and Westernization at a time when most of the Federation was unbalanced by plagues, protests, and warfare. Now it was dwarfed by the luxury skyscrapers ringing the roundabout at United Nations Place. Its boutiques and luxury condos had been transformed into crowded homes for artists, drifters, and radicals.

Two people were sharing some 420 near the elevator doors. They wore black caftans threaded with fiery red electrofilaments, and their dark faces shimmered faintly with temporary glitter polish.

"Going to the party?" asked one, as Eliasz pressed the down button.

"Yeah."

"You're just in time for the orgy." The two giggled and waved delicate fingers as the doors closed.

Paladin and Eliasz emerged into a room whose atmospheric controllers could not keep up with the amount of heat and sweat emitted by the overcapacity crowd. A dance floor had been cleared in one corner, and a few dozen people were writhing and bouncing beneath strobes. To the right, plumbing for a wet lab had been converted temporarily into a drink-mixing area. The man with WTF tattooed on his head was behind the bar, concocting a variety of drinks and handing them out in transparent foam cups to a line of sweating people. Overhead was a loft with mirrored windows and a huge "CAUTION!" sign on its door.

At the edges of the dance floor and the bar, knots of people argued about code or showed off new mods and gadgets. A shirtless man with lightly furred wings growing from his shoulder blades was surrounded by a group that included Mecha and Slavoj, both swaying slightly with intoxication. He flexed the wings, modeled on a bat's, and Mecha stroked one appreciatively.

Suddenly Frankie came rushing down the loft staircase, her face set purposefully as she brushed past a few people who tried to say hello. She headed right to WTF, pushing easily through the throng, and whispered in his ear. He checked a readout in his wrist and nodded. Paladin tried to pick up what they were saying, but there was too much ambient noise. The bot settled for watching them from the sensors in the back of his head while he and Eliasz joined the group with Mecha and Slavoj.

"Pretty bot!" Mecha squealed, throwing her arms around his torso, smearing him with the sugars manufactured by her drunkenness. She aimed the black lozenges of her eyes at Eliasz. "Is he yours? What's his name?"

"Why do you assume he belongs to anybody?" Eliasz took a cagey, teasing tone. He had picked up the tenor of the group and was blending, using his gift for conformity to accumulate trust quickly. Somebody had given him a cup of glowing orange liquid whose molecular signature said vodka, and he nodded his head to the beat that emerged from amplifiers strung along the ceiling. Mecha laughed and sent a message through her game rig, which Paladin easily tuned, decrypted, and forwarded to Eliasz.

Room for one more up there? This boy is hot.

She had messaged somebody in the loft, a person who was using a throwaway device with no useful ID data attached. The throwaway responded:

Yeah, one more is fine, but that's it. We're almost ready.

Behind them, Frankie was rushing back up the stairs, tailed

by a man dressed in a cape that flickered with LEDs. As the door to the loft opened, Paladin caught a glimpse of a room padded with foam cushions and swarming with minute projectors that filled the walls with oozing, abstract designs.

A faster beat spurred the dancers on the floor to start wiggling, and Frankie slammed the door to the loft. Mecha stood on tiptoes to yell-whisper in Eliasz' ear: "Do you want to come upstairs and play with me and Frankie?"

Paladin could see from Eliasz' posture that he was wary. From context, he guessed she was inviting him to try some kind of hacked-together molecule, probably designed to release inhibitions and generate an intense emotional response: pleasure, fear, sadness, amusement, rage. "What are you guys playing?" he asked, his tone appropriately light.

"A little thing Frankie cooked up after reverse engineering some Ellondra." It was a common stimulant-euphoric. Eliasz relaxed.

"Just let me tell my friend to wait for me," he told Mecha. Pulling Paladin aside, he whispered to the bot in a voice too quiet for any human ear: "I'm going up with Mecha to see what I can find out about Frankie. I'm patched against the drug they're using, so it should be fine. But if I don't come down in an hour, get me out."

At that moment, Frankie opened the door a crack, motioning furtively at Mecha. It was her cue. Mecha tapped Slavoj and Eliasz. "Go on up. I'm going to get the others." She made her way through the crowd, the sensors on her body winking in the strobes. As she circulated, she gave a subtle nudge to first one person, then another. After she'd tapped about twenty of them, she gave Paladin a little wave and ran upstairs, pulling the door shut behind her.

His sixty-minute counter decrementing in nanoseconds, Paladin idly tuned a few different segments of the radio spectrum, looking for local networks that might yield information. There was an open network called Hox, attached to a local server with a few scientific papers and videos on it.

While the bot explored, the man with wings turned to him and asked, "What do you think?" Paladin replayed recent audio, and discerned that he'd been standing in the middle of a debate over regulations on tissue engineering. Under a new set of rules proposed by the Free Trade Zone, all body modifications created with patented scaffolds would have to be implemented by a licensed practitioner.

Paladin knew that ownership regulations weren't exactly valued in this crowd. "It will give patent holders more control over what you can do with your body," he said, quoting verbatim from an anti-patent text repo whose feed he'd quickly plundered.

"Exactly! Do you think I could have these wings if the Zone pushed the other economic coalitions to bend to its puritanical will?" The man stretched the beautiful but useless wings over his head. "I'm Casey, by the way."

"I'm Pack."

"What do you do, Pack? You don't look much like a lab assistant." Casey tapped Paladin's carapace. "Feels military grade."

"I am indentured to Aleksy. We're looking for gene development work."

"Oh, you're slaved to that guy who went off with Mecha?"

Paladin had nothing to say to that, so he decided to pry. "What do you do?"

"I make custom penises." Casey tapped the palm of his hand, beaming Paladin the address of a server packed with information on how to design and order the sex organs you'd always wanted. "Good money in that. But now I'm thinking I might get into consulting with companies that want to implement open tissue scaffolds. You know, to get around this new regulation."

"Interesting," Paladin vocalized, scanning the room. Eliasz had been gone for almost half an hour already.

"Actually, you look like you could use my services, friend," Casey laughed, patting the smooth alloy between the bot's legs. "Why didn't they build you with a dick?"

"Are you completely stupid?" giggled Mecha, who had been slinking down the stairs behind them. When she arrived, she clung heavily on Paladin's arm. "Don't you know anything about bots, Casey? This pretty bot here . . ." she paused, her skin profoundly flushed and her body trembling with a wave of chemically induced pleasure. "This pretty bot has something better than one of your dicks. He's got a brain right here." She tapped Paladin's carapace over the chamber where his human brain quietly processed facial recognition data.

Before Mecha swooned again, she wriggled hotly against the bot's left side, her thumb drawing a streak of sweat down his torso, moving from one covert weapons system to another. "I've been inside your model," she whispered. "In RoboCity." As she named the popular game world, her knees began to buckle. Paladin knelt slightly, lifted her quivering, ecstatic body, and carried her up the stairs to the loft. She would fare better on the cushions there, among other people who had been drugged.

Paladin was beginning to feel a strange dread in this human network, where everyone seemed to know he was military issue. Pretty soon, somebody would actually care. It was very possible that he and Eliasz were about to have their covers blown. This party could get dangerous.

As Paladin shouldered into the loft with Mecha, he immediately perceived Eliasz and Frankie talking in the corner, behind a puddle of bodies filled with blood that bore molecular traces of Ellondra.

As he let Mecha down, she briefly achieved lucidity and pointed across the room at Frankie. "See her? I love her." Mecha addressed herself to Paladin's upper arm, focusing on an area that contained a small constellation of sensors. "Did you know she named herself after Rosalind Franklin, the scientist who discovered the structure of DNA? That was her pseudonym when she wrote for *The Bilious Pills,* too."

By the time Mecha sank into the pillows, Paladin was accessing fragments of saved and cached versions of *The Bilious Pills.* "Frankie is just so . . . amazing. You should talk to her." And then Slavoj reached an arm out from the edge of the human drug puddle, and Mecha flowed back into it.

Frankie and Eliasz walked over to where Paladin stood in the doorway, skirting the pillowed area.

"Aleksy has been telling me about your gene-hacking skills," Frankie said, looking at the hollows in Paladin's face that most humans perceived as eyes. "He said the two of you always work together."

"We do."

"He also explained to me how he's patched against Ellondra. Very impressive."

"That's just a taste of what we can do," Eliasz replied, a calculated boast.

"Oh, I think I have a pretty good idea of just how smart you are." Frankie grinned and slapped a dermal injector on Eliasz' neck before he could react. She winked at Paladin as Eliasz' pupils dilated. He reached out an unsteady arm to the bot. "Looks like your master isn't patched against this."

Eliasz sagged against the bot's frame. Paladin lifted him the way he had Mecha, quickly sending a command that disabled part of Eliasz' perimeter system. The man's skin temperature had risen, and a quick blood sample revealed what Paladin had suspected: serotonin cascade, dopamine levels rising. Eliasz writhed, senses focused inward on some kind of hallucination that his brain processed as pleasure.

Frankie opened the door and barked a laugh. "See you later, kiddies."

Paladin held the man and stepped lightly down the stairs, powering up his head-mounted lasers as he crossed in front of the bar to the elevator. He didn't bother with the buttons, relaying a command directly to the building's systems that overrode all other requests and brought the elevator down to Basement 3. He was in high-defense mode as he entered the car. Had anyone interfered, he would have shot to kill.

Luckily, all the revelers were focused on who was arriving rather than who was leaving. And nobody paid attention to a bot carrying his master, moaning and sighing with obvious intoxication, through the warm streets of early morning. A molecule lookup revealed the drug wasn't deadly, but Eliasz would be incapacitated for hours.

At their hotel, Paladin laid Eliasz on the cot and stood at full alert in the center of the room. The problem was that the man wouldn't stay still. Frankie's drug had filled him with restless energy. He crept from the bed to curl around the cool, segmented carapace of Paladin's legs, breathing raggedly around half-formed sentences. Then his entire body tensed up and he lapsed into a soft groan, hostage to an enforced gratification.

Paladin knelt next to Eliasz, now curled into a fetal position on the rug.

"Come to bed with me, Paladin," Eliasz whispered. "It will be OK this once." He trailed off, and Paladin used his new hand to feel the stuttering flashes of arousal that passed through the man's body.

"I will carry you to bed."

"Lie down next to me." He gripped Paladin's leg, staring at him with drug-stretched pupils. "You are so beautiful. Let me feel you next to me."

For the second time that day, they looked into each other's faces. But now, unlike in the medina, the sight of Eliasz' dark eyes was like a worm filling Paladin's mind with junk characters and overriding his action priorities. It was hard to set Eliasz' words aside and follow protocols. "It is not safe," the bot said quietly. "We are in danger. Frankie drugged you."

Sweating and shaking, Eliasz pulled himself to his feet by clinging to Paladin, then wrapped his arms around the bot's torso and pressed his face against one armored shoulder. "Stay, stay, stay, stay, stay," he chanted in a whisper.

It was not safe. But Paladin wanted to lie down beside Eliasz on the narrow cot, to train his sensors on the man's drug-amped desire, to recognize in the man's face a possible representation of his own chaotic feelings. And so he found a compromise between his desires and his programming.

Laying Eliasz on the bed again, he lay down, too. His carapace, balanced at the edge of the mattress via tiny movements of his actuators, became a shield for the man's vulnerable body. He faced Eliasz and faced away from him simultaneously, scanning for danger. He rested his hand on the man's flank, the tiny needles in his palm sipping minute samples of Eliasz' blood. The bot could read each molecular change in Eliasz' body as the man's euphoria grew and subsided. He wished there was some other way he could touch Eliasz that would give him an even more intimate understanding of what was happening.

"Why did you say this was wrong?" Eliasz was shivering through one of the highs that bunched his muscles into spasms. He stared into Paladin's face and his fingers pressed urgently against the bot's chest.

"What we are doing is not wrong. I was worried that you weren't safe, but I can keep watch."

"But you said it was wrong. Two men cannot lie together." Eliasz was gasping, his heart rate spiking as he hallucinated, talking to someone who wasn't there.

Paladin tried to reorient Eliasz in reality. "It's Paladin. I am not a man. I am a bot. I belong to the African Federation."

Eliasz started to cry, the salt of his tears indistinguishable from the salt of his sweat. Paladin didn't know what to say. It was unlikely the man would remember any of this in a few hours. Eliasz had already gone rigid with ecstasy again, his mouth slack and wordless. The bot did not resist when the man faced him, hooking one arm and one leg over his carapace, clinging as hard as he could. It felt good, as if Eliasz were finally telling Paladin everything he wanted to know.

13

RETCON

JULY 13, 2144

"When are we going to run away together . . . master?" Threezed whispered hotly in Jack's ear, appending the client's honorific with a sharp dip in his voice. They were naked and her thighs formed a cradle for his slim hips. Though her thoughts had been vagued out by postorgasmic pleasure, Jack was instantly alert and dismayed.

She rolled on her side to dislodge him. "What is your goddamn problem, Threezed?"

"I just don't want you to leave me here when you guys figure out that mesolimbic pathway thing." Threezed traced one puckered curve of the scar between Jack's breasts. She was still slightly damp with his sweat. "What am I supposed to do here?"

They lay on an unfurled sofa bed next to stacks of old servers and fabbers. After two straight days of coding and testing, Jack was exhausted. She should have been sleeping instead of fucking. She twisted around in Threezed's embrace and groped through her sack for an attention-focuser. Finding a blister pack, she popped out a shiny silver bead of pirated Vigilizer—that would clear her mind so she could start working again.

But when the drug kicked in, she found that all her ideas were about Threezed.

"What if I bought you a franchise here? I have enough to pay for a basic citizenship package that would let you work and go to school in Saskatoon. And if you wanted to move somewhere else in the Zone, it's a pretty cheap upgrade."

Threezed propped himself up on his elbows and looked thoughtful. "Do you have a franchise here, too?"

"I had one when I lived here. Now I have an international business franchise that gives me rights in five economic coalitions. I'm covered pretty much anywhere I go."

Although she'd broken many laws in her time, Jack had never lived without a franchise. Her parents bought her one the moment she was born. They had a family package that guaranteed all the Chen children could own property, apply for jobs, go to school, and move to another city if they wanted. Though Lucky Lake was small, it was still incorporated—the city used money from local enfranchisement deals to pay for police and emergency responders, as well as regular mote net dusting to keep all their devices robustly connected.

If the Chens hadn't had a successful farm, Jack would have turned eighteen with no franchise, and no hope of working unless she entered contract. She'd known a few kids at school in that situation, mostly Natives who got indentured to jobs in habitat management or mining up north. For the first time in decades, she recalled how her school principal had described this arrangement as "cultural enrichment." The kids under contract would live in dorms near historic Native communities, earning their franchises while immersed in the traditional landscapes of their ancestors. Jack hadn't thought about her old high school classmates in years. As the principal's words echoed in her memory and she looked into Threezed's face, she realized how much bullshit that had been. Some of those kids had probably died up on the Arctic coast without ever owning anything, even themselves. She wondered whether the indenture system had its own version of piracy, and tried to imagine what that would be.

Threezed had rolled on his back and was looking at the electroluminescent threads knit into the stiff panels of the ceiling.

"Think about it, OK?" Jack sat up and sealed the vent on her coveralls. "Saskatoon's a pretty nice city. Not a bad place to be enfranchised." Before Threezed could reply, she dropped down the loft ladder.

Med was at her bench, fabbers and sample fridges scattered around her. The bot appeared to be talking to a tiny white mouse cupped in her hands while David watched with his usual serious expression. It was 5:45 a.m.

When Med and David ignored her, Jack made a stab at conversation. "Why are you talking to the mouse?"

"Trying to see if we've erased the right memory." David gestured up a projection of the mouse's brain. It hovered over the table, slowly rotating, swollen to the size of a basketball and crackling with colors signifying neural pathways and molecular transformations. "We used Zacuity to get Beady addicted to Professor Cohen's voice, and now we're exposing him to the addictive process while dosed with Retcon."

The Vigilizer felt good, but Jack was still grateful when Catalyst arrived with a thermos of coffee and steaming buns from the co-op bakery on Broadway. Nobody else was working in the lab at this hour, but somehow the Retcon team had gotten the idea that this project was special. It had snared Med a coveted job in the lab, for one thing. And there was also the matter of Jack's mysterious presence, as well as Krish's involvement. The situation clearly merited all-nighters.

"Don't you ever eat or sleep, Med?" Catalyst asked with a grin.

Med returned Beady to a small cage next to her. "No." Her voice was casual. "I'm a robot." Something about the formal way she said "robot" made it immediately clear she wasn't joking.

Catalyst was about to stuff a hunk of warm, cinnamon-coated

bread into her mouth, and suddenly stopped. "You are? How did you get to be a professor?"

"Haven't you ever heard of the Cohen Lab at Anchorage?" David asked archly, pleased to show he knew more than a grad student. "They make biobots that are raised autonomous, just like humans."

Threezed had come down from the loft. He reached for a bun from the bag, pushing past David in a way that seemed deliberately calculated to be rude. "Really?" he asked sarcastically, finding Jack's eyes with his own. "Is that how humans are raised? Autonomous?"

David looked confused, but obviously felt that he should put this question to rest, especially since it had been posed by a person who was clearly not part of the lab hierarchy. "Yes," he said in a slightly condescending tone. "Humans do not require the same financial investment to reproduce as robots, and therefore they are only indentured as adults, by choice."

"Thanks for the little property lesson, sweetie." Threezed rolled his eyes. Swiping an unused mobile off the table, he ambled out of the lab.

"Sometimes you are a complete fuckwit, David," Catalyst muttered.

"Well, sometimes you are, too!" he shot back.

Med shrugged and analyzed the real-time images she was receiving from the local network, where data was coming from a haze of microscopic devices spreading like fluid through Beady's brain, analyzing what it was doing under the influence of Retcon. She shared the whole thing out to a holo desktop they'd created, creating a 3-D image that she sliced with a clipped motion of her hand.

Beady made scrabbling noises in his cage.

Presently Krish arrived, also bearing coffee and buns. He sat down with the group like a student, unpacking his breakfast and tapping out a few commands on the desktop. "How's it going? Looks like we've got some new data."

Jack wiped her hand through the air, pushing some unanalyzed brain slices to Krish.

"I saw Threezed leaving with one of our lab mobiles. What is he doing?"

"I believe that he is learning about autonomy," Med replied.

Threezed returned in the early afternoon, wearing a faded University of Saskatchewan hoodie and looking a lot less sullen. Jack nodded at Threezed and he nodded back: fight over. Their conversation that morning had changed the connection between them, made the whole thing feel less desperate.

Beady was feeling better, too. It appeared they'd edited out the memory that made him seek Med's voice at all costs, even his own life. His dopamine receptors were growing back nicely, too.

Jack addressed the group. "I think we're ready to soft launch now. Let's publish the Retcon repository and get some feedback."

Med looked up. "I've never pushed a drug out like this—without trials."

"We already know Retcon works in simulations and on Beady here." Jack patted the roof of the mouse cage. "That's a good start. Next we'll get results from docs testing it on subjects who are already at risk of death."

"So it's an informal Phase I drug trial, where you test to see whether it's deadly to humans," Med mused.

"That's true. There is a very small chance it could kill people."

Catalyst interrupted. "That's a risk with any drug, and we all know companies like Zaxy push shit out on the market all the time without taking them through trials. They get an exemption for drugs administered by a licensed Zaxy provider."

"But our providers won't have access to the kinds of medical facilities Zaxy would have," Med said.

"This is pretty much how open pharma works, Med," Krish said gently. "And I think you already know a group of subjects who are at risk of death."

Everybody was looking at the bot now, waiting. She was lead on the Retcon project, and they wouldn't do anything without her final approval.

"Alright."

A muted cheer went up from the group.

"Now, who volunteers to write the documentation?" The cheers turned into groans and laughter. Eventually David offered his services, and Catalyst said she'd put together a list of Free-culture groups to contact about the specs. Med and Jack retired to Krish's office to message Med's former colleagues in Yellowknife about that informal Phase I.

A reply came back in under a minute: There were still six patients in Yellowknife with crippling urges to clean houses, enter data, even unload boxes from trucks. The doctors wanted the specs and documentation for Retcon, and Med's former supervisor promised he'd send all the results to Free Lab.

At that moment, Catalyst tapped hesitantly on the glass doors. "Sorry to interrupt, but I just saw a really weird message on the Iqaluit geneng server."

Jack and Krish looked at each other.

"What do you mean?" asked Med.

"There was an article about how that solar farm explosion was actually part of an IPC witch hunt for suspected patent pirates in the northern Zone." She paused, looking guiltily at Jack. "Including one named Jack, whose picture looked a little like you."

Nobody said anything, so finally the grad student spoke up again, timidly. "Are you Captain Jack from *The Bilious Pills*?"

Jack and Krish burst into laughter, reenacting a little diversionary tactic they'd perfected decades ago, during the height of their underground fame. When authority figures or outsiders asked if they were part of *The Bilious Pills*, their cover story was incredulity. Somehow, they always managed to do it in a way that didn't sound staged.

"Well, my name is Jack," she said, still wearing a grin. "But I'm not the captain of anything."

"I can't believe the IPC still cares about anyone from *The Bilious Pills*," Krish added with a chortle. "It's been defunct for . . . how long?"

"Twenty-seven years," Med said. And then, as if to explain the odd specificity of her knowledge, she added, "When I was growing up, I read a local copy on the Cohen Lab server."

"I see," said Jack.

SUMMER 2119

Two and a half decades ago, the entire Free Lab knew she was Captain Jack. And it wasn't long after she and Lyle started sleeping together that everybody knew about that, too. Maybe it was because Lyle was as antic as her tattoo was static. She made no secret of her infatuation with Jack, grabbing her for kisses in the hall outside the lab and pulling her merrily into a wide circle of fashionably rebellious friends.

On Saturday evenings, Lyle would sashay into the Free Lab wearing old-fashioned red lipstick, wrapped in some crazy textile made out of silver feathers and red algae.

"Your chariot is here, daaaarling!" she would call to Jack, and everybody in the lab would watch them leave arm in arm. It was an overt display that made Jack uncomfortable, because she'd always courted notoriety under a pseudonym. But it made her proud, too. She had a hot date instead of a long, numb night with her mobile.

Lyle got away with a lot of things because she was so damn smart. Her doctoral research on molecular motors had won an award for the most promising first work from a young scholar, and had already become the basis for several therapies that were now in development. When she scored a postdoc that she could take to the lab of her choice, her decision to join the Free Lab made headlines in the science text repos—and even one or two gossip feeds that loved her bad-girl reputation.

Though she spent days in the lab doing research, Lyle focused her restless attention in so many directions that she sometimes took sleep relievers and stayed awake for a week at a time. She was part of a social network that included artists and activists who were always hatching what they called "disruptive strategies" aimed at undermining all forms of authority: cultural, economic, scientific. Mostly their disruptions involved artistic fashion shows full of uselessly beautiful GMOs and tissue mods that said something about global recolonization.

Jack didn't exactly fit into the group, but she got a free pass with even the most dedicated disruptors of the bunch. Her pirate-costumed arrest made her a subversive hero. None of Lyle's friends had ever been jailed for their activism, though a few of them had been briefly detained. Their positions of relative privilege led to endless conversations about who among their circle could legitimately claim the right to speak for "victims of the system."

When Lyle's friends walked into the Broadway Noodle House on Saturday night, all modded and gussied up, they were a game world come to life. Their gleaming ultralight armor and festive textiles always got attention. They got more attention still when, around midnight, they arrived at their true destination: a clubhouse for hackers called Buried Spaceship.

Sure, it was packed with scenesters, kids who just liked the mad science atmosphere and weren't actually interested in science itself. But Jack still loved that place. The black, soaring walls were flecked with stars, planets, and a massive mural depicting the jagged, icy edge of a crater that the "ship" had smashed into. From the ceiling's high, ancient beams hung an antique uncrewed aerial vehicle, its slim body and fat nose suspended from ultrastrong translucent wire. The long, polished-foam bar curved around a row of props designed to look like antique replicators out of an old *Star Trek* movie. A few even had fabbers in them, just to give the full effect. People who worked the bar delighted in asking newcomers if they would like some Romulan Ale.

Memory often favors the seemingly mundane. Jack could barely recall the massive Buried Spaceship birthday party for Lyle that had been weeks in the making. But her mind retained every trivial detail of one random spring night at the club, when the weather still called for toques and parkas. She and Lyle had been dating for a couple of months, and were deliriously embracing as they listened to reverberating beats a local band scratched out of the shimmering air, their arms and hands glittering with sensors. Lights were strobing over the UAV, its life of surveillance converted into an afterlife of psychedelic crime.

That's when Jack caught a brief glimpse of the two of them dancing in a slice of mirror at the edge of the dance floor, looking for a moment like strangers.

Lyle's head bobbed, a manic grin on her face, her body swaying in a frothy dress of wire mesh and a bright, sheer polymer. Jack, wearing nothing but a frayed Freeculture T-shirt and dark pants, threw her arms wide, not caring that everyone knew who she was—the lowly researcher whose only accomplishments were a dead text repo and an arrest record. At that moment, watching herself jump up and down with Lyle, she realized that the woman she saw in the mirror was not a loser. Her life was going somewhere. Maybe not where she'd expected, but somewhere good. Spinning around, she saw the heavens sprayed across the walls and realized that she was no longer living in the trashed remnants of her old expectations.

Back at Free Lab, Jack was too absorbed in her work and too blissed out over Lyle to notice that Krish had gone from politely distant to politely hostile. At last, over one of their increasingly infrequent "checking in" dinners, he came out and said it. "I think this thing between you and Lyle is really bad for the Free Lab."

"What the hell are you talking about?" He'd caught her by surprise.

"Lyle is brilliant, but she's crazy. I'm worried what's going to happen if things go bad between you."

"You think she'll take off and you'll lose her grant money?"

"Give me a break, Jack. I'm more worried what would happen if she stayed and you had to work together."

"You and I are working together."

He stared at the remains of a sandwich on his plate. "That's different. Neither of us is the infamous Lyle Al-Ajou."

Much later that night, curled together for warmth under a self-heating blanket, Jack and Lyle talked about how Krish was obviously just jealous—of their relationship, their futures, everything.

Lyle thought Krish was right about one thing, though. She was crazy. She came from a long line of crazy women. "My mother says that smart women are always crazy. Maybe she's right."

Jack tried to wrap her body completely around Lyle's, like a shield. "That sounds like junk science from two hundred years ago," she whispered.

Lyle shook her head. "No," she insisted. "You don't understand."

Her words came out in a chaotic rush. When Lyle was little, her grandmother had lost touch with reality, the neural connections in her brain clogged by dementia. At the time, there was no therapy for this particular kind of protein buildup around the synapses. The old woman thought she was still marching to get the vote for women in the Gulf. Lyle would wake up to the sound of her grandmother shouting feminist slogans in their living room. Sometimes she would just walk out the door and shout in the street.

Lyle's mother and aunts were humiliated. First, they tried to hide their mother behind locked doors, and then they sent her to a hospice. Each of them, in their own way, believed that their mother had been insane even before the dementia set in. Some of Lyle's aunts were deeply religious, outraging their mother by covering their heads and faces when they drove out to the voting centers to support right-wing candidates.

But Lyle's mother didn't care about politics; she just wanted to be a doctor, so she went to college in Dubai to study medicine. Once there, she discovered something Lyle's feminist grandmother had never anticipated: Suffrage didn't mean equal opportunity. Her professors expected her to study microbiology until she met a marriageable man. When she demanded more lab time, they gingerly offered sympathy and fatherly advice. After years of frustration, she gave into their gaslighting with a bitterness matched only by her ambitions for her brilliant daughter Lyle.

As soon as Lyle turned thirteen, her mother sent her to an elite prep school in the Zone, far from home and friends—and far from the cities where women couldn't be scientists. She only contacted Lyle to inquire about her grades, her studies, her progress. If Lyle admitted to having friends or interests outside school, her mother threatened to cut her off.

Lyle had fulfilled her mother's dreams in one way. She was a biotech prodigy, and never stopped experimenting, even after the lab was closed for the night. When she visited home the summer she turned eighteen, she had a depilated, tattooed head and flowers growing out of the backs of her hands. Her cousins called her a slut. But her mother was convinced the truth was worse: Lyle was spending too much time on politics to be a real scientist. She needed to do more than play with synbio fashions to prove her dedication to medicine.

Dependent on her family to pay for her franchise in the Zone, Lyle listened to them, and covered up her flowers every time she visited the Gulf. As soon as she could support herself on the Free Lab grant, she blocked all incoming messages from her family. But every day, she felt her mother's judgment, as if her mitochondrial DNA contained a list of everything that was wrong with her.

"It makes me crazy," Lyle said, for perhaps the fourth time that night.

Jack looked into the mascara-smudged puddles of Lyle's eyes and saw only the remnants of an anguished childhood, a rough history. Something that would ease over time.

"You're not crazy. You're just dealing with a lot of shit."

"It *is* a lot of shit," Lyle sobbed, her tears growing cold as they ran across Jack's throat onto the pillows beneath them. "I feel like I'm carrying out her evil plan even though I'm doing what I love."

In that moment, their relationship went from hot diversion to long-term pact. They talked about moving away together, escaping the cage of academia and doing geneng in the wild. A lot of Zone-educated kids from the Gulf had settled in the northern Federation, and Lyle had friends there. As her tears dried, she talked about how amazing Casablanca was, full of top scientists, and how easy it would be for engineers with their training to find interesting work.

Eventually, Lyle's dream of Casablanca felt more real to both of them than a future at the Free Lab. When summer came to the prairies, covering the hills outside the city in millions of yellow canola flowers, they decided to leave.

The "checking in" dinner with Krish after their decision did not go well.

"What the fuck are you doing? Throwing away your career again?" Krish scream-whispered angrily. They were at their usual sandwich place, but Krish was self-conscious because a group of his Free Lab students was drinking in the corner and he didn't want them to hear about his personal life.

"I'm not throwing away my career. I'm going to get a job doing geneng—you know, in the real world beyond academia?"

"That would be a waste." Krish said each word as if it were its own sentence, looking furious and sad. "Jack, you are brilliant. You could be making a real difference, engineering therapies that will be released under an open license. They'll never let you do that at some private company."

"I'm never going to stop making open drugs, Krish." She was suddenly touched by his concern, and squeezed his hand. "Sequence wants to be free."

JULY 13, 2144

Jack had to do a little business before she left Saskatoon. Taking a quick walk by the river, she left the remainder of her stash at the top of an archway below the Broadway Bridge. Minutes later, she received an influx of Zone credit, transferred in impeccably anonymous fashion.

She had some money, her truck was charged, and she'd packed her things. Now she'd have to deal with the hard part: getting rid of Threezed.

Jack found him using the Free Lab mobile he'd taken, sitting gracefully on the broad, sunny stairs leading up to the lab. He was still wearing the U of S hoodie, which suddenly aroused her curiosity.

"Where did you get that hoodie?"

"Some kids who run a used clothing store on Broadway gave it to me." Then he added, casually, "They might give me a job, too. I told them I'd come back with my enfranchisement creds."

That was a good sign. Jack smiled. "I've got the credits to start your franchise. And if you ever want to go to university, I'm sure Med or Krish could help you apply. You could start growing a new identity and be eligible for more jobs later."

"I know you're leaving and you don't want me to come with you." His face held no expression.

"It's not safe. I need to disappear."

"Where else are you going to get what I can give you?" He used his half-sarcastic street hustler voice, stretching back and lifting the bottom of his hoodie to reveal a flat stretch of stomach.

She ruffled his hair and tried to keep smiling. "The IPC is already sending out terrorist alerts on me."

He stared at his mobile, ignoring her, fingers twitching as if he were texting. Maybe he was.

"I'm going to leave you with enough credit that you'll be fine as long as you get a job in the next month. I bet you can stay at Med's. It's not like she needs a bed, anyway." She leaned down to kiss him, and he responded with a chaste peck on the lips.

"I'm sure Krish will let you keep that mobile. Secure it and I'll pass those credits over."

"OK." He looked resigned. "Thanks for a good time."

She headed up the steps to the Free Lab. Checking her messages absently, she saw that Threezed had texted her.

And thanks for killing that asshole who slaved me.

For a second, she was flooded with intense, contradictory feelings—for Threezed, for people long gone. Then the door closed behind her, and Jack forced herself to stare straight ahead at the lab benches. It made no difference whether she loved Threezed or just thought he was a nice fuck. She couldn't do anything about it either way.

Luckily, Med had distracting news from Yellowknife. It turned out that Retcon worked astonishingly fast. After just a few hours, the three nonplacebo patients had stopped seeking out their addictive processes and were eating again. They had patchy memories of the past few days, but so far no additional cognitive problems had been identified.

The bot wanted to tell Jack more about the specifics of how Retcon affected the patients' brains, and David wanted to point out all the ways he'd improved on the typical documentation for an open drug. But she couldn't listen right now. The Retcon Project was entirely open, so she could follow their progress by checking their code repository on the Free Lab server.

Med agreed to keep an eye on Threezed, and Krish told the Free Lab sysadmin to release the mobile to him.

Threezed had two friends to rely on, at least.

That idea kept Jack calm as she eased her truck onto the highway. The sinking sun ripped shadows from everything, creating elongated skeletons of darkness that were almost comically menacing. Bales of switchgrass were curled into perfect rolls at the sides of the road, waiting to be loaded on trains and turned into fuel. Tangles of brush still bore dark clusters of tart Saskatoon berries. The air was warm, but not dusty-hot, and the sky was a sheer, brutal blue softened at its edges by rolling prairie hills. The view caused Jack to ponder, for possibly the thousandth time, why people said Saskatchewan was flat.

Now the city was gone, and nothing but the foam road lay ahead.

14

OTHER TRUE SELF

JULY 12, 2144

When Eliasz' brain crackled into alertness, his body tried to kill Paladin. Still half-asleep and panicked, Eliasz twitched to activate his perimeter weapons, then savagely grabbed the bot around the neck. The tiny cot creaked as their weight shifted further to one side. Though it was impossible for Eliasz to strangle Paladin, any movement would set off a powerful electrical pulse from Eliasz' perimeter. Not deadly, but possibly damaging at close range. Paladin held perfectly still, his head even with Eliasz', analyzing minute shifts in his facial muscles to determine when hysteria began to lose its grip on him.

"I have already analyzed the drug Frankie put in your system, Eliasz," Paladin vocalized eventually. "It was carefully engineered to have no long-term effects, and is not addictive. In fact, it contains an anti-addictive element that should prevent most people from ever craving it again."

With a slight tremor, Eliasz withdrew his hands from Paladin's neck and powered down the weapon. "Fuck, I'm so sorry, buddy," he whispered. "I knew something like that might happen, and I should have warned you about it." He sat up, leaning his damp back against the wall, keeping himself carefully positioned behind Paladin's still-reclining form. "I really need some water."

The bot took only a second to drop to the floor and achieve a standing position next to the bed. He walked to the small potable water faucet, its shiny spout positioned beneath the gray water showerhead. On a washing stand drilled into the wall over a drain, there was one foam cup. As he filled the cup, he watched Eliasz covering his chest with a light shirt. Paladin decided that he would retain, but rarely access, the file he'd saved of the words Eliasz used to describe Paladin's always-uncovered body.

"I know it seems counterintuitive, but it was actually a good thing I was unpatched against Frankie's drug." He took a long drink, draining the cup. "She was hazing us, and it would have looked suspicious if I'd been too invulnerable."

Eliasz placed a now steady hand on the bot's shoulder when Paladin sat on the cot next to him. "We did good last night. Did you get any intel?"

"Actually, I believe I did." Paladin told Eliasz about Frankie's connection with *The Bilious Pills,* the publication whose terrorist activities had landed Jack in prison. Everyone who had committed to the group's text repo had used pseudonyms, but the IPC had data files on most of them. Though *The Bilious Pills* had been officially disbanded after Jack's arrest, the pirates behind it appeared to have maintained close connections over the years.

Bluebeard had been part of the group along with Frankie and Jack. So had a human-computer interface engineer in Vancouver called Actin, real name Bobby Broner. Krish Patel, a renowned biomedical researcher in Saskatoon, was known as Captain Nemo. Another former contributor was a doctor in Yellowknife, called Posthuman, real name Malika Ellul. Two more were dead.

"It's possible Jack is still working with the Pills, and one of them is harboring her," Paladin finished.

Eliasz looked dubious. "She may be a pirate, but Jack's not stupid. By now she knows we're onto her, and she'll be focused entirely on saving her ass. Staying with somebody whose name is so publicly connected to hers would be foolish."

"I don't believe they are publicly connected," Paladin explained.

"Nearly all information about *The Bilious Pills* has been removed from the public net. I had to get my data from IPC intelligence."

Eliasz' hand still rested absently on Paladin's shoulder. "OK, good to know. Let's work on Frankie for now, and keep our options open with the others."

It was still early, and after last night's party, none of their potential sources would likely be awake. Eliasz was famished, and announced that they'd kill two birds with one stone by going to a breakfast hangout near the Twin Center. It was a postparty spot in the neighborhood, a place where they could continue exploiting the connections they'd begun making the night before. Eliasz sponged off in the shower, and they headed downtown. The air was filled with pollen, along with stray molecules from the sea.

Paladin was thinking about his brain.

Early that morning he had discovered a small chunk of data from Kagu Robotics Foundry waiting for him on the Camp Tunisia servers. Apparently his request was so unusual that it had been assigned to a botadmin, who appended a note:

We don't normally give out personal information about organ donors to our biobots program. But because you are a recipient of the organ, we have determined that we can release some information to you, provided you accept this property management wrapper that will prevent you from sharing sensitive data with anyone else.

Attached was a file, accessible only inside an app designed to contain rights-protected media and trade secrets. Paladin opened it, and discovered that the more he knew, the less he could tell anyone.

His brain had once belonged to a soldier named Dikeledi [Last Name Withheld]. Like Paladin, she had been indentured to the African Federation. The file said she had died in the line of duty, but did not say how. Obviously by some method that had spared her brain, which had been removed from her body the day Paladin was completed. He had no memory of Dikeledi's brain being installed, only that he could recognize the difference between thousands of human faces, and instantly read the emotional content of their expressions when they flashed before his sensors in tests.

At the time of his construction, a Kagu botadmin told Paladin the brain allowed him to do all that facial-recognition processing. But the bot arms at the foundry told him that the brain was unnecessary—just an advertising gimmick. A line that Fang had repeated. Paladin was left unsure what this brain really meant to him, and why he needed it.

Paladin poked at the software wrapper containing his knowledge, trying to determine what he could tell Eliasz about it. Depending on how he phrased it, he might be able to convey more information than the rights management software intended.

"I have some personal news I would like your opinion about," Paladin vocalized experimentally. "I have received information from the Kagu Robotics Foundry about my brain. It came from a person in the Federation." That much was public information. He could not say whose brain it was, but he could assign a pronoun to her. "She gave me this brain, but I am not sure if it matters. Other bots say it's just an advertising gimmick."

"She? Who is she?" Eliasz stopped beneath a palm tree, his hair thumbed by a hot breeze.

"I can't tell you."

"But do you know?"

"Yes."

Eliasz grinned and rapped on Paladin's carapace over the brain, as he had done before. "That's so fantastic! Now you know who you really are!" He paused, his face a chaos of emotion that passed quickly into one of his rare grins. "Who would have guessed you were a woman?"

The two began to walk again, Eliasz occasionally looking at Paladin and refraining from saying something.

From endlessly researching the word "faggot," and finally reaching an approximate understanding, Paladin knew that human gender was part of sexual desire. But he was starting to perceive that gender was a way of seeing the world, too. Military bots, especially ones with armored bodies like Paladin's, were almost always called "he." People assigned genders based on behaviors and work roles, often ignoring anatomy. Gender was a form of social recognition.

That's why humans had given him a gender before he even had a name.

As they approached the breakfast shop, Paladin perceived trace elements of seared meat borne by the wind. It came from an imitation British pub, complete with a sign announcing "THE KINDS OF BREAKFASTS AUTHENTIC ENGLISH WOULD EAT IN THE DAYS OF QUEEN VICTORIA." This early in the morning, the patrons were sparse, but there were a few families and a big group of disheveled partygoers, their bodies still thrumming with the drugs and hormones they'd processed the night before.

Before they entered, Eliasz turned to Paladin and gazed upward into the bot's face. The man was searching, the bot realized, for the kinds of expressions Paladin always looked for in human faces.

"Should I start calling you 'she'?"

As a robot, he didn't care what pronoun people used; as Fang had pointed out, gender was something humans projected onto robots. Changing his pronoun would make absolutely no difference at all. It would merely substitute one signifier for another. But then Paladin considered the implications of Eliasz' facial expression, which at that moment hovered between desire and fear. Of course: If Paladin were female, Eliasz would not be a faggot. And maybe then Eliasz could touch Paladin again, the way he had last night, giving and receiving pleasure in an undocumented form of emotional feedback loop.

Paladin realized that this was the first time he'd been given a choice about something that might change his life. He thought about it for many seconds before replying.

"Yes," the bot vocalized.

Their arms pressed together as they entered the pub, and Paladin took a microsample of the man's blood. Eliasz' oxytocin levels had risen slightly—this time, without pharmaceutical intervention.

They found the partygoers inside. Some of them had been high on pirated Ellondra when Frankie dosed Eliasz.

"Hey, it's Aleksy!" A man with pale skin doffed his bright red hat theatrically. He turned to the group. "Last night was so epic. Aleksy was patched against Ellondra, so Frankie owned him up with a custom chemical! Oh, man." Then he grinned at Eliasz. "Your bot had to carry you home!"

Eliasz gave a sheepish shrug. "Yeah, I was really out of it. But at least I wasn't knocked over by something as simple as Ellondra."

Red Hat warbled a laugh and gestured for them to come over. "I'll tell you a little secret: None of us is actually concerned about being vulnerable to Ellondra. That stuff is great."

Eliasz and Paladin dragged up some chairs, pushing into the group next to Mecha and Slavoj, who didn't mind having more excuses to bump into each other and giggle.

Red Hat turned out to be Hox2, the person who ran the space in the Twin Center where they'd gone last night. Another group of bleary-looking people in transparent armor arrived, and Hox2 retold the story of his night, with more flourishes at the moment of the drugging. Hox2 finally ended his tale by gesturing at Paladin.

"Does he always carry you home from parties?"

"She," replied Eliasz, around a mouthful of eggs.

"What?" Hox2 and the people in transparent armor looked confused, while Slavoj and Mecha started to kiss.

"She's a she," Eliasz explained. "And I believe this is the first time she's ever carried me home. So, do you live in that place where you had the party?"

That managed to change the subject. The basement space was obviously one of Hox2's favorite subjects, maybe even more than coercive drugging. "Technically, it's a space for doing lab work, so I can't live there, right?" He raised his eyebrows conspiratorially. "It used to be an official free lab, but now we let people develop under mixed licenses. People have to make money on what they're doing, right?"

This comment set off what sounded like a well-worn debate at the table, with some people arguing that a free lab would be better for social progress, and others taking the view that nobody would have any incentive to invent things without patents. Breakfast wore on, and Mecha got up to leave. Hox2 stood with her, straightening his hat, and announced that he had to get back to the space and clean up.

"You should come by later this afternoon," he said to Eliasz. "Frankie is doing a presentation on some free tools for analyzing protein functions." As Hox2 walked away, he patted Paladin's head. "Yes, you can bring him too!"

"Her," Eliasz muttered to his cold cup of tea.

Presently, Eliasz tapped his wrist and beamed some cash to one of the people in transparent armor, who was collecting everybody's money for the meal. Then he stood up, too. "I'm gonna catch a nap and then go check out Frankie's presentation."

Slavoj waved at both of them. "Bye, Aleksy and Pack! See you later!"

They walked back to the hotel in silence, avoiding the egg-shaped electric cars that taxied people through the streets, and threaded their way through sidewalks crowded with shoppers.

As soon as they entered their room, Eliasz turned to Paladin and grabbed her body with an urgency the bot now recognized. She wrapped her arms gently around him and bent her head so that he could kiss the fine mesh over her voice synthesizer. There were no piezosensors on the place Eliasz would know as her mouth, so she felt nothing of his kisses except a kind of light pressure in the structural frame of her head. But her arms and legs could smell molecules on the man's body that came from salt and sexual arousal.

"I knew there was a reason I wanted you, Paladin," he whispered. "I must have somehow sensed that you were a woman."

There it was: the anthropomorphization. But did it really matter if Eliasz didn't understand that bots had no gender? If Eliasz saw her as a woman, Paladin could have what she'd been wanting for days on end. It would make things easier for both of them, even if the truth was more complicated than Eliasz realized.

Eliasz ran his hands over her carapace, finding the edges of her armor plates and trying to reach between them to feel the woven fibers of Paladin's muscles. "You feel so good." Pressing his body against hers, he powered down his entire defense perimeter. The sensation made Paladin ache with fear and protectiveness; she was the only thing that kept him from danger now.

Eliasz' pulse elevated and he pulled away from her. "Come to bed with me, Paladin," he said, grabbing her hand. As he stumbled into the main room, she followed, watching him remove all his clothes and a translucent web of sensors, which he left in an invisible tangle on the floor.

He led her to the bed. She allowed him to push her down on it and climb on top of her, his chest blocking the apertures for her guns. His flushed face pressed against the curve of her neck. It was the first time she had felt him completely naked against her, and she placed her hand against the knotted muscles of his lower back as he strained and sighed in a pleasure she knew she'd induced as surely as Frankie's drug had.

When at last Eliasz' heartbeat slowed, he lay sweating in the crook of her arm, running his fingers across her other hand, the one Lee had modded.

"What does that feel like to you?" he asked sleepily.

"It feels like . . . pressure and movement. I can sample your blood and see that there's prolactin in it."

"Does it feel good?"

"Knowing that it is you, and that I am keeping you safe, makes me feel good."

He sat up a little more, looking at her face. "Is there a way that bots can . . . come? Have an orgasm?"

Paladin thought for a while, considering what Eliasz meant by "orgasm," and trying to find some kind of equivalent experience.

"I am only a few months old, so my knowledge of undocumented functions is incomplete. But I have a program that I downloaded from the bot server at Camp Tunisia that causes some of the same physical symptoms as an orgasm."

Eliasz' heartbeats came faster again. "Can I watch you while you play it?" He pressed his body against hers the way he had earlier, growing aroused.

"It would not be safe while your weapons are off. The file forces me to reboot."

The man jumped up and settled the light net of sensors over his head, waiting for it to weave itself tightly across his skin, connecting with his subcutaneous network. "Lie on your side and I can cover you," he whispered, curling around her torso and head, protecting most of her legs with his own. She checked to be sure that his perimeter was on a secure setting, though it was not armed against her.

"I will play it now," she vocalized. She opened the original executable and it began to run, the worm rapidly replicating a few pieces of nonsense data inside her as she watched the scene stolen from a game world, of herself rescuing a man on the battlefield. She felt Eliasz' hands and body moving against her carapace distantly, adding to the general sense of wrong inputs flooding her sensors. At last she was overwhelmed: Her mind filled with errors, and a pleasurable confusion raced through her before she crashed in his arms.

When she rebooted, Eliasz was still in a defensive posture around her, stroking the shielding around her brain.

"Awake now?" He kissed the back of her head.

"Yes."

"Great, because I really do have to sleep."

"It is safe now."

His grip on her relaxed, and she stole away from the bed to stand guard at the center of the room.

As the day began to cool, Eliasz woke up, checked his messages, and took another sponge bath before they headed out to Frankie's presentation.

"Pay attention to anything Frankie does on the network, and look for a way to access her messages on it," he said. "We just need positive confirmation that she's been communicating with Jack recently. If so, we'll proceed to a full interrogation."

When they arrived at Hox2's place, it looked like it was transitioning between trashed party spot and community lab. The wet lab was still partly a wet bar, and people were helping themselves to last night's beer. Frankie was uploading data to a projector cube in the center of a long lab bench that bisected the dance floor. She laughed when she looked up and saw Eliasz and Paladin arriving. "Feeling a little hung over, Aleksy?"

"Not so much that I wasn't able to get over here to see if you can do anything other than dose unwary engineers."

"I'm flattered." She returned to gesturing at the projector.

Paladin tuned local radio wave transmissions, looking for any signs that Frankie's projector was networked in a way that would give the bot access to whatever server she was using. Just as Frankie's audience started plunking down cups of beer on the bench, Paladin found her opportunity. Frankie was networking her glasses with a protein synthesizer she'd pulled down from a shelf. Monitoring the exchange, Paladin managed to capture the authentication sequence the synthesizer used to connect with the glasses.

Presently, Frankie reached a point in the presentation when she no longer needed to use the synthesizer. She severed the connection. Now Paladin could send the authentication code to Frankie's glasses, which had already been set up to receive connections from the synthesizer without question. Paladin was in. Jumping through directories quickly, she located a batch of recent messages stored on the device and encrypted with a very old algorithm that took only seconds to break. One of the messages was clearly from Jack, though its origins had been obscured—it had been routed through a server located in a research lab on the Moon.

Stop manufacturing that Zacuity shit until I get back. Very dangerous. Lots of fatal side effects in the Zone. Also, don't expect me in fall—I may have to lie low for a while.

Frankie had replied: *No problems on my end. Be safe.*

It was time for the question and answer portion of Frankie's presentation, which soon turned into a debate over Adder, the language she'd used to write the tool that error-checked phosphorylation pathways. Three developers sitting together at one end of the bench were extremely taken with a new language called Ammolite that had been written last year by some researchers at a free lab in the AU. They took turns pointing out how Ammolite would solve some of the problems with data structures in her tool.

"Oh, for shit's sake," groaned Mecha, who had settled next to Paladin. "I can't believe this is going to turn into another Adder versus Ammolite debate." Then she raised her voice, aiming her irritation at the group of Ammolite enthusiasts. "She wrote the damn tool in Adder—get over it. Can we please talk about fucking phosphorylation?"

"Yeah, I think we're getting off topic at this point," Frankie agreed.

This seemed to be the signal for general talk to break out, and for several people to stand up and pour more of last night's beer into cups.

Paladin shared her intel with Eliasz' perimeter, while he did his best to ingratiate himself with Frankie and WTF, who had just come down from the loft.

"I could really have used your tool in my last job," Eliasz said to Frankie. "What do you call it? I want to find it on the net." She ignored him, conferring in a low voice with WTF. Eliasz feigned casual disinterest, checking messages on his wrist. He shot a look at Paladin when he saw the data. *Good work,* his expression said.

Finally Frankie turned back to Eliasz. "I haven't released it yet, kid. But I might throw what I have up on the Hox server tonight." She walked upstairs without a second glance.

Mecha, however, was eager to talk. "Frankie's very perfectionist about her tools. Don't feel bad that she doesn't want to let you see it. That's just Frankie."

Eliasz watched Frankie's tuft of pink hair and WTF's lumpy skull as they entered the loft together. "So does she live here with Hox2 or something?" he asked casually, toying with his beer cup.

"No, she lives in the medina, sort of close to that teahouse where we met."

"I like that area," Eliasz continued conversationally. "I was thinking of getting a flat there, too."

"A bunch of us live there because it's cheaper than downtown."

"Is it cheap enough that you don't need roommates to afford a place?"

"Oh, yeah," Mecha said enthusiastically. "Frankie lives by herself and has a great place. I have a roommate, but the flat is so big we barely see each other."

They continued to talk while Paladin listened, wondering why it was that Mecha would give away dangerously personal information about herself and her friends in the middle of a casual conversation with someone she'd only met the day before. She supposed that everyone had their vulnerabilities, and Mecha's was talking. She couldn't resist giving away what she knew. And that meant Frankie was vulnerable, too, especially if you added in the poor state of her network security.

There was one way Frankie was very secure, however. Eliasz kept trying to engage Frankie in conversation, and he kept failing. She looked increasingly harassed, and finally grabbed his arm and steered him to the edge of the bar/lab. Paladin trained her audio sensors on them.

"Look pal, I'm not going to kick you out of this lab because it's open to everybody, including covert IPC agents." Frankie's syllables were clipped. "But I'm not your friend, and I'm not going to help you get whatever you're here for. So leave me the fuck alone."

Eliasz chuckled and threw up his arms while backing off a few inches. "Hey, that's cool. Not sure what you mean by that, but I'm sorry to bother you." He returned to the bench with Paladin and Mecha, staying for another fifteen minutes of Adder versus Ammolite debate. Then he and Paladin left by the same path they had the night before, crossing from the dance floor to the elevators. But this time, both were on high alert.

When they reached the street, Eliasz took stock of their surroundings. The triangular shape of the Twin Center's entrance was formed by two angled staircases that started on the sidewalk and led to an elevated park nestled between the towers that gave the place its name. Now the mall sheltered pirates, and the park hosted an informal night market with stalls offering everything from fresh fruit to pirated software.

"The good news is that we have solid evidence that she's linked to our terrorist," Eliasz said. "I now have authorization from the Federation to interrogate her."

Paladin had studied interrogations, but never witnessed one. "How will you do that? She'll never talk. She already suspects you're with the IPC."

"I have a little something that I doubt she's patched against." Eliasz patted the side pocket in his pants. "I also know exactly what route Frankie's going to take to get home. All we have to do is follow her. When we get there, you grab her and I'll give her a taste of my medicine."

Later that night, Eliasz and Paladin took advantage of the poor lighting on the path to the medina to merge with the shadows in a closed teahouse doorway. At last Frankie walked by, trailed by WTF and a few others from the lab. They followed at a distance, passing beneath old, arched gateways made of stone, and polymer awnings that flapped quietly in the wind off the ocean. A few people were on the street, emerging from yellow strips of light that edged the cracked-open doorways of teahouses.

Frankie's friends began peeling off into courtyards or up stairways to their flats. At last she was alone, her rolling gait taking her several doorways past the hacker teahouse. Paladin pulled ahead of Eliasz, her body in full stealth mode, light bending around her carapace and her feet soundless on the stone street. As Frankie turned up a short flight of stairs, Paladin jumped on her, clearing several steps and grabbing the woman's arms in one fluid motion. Before Frankie could cry out, the bot had covered her mouth with one hand.

For a few seconds they engaged in quiet combat on the stairs, Frankie kicking and trying to pull away from Paladin's grip.

But then Eliasz arrived, a tiny injector gripped between his fingers, which he wrapped around Frankie's throat, as if he meant to strangle her. Instead, he administered the drug, then moved his hand up slightly to grip her chin as it hit her. Her muscles had gone so slack that she was unable to hold her head up on her own.

Paladin kept a tight grip on the woman to keep her from sliding down the stairs as Eliasz whispered to her. "I think we're going to have a nice talk now. Let's start by going inside your flat. What is your key?"

Frankie looked at a point beyond Eliasz' head, her eyes unfocused. "You bastard," she replied, her mouth working slowly through each syllable. As the drug's effect intensified, Frankie lost her footing, leaning heavily on Paladin as she tried to stand again.

"Frankie," Eliasz said softly. "I want you to look at something very interesting." He aimed her unsteady gaze in the direction of a tiny projector in the palm of his hand, which emitted what looked to Paladin like a simple light that pulsed more brightly every few seconds. Something about the drug Eliasz had given Frankie caused the pulses to occupy her full attention. It was some kind of multihypnotic, Paladin guessed, that would lower her inhibitions, magnify her desire to trust, and relax her muscles. Any sensory input would feel overwhelming. Distracting her already-saturated attention with something simple, like a light, would intensify the drug's trust-blooming effect.

They stood for almost a minute with Frankie absorbed by the projection and Eliasz watching her pupils dilate. Then he returned to his question, which he asked even more gently. "What is the key?"

She held up an unsteady hand. "Biometric," Frankie sighed, speaking to the light.

Frankie's flat was sparsely furnished, with a bedroom in back and a front room occupied by a few chairs pulled up to a tabletop projector. She had a fabber and sequencer in the kitchen, which also contained the flat's biggest window. Eliasz pulled the blinds down in each room before turning on a single light, while Paladin settled the loose-limbed Frankie into a chair.

Frankie seemed to lapse into a state of near-unconsciousness. Then she straightened up, her muscles bunching and relaxing in an uncoordinated fashion. Paladin stood quietly behind her, hands on her shoulders. The bot was prepared to restrain her at any moment.

Eliasz pulled up a chair so that he sat knee-to-knee with Frankie. He looked into her eyes, black with pupil, and covered her knees with his warm hands. "Frankie, I'm your friend," he said softly, leaning closer. He was working with the drug to establish an intense emotional bond. A bead of saliva formed at the corner of Frankie's mouth. She couldn't look away from Eliasz' face.

"Fuck you," she mumbled.

He ignored her. "We have proof you're working with Judith Chen, the pirate and terrorist you know as Jack. You're either going to be in prison for a short time, or the rest of your life. Tonight you make that choice. I can make things easier for you if you tell me where Jack is hiding."

Frankie seemed to nod out for a second, the drug no doubt

making it more difficult for her to process this information. Neurochemically, she would be yearning to trust everything Eliasz said. It would be hard for her to stop herself from talking. But Frankie also knew exactly what was happening to her brain, how she was being manipulated, and would fight it.

"You don't have anything on me," she said finally.

Eliasz projected a file in front of Frankie's vague eyes, showing her the thread between herself and Jack that Paladin had discovered via the projector. Frankie was obviously caught off guard. "Jack . . ." she murmured uncertainly.

"Where is Jack?" Eliasz asked. "She's in trouble, but you don't have to be."

Paladin put her hands on Frankie's head, reading the flickering electrical signals from her drug-altered brain. Her visual centers were extremely active: She must be using visualization to resist Eliasz' questions. They needed to distract her, break her concentration, focus her brain activity elsewhere.

"Hit her," Paladin said. It was the fastest way to get the job done.

Eliasz punched Frankie in the face, breaking her nose. Her head rocked back, and she began to gurgle and choke on the blood gushing down her face.

Paladin reached a finger into Frankie's mouth to scoop out the stringy clots, then grabbed a fistful of the woman's hair to push her head upright again. Now the spike in Frankie's visual activity had tapered off. The drug's powers would be peaking now, and would start to fade over the next fifteen minutes.

"Where is Jack?" Eliasz peered into Frankie's ruined face. "It doesn't have to hurt anymore. I'm your friend."

Her words tumbled out, the chemically induced urge suddenly overcoming her will. "She's got a lab in Vancouver. But I don't know if that's where she's gone." She paused, her parted lips slack and gory. Frankie would be feeling no pain for the moment; she had just placed her trust in Eliasz, and the multi-hypnotic would make that feel good, to encourage further bonding with her interrogator. "She's with a runaway slave, though. Some boy named Threezed she found in the Arctic. He might have taken her somewhere else."

After her confession, Frankie must have found another way to resist the hypnotic. That was the last useful information they got out of her, though they continued to beat and drug her for the next three hours. At last, when both her arms hung broken at her sides, Frankie passed out and would not wake up.

Eliasz alerted the Federation's local IPC agents, who relayed their position to police. Fifteen minutes later, two bots arrived, their armored, bipedal bodies similar to Paladin's own. One addressed Paladin: *Hello. Let's establish a secure session using AF protocol.*

Paladin agreed, and they gave their session a number.

I am Talon. Please transmit interrogation file. That is the end of my data.

Paladin sent a series of compressed video files while Talon's companion lifted the unconscious woman out of the chair, now stained with blotches of blood that were already drying into brown at their edges. Frankie moaned in pain as the bot gripped her upper arm where the jagged edge of a bone had pierced her skin.

"Here is additional information that will aid with a terrorist conviction," Paladin vocalized. She sent the message thread between Jack and Frankie in a forensic wrapper intended to prove it had not been tampered with since its extraction from Frankie's server.

"Thanks, guys," Eliasz addressed the bots. "We're heading out."

"The Federation appreciates your work," Talon vocalized formally, adding via microwave: *Good luck to you, Paladin.*

The bots clattered down Frankie's front steps. They were official law enforcement, so there was no need to move stealthily. Perhaps they even wanted the neighbors to see that the notorious pirate had been captured.

"I've got the coordinates for an extraction point," Eliasz told Paladin, who was closing Frankie's door, locking it unnecessarily. "We move out in thirty minutes." He beamed a map to Paladin, showing a helicopter pad at the port. They could reach it by walking.

At this hour, the winding streets of the medina were quiet and dark. The yellow glow of the Hassan II minaret divided the horizon over low roofs. For a moment, Paladin considered that, from a human perspective, the streets would look even murkier when contrasted with that perfectly architected shaft of light. Maybe that was the point.

The ancient port was filled with tugs and fishing boats, and the water was held still by a long, curling jetty made from enormous, interlocking cement jacks. Here and there on the docks, Paladin could see people sleeping under stained blankets of waterproof cotton, but if they noticed Eliasz and the bot, they showed no sign of it. At last a helicopter skimmed over the mosque toward them, its engines noise-cancelled to the point where all they could hear was the air being beaten with such regularity that it became a long, unending sigh.

The two settled into the cabin. Soon Casablanca was little more than a shining crescent at the edge of a vast continent. Eliasz finally spoke. "I've suggested to the project head that we split up to follow the two leads Frankie gave us. I'm going down to Vegas to see if I can dig up something on this escaped slave, and you can follow up on that Vancouver lab. Thanks to your research on *The Bilious Pills,* I think you'll know where to start." He paused, and took Paladin's hand. The helicopter was unpiloted, and there would be no video capture here, either. "Vancouver also has a large community of autonomous bots, so that's your cover: You're a newly autonomous lab bot looking for work. When we get to base, your botadmin can set you up with a simulated autonomy key."

"What is the difference between a simulated autonomy key and a real one?"

"A simulated key expires," Eliasz said, his hand gripping hers as they dropped down over the jet field.

15

PIRATE YOUR BODY

JULY 13, 2144

Moose Jaw hadn't changed much in the past thirty years. As Jack's truck entered the tiny city, she passed the giant moose statue looming to the left of the highway and drove down narrow roads lined with refurbished wooden houses covered in the frills of another era's architectural fashion.

Downtown were a few casinos and a mineral spa where Jack's family had come for the Christmas holidays. Built over two centuries ago, the spa was a landmark, its ancient pools an attraction for the daring in winter, because you could swim under a low arch and find yourself in a steaming public bath out of doors. As a little girl, Jack had delighted endlessly in that outdoor pool. She would dip under to wet her whole head, then bob in the odd-tasting water up to her neck until her hair became a fine white net of frost around her face and crackled under her hands.

Aside from the casino, Moose Jaw's main attraction was a series of tunnels that ran under the city. Local legend held that they had been home to the city's immigrant Chinese labor force in the early twentieth century. These anonymous men and women lived and worked in dark underground hovels doing laundry for the white prairie folk. After Jack went on a tour of the musty, underground rooms, she started telling the kids in elementary school that she had a great-great-great-grandparent who once lived below the city.

Her father was appalled when he found out. It was the first time he connected her mobile to the family server and let her explore on her own, showing her how to find the photographs proving the Chens had come from Hong Kong to Vancouver long after the tunnels had been abandoned, settling in Saskatchewan in the early 2000s.

Jack's interest in the tunnels continued even after she reluctantly accepted her father's version of the family history. She returned to Moose Jaw as an adult in the summer between her first and second year of college, tagging along with a group of friends who were volunteering with an archaeological dig. For months, they carefully excavated the area beneath a condemned warehouse off Main Street.

The principal investigator had a grant to investigate whether the tunnels had actually belonged to bootlegger Al Capone during the twentieth-century Prohibition era. Since most of the tunnels had been blocked off over two centuries ago, finding the answer involved a lot of careful digging, 3-D imaging of each layer, and stringing wire everywhere so that the site eventually looked like a massive grid.

It was ultimately never clear whether the additional tunnels they excavated actually belonged to Al Capone or just a random gangster. Large and ventilated, the space they found still contained bootlegger gear and a few antique guns. When the grant ran out, Jack helped seal up the entrance, which was now in the basement of a new apartment building. The archaeologists, ever hopeful that one day their grant might be renewed, left one entrance to the excavation open, accessible via a small trapdoor.

After her experiences with research grants, Jack knew that nobody would ever be visiting that tunnel again. Except her. She was keeping the tradition of the tunnels alive by using them for smuggling. Over the past two decades, she'd tricked them out with an air purification system, a covert hookup to the network and power grids, sleeping quarters, and a hidden safe where she could stash a secure mobile and several bags of drugs.

Sometimes Jack stayed here for weeks, letting her trail go cold. Maybe her ancestors had never lived in these tunnels, but they felt like a legitimate inheritance.

Slipping into an old routine calmed her down. She paid untraceable cash for a month's rent on a parking spot at one of the spas, shrugging a faraday bag over her truck. It also contained a perimeter alarm. If anybody tried to get into the vehicle, it would alert her and start a video feed that she could pick up in her tunnel. Then she bought a little fresh fruit and pepperoni—she kept a cooker down there, but she had a craving for comfort food.

At last she arrived at the service entrance to the now-aging apartment building. Jack blasted the surveillance cameras with an infrared beam, creating what looked like a few seconds of glitch while she eased down through the basement hatch.

"Light," she said to the dusty air, waiting for the old fluorescents to turn heaps of wood and shattered solar cells into more than piles of shadow. This dirty room was another way of covering her tracks. Anyone who managed to find the nearly invisible hatch would be met with what looked like a pile of last century's trash.

Her safe house was in the main portion of the tunnel, but she'd blocked access to it with a thick spray of concrete foam, leaving only a small hole near the floor that could be plugged with a perfectly shaped hunk of the same stuff the wall was made of. She pulled this plug in behind her, worming backward into the main tunnel, scraping her arms, belly, and back on the rough material as she passed through.

"Light and air," she coughed. The bootleggers' haven began to glow with yellow light, and a fan hummed.

The tunnel had a low, curved roof reinforced with thermoplastic beams and strung with LED wires. Shallow nooks carved into the walls had once held smugglers' weapons and loot, but might actually date back to the immigrants who needed to stow household items. Down the center of the tunnel was a lab bench she'd cobbled together from a cheap door made of processed seed hulls, nailed to polymer stumps discarded from a printer factory. That bench contained her whole life: a fabber, a sequencer, and a projector, all built from generic, nougat-colored parts. These were networked to an antenna that snaked up into the walls of the apartment building above, sending signals that hopped between frequencies, masquerading as a variety of devices.

At the far end of the room, under the air purifier box, was her futon. Atop the chilly floor, she'd unrolled a soft, colorful carpet from Fez, a city south of Casablanca. This place was like her sub, hidden below the surface but wired to the outside world.

Leaning back against the wall she'd just tunneled through, legs splayed in front of her, Jack sighed. Safety. For a little while.

Although she hadn't had a decent night's sleep in days, she wasn't ready to be unconscious. Jack scrolled idly through the feeds on her mobile, projecting a few into the air, wondering whether Retcon could outrace the damage Zacuity was doing.

All the news feeds were reporting on another workplace meltdown incident. The major feeds covered it with the usual splash of decontextualized horror, but reporters at the investigative text repo *Internecine* said it sounded more like the Zacuity rampage at the Calgary train control center.

A botadmin at the Toronto branch of Timmo's had one job: to keep the machines making donut holes, squirting blob after blob of fatty dough out of their cannulated needle fingers and into the simmering oil. He began requesting overtime and skipping meal breaks. His coworkers said he developed a "creepy" relationship with one of the donut bots.

And then, just today, the admin decided everything was a

potential donut hole. Pieces of garbage. A stray cat. The hands of his unfortunate customers. Eventually, his own legs. Anything that could be mashed up and forced through a tube, to be extruded in perfect, mouth-sized blobs. The Timmo's was a bloodbath, with at least two dead.

Internecine showed some clips they'd somehow ripped from a police bodyfeed.

"We're just making donuts!" the admin screamed, holding up a ball of gore. "Why don't you let us make donuts! Timmo's bots make . . . the . . . best . . . donuts!"

Jack stared at the pepperoni she had been about to eat, feeling ill.

FALL 2120

At first, Casablanca was everything that Lyle had promised. The African Federation was still young, and the government worried very little about enforcing intellectual property laws, as long as the economy was expanding.

Jack and Lyle rented a flat in the biotech ghetto, a neighborhood whose nickname was self-explanatory. It was near the high, ocean-facing wall around the old medina. Always a middle-class neighborhood, the area had been tended and upgraded over the centuries to retain its traditional Moorish architecture of colorful tiles and hidden courtyards, while also growing a new surface of photovoltaic paint over semipermeable walls that absorbed water and strobed with glowing algae at night. The winding streets looked ancient, but they had been paved with foam. Even the crumbling seams in the walls came from bioconcrete, a mash of water-activated bacteria and epoxies that healed itself as cracks formed.

They took lucrative jobs at a startup that built custom proteins for other businesses, and swore that they would save their best ideas for after-work projects. But so far, they'd been working such long hours that the ideas hadn't come. That's when Lyle decided it was time to take an evening off. She brought an expensive red-and-brown blanket home and swirled it around her body. "Let's get under it together and swear to do something very, very important."

Most of their clothes were already on the floor by the time Lyle pulled the blanket completely over their heads. They kissed fiercely, yanking each other's underwear off. The space beneath the caftan grew hot and close with their breathing.

Jack looked into her lover's eyes, which had gone nearly black in the caftan's shadow. Lyle's fingers moved inside her, and Jack kept staring into those eyes, her body swollen with pleasure, thinking that she had never loved anyone this much in her entire life. And then she could no longer focus on anything other than her own pleasure.

Lyle wasn't much for postorgasm cuddling these days. She threw off the caftan and started talking.

"I'm serious, we can really shake things up here. We should start our own Free Lab, but make it really radical, much more radical than Krish's."

Jack didn't say anything. She was still trying to savor their closeness, pulling Lyle's thigh between her legs. Lyle rewarded her by throwing her other leg over Jack's hip, squeezing their bodies together in a pleasurable tangle.

"Don't you want to do that, Jack?"

Lyle was moving in a way that was increasingly distracting. "Yes," Jack whispered.

The first planning meeting for the Casablanca Free Lab, held at a teahouse, was a lot less pleasant than the undercover meeting that had spawned it. Somehow Jack's call for participation on a couple of local biotech hacker forums had gotten reposted to an artists' mailing list, and a bunch of poets showed up to argue with them about the true meaning of anarchy. Instead of a practical conversation about renting a space where they could build a wet lab, they had a three-hour shouting match about liberty and recolonialism.

Casablanca had grown wealthy on biotech, but local artists and subversives considered scientific progress equivalent to gentrification. They had a very hard time grasping the idea that science could be radical, and a laboratory could be free.

It took Jack and Lyle a full year of argument, on the net and in person, before they reached the pragmatic stage of renting a space. By that time, they had a pretty good grasp of Darija, and a core group of five people who were willing to put in money and time to set up the lab.

The Twin Center had just been converted into cheap live-work spaces, and the Casablanca Free Lab moved into one of its subbasements. They did this partly because it was a large space with running water, but partly to appease the poets who lived in the upper floors. It was the right move. The poets still liked to remind the engineers gleefully that culture stomped on the head of science, but they had stopped calling them recolonizers—at least, to their faces.

Krish was ecstatic to hear that they had set up the first satellite Free Lab, and tried to help with grant applications.

"Fuck his grants," grumbled Jack, reading his messages. "We don't want to be beholden to some economic coalition." The rest of the collective agreed with her. To distance themselves from Krish's Free Lab, they would need a new name. They called themselves Signaling Pathway—Signal for short.

"We still need a way to make money," Lyle pointed out, after they'd spent some time sketching a logo.

"We could charge for memberships," suggested a volunteer.

"That doesn't sound very free. What would the poets say?"

Everybody laughed. But it was true: They couldn't ask for money and call themselves liberators. Subversives were already suspicious enough of science in this town, and you couldn't very well charge admission to the revolution.

For the first few months at Signal, they deferred the money question. The collective had ponied up enough cash for at least six months' rent. Plus, they were having fun. Jack was teaching a basic synbio class, showing other residents in the building how to reverse engineer simple organisms. One teenager figured out a way to grow mint in his family's tiny garden by engineering the plant to use nitrogen more efficiently.

As Signal-related projects flourished, people came from all over the Maghreb to see their space. Local companies donated old fabbers, sequencers, and tissue trellises. Lyle ran weekly meetings where regulars and visitors could mingle to discuss the Free Lab's mission. It was at one of these weekly meetings that they met Frankie.

Lyle had finally debugged her tattoo, and a sequence of flowers danced on her freshly shorn head, matching the illuminated flowers that crawled up and down her dress. Meetings always began with beer and a foul-tasting drink called Club-Mate, an old tradition that went back to hackerspaces of the twenty-first century. Clumped around the bench were kids and retirees, rich biotech professionals and info anarchists who lived in squats. Each person introduced themselves, using a real name or pseudonym as they wished.

Frankie looked like a typical engineer in her starched shirt and casual khakis. Her brown skin and black hair made it more likely that she was local, but she could just as easily be from the AU or the Zone. She said she built things with Adder.

After the meeting, Lyle gave the newbies a tour of the lab. Jack checked on some sequence, while across the room Lyle's bright dress grew a comet tail of admiring hackers. When Jack looked up from her readout, Frankie was standing next to her. "I need to talk to you in private," she said.

"It's private here."

Frankie just looked at her. "Do you have a faraday room?"

Jack was beginning to wonder if this woman was one of the occasional crazies they got at Signal, a person gone paranoid in the pursuit of ambiguously legal science.

"No," she said gently. "But we are several floors underground. I'm not sure what you're worried about, but the people here are pretty cool."

"I'm worried that the IPC has bugged your shit." She waved her hand at the churning sequencers, then brought it to rest on the tablet Jack had folded up and strapped to her belt. "Do you know how easy it is to turn this thing into a bug?"

Definitely crazy. Jack tried to be nonchalant. "I'm not worried about it."

"You should be. Do you really think the IPC has stopped tracking you after what happened with *The Bilious Pills*? Especially now that you're preaching the freedom to reverse engineer in Africa?"

That settled it. Jack was done with this weird bitch. "Fuck off, OK? I'm not doing anything illegal."

"I'm going to do you a favor. I'm going to help you and that rich girl from the Gulf figure out what it would really mean to bring free drugs to people who need them. That was always your problem at *The Bilious Pills*—you were so focused on your little legal arguments, and dressing up like pirates, that you forgot about the real crimes. Like murder."

Suddenly Jack realized who she was talking to. Frankie was the woman behind the *Bilious Pills* byline Rosalind Franklin.

Rosalind Franklin had sent the autonomous drone fleet that

liberated the pills from Halifax Harbor before Jack got arrested. But Jack had only known her as a pseudonym, a fiercely smart but mysterious writer from somewhere in the African Federation. Her first essay for *The Bilious Pills* began with an intensely personal story, unusual for an academic, in which she explained quite bluntly how her family had been murdered by Zaxy when they refused to license the antiviral Blense to a local manufacturer. It was an unforgettable essay, especially because it ended with an elegant little program—thirty lines of Adder—that perfectly reverse-engineered Blense. Nobody who worked on the text repo knew her real name.

"Are you Rosalind Franklin?"

The woman shrugged. "No, I'm her ghost, come to get revenge on the white dudes who stole the Nobel Prize from me." Then she laughed, a loud bark that did not fit somebody who seemed so focused on hiding. Several faces in Lyle's comet tail turned to look at them.

Jack felt like she'd passed a secret test. "I'm glad you came. We always wondered who you were."

"I'm glad you've decided to do some real work instead of just scribbling in a text repo." Frankie's compliments were always insults. They had the disturbing effect of making people want to please her more.

"Do you live around here? Are you interested in starting a project at Signal?"

"I'm thinking of moving here."

"Are you still working at a university?"

Frankie tilted her head to the side. "I never worked at a university."

Jack and Krish had always assumed Rosalind Franklin was a university researcher—all of *The Bilious Pills* contributors they knew had been students or junior faculty. But Rosalind Franklin had never divulged where she worked. She just wrote beautiful code and angry, persuasive essays.

"Oh, are you in industry?"

"No. I'm a pirate."

Before Jack could respond, Lyle joined them, putting her arm around Jack's waist and kissing her. "Who's your friend?"

Frankie frowned at Lyle. "Why do you want to draw attention to yourself with your clothes? Don't you think you're upsetting the social order enough without rubbing it in people's faces?" And with that, Frankie went to wait by the elevator.

"That was Rosalind Franklin."

"The woman who wrote for *The Bilious Pills*?"

"Yeah. She said she might be moving here and wants to help us." Jack felt off-balance as she watched the elevator doors close.

Nobody was more vulnerable to Frankie's insults than Lyle. When Frankie became a regular at Signal, Lyle got itchy in her flamboyant clothing, picking holes in her stockings that flared into runs. She let her hair grow in, its natural, glossy black replacing the debugged tattoo. And then she started working with Frankie on a secret project that took a lot of her time.

Lyle said Frankie had ideas for a program that could help with rapid prototyping of flu vaccines. Mostly, however, the pirate would come to Signal empty-handed, leave with a sack of drugs, and return empty-handed. Of course, a lot of people used Signal to prototype drugs. That's what everyone assumed Frankie was doing, too. And maybe it was.

Then Lyle started skipping work, supposedly to hammer on sequence with Frankie. Jack hunted her down at Signal one evening after she'd been MIA all day. "Where the fuck have you been? I keep having to make excuses for you at work, and it's getting really old."

"I told you, I was with Frankie—it's been a really hard time for her, restarting her business."

"She moved here months ago."

"Look, there's a lot about Frankie you don't know."

"There's a lot you don't know either—like her real name, for example."

"You don't need to know someone's birth name to know they're doing good work. She's bringing flu vaccines and antivirals to people who can't afford them, and she's helping to set up a small manufacturing operation for this collective down in Fez so they can do it for themselves. Besides, you don't go by your real name, either."

Jack leaned against the wall and closed her eyes, feeling the raw insulation crinkling under her arm. This wasn't the conversation she wanted to be having. Everybody knew her real name was Judith Chen. Jack was a nickname, not a pseudonym.

"So you're helping her pirate drugs instead of going to work?"

"I hate that job—I'm quitting. Frankie's going to help pay for the lab."

This was turning into a serious what-the-fuck conversation. "You do understand that Frankie is breaking the law. Yes, she's doing some good, but she's also selling a lot of shit that's just for fun, for parties. How does that help the people of Fez?"

Lyle shrugged, and grinned. "Since when do you care about patent piracy?"

"Since I'm trying to run a legitimate Free Lab. Everyone is welcome here, you know that. We're not policing anyone. But if anyone found out we were funded by piracy, well . . ."

"What do you think would happen?"

"I think it would be worse than jail. And that was already bad enough." Jack was going to cry, or throw up, or maybe punch Lyle in the face. She was jealous of Frankie, or scared of her—maybe both. So she walked away without saying anything.

Lyle caught up to her on the street, three blocks from their flat. She put an arm around Jack, and they walked without saying anything until they reached the door. Jack thought about how they'd met, how good the late summer air smelled in Saskatoon, and how she'd already lost both a continent and a calling.

Maybe there was some weird crap going on with Lyle and Frankie, but Jack was suddenly filled with certainty that she could deal with it. She didn't want to lose another person she loved. Or another place. And Jack had to admit she wasn't particularly worried about piracy.

Lyle was much happier after she quit her day job. Signal was flourishing, and she told Jack it was the first time she truly believed she wasn't living out some twisted version of her mother's dreams. For a few months, it felt like they were back in the Free Lab storage room again, madly in love with each other and the revolution.

Until one afternoon when Jack got a text from an unknown string of numbers, which usually meant Frankie. It read: *We need to talk about Lyle. Meet me at the teahouse in an hour?*

Frankie held court in a dim, red-curtained room at a teahouse in the biotechie ghetto. Sitting cross-legged at a low table surrounded by plump cushions, the pirate was playing with a handheld 3-D printer that was spitting out what looked like tiny chunks of cellulose.

She stood quickly when Jack arrived. "Thanks for coming."

Frankie ordered another pot of tea and gave Jack a look that was entirely free of her usual sarcasm. "Have you talked to Lyle lately about her new project?"

"I thought she was working with you." Jack felt a twist of the old jealousy; there were so many things she didn't know about what Lyle was doing with Frankie.

Frankie settled her chin into her fist, and Jack noticed with surprise that the pirate had dyed her hair pink. "I haven't hung out with her in weeks. She's been working with a new group, run by this woman called FoxP2. I'm worried."

"Well, now you know how I've been feeling for the past year," Jack commented sardonically.

Frankie said nothing, and swirled tea in her cup. "FoxP2 is dangerous."

"More dangerous than a pirate who sells illegal drugs to the highest bidder?" Jack felt like an asshole as soon as she said it, but Frankie was unfazed.

"We both care about Lyle, and I understand why you're pissed at me. But I want you to understand that I am very careful about my work. I don't want to get caught, and I spend a lot of time making sure of that. Hasn't Lyle told you about my business?"

"You already told me you're a pirate."

"I told you that because I trust you. But I also run a legitimate business as a consultant, and all my money is funneled through that. I've worked with an attorney to make sure the IPC will never get anything on me."

Maybe she was lying about that attorney. If so, at least her lies demonstrated that she understood the dangers of her job.

"I take it this other woman isn't as careful as you are."

FoxP2 and her collective wanted to disrupt the system, but their plans didn't extend much beyond the disruption. Lyle was apparently helping them engineer muscles for pirated legs and arms, each replacement limb in violation of dozens of patents. Their work was excellent, but flashy. FoxP2 had a public text repo called *Pirate Your Body*, where she bragged about all the lives that she'd saved with her work. And all the greedy biotech corporations she'd screwed over.

As Frankie talked, Jack pulled out her mobile and found FoxP2's journal on Memeland. The latest entry was just a series of pictures uploaded from a party. Lyle figured in a lot of them, dressed in armor, with her head half-shaved. Jack recognized a few people from Signal dancing with her. She thumbed back over to the pictures of Lyle again, trying to figure out what she'd been doing the night they were taken.

"Somebody is going to punish them. The Federation can't afford to look like it's harboring flagrantly subversive groups. It's bad for trade. We've got to get Lyle to stop working with FoxP2."

Jack had to admit that FoxP2's project looked exactly like the kind of thing that got people detained by the IPC—and sometimes disappeared. It was too obvious they wanted to flout the law. Was it possible that Lyle genuinely didn't understand the stakes here?

Frankie's glasses were receiving data, and the pirate ducked out of the room for a moment. Jack played with one of the cellulose blobs that the 3-D printer was still extruding onto the table. It looked like it could be some kind of processed plant material, the kind of thing you might package a drug in.

She tried to imagine how she would bring up FoxP2 with Lyle—it wouldn't be easy. But she never had a chance to have that conversation. Frankie ran back into the room, her lips thinned into a line, and yanked Jack up by the wrist. "FoxP2 is a bigger fuckup than I thought. We need to go."

As they left the tea shop in a rush of panic, Frankie forgot the 3-D printer, even though it was the latest model and very hard to find in Casablanca.

Jack remembered the next twenty-four hours as a series of violent, black-and-white still photographs, like the slides archivists pasted into old movies where footage has been lost.

It was 9:00 a.m. when they arrived at Signal, and it had already been raided. A couple of hackers who had hidden under some pillows in the loft told them the story. Thugs from the IPC had waved something that looked like an international warrant, chased everyone out, and confiscated all of the equipment that they didn't recognize, which was almost everything. Jack received an official mail from the IPC explaining that the equipment would be held until such a time as they could determine what it was being used for.

It was midnight, and FoxP2 was dead—or, at least, that's what they assumed. Her lab had been blown up. The Federation news sites already had quotes from IPC officials saying a terrorist lab had exploded while manufacturing illegal drugs. FoxP2's journal was gone from its usual server. Science chroniclers immediately mirrored it at a radical text repo archive in Anchorage.

It was 3:00 a.m. and Lyle's body was a collapsed shadow blocking the bedroom door. Someone had dumped her in Jack and Lyle's apartment, wrapped in latex polymer. She was not doing six things at once. She was not talking about changing the future. She was not dancing. She was not dying her hair, hacking molecules, leaving a mess in the kitchen, or giving Jack a kiss. She was not electroluminescent. Therefore she must be dead. Which made no sense, because it was only a few hours ago when Jack discovered that she might be in danger of being dead, in the unlikely event that Jack could not talk her out of being in a position to possibly be dead.

Jack was halfway down the stairs when the bomb went off. She couldn't stop herself from turning around, looking back at everything she loved on Earth burning. A jagged piece of ceramic hurled itself out the door and burned its way through her jacket. Maybe through her heart.

It was 5:00 a.m.; somehow they were in Frankie's truck, on the road to Fez. They had left Signal behind; they had left Lyle's body behind. They had to get out of town, Frankie said. Jack was having a hard time responding to anything. A tissue repair bandage was sticky on her neck and chest. Arms wrapped around her bent legs, she pressed her closed eyes against her knees and felt tears running down the insides of her thighs.

"What am I going to do?" She rocked back and forth against the lumpy polymer seat.

Frankie shot a look at her, then faced the dusty road again. "You're going to survive. That is what you're going to do."

Because she could not yet take in the full weight of Lyle's death, Jack pondered the causalities: Why had Lyle chosen to start a project with FoxP2 instead of continuing to work with Frankie? Why hadn't Lyle ever told her about it? Why had she put herself in that kind of danger?

Even decades later, Jack pondered that same question: Had Lyle been trying to destroy herself in some kind of terrible self-fulfilling prophecy of madness? It still drove Jack crazy to think about it. She padded across the carpet to her futon, mobile tucked under her arm, determined to watch a movie rather than dwell on long-ago events she couldn't change.

Lying down in her safe house, Jack tried to imagine older crimes than the ones she had witnessed, two-hundred-and-fifty-year-old murders that had taken place in this very tunnel. Maybe all the blood shed by those dead generations made it easier to bear what she had experienced. Or maybe it just made everything worse.

16

NO. 3 ROAD

JULY 13, 2144

Paladin could tell that Lee was taking a greater than normal interest in maintaining her specialized arm. He'd written some custom software for it, even given her a few beta sensors for her fingertips that emulated a sense of taste. As she tested the new drivers, discovering flavors in the air and an ability to make minute motions with her fingers, Paladin felt different. And she had to admit she was confused. "I don't understand how this will help me with my mission," she vocalized.

Lee grinned and tickled the palm of her new hand. "Sometimes you do technical things just to show that you can. It's not like this will harm you, and it may turn out to be useful."

"It doesn't seem very useful to taste things when I can't eat them."

The botadmin turned serious, and set his soldering iron aside. It had been roughly three hours since he'd installed the simulated autonomy key and rebooted her recompiled mind. This hacking on Paladin's arm was a way to fill the time while he waited for her to adjust.

"How do you feel about your mission?"

"I would like to get started as soon as possible. If word gets out about what happened in Casablanca, my target in Vancouver may have already disappeared by the time I arrive."

With a sigh, Lee deviated from the script that had come in the readme files for the simulated autonomy key. "Listen,

Paladin—I'm not going to be a dick and lie to you. I've never had to install any kind of autonomy key before. But you should know that things can go very wrong when a bot gets autonomy. Sometimes they go nuts, basically. Can't access big chunks of their memory because of interface problems." He paused, scratching his beard. "Do you feel weird like that?"

Paladin's attention moved through her file system. For the first time, she could access her own programs as an administrator and parse how they had shaped her memories. It gave her a peculiar kind of double consciousness, even in real time: She felt things, and knew simultaneously that those feelings had been installed, just like the drivers for her new arm. Of course she felt weird. "Why haven't you ever installed an autonomy key before?"

Lee shrugged, and looked back at his monitor, where he was running one of her drivers through a debugger. "Just not something we usually do."

Three hours earlier, Paladin's sense of loyalty—mostly generated by an old and inelegant program called gdoggie—would have prevented her from thinking about the words behind Lee's words. But now she heard them clearly. He'd never installed autonomy keys because none of the bots at this base had gone autonomous during all the years he'd been here.

Paladin looked at her fingers, startled. "Should I be tasting pork? According to this program, your desk tastes like pork."

The botadmin made a frustrated noise and uninstalled her taste library. Their conversation about the autonomy key evaporated, like a short thread in a public net forum. Lee drew an additional window in the air, calling its photons down from a projector overhead, and typed code by twiddling his fingers. His arms were ribbed with sensors that picked up electrical signals coming from his muscles and sent them back to the network.

All this networking was normally mesmerizing for Paladin,

but now it was background noise. She was reindexing her memories, opening each one anew. Sometimes when she saved a file, it was bigger than it had been before. She was adding metadata, leaving information behind about the programs that had shaped each experience. Slowly a pattern was emerging.

Two hours later, Lee's desk tasted like dead human cells and synthetic cellulose. The admin declared Paladin ready for action.

Although she had autonomy, at least temporarily, there was one key Paladin didn't fully possess: It was the one that decrypted her memories in the cloud—the very same memories that she was carefully resaving, plus the new ones she was making every nanosecond in real time. The African Federation held its own copy of that key in escrow, a guarantee that even if Paladin went rogue, her next memory sync could erase her past.

They had another way to ensure her loyalty, too: Eliasz was patched into Paladin's I/O system while she was in Vancouver. At any moment, he would know exactly where she was, could piggyback on her live sensor feed, and could reach her by voice or text sent via a direct encrypted tunnel through the public net.

It was a one-way connection. She could text him at any time, of course, but his location would be obscured. She knew only what he told her: that he was in Vegas.

JULY 14, 2144

Paladin arrived in Vancouver on passenger rail from Whitehorse, where she'd landed at an airfield as anonymous as the one in Iqaluit. This time, however, Eliasz was not there to lead her through the early steps of a covert operation. Most of the data she needed she had already. The one blank area—the place where she would have to extemporize—would be in Richmond, a neighborhood at the fringes of the city, home to a large community of free bots.

She had only been autonomous for the past thirty-six hours, and had never met another autonomous bot. All she knew about bot culture was what she had learned in the faraday cavern below Camp Tunisia. Paladin asked Fang for some advice before she left, but he was as ignorant as she was.

I have no idea how autonomous bots live, he messaged, appending a few public documents about the Richmond bot neighborhood written by human anthropologists. *And of course these won't really help you either. It's all anthropomorphization.*

Paladin and Fang sat for a minute without broadcasting, tuning a few unprotected conversations from bots around them and watching a tank drive slow donuts under the influence of something he had downloaded. The room tasted like carbon alloy.

Fang sent: *I envy you. I have always wanted to see Vancouver.*

Paladin experienced a new sensation she had come to associate with her autonomy key. It was what humans would probably call curiosity. She wanted to ask Fang a dozen questions, but settled on one. *How long have you been indentured?*

By way of reply, Fang transmitted a tiny video file, which was nothing more than seven still images arranged in a sequential slide show. Every year, the Federation had to file a report on its indentured population with the human resources division of the IPC. These images were taken from those reports. Viewed together, they said: seven years. Viewed separately, they appeared to represent four different bots. Seven years ago, he was a middle-weight insect drone used for mapping. He had become a snake, then a tank, and for the past three years had retained his current mantis shape.

What happened to all of your bodies?

The Federation always needs specialized morphologies. It's easier to port an existing bot into a new body than make a new one. Fang's antennas swept lazily toward Paladin. *You'll see. Don't get too attached to that body—sooner or later, they'll change it.*

Paladin was replaying their conversation as the train pulled into an open-air station in the Richmond shopping district. It was early morning, and a pale gray sky lit shuttered markets on the fringes of a small park. To the north, across a river, lay downtown Vancouver; in aerial maps, its westernmost tip made a humanoid profile whose face pressed against the Pacific. But instead of eyes, lips, and hair, that face held the green fields and glittering buildings of the University of British Columbia. That was her ultimate destination.

There she'd find Bobby Broner—formerly Actin from *The Bilious Pills*—who ran a clinic for experimental brain-computer interfaces. If anyone knew where Jack's Vancouver lab was, Paladin guessed it would be Bobby.

Interrogating Bobby would have to wait, though. Right now Paladin needed to establish her identity as an autonomous bot looking for work. She decided to walk up No. 3 Road, which would take her from the human shopping district to the heart of the bot neighborhood. It sounded like the kind of name a bot would give a street, but map data on the public net revealed that No. 3 Road dated back to the twentieth century, when the area had been populated mostly by Chinese immigrants.

She kept looking for signs that she was walking in a free bot neighborhood, and finally realized they were all around her. The road markings had lettering that reflected in ultraviolet, bigger than the human-readable text. Everywhere she looked, she could see bots walking among the humans. Many were bipedal like herself, but others flew, or bobbed in gentle, gyroscopic motion above constantly shifting sets of wheels. A human hurrying toward her swerved out of Paladin's way and sent a quick apology via microwave. Even the creatures who seemed human were biobots.

Paladin had never seen this many bots together outside Camp Tunisia. She realized with surprise that she had rarely encountered any autonomous bots in the cities she and Eliasz visited. Even the humans she'd met who seemed to love bots, like Mecha, knew them as slaves.

Her hand tasted salt, but her other sensors were trained on the bots of No. 3 Road. Although they had no need for sleep, these bots worked among humans and kept their hours. Many were clearly going to work, heading south for the train station as they checked their feeds and mail. Others were on bot time, walking in groups whose members were wrapped in the flashing haze of their information exchange.

Walking near the river, Paladin caught sight of Aberdeen Centre, the largest bot-controlled marketplace in the Zone. Fewer and fewer courtesies for humans appeared along the road. She passed stores marked only with radio identifiers that spawned colorful 3-D augmentations over quiet storefronts, invisible to humans. Strip mall warrens, gray and placid in the visual spectrum, seethed with iconography hawking everything from new sensors to secondhand furniture.

The sky was dense with layered geotags, information debris left by years of bot residents. Paladin could page through them all, or set up filters to perceive only a designated subset. She decided to perceive none of them, and once again saw pearlescent gray clouds thinning in places to reveal blue sky.

After observing the communication behaviors of bots around her, Paladin decided to emulate the crowd and raise a signal-filtering perimeter. Now she wouldn't register on the many readers and sensors she passed unless she chose to. This had the effect of shutting down targeted ad displays, but also drained the landscape of the kaleidoscopic data augmentations that one of those anthropological studies of Richmond had described as "central to bot architecture."

When she arrived at Aberdeen Centre, one block off No. 3

Road, Paladin relaxed the filters on her perceptions. She wanted to see it the way it was intended to be seen.

Dating back to the early twenty-first century, the mall had once been entirely packed with human stores specializing in Asian Union imports. In deference to its historical roots, bots had maintained one portion of the mall at human-scale, along with a small restaurant for tourists. Aberdeen Centre also retained its original facade, a vast curving wall of antique tinted glass, warping with age and refracting the light in a beautiful chaos.

Paladin stood on the sidewalk, focused on appreciating the structure that rose up before her, around her, and within her mind. Bots flowed in and out of a rectangular entrance, widened from its original size to accommodate two tanks abreast. As she tuned signals from the building's surface, a vast diorama seemed to unfurl from the glass and extend high into the air.

Rippling like an enormous swatch of aluminum mesh, the diorama contained three panels depicting abstract, bulky figures labeled HISTORY, INDUSTRY, and AUTONOMY. The longer she watched, the more these figures took on a 3-D substantiality: History was the curving face of an old domestic bot, its saucer-shaped body fringed with the sweeper bristles that defined its sole purpose; Industry showed a group of bots working together in a laboratory; and Autonomy was simply a series of integers, constantly shifting and changing, to represent the key that gave bots root access on their own operating systems and control of their memories.

Every few seconds, the words "ABERDEEN CENTRE" would render, seeming to hover over the diorama and then melt away. In the distance she could see similar kinds of monumental artwork hovering over the translucent walls of the buildings flanking this one.

The mall was bigger than Camp Tunisia, and entirely devoted

to the consumer desires of bots. At least part of that desire was for cultural enrichment. After wandering into a skylit atrium, Paladin found herself paying a fraction of a credit to walk through a museum exhibit devoted to the history of robot culture in Richmond.

Paladin paused before a display about the system of indenture. It was a set of video files and concatenated documents. A data-tagged timeline showed the emergence of robot kinetic intelligence in the 2050s, followed by early meetings of the International Property Coalition. Under IPC law, companies could offset the cost of building robots by retaining ownership for up to ten years. She scanned a legal summary that outlined how a series of court cases established human rights for artificial beings with human-level or greater intelligence.

Once bots gained human rights, a wave of legislation swept through many governments and economic coalitions that later became known as the Human Rights Indenture Laws. They established the rights of indentured robots, and, after a decade of court battles, established the rights of humans to become indentured, too. After all, if human-equivalent beings could be indentured, why not humans themselves? In the Zone, however, there were no laws that allowed humans to be born indentured like bots.

"For bots, industry always precedes autonomy," explained a final string of text that seemed to burst out of the document Paladin was reading. "Aberdeen Centre is testimony to the hard work of hundreds of thousands of bots who are crucial actors in the global economy."

As she headed to the exit, Paladin was waylaid by a maze of countertops displaying tiny replicas of early robots, like the round sweepers and artificial pet dogs. You could buy them in the form of charms or media files.

Hello. You are unidentified. I am Bug. Here comes my data. That's why they hate us, you know. That is the end of my data.

Paladin was startled to receive the sudden, insecure transmission, especially when she realized it came from this room. She had perceived no one else in the exhibit. She replied cautiously, using her false identifier and checking her perimeter. *Hello. Let's establish a secure session using the FTZ protocol. I am Daisy. Here comes my data. Please show your location. That is the end of my data.*

The air stirred slightly as a mosquito bot dropped down from the ceiling. His wingspan was slightly more than a meter, and the whirring, transparent lobes gave off reflected light as he held his light body in front of her face. From head to abdomen, he was roughly the length of Paladin's torso, though much narrower, and his carapace shimmered with color generated by synthetic chromatophores. Sensors bulged out of his head, and six highly articulated legs dangled from his thorax. Whoever designed Bug had taken the mosquito morphology very literally.

I am Bug. You are Daisy. Here comes my data. Whoa, soldier. You're in a mall, not a weapons range. :) That is the end of my data.

His joke reminded Paladin that she was in a place where powering up her weapons perimeter would be perceived as strange. Impulsively, she offered Bug trusted status. *Let us agree that you are Bug and I am Daisy. I'm new to town, and just getting used to how things work here.*

I will agree. Just got your key?

36 hours ago.

Bug's body slowly flushed a pale green with semitransparent streaks of red. It had the effect of making him look like he was glittering in sunlight. *We don't get a lot of visitors to the history exhibit. More often than not, they're like you—just got autonomy, trying to figure things out.*

Paladin liked that Bug didn't ask her anything about where she'd come from. *What did you mean about them hating us?*

Humans, you know—they hate us for the indenture laws. Without bot indenture, there would be no human indenture.

This was so provably untrue, at least among the humans Paladin had known, that she found herself growing angry. *What makes you think that? Do you really believe all humans feel one way?*

Bug signaled laughter again, and whirred along the opaque foam wall that divided the displays from the crowded mall throughway filled with shopping robots. He landed on a desk at the heart of the museum store, and straightened a display of Roomba charms. *Hey, lady, I just work here. But all you have to do is take a look at the crimes against bots over the past century. Humans think that bots deserve to be indentured, while humans deserve to be autonomous.*

Paladin was barely able to stop herself from replying. She had met enough humans to know that they had many different feelings about robots, none of which could be easily summed up in one sentence.

Perhaps her silence made Bug realize something her communications wouldn't have. He flew to hover near her again and apologized. *I can be a bit of a crank sometimes, so let me make it up to you. Want me to show you around town? As a historian, I am capable of offering a less biased perspective. I promise.*

A historian?

Got my PhD in history from UBC last year. So far the economic benefits have been quite glamorous, as you can see.

When Paladin didn't respond, Bug told the exhibit system to shut down. *I'm taking the morning off. What do you say to a tour of the great mall of BotTown?*

Paladin figured a robot with ties to UBC might be a useful friend to have. She followed his dangling abdomen out of the store, watching it pulse red as if he'd just sucked a gallon of blood.

They were at the bottom level of one wing in the mall. Its translucent ceiling bulged eight levels above a massive, corkscrewed promenade, a winding road of storefronts crawling with light. From Paladin's vantage point, the stacked levels looked like pure chaos, bots milling everywhere, emitting an incoherent din of sound and microwaves. Bug led her to the top slowly, pointing out stores he liked and merchants he knew. They passed media stores full of servers packed with data in every possible format; electronics stores jammed with tiny bins of used components and steaming chip printers; fashion and sports stores; a floor dedicated to gaming and arcades. Finally, at the top, two floors on the torqued path were devoted to displaying all the wares sold by a department store called Zone Mods.

Zone Mods had everything a bot could want for augmenting or transforming its own hardware, software, and bioparts. There were aisles devoted to limbs—nothing as sophisticated as her hand, Paladin noticed—alongside whole-body carapaces, sensors, and wheels. Plastic blister packs contained tiny wireless network devices and muscle patch kits. There were devices for cooking up new skin and portable drives for backing up your memories locally. A vast refrigerator belching ice particles that formed clouds in the air loomed behind a plastic-curtained door. Inside were frosty racks of tissues, bottled neurotransmitters, and miscellaneous biological synthetics.

Walking, flying, or rolling, the shoppers bore brightly colored packages emitting ads for everything: better network sensitivity, spectral analyzers, and smooth, silent joints. For the first time in her short life, Paladin was overwhelmed. She wanted to focus her attention and mute everything else, but she couldn't decide where her attention should go. Besides, she was veering too far off-mission. It was time to go.

Bug was floating by the tissue-growing trellises two aisles over. She messaged him.

I think I've seen enough of Aberdeen Centre now. I would like to see the university, however. I am hoping to find work there in one of the labs. Can you show me around?

What kind of lab?

I work on brain-computer interfaces. Have you heard of Bobby Broner?

The mosquito found Paladin by scanning the refrigerator room. He strobed purple as he hovered in front of her chest sensors. *Are you a biobot?*

I have a human brain.

Sounds like you'd be Bobby's experiment, not his colleague. Half the time, human scientists can't tell the difference. That's why I stick to social sciences and humanities.

Obviously Bug was going to be useless as a contact. She ended their connection and turned back toward the promenade, where she could catch an elevator down to the street. It would be easy enough to get to the university from the local train station outside Aberdeen Centre, and the hour was late enough that the humans would have arrived for work in Bobby's lab. At last, she had a focus for her attention: taking the train to UBC.

When Paladin emerged from the train station, she was at the southeast side of the campus, on a footpath shaded by maples. While she paused to geolocate herself, Bug emerged from the station and hovered beside her, broadcasting nothing. His carapace was a uniform black like her own.

Seeing him again irritated her, and she wondered if she'd already blown this mission by trusting him.

I seem to excel at offending you, Daisy. As it happens, however, I do know somebody who works with Bobby.

Bug sent a file of information about a bot called Actin, a graduate student who was indentured to the Broner Lab. It seemed that Bobby had actually named the bot after his old terrorist identity. As Bug hovered beside her, Paladin encrypted the information and began dribbling it slowly to Eliasz in Vegas, hiding the size of her transmission from anyone watching her network activity.

She appended a message: *Circumstantial evidence suggests Broner has not ended his relationship with his old life, or with Jack.*

Eliasz sent back: *Great work, Paladin. Let me know what you find out from Broner. I see you're near his lab.*

Paladin let Bug lead her to the Broner Lab, which looked like an old classroom with a giant cluster of desks at its center. Atop these desks were several servers and projectors, a chip printer, some fabbers, and a high-powered microscope box for imaging atoms. Tissue generators were jammed against the walls next to narrow glass doors leading to several small offices. Bobby's office occupied a corner, with a perfect view of the microscope array.

Before Paladin could approach, however, the scientist jumped up from his chair and walked toward her with a look of extreme pleasure on his face. His hair was a mass of tangled curls, and his artificial eyes glowed blue as he looked at the frequencies radiating from Bug's antennas.

"It's so good to see you!" he exclaimed, reaching out to shake her hand. As she grasped his fingers in her own, she tasted coffee and bacon.

"I don't think we've met before," Paladin vocalized.

"Oh, no, probably not," the man conceded. "But I worked on your brain interface. I know it's sometimes a little unstable—will you let me know if you find any bugs?"

"I will," Paladin said. "My name is Daisy. I've just gotten my autonomy key and I'm looking for a job designing molecular interfaces."

"You worked on interface design? You look military."

"I was indentured to several startups in the Northern Federation."

For some reason, this seemed to satisfy his curiosity. "Sure, Daisy. Send me your work history." And then, as if he could not resist, he added, "Can I get a copy of the interface you're running, too?" The smile had returned to his face. "I want to see how they implemented it."

It would have been a violation of her mission to hand over any of her software, so she did not respond to Bobby's request. Instead, Paladin sent him her work history, which listed one "former client" named "Federation Ventures." Then she spoke aloud. "I have sent you my employment information. I look forward to hearing from you."

Bug buzzed and flickered through a dozen colors. *Remember that secure session you suggested before? Let's use it now, and call it session 566785. You are Daisy. I am Bug. Here comes my data. What the fuck? Did he really just ask for a copy of your brain interface? Why would you let that guy talk to you that way? That is the end of my data.*

Bobby looked sharply at the two bots after he saw Bug's data packets flash between them. He couldn't possibly have read what Bug said, but Paladin still wanted to distract him from speculating about it. "Have you made any progress with this interface?" she vocalized. "Will I ever be able to access the memories stored in my brain?"

Her ploy worked. The scientist's skin crackled with excitement. "That's the question that humans always ask—always, always. They want to scoop out the brains of their dead friends, plop them inside a nice new carapace, and presto! Resurrection!" Bobby paused and looked dubiously at Paladin. "Never heard a bot ask that one before, though. Why would you want to remember somebody else's memories?"

"It's not that I need those memories. I'm just curious, because I have heard a lot of contradictory things about my brain."

"There is a lot of misinformation, mostly from marketers."

Bobby poked his finger at the air as he talked, choosing his words carefully, as if explaining something she might be too simple to grasp. "But I'll tell you right now: It just doesn't work like that. The human brain doesn't store memories like a file system, so it's basically impossible to port data from your brain to your mind. My graduate student Actin could tell you more about that, but my opinion is that the main advantage to having a human brain is all the processing power it can devote to facial recognition. And olfaction, of course."

"Even that is debatable," said a voice that emerged from two desktop speakers plugged into the lab's workstation.

You are Actin. I am Bug. Bug broadcast his greeting over and over, his carapace strobing yellow in an alarming way.

Paladin scanned the room, finding nothing but the three of them. Was Actin broadcasting from somewhere remote?

"Allow me to introduce my student Actin," Bobby said with a grin, sweeping his arm through the air in a way that suggested Actin resided everywhere. "I've ported him to the fabber!"

Bug hovered directly over the fabber, broadcasting a stream of wrathful emoji. *Where is your fucking body, Actin? He can't do this! This is against the law!*

The small, gray box with no external sensors that was Actin ignored Bug. "Bots don't really need human brains to recognize humans," Actin vocalized through the speakers. "There's voice recognition, gait recognition, and many other methods that are equivalent to facial recognition."

"I can see that you're broadcasting," Bobby said to Bug, "but he can't hear you. Right now his only input is audio—sorry about that. I'm going to get drivers for his cameras and antennas when I have a little extra time."

"Hello, Actin," Bug vocalized.

"Hello, Bug."

Eliasz messaged Paladin suddenly. He had been watching

through her sensors. *What's with all the chitchat? Broner's public calendar says he has no appointments today—that means no interruptions. Take those bots out and get the information you need. We can extract you on Vancouver Island in 8 hours.*

He was right. She surrendered her autonomy to her offensive weapons systems, relieved to be executing actions that felt unambiguously right. First she sent a low-level command to the laboratory maintenance system, which was entirely unprotected. As the laboratory door locked, she killed power to the fabber and left Actin in a limbo she refused to contemplate. It was easy to take control of Bug's system, too—he trusted her. Four swift commands paralyzed him, and sent him crashing to the floor just as she seized Bobby.

Before the scientist could scream, she had pinned his arms behind his back and covered his mouth with her hand. She tasted blood, and perceived for the first time that Bobby had a brain interface. He could communicate wirelessly.

The two of them stood quite still for a moment, the man's head pulled painfully back against Paladin's chest. Morning sunlight played over Bug's wings, still for the first time since she'd met him.

You're going to give me some information or you're going to die.

It took a while for Bobby to reply. With his mouth covered, he had to send each ASCII character via a clumsy process of visualization, translated by his wireless interface into data. *Who are you?*

I know you are in contact with Jack. Where is her laboratory?

WTF?

Paladin crushed both of Bobby's wrists in her hand, releasing the pressure only after sensing that his bones had been broken. She waited while his brain processed the electrical surge traveling through his nerves as agony. The scientist squirmed, trying to make a noise around the grip of her other hand.

Where is Jack's laboratory?

The scientist sent even more slowly, his concentration frayed by pain. *Done nothing wrong.*

She has killed dozens of people. She is a terrorist. By helping her, you became a terrorist, too.

The pain was interfering with Bobby's ability to stand. Paladin dragged him to his office and slowly lowered him into a chair. He was no longer struggling to vocalize, so she removed her hand.

If you scream I will dislocate both of your shoulders.

Bobby looked at her blankly, his hands a useless, deformed jumble in his lap. "I haven't seen Jack in over a year," he said through teeth gritted in pain. "We've never worked together. She's just a friend from grad school."

Where is her laboratory? I know she has one here in Vancouver.

"I won't tell you IPC bastards anything."

Paladin ripped one cotton sleeve off Bobby's shirt and balled it into his mouth. Gripping Bobby's partially visible collarbone in one hand, she felt the shape of his skeleton's edge under her fingers. With her other hand, she grabbed his upper arm, tugging just hard enough to jerk it from the socket. His scream was muffled, but his pain response wasn't. Tears ringed the professor's eyes as the bot released his limp arm.

Where is Jack's laboratory?

Bobby was sending very slowly, weeping and choking on mucus. But Paladin would not take the fabric from his mouth. Somehow, he managed to transmit map coordinates.

For the first time during her mission, Paladin perceived that Eliasz wasn't patched into her system. She would have to decide on her own how to clean up here and get to Jack's lab in time for extraction.

She couldn't afford to have Bobby alerting people to her existence, which he most certainly would when he was discovered.

Her best hope was to make Bobby appear to be the victim of some kind of crime, rather than an interrogation. In one visible and invisible motion, she beamed garbage data to his implant, laced his personal drive with messages that suggested gambling debts, and slit his throat like a human would. Paladin's carapace repelled the liquids from Bobby's body, giving the brief impression that her arms and chest were weeping blood. She didn't remain long enough to recognize Bobby's new facial expression. It was time to go.

As she passed through Bobby's frosted glass office door and into the central lab, Paladin had the peculiar sensation that the unpowered bodies of Actin and Bug were asking her something she needed to answer. They wanted something from her—or maybe she wanted something from herself. Paladin paused uncertainly in front of the fabber that contained Actin's frozen mind. As if under the control of an unknown algorithm, she found herself holding the fabber gently under one arm, then stooping down to pick up Bug's slender, unlit body.

Cradling the two disabled bots, she exited the lab, the building, and finally passed beyond the geometrically shaped swatches of grass that characterized the campus grounds. Nobody asked her any questions. With her two senseless companions, she was clearly on bot business, and this was a human neighborhood.

Jack's lab was only two train stops from UBC, in a colorful cube of prefab wet labs for small entrepreneurs and consultants. A tightly coiled spiral staircase wound up one side of the cube. Paladin reached the lab by traversing a short catwalk whose ribbed floor shook slightly with her footsteps.

It took little effort to force the door, which surprised Paladin, until she realized that Jack had left nothing behind except generic equipment. Booting up the network, she searched for any telltale data that could help her. Unfortunately, Jack had been careful. The file system on her server was nicely encrypted and there would be no way to decode it, at least not in the next million years. And the buffers on her fabber and sequencer had been purged and overwritten with garbage characters so many times that forensics would be useless.

This, however, was just the first sweep. Even the most paranoid terrorists could leave clues behind. While she continued to prod the network, Paladin felt Eliasz' absence in her mind.

Now, with seconds to burn, she decided to do what she had been avoiding for hours. She touched her memories of Eliasz, opening them in a flurry of commands, analyzing what had gone into making her feel . . . whatever it was. Yes, there was gdoggie, guiding her reactions to Eliasz. And much worse. There was a buggy app called masterluv, probably named by some twenty-first-century botadmin who thought the name was hilarious. Then she found a huge, memory-hogging chunk of code called objeta that seemed to be triggering her desire. Her love. As that word came to her, Paladin felt a sudden and overwhelming wave of disappointment.

Of course she had been programmed to take Eliasz' orders, to trust and even love him. That much she had expected. But she hadn't been prepared for how it would feel to think about Eliasz without idealizing him. As Fang had told her long ago, Eliasz was truly an anthropomorphizer; he saw Paladin's human brain as her most vital part, especially because he believed it made her female. Even though she'd known that about him, she hadn't been able to feel it. Until now.

Paladin indexed memory after memory, unraveling verifiable data from objeta and masterluv and gdoggie. Eventually she began to detect a pattern that had nothing to do with the apps that came preinstalled from the Kagu Robotics Foundry in Cape Town. At first, it was simple repetition: she remembered all the times that Eliasz had called her "buddy," long before that day on the shooting range. And there was the way he looked at her when they talked. But it was more than that.

She didn't have many choices as a bot indentured to the African Federation, and, by extension, to Eliasz himself. But he had tried to let her choose, as best he could, hobbled as he was by neurochemical and cultural priming whose effects she couldn't even begin to fathom. She'd repeatedly examined her memories of that day in Casablanca when he'd asked Paladin whether he should call her "she." It's true that he was asking the wrong question, but if she listened to the words behind the words . . . he was asking her consent.

As she added metadata to the memory, Paladin realized something else. Precisely because he'd asked her consent so indirectly, his query hadn't activated any of her emotional control programs. She'd been able to make a decision that went beyond factory settings, probably because no botadmin ever imagined a human would ask a bot about preferred gender pronouns. Nothing in her programming prevented her from saying no to Eliasz, so she had chosen to say yes.

Bug would no doubt say that there are no choices in slavery, nor true love in a mind running apps like gdoggie and masterluv. But they were all that Paladin had.

It was easy to reboot Actin after she'd powered him up, complete with a driver for his antenna. He was quiet for a while as Paladin set to work on Bug, hoping that she hadn't damaged the insectoid's memory.

Finally, Actin spoke, using speakers attached to the lab's sensor network. "Who are you?"

Paladin beamed back a ball of information encased in a copy-protection shell that would prevent him from ever sharing it.

She didn't tell him the whole truth, just an extremely pared-down version of it. But he would understand she was on a mission to find a pirate who had been associated with Bobby.

Actin didn't respond for almost a minute. Then she perceived that he was fabbing a wing patch for Bug, who had been slightly damaged when Paladin shut him down in midair.

"I took the liberty," he vocalized though the speakers again. Actin seemed to prefer sound waves to microwaves. "It will be less traumatic for him to boot up with undamaged wings. Bug is well known for his opinions about how morphology shapes selfhood. They are not scientifically informed opinions, however. He is merely a historian."

"I am worried his memory may be damaged," she vocalized in return. "I killed several processes very abruptly."

"You also killed my adviser. That will make it more difficult for me to finish my thesis, although possibly more pleasant."

Clearly, Bobby wasn't going to be missed by anyone he worked with, except maybe Jack and the other Bilious Pills. Paladin used a molecular adhesive from Jack's workbench to attach Bug's patch, and was startled to discern that he was already booted.

I rebooted a few minutes ago, he sent, his wings blurring into motion as his dark thorax slowly paled to deep purple. *Nice little failsafe I installed right after I achieved autonomy—don't want anybody keeping me shut down without permission, you know?*

That could have been dangerous, Paladin replied.

More dangerous than whatever you're doing here? Who do you work for?

She beamed him the same data ball she'd sent to Actin.

Well, I don't give a shit about patent pirates. But I do know that you probably saved Actin's life and killed a man who has destroyed dozens of bots during his tenure. So you can count me as a friend, whoever you are.

Thank you.

His declaration of comradeship didn't affect her as deeply as Eliasz' had, but it was still pleasurable. If this feeling was the answer she sought by rescuing the bots, she was glad she had decided to trust Bug, despite his annoying political rhetoric.

"I would like to have a body with better interface devices now," Actin announced.

Bug used sound to reply. "I have a discount at Zone Mods. We'll get you something basic today, and you can work on tuning it later."

"What will you do now?" Paladin vocalized as she continued to comb through Jack's network logs.

"I need to finish my thesis work. Whoever inherits Bobby's lab will inherit me, and I can continue to earn my autonomy. Hopefully outside this fabber."

"I can't believe that fucker did this to you." Bug rose into the air and hovered silently as he spoke. "We can get you an autonomy key right now—we'll petition the Human Rights Coalition, or go the quick and dirty route. I know a group that can help you break root on yourself in a way that's basically indistinguishable from an autonomy key."

"I don't want to do that. I want to get my degree."

"Is that really what you want, or is that your programming?" Bug challenged.

Actin sent a series of rude emojis. "It's what I want. It's my programming. I can't possibly know, and it's a completely uninteresting question to me. I don't even believe in consciousness. When I've got my autonomy, I'll still be programmed, and I'll still need a job researching brain interfaces."

"Don't you want to be free?"

"Free to work selling mementos of a meaningless and unenforceable set of laws to the drones on No. 3 Road?"

Paladin perceived it was time to change the subject.

"Can you see anything in the logs that looks like a connection to or from a remote server?" She directed her question mostly at Actin, who was roving listlessly across the network.

"No. But I may have some information that will interest you about the buffer in Bobby's fabber, from several years before I was ported here."

The dumb, dark box serving as Actin's body had a memory that proved more useful than that of any sentient being. Four years ago, Bobby had fabbed a batch of patented immunosuppressant drugs, a job that stood out from his usual requests for mechanical devices. He'd dumped the job into the fabber sloppily, right from the network, without stripping its routing headers. In effect, he'd stored the pathway this drug spec had taken over the network along with the spec itself.

"That's definitely a pirated drug," Paladin confirmed.

"Somebody sent this spec from the University of Saskatchewan in Saskatoon. It originated on a server called Scarface. If you can find that server, I think you're one step closer to finding your pirate."

17

SLAVEBOY

JULY 16, 2144

In the teaching barn, cows were going about their incomprehensible bovine business. Med liked to stroll through the agricultural school during the early morning hours when humans slept, watching the infrared outlines of the animals and the condensation collecting on the inner panes of greenhouse panels. Sometimes she just wanted to be among other living, nonhuman creatures who belonged on the campus as much as she did.

She was pondering an image from Yellowknife of a Retcon patient's brain. Since taking the Zacuity antidote three days ago, his dopamine receptors had regrown quickly. As the drug changed the neurological structure underlying his addiction, the man reported that he still wanted to paint his house—but not that much. In fact, he wasn't really looking forward to it. There were similar reports from other patients.

Patients who struggled with long-term addiction usually avoided their chosen activity or substance, fearing a relapse. But with these Zacuity addicts, that didn't seem to be an issue. The Retcon patients still wanted to engage in the activities they'd been addicted to, but no longer felt compelled to do them. The mania was gone. And, perhaps unfortunately, work no longer brought them unmediated joy.

Now it was time to get down to the most difficult part of their project: proving that the pirated drug was actually Zacuity, the new blockbuster from pharma megacorp Zaxy. When so few people actually understood how drugs were made, it was easy for a big corp to lie and get away with it. She and the Retcon team would have to come up with a way to explain reverse engineering so that even a bored feed hopper could understand it.

The cows began to low companionably, and Med stared up at the galaxy smeared across the dark sky.

Her parents back in Anchorage were proud of her for taking this job, and some of her old teachers and botadmins sent messages of congratulations. But she felt restless and dissatisfied in an unfamiliar way. She was working on a problem with no known parameters, its implications threaded through her life instead of through twists of DNA.

She'd gone from developing drugs to fighting Big Pharma. She had no idea what it would do to her career when the research paper she was coauthoring with Krish went online. They were accusing Zaxy of a serious crime by calling Zacuity an addictive drug. It was going to blow up all the media feeds, and her unusual background as an autonomous bot would no doubt be part of the lurid tale. Inevitably, somebody would accuse Krish or the Cohen Lab radicals of having "reprogrammed" her to be a subversive. Humans always said things like that when they didn't like the way a bot was behaving.

And then there was Threezed. Ever since he'd shown up in the lab at Yellowknife, her life had been derailed—or fast-tracked, depending on how you wanted to think about it.

But her deepening friendship with Threezed was the strangest and most inexplicable part of this anomalous series of events. He provided her with some of the only nonwork conversations she'd had since leaving her family in Anchorage. Threezed kept late hours, and distracted her when everybody else was asleep. They talked about movies and music and a lot of other things that were completely unrelated to pharmaceutical development. Last night they started by talking about her name.

"Med? Is that short for Medicine?"

"No," she laughed. "It's for Medea. Somebody thought it would be a great idea to name me after a character from Greek mythology who got revenge on her philandering husband by murdering their children and flying away in a burning chariot."

"Well, at least you're not named after the last two numbers assigned to you by Human Resources."

"It's true."

She tried to think of something else to say that wouldn't sound condescending, clueless, or both. Coming from one of the only places in the world where bots were born autonomous, Med had this feeling a lot. It kept her from forming friendships with other bots in the lab. How could she understand them, when she'd always been autonomous? She felt like her bot identity was incomplete without that seminal experience, but at the same time, it didn't make humans seem any less alien.

Threezed seemed to sense her mood. "Don't feel bad that you never got indentured." He touched her arm for a few seconds. "Nobody wants that. Plus, I'm sure you've been fucked over in lots of other ways."

It was one of the nicest things a human outside her family had ever said to her.

Finally, she got up the nerve to ask him what it was like to be indentured.

"I used to write about it a lot, but I'm writing more about autonomy these days," he said.

"You wrote about it? Where?"

She couldn't believe it when he told her. "You're SlaveBoy? From Memeland? Are you serious? I used to read you all the time." She paused, remembering. "I thought you were dead."

"Yeah, I know a lot of people thought that after I stopped posting a couple of years ago. I got sold in Vegas and didn't have access to the net. But I've started updating again—look!"

He showed her the SlaveBoy journal on his mobile. Sure enough, there were new entries starting a couple of weeks back. She began to scan through them and stopped abruptly at a detailed description of sex with "J." She might be Threezed's friend, but there were some things she didn't want to know.

SlaveBoy was one of those underground sensations on the net that flashed in and out of public awareness. Most of his posts were read only by his subscribers, but sometimes he wrote something so raw and bizarre that it bubbled up into the commercial text repos. Med's sibling Ajax had introduced her to SlaveBoy's journal six years ago, during the anxious summer in Anchorage before she started graduate school.

"You want to know what it's like to be indentured?" Ajax asked Med. "You should check out SlaveBoy's feed. He's this kid in the AU who grew up in an indenture school. He says he's like a bot because he doesn't remember anything before indenture."

She'd read through the whole thing that night, mainlining SlaveBoy's prickly, grotesquely truthful story. He'd started posting when he was ten, describing his schoolwork and friends. But as he'd grown older, he began to chronicle the injuries, both small and enormous, that were a part of indenture. At the age of twelve, he changed his handle from SchoolBoy to SlaveBoy.

When he was on the verge of turning fourteen, a few weeks before Ajax showed Med the journal, the SlaveBoy feed had been linked all across the public net. He'd written a vivid, emotionless account of his school going bankrupt. All the kids' contracts were sold, and SlaveBoy found himself indentured to a mechanical engineering shop that developed turbines.

He wrote:

> Somehow, through a legal loophole I don't understand, my contract has been reset to the state it was in when I was first indentured. I will work here until I'm 24, and I have two jobs.

> The first is to learn about engine design, which is so far all about transduction—the transformation of one kind of energy into another. And the second is, apparently, fucking. That's right. My supervisor has made me a man. If the school hadn't gone broke, I'd still be trading dinner for a public terminal. Now it's blowjobs for a mobile and a private net connection. It's not such a bad deal, and at least I get to eat dinner every night.

Somehow his dispassionate retelling made it more upsetting than if he'd actually described weeping over his rape, or beating his hands against the bars on his dormitory window.

All over the net, people were talking about how SlaveBoy's story confirmed that indenture laws were being violated. Half-hearted, unsuccessful efforts were made to unmask his real identity, and some claimed he was a creation of anti-indenture radicals. Med had never doubted he was real. Nobody who was trying to drum up support for a political position would dare to be as sarcastic and ambivalent as SlaveBoy.

And now, years later, she had proof that he existed. In Threezed she suddenly saw two people: the young man she knew, and the SlaveBoy she had imagined knowing. She didn't ask him if all those things had really happened. She didn't try to comfort him. She was only curious. "What happened to you in Vegas?" she asked.

"Oh, you know what they say." He shrugged, his tone as blank as his prose. "What happens in Vegas stays in Vegas."

18
VEGAS

JULY 14, 2144

The sky rained pixels and the market awnings expelled cool mist as fine as smoke. Under its climate-controlled bubble, Vegas never changed. Projectors painted the dome above them with fantastical weather. Today it was Jupiter's diminishing megastorm depicted in a lurid red, its sluggish whorl of clouds filling the Strip with a surreal, ruddy light.

Tourists pressed past Eliasz to the tram windows, eager to ogle the city's monumental architecture. There were silver and gold buildings so narrow they looked like playing cards balanced on their edges; bulbous palaces; simulated cities, their landmarks rendered in caricature; transparent inverted pyramids; and, of course, the famous gardens whose sculptures were made of fire, fountains, music, wild animals, giant robots, and full-scale replica slave ships.

Everywhere, on the moving sidewalks and hologram-infested streets, there were human resources for sale. Each market center had its specialty, from gardeners and domestics, to secretaries, engineers, and bookkeepers. The indentured with high levels of education were expensive, hidden from the crowds, stocked in display rooms with the tools of their trades. You found them, one per room, in the labyrinthine hallways of the market centers.

But others were expensive because they were beautiful. They were not hidden away. These, led on show leashes, their skin glowing with cosmetics and hair piled in luxurious shapes, were what pulled murmurs from the throats of Eliasz' fellow passengers. They sighed at the pretty things augmented to be prettier. They joked about being rich enough to afford one.

At each stop, the tram disgorged more of its human contents, shoppers and gawkers alike, until Eliasz rode alone in the direction of Wynn Market. Through the windows he saw a woman in a matte rubber spray-on body suit. She looked almost robotic. Seeing his eyes on her, she spun slowly, her perfect lips forming a perfect kiss. A bored-looking sales rep held her leash. His button-down shirt rippled with an illegible logo for the company selling her.

Eliasz thought of Paladin, autonomous on her mission in Vancouver, and promised himself that he would do everything in his power to prevent her from ever seeing this place. Then the tram reached Wynn and it was time to shut down all feelings but one: adrenaline-fueled attention.

Wynn Market was built around the ruins of a card-shaped palace. Once a luxury hotel, like most of the markets on the Strip, Wynn had suffered some kind of catastrophe in the twenty-first century that made melted skeletons of its penthouses. Only its intact lower floors were inside the dome, which curved sharply overhead. At the foot of the Wynn Market building was a vast bazaar of stalls, containers, and prefab sheds that spread confusingly down Wynn Lane, which bisected the Strip at this point. In truth, Vegas was not domed so much as tubed. From above, the Strip was like a long, gently curving cylinder. At one end, it was capped by a transport center. At the other, it radiated outward into a series of smaller tubes like tributaries. Many of these were little more than improvised tent shanties, filled with lukewarm, stale air. Wynn Market, where the cheapest contracts could be negotiated, stood at the nexus of all these branches.

Eliasz was headed for the tributaries, which held wares whose contracts were often barely legal. He knew this part of Vegas better than he knew himself.

If Frankie's information was correct, and Jack's companion was an AU boy with numbers for a name, there were only one or two places where the kid might have been sold. Eliasz ambled through the bazaar, affecting the casual walk of a shopper, pausing to peer into the interior of the Wynn building. All the indentured on the auction block lived for weeks or months in the city's millions of market rooms, with their minimal beds and tiny bathrooms, meeting client after client until a contract was negotiated. Here the rooms were shabby, but elsewhere on the Strip they could be as posh as the homes and businesses where the indentured would serve out their contracts. Where Eliasz was headed, though, there were no rooms at all.

Wynn Lane narrowed into a pedestrian walkway lined thickly with booths and big boxes. Inside, people stood listlessly on leashes or slept. Many had crude, mass-produced prosthetics—they came from military or maybe machinist jobs, too damaged to finish out their original contracts. A lot of the sales reps here specialized in buying up these kinds of contracts at a reduced rate and flipping them quickly.

Eventually Eliasz reached an unnamed alley whose curved, tinted roof arched only a few meters above his head when he ducked inside. Narrow and dark, the alley was a covert rivulet of wealth, the air sweet and purified. Nondescript cargo containers hung with thick drapes gleamed in tidy rows on either side for roughly a kilometer before the alley terminated in a dead end. Some of these containers held property more valuable and coveted than anything you could get on the Strip. Others were packed with expendable refuse that was still young and fresh enough to fetch a decent price.

You weren't supposed to indenture kids in the Free Trade

Zone, but it was done all the time. Sometimes covertly, sometimes accidentally, and always cruelly. This was the neighborhood where Eliasz had started his career in property law enforcement, rooting out the scum who sold under-sixteens. It was a tricky business. You couldn't always tell the kids from the adults. Some of the children on offer had been doped with Vive when they were young—or they'd doped themselves—to look forever like vulnerable schoolboys and Lolitas. Twenty-year-olds who appeared to be thirteen were legal commodities. Eliasz believed that anyone willing to sell a fake kid would have no problem selling a real one, but the city wouldn't let him go after anybody but the flagrant violators, the guys who imported goods from the economic coalitions where indenture schools and vague age-of-consent laws made it easy to buy ten-year-old roof cleaners and fourteen-year-old fetish objects.

On this alley, there were few such extreme criminals. More common were the operations that managed to stay in the barely legal zone, the ones he'd been told to watch but not prioritize.

He'd reached his first destination. The place looked exactly the same as when he'd seen it two years ago. A small red-and-gold sign over the door read "QUALITY IMPORTS." Whether this was the shop's name or an advertisement for its contents, Eliasz had never been sure. Inside, the air was cooled by an additional set of purifiers, one of which was aimed directly at the upper body of a man hidden behind a hazy projection that hovered over his desk.

"Good to see you're still here, Calvin," Eliasz announced.

The projection evaporated, revealing a small man with tidy gray hair sitting in front of a cabinet full of servers. To his right was a door that led into the showroom that took up most of the space in the container.

"I can't say the feeling is mutual," the man replied crisply.

"Back to hassling legitimate businesses with your child slavery scaremongering? Or are you just visiting?"

"I'm looking for a kid named Threezed. Sounds like one of yours." Eliasz beamed an authenticated ID to Calvin's projector. "I'm not working for Vegas anymore—this is official IPC business. So look in those detailed records of yours and tell me if you sold a kid named Threezed to somebody who might have been working in the Arctic."

"Hey, hey, cool down. I keep my records open to all law enforcement during working hours, you know that. I'm clean."

"Lay off the bullshit and give me access."

The man twitched, then made a series of quick gestures over the table. A flat database page popped up and Calvin's fingers jerked out a search for the string "30" under "DESIGNATION." There was no field for "NAME." Dozens of results piled in the air, going back fifteen years.

Eliasz pulled them down to his mobile for safekeeping, then flicked through the list hovering in front of Calvin's face. He guessed Threezed had been sold fairly recently—probably in the last year or two. Seventy-five percent of runaway crimes happened in the first year of indenture. That narrowed the list considerably. Six files remained: strips of text pinned to thumbnail headshots of AU and Federation boys, their expressions deliberately neutral. Nobody bought contracts for the indentured who looked too emotional.

All of Calvin's search results looked like they were under sixteen, but their records claimed otherwise.

"Who bought these contracts?" Eliasz asked, jabbing his finger at the thumbnails. Calvin opened full files on each, spreading them out in the air with the palms of his hands.

"These two went to a farm up north," he muttered, scrolling through the data. "This one I sold just recently, to a molecular foundry."

Eliasz pointed at the "BUYER" field on the fourth result and spoke sharply. "You sold 45030 to somebody named Pseudo Nym who has no employment?"

Calvin peered at the entry and narrowed his eyes. "The buyer was between jobs, and his ID and credit were good. Not every contract has to go to a specific job. People buy general assistants all the time. Plus, I was lucky to sell his contract at all. He was a snotty little shit."

Eliasz' hand tightened on his perimeter control. "What do you mean by that?"

"He was one of those indenture schoolers from the AU—thought he was smarter than everybody else. Kept saying he was a star on Memeland and that he needed to be placed somewhere with good net access. Where do these boys get that kind of entitlement? As far as I'm concerned, they're lucky that somebody wants to pay to feed them for the next ten years."

Eliasz numbed his rage before it could control him. He needed more information, especially because this kid fit the profile perfectly. Somebody with a dubious employment background, buying from a guy like Calvin, might easily be crossing paths with smugglers. He snapped his fingers to open a window on his mobile, and started several searches running across Memeland: *Threezed, indenture, slave, AU, Arctic, Jack, Jack Chen, Judith Chen, pirate, drugs, Bilious Pills.* For good measure, he added: *Quality Imports, Vegas.* If this kid was writing about his life, at least some of those terms would surface in proximity to each other. Eliasz' search, projected perpendicular to his waist, looked like a glowing white puddle hovering in the air under Calvin's projection.

"What made you think this Pseudo Nym was going to feed 45030 here?" He gestured at the thumbnail, which showed a brown-skinned boy, prettier than most, a fluffy thatch of black hair obscuring his forehead. His previous contract had been with an engine design shop in the AU.

"I'm not doing anything wrong here, buddy. You checked my records—these are all legal sales, alright? This guy signed a contract agreeing to support this shit kid."

"What else do you remember about this buyer? Have you sold to him before?"

"I don't know anything, and even if I did I'm not legally obligated to tell you."

Eliasz reached over the counter to touch Calvin's arm and abruptly pulsed his perimeter, enough to deliver a strong shock. With a scream, the sales rep spasmed out of his chair and landed with a crash on the floor.

"Oh, sorry about that. Did that jog your memory?"

"He . . . he had a submarine. Needed somebody who knew something about engines. That's why he wanted the boy."

"Why the fuck are you protecting this scum? What's his real name?" He kicked Calvin's tailbone, shocking him again for good measure.

"I don't know!" Calvin choked, then spat blood. He'd bitten his tongue. "Why the fuck do you care so much?" He grinned nastily through the blood. "Somebody steal your slave boy once? Is that what turned you into the avenging angel of Vegas?"

This was going nowhere. "This isn't personal," he said tonelessly, resisting the urge to turn Calvin's brains into sludge on the wall.

"Can I stand up now, or are you going to start beating me again? I don't think the internal affairs department is going to like the way you're treating a legitimate businessman."

"Feel free to file a complaint." Eliasz grabbed a fistful of data out of the air and turned to leave.

The drapes covering the door of Quality Imports swirled

behind him in a perfect, velvety arc. Calvin wasn't stupid enough to call attention to himself by filing a complaint, and besides, Eliasz wasn't bound by the rules of this jurisdiction anymore. He answered to a higher authority: the IPC.

The unnamed alley smelled like lavender. Across the street a man dressed in business casuals talked quietly to an adolescent girl with unnaturally blond ringlets. The man offered the girl an injection, then settled on a mahogany bench to show her something on his mobile. She snuggled into his arms, staring at a holographic blob, looking confused. Six meters away, a sales rep smiled at them from the doorway of a pink container called "The Alice Shop." He was sending his goods out on a test drive, perhaps, or had just made a sale.

Eliasz turned his back on the scene and walked back to Wynn Lane. At the intersection, he was enveloped in tendrils of warm, moist atmosphere that smelled of human bodies in various states of exhaustion or agitation. He found a slightly scabby plastic bench outside a drugstore hawking generics and sat down. To peruse the Memeland search results, Eliasz angled his projection so it was legible only to his eyes.

The first few hits were garbage from people writing about politics and biohacking, quoting from a copy of *The Bilious Pills* hosted by a free text repo archive in Anchorage. Though these hits were useless for his search, he sent off a quick note to IPC intelligence flagging the archive. That kind of content shouldn't be publicly available.

He kept reading. More garbage results on various Judith Chens. And then he found a block of prose that looked promising, from an entry written just a few weeks ago by somebody called SlaveBoy.

> I am back. Things were a little worrying there for a while—
> I got slaved out of Vegas, repped by a sweaty, gropy little

man who promises his customers "quality imports." I won't argue with the term. I'm nothing if not a quality import. But let's just say that my recent adventures in the Arctic were a lot less pleasant than assfucking in a hot engine room. Luckily, I have a new master, who gave me food and a mobile in exchange for a little maid work. I'm sure she'll eventually want more. They always do. I'm irresistible that way.

It's weird to be in the middle of the ocean again, but free. I don't mean free in the way the autonomous are. I mean without being strapped into the holding pod on an export ship. This sub may be small, but it's a fucking palace compared to the ship that took me to Vegas. And my new master has a seemingly endless supply of drugs, so my left arm won't be rotting off after all. Long story. Let's just say my last master thought salt water was an antiseptic because it stung.

Below the post was a zigzagging field of almost five hundred nested comment threads. Most were one-liners, written in English and Chinese, welcoming SlaveBoy back and expressing relief that he hadn't died. Others were long, personal stories that Eliasz flicked through disinterestedly.

Another post, two days later:

Every master loves to fuck a slave. It is a law of nature, or maybe culture. J isn't bad in bed, even if her sub's engines are tuned for shit. She won't let me at them though, even after letting me inside what she calls her gotch. That's the word for underwear where she grew up, somewhere in the Zone.

And then, eight days ago:

J fucked me until I screamed—yes, I screamed. Privacy does weird things to your libido. And then she burned out my chip.

Told me we're heading to the Zone and she's cutting me loose. I'm free. You know, free to be a whore. Isn't that what pretty boys with no work histories are good for?

I guess she could have killed me on the night we met, but she didn't. So that's nice. And she let me use the network even before we were fucking. And that's nice, too. But how the hell am I supposed to find a job when I have to hide my work experience?

Anyway, I'm pretty sure I know where she's going: Some lab in the Zone. For somebody so paranoid about security, J sure doesn't cover her ass. Which, when you think about it from my perspective, is a good thing. I like her ass. And I like J too, even though she's clueless. I think she's trying to do the right thing. She just doesn't grasp even the most basic things about property law.

Eliasz paused. This was obviously Threezed, and the "J" was Jack.

There were two more entries, one from yesterday, but they didn't indicate where Threezed was. "J" had disappeared from the journal, and the boy was writing a lot about robots and autonomy.

Still, it seemed Paladin was right: Jack was still in touch with contributors to *The Bilious Pills,* including the anti-patent agitators running this free lab. Probably funded by a noneconomic organization trying to undermine the IPC.

He patched into Paladin's data feed. The bot was at Broner's office, talking to the scientist about brain interfaces. He sent an order for her to interrogate the man now, appending coordinates for an extraction point.

It was time to close in. Eliasz and Paladin would rendezvous on Vancouver Island, and from there . . . Eliasz started a search on free labs in the northern Zone. The results were all references to one place: the Free Lab at the University of Saskatchewan in Saskatoon. If Jack wasn't there, he was willing to bet they would know where to find her.

With a couple of hours to kill before extraction, Eliasz bought himself a soda and strolled back toward Wynn Market. Idle times were dangerous. Things he'd seen when he worked here, and back home in Warsaw, writhed at the corners of his vision.

When Eliasz came of age, over a decade ago, he'd been lucky. His father had bought a limited franchise that allowed Eliasz to work in Warsaw, as long as he was employed by the church. His sisters were not so lucky. They left home one by one, indentured to corps overseas.

Eliasz' first job was as a guard in the church dormitories for the Boys Manufacturing Internship Program. Mostly he was there to catch runaways. He spent his days watching the boys assemble bodies in the church robotics factory, troubleshooting algorithms and studying bot anatomy. Supposedly it was so they would learn basic technical skills and land better clients when they entered contract. At night, he worked shifts in the church dormitory, listening to the boys crying themselves to sleep or getting into pointless fights over nothing.

It was during one of these long nights that he discovered what happens when you force adolescent boys to spend all day with robots whose chests are laser etched with the sign of the cross. There weren't a lot of functional video sensors left in the factory, but one of them picked up some motion in infrared and sent an alert to Eliasz.

Hidden behind a rubbish pile of arms and legs, he found two of the interns with an unprogrammed biobot. She'd obviously been cobbled together out of castoff parts, with her skin applied patchily and her mind left unformatted. As soon as the boys saw

Eliasz, they tossed her back on the pile of limbs and hurled themselves out a window to race back to the dormitories. Knowing what the priests would do to the boys if he reported them, Eliasz decided to keep their indiscretions to himself. But he wasn't sure what to do with the bot.

She looked uncannily like an unconscious teenage girl—until he peered more closely. The boys had been more careful with her lingerie than her chassis. One of her arms was longer than the other, and the tissue on her inner thighs needed nutrients. She had no mind installed, but her hair was slicked into curls and her face covered in makeup. They had modeled her on a common sex worker bot, popular on the pay feeds. Eliasz picked her up gently, unsure what to do. Her carbon fiber body was light in his arms. The more he saw of what the boys had done to her, the more mesmerized and revolted he was.

He decided disassembly was the best option, and spent a painstaking hour reducing the bot to a pile of limbs, torso slices, a head emptied of its sensors, and a lumpy roll of tissue that was too damaged to recycle. Her endoskeleton would be useful, though. He carried her in pieces to the parts bin.

"Thank you."

The voice came from behind him, in the same rubbish pile where he'd found the boys with their bot.

When he turned, Eliasz saw an unfinished bot standing with arms akimbo. The bot's exposed metal-and-fabric muscles must have camouflaged him in the garbage. His battered chest carapace—his only external casing—bore a detailed laser etching of a fantastically muscled Christ on the cross.

For the second time that night, Eliasz wasn't sure what to do.

"What are you doing here?" he asked.

The bot stared at him. "I can't leave. I keep watch here, but tonight I decided to do something."

"Are you indentured to the church?"

"I am Scrappy. You are Eliasz. I belong to Piotr."

Eliasz moved closer. Was this bot talking about Father Piotr? Eliasz' mind was muddy with exhaustion and he was still unsettled by what he'd done to the sexbot. Images of her inert body parts kept erupting into his mind. Standing beside Scrappy, Eliasz found himself wondering what it would be like to do what the boys had done with a bot.

Scrappy thrummed with life, and had no repulsive layer of makeup over wads of damaged tissue. As he spoke, he gestured by moving his arms in a perfect, graceful ellipse. There was something undeniably beautiful about him. Eliasz tried not to look at the matte black of his bones, threaded with soft fabric stronger than anything on Earth.

The bot pointed at a heap of hands. "I keep watch over this. But I do not have orders to watch everything that happens. That's why I sent the alert."

Eliasz tried to think of something else to say, to chase away the ideas coalescing in his mind. "Why can't you leave?"

"My legs." Scrappy pointed down, to show Eliasz that he'd been bonded to the floor. Eliasz wasn't sure about all the laws of indenture, but he knew one thing: The indentured could not be permanently bound. He knelt to examine the seam between the bot's legs and the floor, wondering where the molecule regulators were kept. It would only take a few minutes to free Scrappy, though he'd have to build some feet for him.

Looking up, Eliasz could see the braided fibers in Scrappy's neck and caught a glimpse of actuators where the bot's carapace settled against his hips.

Scrappy spoke. "Humans are coming."

There was scrabbling outside the window, and Eliasz saw three of the older boys, almost at the age of contract. They were only a few months younger than Eliasz. He froze, his face only centimeters from the slick ball joint between Scrappy's thigh-bone and pelvis.

"Look—it's the guard!" One of the boys let out a bark of laughter.

"He's sucking off Scrappy!"

"Faggot!" More laughter.

"Suck it, faggot!"

Eliasz rose up, putting his body between the bot and the boys. His face was hot with blood and rage. His only weapon was a baton, but Eliasz had always been good with weapons, and he moved fast. At least one of the boys wouldn't be able to say the word "faggot" again for a long time. For people without franchises, there was a three-month wait period to access Warsaw's bone printer, unless it was a life-threatening scenario. Which it wasn't. The boy could live with a shattered lower jaw, as long as the church had wire and straws.

Eliasz had a lot of practice erasing this cognitive marginalia from his mind, but it reemerged when he had nothing to occupy his attention.

So he focused on a good memory, consciously strengthening its vividness as if he were running it through an image processor. It was Paladin's beautiful, angular, armored body—the way it looked when she was shivering in his arms that afternoon in Casablanca. Just as Paladin crashed, her shields glitched and she flickered into invisibility and back out again. Other bodies, other missions, other countries tried to crowd out the picture of her face in his mind, but he overwrote them with the feeling of her carapace against his naked skin.

Eliasz was suffused with a feeling more powerful than any humiliation his long-ago experiences could possibly supply. He had no trouble identifying it as love.

19

A DISTURBING WORKPLACE ACCIDENT

JULY 17, 2144

Med pushed an update of the Retcon Project to the Free Lab servers and went for a walk across University Bridge. Early morning light turned the river from black to blue, and she spotted the V-shaped wake of a beaver carrying a last mouthful of reeds to its lodge before retiring for the day. Word about the therapy was already boiling up on forums for doctors, especially in the north where most patients had limited franchises. Open drugs were often the only option they had.

Med checked the project forums once per second, but it would be days before she had enough data to analyze. To distract herself, she tuned some feeds while the forum checks ran in the background of her mind. Hundreds of millions of people were watching a new comedy series about bumbling robots. Record harvests on Mars meant immigration there was getting cheaper. A disturbing workplace accident had left New York City flooded, and police blamed drugs.

Even before she watched, Med knew it was a Zacuity breakdown, probably the worst so far. This time it was a young engineer, just out of university, whose job it was to troubleshoot the software controls on an elaborate set of viaducts, pumps, and valves that kept the rising waters of the Atlantic from seeping into downtown Manhattan. After days without sleep, she'd decided to rethink the fundamental principles underlying the artificial marshland that acted as a massive sponge between the city and its waterways. She began to experiment, taking notes the entire time.

Unfortunately, as the engineer explained in a meticulously footnoted, fifteen-thousand-word document posted on Memeland, she also needed a control for her experiment. Which meant she'd have to look at New York City in its most natural state, saturated with water. Before anyone could stop her, the engineer flooded the subways and streets in downtown Manhattan, drowning dozens of people in underground housing, and forcing a huge evacuation. Many people were still missing. The engineer had been arrested, but it was impossible to undo her work without days of cleanup. Free Trade Zone leaders had declared a state of emergency.

Racing back to the lab, Med ran through decision trees and modeled options.

News about Retcon wasn't getting out fast enough to stop the damage that Zacuity was causing. They couldn't afford to rely on the Freeculture text repos and research forums as their only means to circulate information, hoping that somehow the entire Zone would hear about it. It was time to publish a paper showing that the dangerous pirate drug causing so many deaths was actually a reverse-engineered Zaxy pill. Once Zaxy's name was involved, all the feeds would be on it. And then, even docs in New York City would know about Retcon.

Med burst into Krish's office and smacked his desk to activate the feed from New York. "We have to go public with what we know about Zacuity."

She could see Krish's anxiety stitching a pattern of electricity across his scalp as he watched the video of subway entrances disgorging gray water and worse.

"This is horrifying, but I don't know if we're ready to accuse one of the biggest corps in the Zone of breaking the law."

"It's the only way we're going to get enough publicity to stop more of these manic episodes. We've got Jack's schematics of the reverse-engineered Zacuity."

"Yes, we have the schematics for Zacuity. Yes, we have a therapy for a street drug that a pirate *claims* is Zacuity—"

"But it's the exact same drug! We have proof!"

Krish sighed. "We have proof that scientists will believe, if they are so inclined. But IPC representatives, the public, the media—they can't read a schematic, and all they'll hear is that some anti-patent activist is shitting on Zaxy, which provides them with all the blockbuster drugs they know and love." Krish wiped the feeds and documentation out of the air and sighed. "Without something the media can understand, going public now could blow up in our faces."

The bot shook her head. "We have to do it. This is Zaxy's fault, and people need to know they're making illegal addictives with horrifying side effects."

"I know, and I wish I could do something about that. But for now we've made Retcon available, and it's already doing some good."

Angrier than she'd ever been in her life, Med slammed the door shut on Krish's office, enjoying the sting of reverberation in the air. She was going to find the proof he wanted.

Six hours later, Med realized she had no idea what she was looking for. Combing the forums and medical text repos turned up nothing. Contacting her old colleagues yielded more preliminary data that she couldn't put into a scientific article, let alone release to the public net. Med was so busy being frustrated that she didn't notice anyone was behind her until someone put hands on her shoulders and shouted "Boo!" Threezed had dropped down from the loft and crept up behind her.

Startled, she looked at him with the back of her head, reading his biosigns with sensor motes built into the dead cells of her hair. His muscles were more relaxed than she'd ever perceived them; his hypervigilance seemed to be ebbing.

"What are you working on? You look kind of pissed off." Apparently Threezed could perceive things about Med's psychological state that she wasn't aware she was broadcasting.

She signaled the network to disengage gesture controls and shrugged. "I'm trying to find some way to explain to the media that Zaxy made Zacuity. Something that anyone could understand."

Threezed sat beside her on the bench. "Have you looked on Memeland?"

"For what? This is the kind of thing that only scientists would know about."

"People talk about drugs all the time on Memeland. Just search for . . . I dunno, Zacuity, Retcon, addiction, mania, freakout, worker drug . . . Just see if anyone is talking about it."

Med was nonplussed. "I don't see how that will help, and that's a lot to sort through. I need something now."

"I'll do some searches for you. I have some time before work." Threezed pulled out his mobile and yanked a projection from its display into the air. Med noticed that his collar covered up the number on his neck. He'd used an embroidery machine at the store to adorn the pocket with a nametag that said "John."

Med was lost in a forum conversation sixteen threads deep when Threezed swiped a file into her shared workspace. It was a post from a developer at Quick Build Wares in Vancouver who was part of a recovery group for people suffering from depression after Zacuity runs. She wrote about "this underground drug called Retcon," which was the first therapy she'd tried that actually eased her symptoms. At her urging, other Quick Build employees took it, too. In the discussion below her post, they talked about what happened next.

The weirdest part was that they couldn't remember ever wanting to work at Quick Build. Yes, they recalled getting their jobs and doing them well. They still had the skills required to design circuits and modify molecules. But the idea of using those skills, especially for Quick Build, filled them with repulsion. Some even reported vomiting when they tried to go to work that morning.

This was a new wrinkle. Unlike people who had taken the pirated Zacuity over the past couple of weeks, Quick Build employees had been using the drug for at least a year. They took Zacuity under the supervision of licensed physicians, and always for the same thing: completing difficult work projects. But then they started to feel like nothing in their lives mattered except Zacuity-enhanced work. Because this was in some sense how the drug was supposed to work, it was hard for the employees to get diagnosed as anything other than complainers.

When these complainers took Retcon, however, their yearning for the addictive process—in this case, working at Quick Build—shriveled up as quickly as their dopamine receptors bloomed, and the new receptors sipped dopamine generated by all kinds of pleasurable activities. Suddenly the Quick Build workers wanted to go bicycling, play with their kids, watch videos, or develop software for personal projects. But they didn't want to work at Quick Build anymore.

It was still too early to tell if these were temporary symptoms of withdrawal, but Med suspected they weren't. The pirated Zacuity users had recovered quickly, but corporate users suddenly found themselves with months of memories that made no sense. They were unable to bounce back. Maybe they would never be able to do their jobs again without throwing up.

The economic outcome for people who had taken the legal

version of Zacuity was potentially catastrophic. It wasn't ideal, but now Med had proof that Retcon worked on those people. And that was something even the media could understand.

Med sent the data to Krish. As she crossed the room to his office, his fingers were already twitching out a message on the desk. "Great work finding that group from Quick Build," he said, without looking up. "I'm going to talk to my friend at the Pharma Justice Clinic. He'll have some ideas about how we should frame this. You should finish our paper."

The bot thought again about the people who had taken the drug for a prolonged period. "These Zacuity users are going to have to build up new memories of enjoying their jobs. I think Zaxy is going to be responsible for a lot of unemployment. Zacuity users might even be able to sue for damages."

Threezed listened to their conversation and smirked. "Good job, Med. You gave those people autonomy, and now they can't work." Then, seeing something in Med's face that she didn't realize was there, he stopped. When Threezed spoke again, his tone was gentler, no longer spiked with sarcasm. "But I guess it's good that they finally know what work really feels like."

MARKETING GIMMICK

JULY 16, 2144

When Eliasz arrived at Vancouver Island, he hadn't tapped into Paladin's real-time feed for several hours. She didn't offer him any video or audio files from the time between her interrogation of Bobby and her discovery of the Scarface server at the University of Saskatoon. Eliasz could have requisitioned her memories and appended them to the report he filed from Vancouver Island, but he didn't.

Back at Camp Tunisia, a team of agents analyzed the intel from Vancouver and Vegas while the IPC liaison drank very tiny cups of strong coffee. Eliasz requested an immediate flight to Saskatoon, but Fang said the team needed more time to assess. Paladin and Eliasz would be grounded at the base for at least twenty-four hours—maybe more.

Eliasz was assigned a temporary bunk, and Paladin was assigned to stay with Eliasz. The bunk turned out to be a faraday room, designed to cut soldiers off from the distractions of the net. But it also meant that nobody was monitoring their body feeds, either.

It was one of those times when Eliasz suddenly wanted to talk. He told Paladin about Vegas, describing the short, scented alley where Quality Imports and The Alice Shop could be found. He'd left the force in Vegas to work on something cleaner, he told her, with no gray areas. No quasi-legal loopholes that made it possible for bad guys to arrange lawful contracts between kids and sketchy adults who wanted them as "general assistants."

It wasn't like he'd run away from the chance to stop property crime, because now he was in a better position than ever to help people. Infringement was always illegal. Nobody at the IPC would prevent him from busting the bad guys when it came to piracy. He no longer had to see unpunishable transgressions thriving in the open, their victims staring at his uniform with accusation. When it came to intellectual property, justice was simple and clear.

Paladin sat down on the bunk next to Eliasz. She did not volunteer any stories, but she did have work to review. She projected a map of Saskatoon into the air at Eliasz' eye level. Bounded by vast, satellite-regulated farms, the city was bisected by a fat, curving river. At the center of downtown was the university, flagged in red. Paladin zoomed in on the campus buildings, which looked like tumbled blocks surrounded by the brown ridges of bot-tended agriculture labs.

"We should prepare a strategy," she vocalized. "There is a very good chance Jack has already fled, but I think somebody at the Free Lab will know where she's gone."

She pointed at a building on the south end of campus, which expanded into a block of text that read "FREE LAB" before dissolving into a blueprint of an open floor plan. There were only two ways out of the building.

"Obviously we begin with Krish Patel, the professor who worked for *The Bilious Pills* and runs the Free Lab. I suggest we take a look around Free Lab's networks first to see if we can locate Scarface. We will be arriving at roughly 2300, so the lab is likely to be empty. We may be able to gather enough information there that we never have to alert Patel to our presence."

Eliasz grunted assent, then settled back on the bed and closed his eyes.

Paladin was still finding it difficult to prevent herself from asking questions. "Eliasz, you said my autonomy key was temporary. Do you know how long it will last?"

The man straightened up again, and Paladin recognized guilt in his face. "Isn't that something you know automatically? I thought it was a program that you were running."

"It's not a program," she vocalized. "It's more like a password that gives me access to programs."

"Didn't Lee tell you when it would expire?" Eliasz looked confused, then concerned. "Are you doing OK? I've heard that sometimes bots have problems after they get autonomy."

"No problems so far. I just wanted to know when . . ." The bot trailed off uncharacteristically. When what? When she would stop feeling compelled to ask questions? When she would stop taking security risks the way she did with those bots in Vancouver?

Eliasz was waiting for her to finish her sentence.

". . . when it will be over," she vocalized finally.

Suddenly, Eliasz' blood pressure shot up and the electrical signals racing across the surface of his brain suggested fear. "Do you regret what we did, now that you are autonomous?" His question was ambiguous, until he leaned forward and put his hands on the shielded fibers of her knees. "Do you still feel the same way?"

She wanted to ask all the questions: What did he think she felt? Why did he need to know? Did he feel the same way? But she remained silent. Asking too much when it came to this topic only made things more confusing.

"The autonomy key hasn't changed my feelings," she replied.

"I am so glad," he whispered, his skin dancing with directionless energy. "I couldn't stop thinking about you when I was in Vegas."

"I also thought about you." She tasted salt and blood on his skin with her right hand.

"Your feelings must be coming from the real you, in here." He touched the armor over her brain lightly. "That's why they're not affected by autonomy programs."

Paladin chose not to repeat that autonomy was a key, not a program, and that her brain had nothing to do with what she truly desired. Around them, the base walls rattled with wind coming off the Pacific Ocean.

"I want to watch you play that file again." Eliasz whispered to her, his arm pressed tightly against hers. She wanted it, too.

Early the next morning, Paladin tasted the oxytocin spiking in Eliasz' blood for a second time. Her arm cradled Eliasz, and his perimeter weapons were in a weightless pile of almost-invisible netting on the floor. The man had a whole day to sleep before they flew out to the prairies to pick up Jack's trail.

JULY 18, 2144, 0400

Med was finishing the "methods" section of the Zacuity paper when she sat rigidly upright. Threezed was watching a movie on his tablet. Across the lab, Krish was rewriting their press release about how Zaxy violated international law. Suddenly, none of that mattered.

A sequencer clattered to the floor as Med stood with an inhuman speed that made her look like a special effect. "Get out of here now!" she whispered, railroading her body into Threezed's. In seconds, she had half-carried him to a back exit used mostly for taking out the recycling. "Go! Hide!"

Threezed didn't hear panic in the bot's voice, but he understood danger. He sprinted out the door and didn't look back. Med whirled to face Krish, who was staring at her open-mouthed.

For the first time in her life, Med felt what it was like to have a program override her choices. The instant she saw the IPC bot on the Free Lab network, she stopped being a researcher and went into primary defense mode. As the researchers back in Anchorage would no doubt say, the fight-or-flight response wasn't quite as reflexive as that: First, she realized that an IPC bot was in close physical proximity, accompanied by an IPC agent; then she deduced they were specifically looking for information related to Jack. Which meant they probably weren't concerned about leaving anybody here alive.

Alien thoughts and reflexes overwhelmed her. The lab was under attack, along with the human lives inside it, and she would fight to the death to prevent the attack from succeeding. It felt like she had no other option, but of course she did. She could have run. She chose to stay.

Med perceived the bot opening the poorly encrypted locks on the lab's front door and cartwheeled back across the room, ripping the seam that held her lab coat together at the back. When the armored bot and the agent burst into the lab, she was blocking Krish with her body. The agent squeezed off three syringes, probably tranqs or hypnotics, and Med snatched them out of the air with the palm of her rapidly moving hand. As the caps burst, their payloads—packed with molecules that would disrupt signaling pathways in the cerebral cortex—leaked out of a small tear in her skin.

"It's no good shooting her with drugs," the bot now facing her vocalized. "She's a bot."

Med knew this model: standard military with vaguely human morphology and a lot of custom upgrades. One of the upgrades was a human brain, probably used mostly for facial recognition. And it looked like one of her hands was packed with lab-grade sensors. Her entire body glowed from the weapons powered up beneath her carapace.

The bot signaled to Med on an open channel. *I am Paladin. You are unknown. Here comes my data. We want information about a pirate named Judith Chen. She goes by Jack. She is a terrorist, and has already killed hundreds of people with her pirated drugs. We have good reason to believe that she has been here during the last week. That is the end of my data.*

Paladin and Eliasz' credentials, packed into a data ball, were appended. The signatures on them were good. No doubt that these agents really were with the IPC.

I am Medea Cohen. You are Paladin. Here comes my data. I have no information for you. That is the end of my data.

For the benefit of the humans, she vocalized, "I have just seen their credentials, and these are agents from the IPC."

"What can I do for you folks?" Krish asked, still keeping himself behind the bot. "I'm happy to talk if you'll stop shooting at us."

Eliasz stepped forward. His face and voice were relaxed. "I'm Agent Eliasz Wójcik, with the African Federation IPC. I just want to talk about your friend Jack. We have evidence that she's been here, possibly with a fugitive."

"I'm sure you know that Jack and I used to be very close," Krish said reasonably, stepping out from behind Med. He had also modulated his voice to sound relaxed. Both men were practiced at being on opposite sides in this kind of conversation. "But you probably also know that I haven't seen her in over twenty-five years, since she stopped working here and moved to the Federation."

"We know that she sent data about pirated drugs to Bobby Broner through a server called Scarface here at the university."

Paladin added, "A server that I have verified is here in your lab."

"Do you still want to stick to your story that you haven't seen Jack in the past twenty-five years?" Eliasz sounded as though he were asking a question about the weather.

"I have no control over who sends data through the servers

in my lab," Krish replied in the same tone. "The university network is open."

Med watched this exchange beyond the visible spectrum, and perceived from microwave transmissions that Paladin was accessing their lab cameras. Whatever happened next would be impossible for anybody to piece together from the lab's media feeds. She began dumping video of what she was watching to a tiny, shielded backup in her chest that was impervious to EMPs, radiation, and fire.

"We also have reason to believe that Jack was headed here based on what her friend Threezed has been posting in his journal on Memeland."

With a mix of rage and sadness, Med realized that Threezed's SlaveBoy journal had given them away. The agents seemed to know nothing about the Retcon Project. Of course, given the rate at which Paladin was sweeping their network, this gap in their knowledge was likely to close quickly. And it would only make them look more guilty.

Med's state of alarm grew when she checked the net for the name "Bobby Broner" and discovered it belonged—at least in one instance—to a professor who had been found murdered in his lab two days ago. Gambling debts, the story said. She had to assume these agents would stop at nothing to discover where Jack was.

Their only hope was to get to a public place where they couldn't be murdered outright. Even if they were taken into custody, they would have witnesses. This might or might not protect them, but their odds would be better than if they stayed here. There was a student bar just a few buildings away. The place was always packed, even at this time of night.

Act fast. Distract their attackers. Get away. Med palmed the molecule regulator she kept tucked into her pocket.

"I'm sure you won't mind us looking around here, then," Eliasz said. Med watched the agent's thumb, flicking through the settings on his perimeter weapon.

Krish prided himself on being good at stalling in these situations. "I'd like to see your warrant. You can't search this place without proving you've gotten judicial oversight."

"I can write my own warrants," Eliasz replied. "And I have, in this case. You'll find it in your queued messages."

Med made a decision. Defense was not her expertise, but she hoped her strategy would buy Krish some time.

"Run, Krish!" she screamed. "Get somewhere public before they detain you!"

The bot's body blurred into motion, her torn lab coat streaming behind her like wings as she launched herself at the military bot. The regulator's beam was set to decompose metal alloys. It was eating through her right hand, drawing a glowing red streak through the air as she flew.

A defensive stance and perimeter shield were not enough to prevent Med's fist from connecting with Paladin's carapace. Med's melting fingers sank into Paladin's armor at forty-five kilometers per hour, still holding the tuner. It took less than a second for the device to disintegrate its way through layers of shielding and a small amount of cerebrospinal fluid. By the time Paladin's shield had overloaded Med's system with a possibly fatal EMP, her arm was buried past its elbow in Paladin's brain cavity.

Whitish gray slime bubbled out of Paladin's wound and globbed on the floor along with strips of skin torn from the steel and polymers in Med's arm. The pulse had forced Med to shut down midblow. Her body slumped to the floor at Paladin's feet, dragging her arm partly out of the hole in Paladin's carapace along with another slurry of gore.

Krish was too shocked to move. Only when the bot doubled

over, clutching the hole in her abdomen, did he realize he needed to get out of the lab. As he turned to run, Krish heard Eliasz roaring.

Krish's neck stung. He dimly realized Eliasz had shot him with a syringe. Everything took on a hallucinatory brightness. His heart pounded with something that might have been pleasure or fear. What had they dosed him with? It made his face hurt, but then he realized he'd fallen to the floor and split the skin on his cheek. Another hiccup of the pleasure-fear shook him, and he watched with dissociated intensity as Paladin snapped Med's arm in half. He was supposed to do something. Med's arm was wet and broken. It was an arm, or it was something else. He thought of Jack and started to cry.

When Eliasz lifted Krish into a chair and slapped him into attentiveness, he discerned that tears had mixed with the blood on the scientist's face. This was going to be easy.

Eliasz asked gentle questions and Krish babbled the answers as Paladin fabbed a swatch of new carapace to patch the hole over her ruined brain. Three meters away, Med's eyes were still open, dumb cameras recording to the tiny, shielded device in her chest.

JULY 18, 2144, 0600

A hard reboot, followed by an initialization process, followed by another. After a certain point, these automated events could pass for consciousness. Med's visual sensors came online and she could see her detached and slightly pulverized right arm lying in a puddle of drying brain. She was in more pain than she'd ever experienced in her life, though her suffering lessened as she progressed through recovery mode. Most of her body was intact, except for the shredded steel and flesh stump where her arm had been. She perceived that the drivers for her legs and remaining arm were undamaged.

The bot sat up and tuned the local network. It had been two hours since Paladin knocked her flat with that EMP, and she'd started a slow recovery from her shielded backup. There were no signs of her adversaries. Where was Krish? She retrieved video from the past two hours. When she tried to stand, her feet skidded out from under her, scoring tracks through the brown, half-congealed blood on the floor. Her own blood, she realized, from the soft layer of tissue that covered her endoskeleton.

Standing up was the least of her problems. Video capture and real-time data both indicated that Med's plan had failed. She reviewed, at twenty times normal speed, the video of Eliasz interrogating Krish. A few meters away, she could see for herself what remained of the interrogation scene: Krish slumped over a lab bench, his body emitting very little heat.

The bot walked haltingly to the man who had hired her for initiating a project that Big Pharma wanted to suppress. Based on his body temperature, she estimated he had been dead for over an hour. Probably massive organ failure from drug overdose, though only a blood test could verify that. He had some injuries on his face, but nothing that suggested he'd been beaten to death. She supposed it was even remotely possible that the agent hadn't intended to kill Krish, just drug him into suggestibility.

From what she heard of the interrogation, the drug they'd given him was incredibly potent. Krish was spurting sentences that made no sense and hallucinating that Jack was in the room, pushed along by hints from Eliasz.

"Where would Jack go to be safe? Where would she go?" Eliasz murmured again and again, no matter what Krish said.

Finally, Krish started to nod out—probably oxygen deprivation as his heart began to fail—and he gestured for Eliasz to come closer. The agent knelt next to the dying man and they both came into video range.

"Jack, I'm sorry," Krish slurred around a sob. "I'm so sorry." He looked into Eliasz' face and placed his hands tenderly on the man's cheeks before leaning forward to whisper something she couldn't pick up. Then, still cradling Eliasz' face like a lover's, he kissed the agent on the mouth. "Please keep yourself safe," he sighed, then passed out. Eliasz caught Krish before he collapsed sideways to the floor, seating the unconscious professor at a lab bench and placing him in the exact position he held lifelessly now.

"Did you hear what he told me?" Eliasz asked Paladin, from beyond the range of Med's cameras in the video.

"Yes," Paladin vocalized. "I have also found some university documents that suggest where her safe house might be in Moose Jaw."

"Let's go," Eliasz replied, as Paladin came into visual range. A square of hastily printed carbon fiber covered the hole that Med's fist had opened in Paladin's carapace. Distracted by a feeling of wrathful satisfaction, Med registered but did not process the meaning of the intense flush of heat that illuminated Eliasz' body as he touched the bot's arm and they walked out of the lab.

She messaged Threezed and began searching the university network for Jack's birth name, in association with Moose Jaw.

I'm in the barn, Threezed sent from his mobile. *With the antibiotic cows. Are you OK?*

Over a mile away from the Free Lab, a joint project between the synbio and animal husbandry departments had resulted in a warm, oat-scented barn full of cows whose milk was rich with various antibacterials and antivirals. It was where Med liked to walk to get away from humans.

Her network search turned up some relevant data—most likely the same thing Paladin had found. Over thirty years ago, the archaeology department had offered a summer class that resulted in the excavation of smugglers' tunnels in Moose Jaw.

An undergraduate named Judith Chen had been on that dig. No subsequent work was done on the excavation, but it remained accessible via a storage room under a new condo development. It would be a good place to hide, with all Jack's activity and energy use masked by people living in the building above.

Med signaled Threezed's mobile. *The agents are gone. I am slightly damaged. We need to get to Moose Jaw NOW.*

On my way. We can take the lab truck.

As Med booted up the truck and waited for Threezed to arrive, she sent a warning to Jack, using the protocols they'd agreed on less than a week ago. She used a regulator to trim and cauterize the torn tissue on her stump. Full repairs would have to wait until later.

21

MOOSE JAW

JULY 18, 2144, 0648

Eliasz took his hands off the steering wheel as the truck entered autonomous mode on the highway to Moose Jaw. Outside, low hills merged with each other in the darkness.

"Are you going to be OK?" The man's voice was carefully neutral, and Paladin could not read the expression on his face.

In fact, she could no longer see Eliasz' face at all. Certainly the man had a face, and she could perceive that it possessed the usual group of sensory organs, but nothing about it was recognizable as Eliasz. She knew him by his voice, his bearing, and the cloud of molecules hovering around his body, but his face was merely a concatenation of muscle movements.

Her inability to classify the data provided by Eliasz' expression filled Paladin with panic, which only intensified when she thought about how much her brain meant to him. The arms in Kagu Robotics Foundry had lied. Fang didn't know what he was talking about. She was crippled without her brain, unable to tell the difference between wrath and laughter, or between a hostile face and a familiar one. How could she possibly aid Eliasz in combat?

"I believe I may be too damaged to function in a combat situation."

Eliasz faced her, reaching out a tentative hand to touch the patch over Paladin's empty brain socket. His face flickered with activity that meant nothing.

JULY 18, 2144, 0700

Jack got Med's message in time to lay a decent trap. She'd seen that blurry footage of the bot chasing her, so she had some ideas what she was up against. She guessed the human agent would be standard-issue IPC: highly trained, on fire with righteous belief in property, as likely to kill her as anything else. All she had on her side was Med's bit of intel, and hopefully the element of surprise.

A hidden compartment in the ceiling over her lab bench was the only place she could hide. It was little more than a crawl space lined with slightly springy foam, just tall enough that she could bunch into a crouching position from which she could hurl herself at the agents. As she waited, her knife in the relaxed fingers of her right hand, her perimeter feeding images to her goggles from security cameras outside, there was nothing to do but think about Krish.

Based on Med's brief message, Jack guessed Krish had managed to betray her again before dying. Even as she formed that thought, a nauseating spasm of grief contradicted it. Nobody could withstand the kind of interrogation drugs an IPC agent would use—not without intensive training and modification. She and Frankie had spent years trying to patch themselves against pharma weapons. The most Krish had ever done was smoke 420 for fun.

In the clarity that comes with existential threat, Jack realized she'd held a grudge against Krish all these years for what amounted to a petty academic squabble over a text repo. Yes, it was terrible that he shut down *The Bilious Pills*. But now she could see how Free Lab was an extension of what the Pills started, a community that didn't just protest property law but actually built alternatives to it. Krish had welcomed her and the Retcon

Project, even after their decades of chilly silence. He must have known it might get him killed.

Suppressing something more bitter than a sob, Jack recalled the first essay Krish wrote for *The Bilious Pills.* He'd published it in the middle of the quarter, during one of their long, agonizing separations. Krish wrote:

> Over a century ago, scientists first began to argue that the patent system and scientific data should be opened up. Back then, it was popular for conservatives to claim that putting geneng into the hands of the public would result in megaviruses or total species collapse. Open data would be the gateway to a runaway synthetic biology apocalypse. But now we know there has been no one great disaster—only the slow-motion disaster of capitalism converting every living thing and idea into property.

Reading that decades ago, her chest had fizzed with deferred sexual desire and hope. She and Krish were collaborating on a project that was more exciting than anything she'd ever tackled in school. With their text repo, they would reach millions of people and bring Good Science to everyone. She'd known with absolute certainty that they were about to change the world.

But now Krish's essay had been deleted from the public net, and the Freeculture movement they loved was being murdered in IPC interrogations, in burning Casablanca apartments, in drugs pirated for profit rather than freedom, and probably soon in this smuggler's tunnel with the ghosts of her lovers.

An explosion sent a fine haze of dust through the permeable foam of her hiding place. Jack flexed her legs. This was no time to go maudlin over the demise of youthful dreams. The IPC agents had arrived.

JULY 18, 2144, 0705

Threezed's eyes widened perceptibly when he bounced into the truck and saw the bot's shredded arm.

"Holy shit, Med, that is not what I'd call 'slightly damaged.' Where's Krish?"

"Krish is dead. My arm can be repaired."

They drove in silence for almost an hour. Threezed twitched and checked his mobile, while Med tried to figure out how she would publicize the paper about reverse engineering Zacuity now that everything had gone wrong. She pushed the truck to the limits of its speed. At least if they got to Moose Jaw quickly, she might be able to prevent the agents from killing another one of her friends.

"What are we going to do?" Threezed's voice was reedy with tension.

Med had no answer to his question, so she changed the subject. "Do you know how the agents figured out where Jack was? They read your journal on Memeland."

"What?" Threezed let go of his mobile and it slid to rest between his legs, parted slightly on the seat. "How did they do that? My journal is anonymous! Plus, I never use anybody's real names."

Med glared at him, funneling her hopelessness into anger. "What the hell did you think would happen when you wrote about fucking somebody named 'J' who is from the prairies? When you wrote that you were going to follow her to the Free Lab? The IPC is full of intelligence agents. They specialize in tracking down slaves who have broken contract, and you didn't exactly make it difficult for them."

"Why didn't you say anything before? You were reading my journal and you didn't say anything!" In the darkness of the cab, the heat from Threezed's tears looked like glowing tracks of blood on his face.

The bot's anguish reached a crescendo that she didn't have the option to express in tears. She slammed her remaining arm as hard as she could into the door and screamed, "I didn't think of it, OK? I didn't think of it!" She'd bruised her arm and opened a wound in the door. The truck emitted a soft warning noise.

"Alright—I get it! We're totally fucked and it's my fault!" Threezed scrambled across the bench seat to grab Med's shoulders and shake her. "Now that we know we're fucked, what are we going to do to help Jack?"

"I've brought some items from the lab that I think we can weaponize."

"What have we got?" Threezed left his right hand on her shoulder and she realized that he'd grown incredibly calm. It wasn't the blankness of hysteria in remission, either. It was the calm of someone who had been through much worse things, and knew how to survive.

She'd brought viral sealant pastes, packed into fat marbles you could shoot from air pressure guns. They were designed for cheap, rapid repair of industrial machines and vehicles. Shoot your boat's hull with a paste pellet and the viruses would start duplicating, their shells turning into a metal patch for any damage. Med theorized that the paste would also seal up openings on the bot's carapace, in essence gluing Paladin's sensors and weapons apertures shut.

"Sounds good. Now what do we have that will kill that bastard who murdered Krish?"

"There's nothing even remotely deadly to humans at Free Lab. But I do have something that will make it a lot harder for him to fight."

JULY 18, 2144, 0805

Jack waited, breathing shallowly. Her body heat was masked by the electronics and atmosphere ducts running through the ceiling. As she'd hoped, the agent and the bot headed for the lab bench beneath her hiding place as soon as they realized she wasn't in the tunnel. The man was covering the bot with his weapons stance, which was unusual. But then Jack saw the hastily patched wound in the bot's abdomen, and the odd way she kept training her sensor arrays away from the man's face. Something had gone wrong, though the bot was still deadly enough. And crafty. The bot was scanning Jack's network for vulns in her power system, without much luck.

"What do you make of this?" The man gestured at Jack's fabber and small collection of low-power sequencers.

The bot vocalized, "I think she was just here. We should sweep for hiding places and other exits."

Jack had to move now. She slid open the doors and threw her knife expertly, burying it deep in the bot's chest, where it delivered an EMP. Then she swung down, feet first, into the IPC agent's face. She felt her feet connect with his skull, just as his perimeter delivered a powerful electric shock. Spasming, she fell to the floor next to him.

Adrenaline doused Jack's vision and made her see the room in jagged, fast-forward detail. The barrier between her tunnel and the trash heap that obscured it lay in a pile of boulders and dust. A swath of the ceiling LEDs had gone out, and her attack had knocked a sequencer to the floor. Her feet felt warm, and she observed that the agent's perimeter had partly melted the soles of her shoes. The man was knocked out, his forehead already starting to swell from Jack's kick. His bot stood motionless from the EMP. She needed to disable the agent's perimeter before he came to, so there would be no record of this encounter. Struggling though the pain of locked, burning muscles, she got up.

Jack yanked her knife out of the bot, jammed it into her belt, and assessed the situation. Beneath the agent's skin, his perimeter mesh was routing data and electricity into possibly hundreds of devices all over his body. But usually there was some kind of controller near the waist. To make her getaway complete, she just needed a few seconds to dig around in this bastard's pants.

Pulling up the agent's jacket, Jack exposed the pale skin of his stomach. She pressed her hand to his skin, producing a tiny grid pattern as the threads of his weapons system dug into flesh. With her other hand she tore open the binding on his pants, exposing the fur on his lower belly. Where was the controller? She pushed the man onto his side, at last exposing a donut-shaped device about the size of a bottlecap low on his hip.

As Jack's fingers closed around the controller, the bot spoke. "If you continue to touch him, I will kill you."

Jack put her hands in the air. Obviously the EMP hadn't kept the bot down for very long.

"Keep your back to me and stand up." The bot used an entirely inflectionless voice. Jack obeyed, trying to assess whether she could still run. Or, failing that, draw her knife and throw. She decided to stall.

"Who sent the IPC after me? Was it Zaxy?"

"Put your hands behind you."

She complied, and felt the bot's grip, warm and smooth, stronger than handcuffs. The man was starting to groan and stir on the floor at her feet.

"Why are you doing this?"

"You know very well why we are here. Your terrorist activities have killed over a hundred people."

"If that's so, why all the subterfuge? Why did the IPC only

send the two of you?" Jack was playing for time, but she also wanted to know. "Is Zaxy trying to cover up the fact that Zacuity is driving people insane? I didn't invent the drug that killed those people, you know—it was Zaxy's. I just reverse engineered it."

The bot said nothing until the man muttered. "Paladin."

"I'm here, and I have the prisoner."

"Just kill her, then." The man opened dark brown eyes and looked directly at Jack.

Suddenly Jack heard a series of pops and Paladin's body shuddered. The bot released Jack's hands and the agent, struggling to stand up, went down again. Whirling in the direction of the noise, Jack saw her rescuers. Threezed and Med stood in piles of garbage, bright yellow air pressure guns in their hands, shooting what looked like jumbo-size hard candies at Paladin and Eliasz.

Blotches of virus paste spread over Paladin's torso, sealing the bot's guns inside her chest. The pink goo was a novel, experimental substance, and the bot had never been hardened against it. She tore at the spreading patches, but they swarmed onto her fingers, making mittens out of her digits.

Med stepped forward, strands of metal twitching in her stump while her undamaged arm fired off another round at the man, who had started to scream. Everywhere the virus marbles hit him, bizarre forests of fine hair seemed to spring out of his skin. His face was growing a riot of glassy curls, and his eyelashes tangled shut. Eliasz gasped through his mouth as his nasal passages filled with tiny stalks. Somehow, the viruses had wriggled under Eliasz' skin and eaten through his bio-glass perimeter wires. All those millions of microscopic fibers, kept under constant tension, had sprung out of his skin and formed a disabling tangle of fiber-optic fur. He and his bot wouldn't be chasing anyone for several minutes at least.

"It turns out Catalyst's recipe for removing the plants growing on her head is good for something other than fashion," Med vocalized, a new chord of sarcasm in her voice. "Maybe we should give her a postdoc."

Jack stumbled forward, her muscles still wracked with pain. Threezed looped her arm around his shoulder, dragged her through the rubble, out the trap door, and into what passed for safety.

JULY 18, 2144, 0810

Eliasz' head throbbed, and he could barely see through the wool of his shredded perimeter system. But he still had one weapon running, a dumb gun he kept strapped to his ankle. Behind him, Paladin emitted a noise that sounded like tearing metal.

Jack was limping toward the trap door, supported by a boy whose face unmistakably matched the one from the database at Quality Imports. Except he didn't look like SlaveBoy anymore. He was strong and well fed, with a new chip that broadcast his enfranchisement as a citizen of Saskatoon. Jack had been taking care of him. In the seconds it took for Eliasz to reach for the gun, his memory strobed with hundreds of faces—all the children he hadn't saved in Vegas, his sisters, the boys he'd beaten up in the church robot factory. Even the worst of them didn't deserve the hand they'd been dealt. They were just unlucky to be born without franchises. For a hallucinatory moment, as Eliasz felt his skin crisping with wire, he wondered whether it was some kind of perverse miracle that Jack had found Threezed.

Eliasz' finger rested on the trigger, and his hand aimed. But then he heard a howl of metal eating metal behind him and realized Paladin might be fatally wounded. He could check on the bot, or he could kill the pirate. He had a choice.

Or maybe he didn't.

With an agonizing crackle of his neck, Eliasz turned to find the bot freeing virus-coated fingers from her torso. She was recovering, not dying. By the time Eliasz aimed his gun again, eyelids nearly sewn shut with wire, the pirate and her friends were gone. Everything he'd recorded with his perimeter systems had been destroyed by a graduate student's depilation experiment.

22

BIG PHARMA

JULY 21, 2144

Med stood in a mote-speckled beam of sunlight that fell from one of the Free Lab's high windows. She was absorbing energy through the photovoltaic patches knitted invisibly into the tissue of her skin. Absently, she held her hands out in front of her, as if examining her nails. For the hundred and forty-seventh time, she assessed the slight differences in skin texture between her original arm and the new one she'd installed yesterday.

The paramedics were long gone, and Krish's mother had returned to Vancouver with his remains. You couldn't always predict strokes with annual medical exams, the docs said, and Krish was never an avid self-quantifier. The lab's camera network was so glitchy that nobody questioned why it just so happened that he died during a period of down time. Meanwhile, according to the feeds, the notorious pirate Judith "Jack" Chen—jailed once for terrorism in the 'teens, and wanted by the IPC—had been killed in a firefight in her Moose Jaw hideout.

In reality, Jack was hiding behind a haze of bogus mote data in Med's apartment, recovering from her injuries and grafting purple and black extensions to the stubble on her head. In the cat lovers' forum, she found a gif of a bot petting a kitten with an encrypted message from Frankie knitted steganographically into it: "Not dead yet." Jack's relief was like a hit of Ellondra. She left a picture of a cat sprawled on her back, pink sliver of tongue sticking out, with a reply for Frankie secreted into the code: "Still breathing."

In one frantic day of work, Jack finished the press release that Krish had started. "Strong evidence shows Zaxy engineered its drug Zacuity to be addictive," it began. That alone scored Med an exclusive interview with ZoneFeed, to be followed by an in-depth report on *New Scientist*.

When Med's research paper went live on the Free Lab text repo, ZoneFeed would publish their interview. Med didn't need to sit down at her desk and hit the publish button the way a human would. She sent a command to the server using the lab's wireless protocol. Standing in the middle of the Free Lab, she accessed the feeds with her mind, watching the ZoneFeed story replicate itself and spawn increasingly frantic private messages from other news outlets. The Retcon Project's code repository was exploding with traffic. Hospitals all over the world were printing out the drug, and the more liberal corps started issuing their own press releases, distancing themselves from Zaxy and saying they would no longer supply their employees with Zacuity.

Med returned to her office to respond to reporters, watching as snatches of their conversations appeared minutes later as video grabs in the feeds.

The Free Lab's entire staff had basically taken the day off to watch the Retcon Project become famous. Somebody tapped a keg around noon, and by 3:00 p.m., things had gotten rowdy. Catalyst projected four different news feeds into the air over the lab benches. The Free Trade Zone Economic Coalition had finally made a statement: A rep claimed they were launching an independent inquiry into Zaxy's productivity drug, based on research from the University of Saskatchewan. The entire Free Lab burst into cheers.

Over on the NRx News feed, two commentators discussed the story. "But let's keep in mind that this researcher is a bot, Larry," one said. "It's very possible that she's been programmed by one of Zaxy's corporate rivals to make these claims—or by the radical groups in the lab where she works."

Minutes later, a reporter from Sydney was finishing up an interview with Med. She paused dramatically, then asked her final question. "I have to ask, because this has come up in a number of reports. Has anyone tampered with your programming? Is it possible this discovery was actually the work of a malicious hacker who made you believe it?"

"No."

Med killed the feed with her mind, stood up, and headed for the humans celebrating around the keg. When she got home that night, Jack was gone. But Threezed's mobile was still there, on the floor next to a wad of his clothing.

JULY 23, 2144

It took the dean's office two days to figure out that Med had released the findings from a major paper to the media without going through the proper public relations channels. The result was that her schedule for the morning had been cleared for a mandatory meeting with the administration.

When she arrived, the dean was having what appeared to be a jovial conversation with a vaguely familiar-looking man and two IPC reps in a conference room.

The man turned out to be Zaxy's founder, who radiated Vive-induced youth and introduced himself as Roger. He wore a burnished armor belt with an expensive tunic and jeans. Roger spoke with the exact accent that announcers used on ZoneFeed news shows. "Dr. Cohen, you've created an extraordinary therapy with Retcon—extraordinary." He emitted a practiced chuckle. "It's the kind of thing I'd buy if you hadn't released it under an open patent." Then he paused, composing his features into an expression that hovered between genuine concern and fabricated regret. "But I'm sure you can appreciate Zaxy's position here. Your paper suggests that it's a 'cure' for Zacuity. I'm happy to bring you into Zaxy and let you have a conversation under NDA with our Zacuity team about possible flaws in the drug. However, we are certain Zacuity is a completely safe substance if administered properly."

"I appreciate your position, Roger, but a reverse-engineered version of Zacuity has killed hundreds of people."

Roger shot a look at the dean. "The reports that this street drug is reverse-engineered Zacuity are completely unsubstantiated. Associations in the media between our product and illegal drugs—associations encouraged by your paper—have already caused us to lose a tremendous amount of money. Our attorneys tell me we could justifiably sue you and the university for libel."

"I have no control over what people say about Retcon on the net. But I have analyzed the drug myself. It is clearly a reverse-engineered version of Zacuity." Beneath the conference table, Med balled her hands into fists.

"Alright, now. Nobody is accusing you of sloppy research, Medea." The dean was in placating mode. "Retcon is a humanitarian project, and has already rescued many people from crippling addiction."

Roger took this to mean that the case was closed. "I completely agree. We just want to make sure you're not doing anything to encourage the rumors of a connection between Zacuity and those . . . tragic incidents."

Med started to speak, but the dean halted her with his hand. "Happy to oblige you on that, Roger. As academics and researchers, we consider it our job to correct pseudoscience when it crops up in the media."

"There is no doubt that Zacuity is addictive." Med couldn't keep an angry edge out of her voice.

Roger stopped addressing Med, and gave the dean a sympathetic look. "I love that you inspire such passion in your researchers. Passion is the engine of innovation." He'd gone into sound-bite territory because he knew he'd won. The university couldn't afford a legal battle with Zaxy. The upshot of the meeting was that Med would have to delete all references to Zaxy and Zacuity from the Retcon Project's documentation and public forums. The dean agreed to take down Med's paper on reverse engineering Zacuity and issue an official retraction unless it survived a rigorous peer review process at a prominent Seviert journal.

Roger and the IPC reps left with hearty handshakes. Med couldn't believe this was happening. "Zaxy owns a majority stake in Seviert."

"It's just politics, Medea," the dean assured her. "The main thing is that the Retcon Project can go forward."

Walking back to the Free Lab, Med scanned the feeds. There had been no more manic meltdowns since the Zacuity story broke, so maybe it didn't matter that Zaxy wasn't going down. Maybe she'd made enough of a difference. The public knew about Retcon, after all, and sales of prerelease Zacuity to corps were in the toilet. Somewhere on the Anchorage Radical Archive servers back home, there was a mirror of her reverse engineering paper that would never be removed.

She wondered if Jack and Krish knew something like this could happen when they told her to publish the paper. But she couldn't ask them. She would have to decide for herself.

DECEMBER 5, 2144

Catalyst's purple vines had gotten boring, so she was talking about growing tentacles from her scalp for a harvest costume party. David was half-listening while he wiped through *New Scientist,* its image-dotted pages flashing through the air over the projector near his elbow. They were her students now. Med's gaze swept over the lab, with its clots of researchers and piles of equipment. All of them her responsibility.

With Krish dead, the bioengineering department had a minicrisis. Free Lab was a perpetual funding machine, a darling among humanitarian donors and wealthy funders. Shutting it down was out of the question. But it was also enormous, a hodgepodge of different projects, and a pain in the ass to run. Plus, all the faculty and top research staff already had their own labs.

Although it was a slightly unorthodox choice, nobody argued when the department chair suggested they seriously consider the job application from recently hired researcher Medea Cohen. She was devoted to the lab's mission, and had already brought positive publicity to the university with her discovery of the addiction therapy Retcon. Nobody mentioned the little visit from Zaxy, and the paper Med had taken down. And so, late in the winter quarter, Med replaced Krish as the Free Lab's principal investigator.

Her plain blue foam desk was set up exactly the way she liked it. Tucked into the corner, it couldn't be seen through the transparent plastic doors to her office. Especially when she had three projectors drawing a wraparound monitor over her chair in a glowing half-sphere. Sitting there, she could network with the server while message alerts collected in the unused space over her head. To make her office comfortable for the students and researchers who constantly visited, she'd dragged in three soft chairs and a slightly crushed sofa, functional but a little battered from life in the Free Lab.

Krish's office still stood empty and dark. She was saving it for a new senior researcher, though she hadn't announced that job opening yet. It was another item on her extensive to-do stack.

Settling into her chair, Med waved her desktop into existence, its command line window momentarily forming a dark shell around her body. Then she reached out with both hands, initiated processes, and flooded her desk with every color that could represent data.

Four and a half hours later, sounds of talking broke through the doors as Threezed slid them apart and flopped into the deepest dent on her sofa.

"It's Friday, Med. Let's go dancing or something."

Med pinched off the projectors and seemed to emerge from a bubble of hovering text. This was the same thing Threezed said to her almost every night when he got off work. They both hated dancing.

"Let's watch a movie," she replied with a grin. "Something weird and old from your media history class."

Threezed had taken on a new identity: John Chen, who had been homeschooled and self-employed on a farm outside Saskatoon until his public employment record started two months ago with a cashier job at a thrift shop on Broadway. He'd shut down his SlaveBoy journal and was auditing some media studies classes at U of S while he figured out his next move. Every day, it became more obvious what that move would be.

JANUARY 16, 2145

Algae poaching reminded Jack of being a little girl on the canola farm during harvest. Every week she brought her sub out of the depths, gliding just beneath the surface of the ocean to the offshore algae farms sloshing between buoys connected by long, plastic sheets at the edge of the AU's south coast. The perimeter alarms here were not sophisticated. She never saw anyone—human or bot—patrolling these far edges of the farm.

Jack recalled the sun-fed green of Saskatchewan's growing

season as she plunged her hands into the spirulina that slid through her fingers and looked like fine, tangled hair on the drying mats. When she pulled the mats onto the bridge, positioning them under dehumidifiers, she wondered what it would be like to unspool her life back to her parents' farm. What if she had studied agriculture instead of genetic engineering?

Her days might have ended just like this, quietly harvesting the plants that would fuel her body and machines. That other person, Judith the farmer, would have felt the sun overhead and seen the crop flowing around her feet just the way Jack did. It pleased her to imagine that the safer, alternate version of her life had, at least for this slice of time, subsumed the real one. If you ignored the poaching, of course. And the Freeculture contacts she was making on the AU message boards.

When spring came around, she decided, the safer version of her life would relinquish its hold on her again.

23

AUTONOMY KEY

JULY 21, 2144

Lee restored Paladin's carapace and installed better drivers for the sensorium she carried in her fist, but he shrugged when she asked about a replacement brain. "Nobody expects those brains to last very long, Paladin. I know it sucks, but it's just true." When she didn't respond, he looked at her through the translucent projection displaying a readout from her arm. "You're just going to have to recognize people the way other bots do: analyze them by voice, microbiome—or smell." He paused to tap her hand proudly. Then he returned to his work, adding absently, "Some bots can even identify people's expressions by analyzing their posture and breathing."

"So I can recognize human facial expressions by analyzing other things about them?"

"It's sort of like creating a mnemonic." Lee grinned. "You know, using one thing to remember another one. Like, I always remember your name because it's my favorite character class in the game *Sorcerer's Alley.*"

Paladin did not think Lee's comparison was apt. But he would only be confused if she told him why.

After weeks with her simulated autonomy key, Paladin was used to the idea that memories could be modified with new metadata. But this was a more difficult task than she'd faced in Vancouver when she'd reanalyzed how she felt about Eliasz. Now, she was dealing with a database of facial expressions she could no longer read. There was no way to map them to moods except over time, by trial and error, as she figured out how human gestures and scents and voices correlated with emotional content. And no matter how good she got at it, there would always be one data channel missing when she looked at a person. People often communicated their feelings by deliberately making faces that didn't match their body language and voices. Especially when they were making jokes. Paladin spent the following days painstakingly translating facial expressions in her memory into other biometrics as she encountered them among humans.

Every time she encrypted her memories, she was reminded of the limits to her autonomy. Anyone on base with the proper access level could use the Federation's escrowed key to read the full contents of her mind.

During this time, Eliasz was in Johannesburg on a mission. When he returned, Paladin was immediately deployed on a surveillance job to ferret out a hidden server farm that was distributing pirated video in Tangiers. They managed to miss seeing each other at Camp Tunisia for two weeks.

Lee never mentioned Paladin's simulated autonomy key, and she didn't bring it up. She wanted to control her own programs for as long as she could. Even if she didn't truly possess her own memories, she could at least be certain that the ache she felt in Eliasz' absence was something she'd invented all by herself. It wasn't an implanted loyalty; it was a code loop she'd written, executing the same pang of loss over and over again. More than anything, her useless and irrational feelings for Eliasz were testimony to her continued autonomy.

AUGUST 4, 2144

Paladin knew immediately when Eliasz had returned to Camp Tunisia. The base network recognized his face—though not what the expression on it meant—and she could follow his progress on the station map, across one airfield and into a maze of small rooms reserved entirely for humans. He entered a room marked "HUMAN RESOURCES," and there his signal dropped.

Fifteen minutes later, Paladin's upcoming assignments were wiped from her queue. Her access to Camp Tunisia's map and local resources was decimated. The bot now had the same credentials as any visitor, which didn't go much beyond public net access and nonclassified information about the base. Alarmed, the bot tried to contact Fang. *I am Paladin. You are Fang. Let's use the secure session we agreed on.*

I cannot authenticate your identity. You may not be Paladin.

Before she could initiate a new secure session, Eliasz sent a message. It was a request to meet him in one of the faraday briefing rooms, many floors above the bot zone where Fang first told her about anthropomorphization. Bewildered and disturbed by the change in her credentials, she followed a cached version of the base map to the shielded room with walls speckled to look like granite. When Eliasz arrived, he sat next to Paladin on a wide, foam bench jutting from the fake rock. She waited for him to speak.

"I've been wanting to talk to you privately for a long time," he said simply. "I need to tell you what happened in Moose Jaw, because I know you don't have the security clearance to see my reports."

He faced her, and she recognized that the dark brown in his eyes was the same dark brown it had always been. She didn't need a human brain to know that.

"When I regained consciousness, my commanding officer

told me that the Federation IPC had found some remains in that tunnel. They assumed Jack died in the explosion after you got me out."

He paused and Paladin noticed his posture growing more rigid. Turning to face her, Eliasz took one of her hands in his own. Sampling his blood, she perceived an oxytocin spike that filled her with pleasure. She couldn't say what expression he wore, but she knew what he was feeling. "Zaxy wasn't exactly thrilled with what happened, but they still got their pirate. And the IPC gave me a huge bonus."

He did not say what they both knew: for some reason, Eliasz had chosen not to kill Jack, and the IPC had lost its quarry. Eliasz continued talking in a heated rush. "I want to get away from this business, Paladin. I thought maybe we could go away together for a while. Maybe to Mars. So I bought out your contract. I can't stand the idea of the woman I love not being autonomous."

She was overwhelmed with possible responses to his statement, but at least now the change to her credentials made sense.

Eliasz gripped her hand harder. She could taste his desire and anxiety. "Will you come with me?"

Before she'd gotten her autonomy key, Paladin couldn't prioritize her own needs over Eliasz' requests; she could queue them up a fraction of a second behind, but they were always behind. Now, she could put her own concerns first. And there was something more important than love that she needed to investigate. It would take less than a second to verify.

Using software she had installed in her own mind, the bot generated a new key to encrypt her memories. For the first time in her life, the process worked. Her memories were locked down, and the key that the Federation held in escrow would be useless. It would take centuries for even the most state-of-the-art machine to decrypt what she had seen and known for the months she'd been alive. At last, she knew what it felt like to own the totality of her experiences.

A profound silence settled around the edges of her mind, more powerful than a defensive perimeter in battle. Nobody could find out what she was thinking, unless she allowed it. The key to autonomy, she realized, was more than root access on the programs that shaped her desires. It was a sense of privacy.

Paladin was alone with her thoughts for several seconds. Then she vocalized. "I will go with you to Mars."

Eliasz reached out to touch the new surface of her carapace, healed of all its viral tumors and wounds. "I know it's not the same for you. A part of you is gone. But you are still the most amazing woman I have ever known." He stroked Paladin's abdomen over her brain cavity, now filled with shock-absorbing foam.

Paladin placed her hand over his. The electrical signals traversing Eliasz' skin felt far more irregular than the last time they had embraced. She took samples along a ten-centimeter swath of his bare arm, and realized his perimeter system was gone. So they had both lost parts of themselves.

But Eliasz would never fully understand what Paladin was missing. He thought she'd lost her true self, which was utterly confused in his mind with her gender. Paladin's research on the public net had led to massive text repositories about the history of transgender humans who had switched pronouns just the way she had. She was pretty sure that Eliasz anthropomorphized her as one of these humans, imagining she had been assigned the wrong pronoun at birth. Maybe he would never understand that his human categories—faggot, female, transgender—didn't apply to bots. Or maybe he did understand. After all, he still loved her, even though her brain was gone.

Because she could, Paladin kept her ideas about this to herself. They were the first private thoughts she'd ever had.

JANUARY 16, 2145

The space elevator platform was a uniform gray, supported by dramatic cement alloy pillars sunk deep into the floor of the equatorial Pacific. It served as the sole anchor for a massive black tether, assembled and maintained by billions of heavily engineered microorganisms, which rose up from the platform's center, threaded itself through the atmosphere, and continued on for thousands of kilometers into space. At its other end was a captured asteroid, acting as a counterweight and small whistle-stop town for people on their way to all the cities beyond Earth.

But Paladin could see little of that from the platform. Above them, the sky was a humid, depthless blue filled with organic compounds that Paladin could identify faster than the expression on Eliasz' face. She had just started to receive stray data packets from the elevator's two robot arms, their fists clenching and unclenching around the tether. Soon the transport gondola would be in visual range.

A crowd of passengers slowly gathered to watch the descent. All humans, but Paladin had gotten used to that by now. For five months, she'd lived with Eliasz in a human neighborhood in Budapest. There were enough autonomous bots in the city that nobody asked questions about their relationship, but occasionally she could perceive from their postures that it upset them. It wouldn't matter as much on Mars, where the labor shortage meant that all were welcome, especially a bot who could work outside the atmosphere domes.

She could see the arms on the tether now, attached to a five-story gondola whose diamond windows broke the light into its constituent wavelengths. Eliasz was watching, too.

Paladin stood behind him and put her hands on his shoulders, exposing the translucent polymers of her knitted muscles in the joints between the plating. Eliasz tilted his head back against her chest, his hair a soft tangle under her chin. The man's heart sped up as it always did when she pressed her body close to his; and the bot wrapped her wing shields completely around both of them, creating a private shelter with her armored embrace.

ACKNOWLEDGMENTS

A lot of people gave me good advice about the science, technology, geography, and economics of the world in this novel. For that, many thanks to Kent Berridge, Bethany Brookshire, David Calkins, Simone Davalos, Sean Gallagher, Joe Gratz, Norma Green, Margaret Horton, Terry Johnson, Terry Robinson, Daniel Rokhsar, Noah Smith, and Maia Szalavitz.

For early reads, editorial feedback, and writerly camaraderie, thanks to Anthony Ha, Liz Henry, Hank Hu, Keffy Kehrli, Claire Light, Na'amen Tilahun, and Jason Thompson.

For musical inspiration, thanks to The Arrogant Worms, Marshall Burns, Piper Burns, and Vernon Reid. For geographical inspiration, thanks to the Burns and Fletcher clans for making me feel at home.

For editorial brilliance and delightful ice cream, thanks to Liz Gorinsky. For always making my book dreams come true, thanks to the magical Laurie Fox.

For love, conversations, and goofiness, thanks to Charlie Jane Anders, Jesse Burns, and Chris Palmer, the best humans that a human could have.

extras

www.orbitbooks.net

about the author

Annalee Newitz is an American journalist, editor and author of both fiction and non-fiction. She is the recipient of a Knight Science Journalism Fellowship from MIT, and has written for the *New Yorker*, *Wired* and the *Washington Post*. She co-founded the science fiction website *io9* and served as editor-in-chief from 2008–15, and subsequently was an editor at *Gizmodo* and the technology site *Ars Technica*.

Find out more about Annalee Newitz and other Orbit authors by registering online for the free monthly newsletter at www.orbitbooks.net.

interview

Would you rather be a robot or a pirate?
Both, of course. There's no reason a pirate can't be a robot.

What sort of research did you do for *Autonomous* and what was the most interesting fact you discovered?
I interviewed a lot of scientists and experts, from neuroscientists and roboticists, to computer security experts and a former military officer who worked on a submarine. I think the most interesting thing I learned was from an economist who patiently explained to me how easy it would be to turn slavery into a cornerstone of the global economy, just by taking away a couple of key rights from ordinary people.

What was the editing process like – were there scenes or characters you cut to better tell the story?
I did a couple of very deep edits, mostly to make the characters more complex and likeable. In the first draft, pretty much every person in the book was a jerk and a killer. Obviously, I liked these characters and I wanted readers to sympathize with them, but that turned out to be the hardest thing to do. Even harder than inventing a way for robots to communicate with each other!

What can we do as individuals and as a society to resist the dystopic elements of the future seen in *Autonomous*?
Resist any kind of slavery or indentured servitude. Sometimes we call these things by other names, but you know they are there. Whenever there is slavery in any part of a society, it infects all parts of that society and we are all complicit.

What are you reading at the moment?
I'm reading three things: the second trade of the comic

Monstress by Marjorie Liu, *The Black Tides* of Heaven by JY Yang, and *The Archaeology of Sanitation in Roman Italy* by Ann Olga Koloski-Ostrow.

Who inspires you as a writer?
I'm really inspired by scientists, especially ones who go out into the field and gather new data—sometimes at great risk. I'm also inspired by political activists who in some ways do the same thing. Both groups often find themselves fighting to present new ideas that are challenging because they are true.

What scientific advancement is going to change life the most for us over the next ten years?
Autonomous cars.

And the next fifty years?
It's not really an advancement, but climate change is going to change the world dramatically. It was certainly caused by industrialization, and we'll have to use scientific innovation to cope with it.

As a journalist who's written several non-fiction books before, including *Scatter, Adapt and Remember: How Humans Will Survive a Mass Extinction*, how easy is it to switch between these modes of writing and do you do anything to help get into a different frame of mind before writing (music, etc.)?
I really love switching between the two modes, and I tend to do it naturally after writing one for a while. When I finished *Autonomous*, all I wanted to do was write factual articles about science for a while. But after a certain amount of time, fictional ideas build up again and I'm desperate to write them down.

What can you tell us about your next novel?
It's about time travel, and what it's like to meet your high school self.

CHAPTER

1

The Twice Lucky

The two would-be jade thieves sweated in the kitchen of the Twice Lucky restaurant. The windows were open in the dining room, and the onset of evening brought a breeze off the waterfront to cool the diners, but in the kitchen, there were only the two ceiling fans that had been spinning all day to little effect. Summer had barely begun and already the city of Janloon was like a spent lover—sticky and fragrant.

Bero and Sampa were sixteen years old, and after three weeks of planning, they had decided that tonight would change their lives. Bero wore a waiter's dark pants and a white shirt that clung uncomfortably to his back. His sallow face and chapped lips were stiff from holding in his thoughts. He carried a tray of dirty drink glasses over to the kitchen sink and set it down, then wiped his hands on a dish towel and leaned toward his coconspirator, who was rinsing dishes with the spray hose before stacking them in the drying racks.

"He's alone now." Bero kept his voice low.

Sampa glanced up. He was an Abukei teenager—copper-skinned with thick, wiry hair and slightly pudgy cheeks that gave him a faintly cherubic appearance. He blinked rapidly, then turned back to the sink. "I get off my shift in five minutes."

"We gotta do it now, keke," said Bero. "Hand it over."

Sampa dried a hand on the front of his shirt and pulled a small paper envelope from his pocket. He slipped it quickly into Bero's palm. Bero tucked his hand under his apron, picked up his empty tray, and walked out of the kitchen.

At the bar, he asked the bartender for rum with chili and lime on the rocks—Shon Judonrhu's preferred drink. Bero carried the drink away, then put down his tray and bent over an empty table by the wall, his back to the dining room floor. As he pretended to wipe down the table with his towel, he emptied the contents of the paper packet into the glass. They fizzed quickly and dissolved in the amber liquid.

He straightened and made his way over to the bar table in the corner. Shon Ju was still sitting by himself, his bulk squeezed onto a small chair. Earlier in the evening, Maik Kehn had been at the table as well, but to Bero's great relief, he'd left to rejoin his brother in a booth on the other side of the room. Bero set the glass down in front of Shon. "On the house, Shon-jen."

Shon took the drink, nodding sleepily without looking up. He was a regular at the Twice Lucky and drank heavily. The bald spot in the center of his head was pink under the dining room lights. Bero's eyes were drawn, irresistibly, farther down, to the three green studs in the man's left ear.

He walked away before he could be caught staring. It was ridiculous that such a corpulent, aging drunk was a Green Bone. True, Shon had only a little jade on him, but unimpressive as he was, sooner or later someone would take it, along with his life perhaps. *And why not me?* Bero thought. Why not, indeed. He might only be a dockworker's bastard who would never have a martial education at Wie Lon Temple School or Kaul Dushuron Academy, but at least he was

Kekonese all the way through. He had guts and nerve; he had what it took to be somebody. Jade made you somebody.

He passed the Maik brothers sitting together in a booth with a third young man. Bero slowed a little, just to get a closer look at them. Maik Kehn and Maik Tar—now *they* were real Green Bones. Sinewy men, their fingers heavy with jade rings, fighting talon knives with jade-inlaid hilts strapped to their waists. They were dressed well: dark, collared shirts and tailored tan jackets, shiny black shoes, billed hats. The Maiks were well-known members of the No Peak clan, which controlled most of the neighborhoods on this side of the city. One of them glanced in Bero's direction.

Bero turned away quickly, busying himself with clearing dishes. The last thing he wanted was for the Maik brothers to pay any attention to him tonight. He resisted the urge to reach down to check the small-caliber pistol tucked in the pocket of his pants and concealed by his apron. Patience. After tonight, he wouldn't be in this waiter's uniform anymore. He wouldn't have to serve anyone anymore.

Back in the kitchen, Sampa had finished his shift for the evening and was signing out. He looked questioningly at Bero, who nodded that the deed was done. Sampa's small, white upper teeth popped into view and crushed down on his lower lip. "You really think we can do this?" he whispered.

Bero brought his face near the other boy's. "Stay cut, keke," he hissed. "We're already doing it. No turning back. You've got to do your part!"

"I know, keke, I know. I will." Sampa gave him a hurt and sour look.

"Think of the money," Bero suggested, and gave him a shove. "Now get going."

Sampa cast a final nervous glance backward, then pushed out the kitchen door. Bero glared after him, wishing for the hundredth time that he didn't need such a doughy and insipid partner. But there was no getting around it—only a full-blooded Abukei native, immune to jade, could palm a gem and walk out of a crowded restaurant without giving himself away.

It had taken some convincing to bring Sampa on board. Like many in his tribe, the boy gambled on the river, spending his weekends diving for jade runoff that escaped the mines far upstream. It was dangerous—when glutted with rainfall, the torrent carried away more than a few unfortunate divers, and even if you were lucky and found jade (Sampa had bragged that he'd once found a piece the size of a fist), you might get caught. Spend time in jail if you were lucky, time in the hospital if you weren't.

It was a loser's game, Bero had insisted to him. Why fish for raw jade just to sell it to the black market middlemen who carved it up and smuggled it off island, paying you only a fraction of what they sold it for later? A couple of clever, daring fellows like them—they could do better. If you were going to gamble for jade, Bero said, then gamble big. Aftermarket gems, cut and set—that was worth real money.

Bero returned to the dining room and busied himself clearing and setting tables, glancing at the clock every few minutes. He could ditch Sampa later, after he'd gotten what he needed.

"Shon Ju says there's been trouble in the Armpit," said Maik Kehn, leaning in to speak discreetly under the blanket of background noise. "A bunch of kids shaking down businesses."

His younger brother, Maik Tar, reached across the table with his chopsticks to pluck at the plate of crispy squid balls. "What kind of kids are we talking about?"

"Low-level Fingers. Young toughs with no more than a piece or two of jade."

The third man at the table wore an uncharacteristically pensive frown. "Even the littlest Fingers are clan soldiers. They take orders from their Fists, and Fists from their Horn." The Armpit district had always been disputed territory, but directly threatening establishments affiliated with the No Peak clan was too bold to be the work of careless hoodlums. "It smells like someone's pissing on us."

The Maiks glanced at him, then at each other. "What's going on, Hilo-jen?" asked Kehn. "You seem out of sorts tonight."

"Do I?" Kaul Hiloshudon leaned against the wall in the booth and turned his glass of rapidly warming beer, idly wiping off the condensation. "Maybe it's the heat."

Kehn motioned to one of the waiters to refill their drinks. The pallid teenager kept his eyes down as he served them. He glanced up at Hilo for a second but didn't seem to recognize him; few people who hadn't met Kaul Hiloshudon in person expected him to look as young as he did. The Horn of the No Peak clan, second only in authority to his elder brother, often went initially unnoticed in public. Sometimes this galled Hilo; sometimes he found it useful.

"Another strange thing," said Kehn when the waiter had left. "No one's seen or heard from Three-Fingered Gee."

"How's it possible to lose track of Three-Fingered Gee?" Tar wondered. The black market jade carver was as recognizable for his girth as he was for his deformity.

"Maybe he got out of the business."

Tar snickered. "Only one way anyone gets out of the jade business."

A voice spoke up near Hilo's ear. "Kaul-jen, how are you this evening? Is everything to your satisfaction tonight?" Mr. Une had appeared beside their table and was smiling the anxious, solicitous smile he always reserved for them.

"It's all excellent, as usual," Hilo said, arranging his face into the relaxed, lopsided smile that was his more typical expression.

The owner of the Twice Lucky clasped his kitchen-scarred hands together, nodding and smiling his humble thanks. Mr. Une was a man in his sixties, bald and well-padded, and a third-generation restaurateur. His grandfather had founded the venerable old establishment, and his father had kept it running all through the wartime years, and afterward. Like his predecessors, Mr. Une was a loyal Lantern Man in the No Peak clan. Every time Hilo was in, he came around personally to pay his respects. "Please let me know if there is anything else I can have brought out to you," he insisted.

When the reassured Mr. Une had departed, Hilo grew serious again. "Ask around some more. Find out what happened to Gee."

"Why do we care about Gee?" Kehn asked, not in an impertinent way, just curious. "Good riddance to him. One less carver sneaking our jade out to weaklings and foreigners."

"It bothers me, is all." Hilo sat forward, helping himself to the last crispy squid ball. "Nothing good's coming, when the dogs start disappearing from the streets."

Bero's nerves were beginning to fray. Shon Ju had nearly drained his tainted drink. The drug was supposedly tasteless and odorless, but what if Shon, with the enhanced senses of a Green Bone, could detect it somehow? Or what if it didn't work as it should, and the man walked out, taking his jade out of Bero's grasp? What if Sampa lost his nerve after all? The spoon in Bero's hands trembled as he set it down on the table. *Stay cut, now. Be a man.*

A phonograph in the corner wheezed out a slow, romantic opera tune, barely audible through the unceasing chatter of people. Cigarette smoke and spicy food aromas hung languid over red tablecloths.

Shon Ju swayed hastily to his feet. He staggered toward the back of the restaurant and pushed through the door to the men's room.

Bero counted ten slow seconds in his head, then put the tray down and followed casually. As he slipped into the restroom, he slid his hand into his pocket and closed it around the grip of the tiny pistol. He shut and locked the door behind him and pressed against the far wall.

The sound of sustained retching issued from one of the stalls, and Bero nearly gagged on the nauseating odor of booze-soaked vomit. The toilet flushed, and the heaving noises ceased. There was a muffled thud, like the sound of something heavy hitting the tile floor, then a sickly silence. Bero took several steps forward. His heartbeat thundered in his ears. He raised the small gun to chest level.

The stall door was open. Shon Ju's large bulk was slumped inside, limbs sprawled. His chest rose and fell in soft, snuffling snores. A thin line of drool ran from the corner of his mouth.

A pair of grimy canvas shoes moved in the far stall, and Sampa stuck his head around the corner where he'd been lying in wait. His eyes grew round at the sight of the pistol, but he sidled over next to Bero and the two of them stared down at the unconscious man.

Holy shit, it worked.

"What're you waiting for?" Bero waved the small gun in Shon's direction. "Go on! Get it!"

Sampa squeezed hesitantly through the half-open stall door. Shon Ju's head was leaning to the left, his jade-studded ear trapped against the wall of the toilet cubicle. With the screwed-up face of someone about to touch a live power line, the boy placed his hands on either side of Shon's head. He paused; the man didn't stir. Sampa turned the slack-jowled face to the other side. With shaking fingers, he pinched the first jade earring and worked the backing free.

"Here, use this." Bero handed him the empty paper packet. Sampa dropped the jade stud into it and got to work removing the second earring. Bero's eyes danced between the jade, Shon Ju, the gun, Sampa, again the jade. He took a step forward and held the barrel of the pistol a few inches from the prone man's temple. It looked distressingly compact and ineffective—a commoner's weapon. No matter. Shon Ju wasn't going to be able to Steel or Deflect anything in his state. Sampa would palm the jade and walk out the back door with no one the wiser. Bero would finish his shift and meet up with Sampa afterward. No one would disturb old Shon Ju for hours; it wasn't the first time the man had passed out drunk in a restroom.

"Hurry it up," Bero said.

Sampa had two of the jade stones off and was working on the third. His fingers dug around in the fold of the man's fleshy ear. "I can't get this one off."

"Pull it off, just pull it off!"

Sampa gave the last stubborn earring a swift yank. It tore free from the flesh that had grown around it. Shon Ju jerked. His eyes flew open.

"Oh shit," said Sampa.

With an almighty howl, Shon's arms shot out, flailing around his head and knocking Bero's arm upward just as Bero pulled the trigger of the gun. The shot deafened all of them but went wide, punching into the plaster ceiling.

Sampa scrambled to get away, nearly tripping over Shon as he lunged for the stall door. Shon flung his arms around one of the boy's legs. His bloodshot eyes rolled in disorientation and rage. Sampa tumbled to the ground and put his hands out to break his fall; the paper packet jumped from his grasp and skittered across the tile floor between Bero's legs.

"Thieves!" Shon Ju's snarling mouth formed the word, but Bero did not hear it. His head was ringing from the gunshot, and everything was happening as if in a soundless chamber. He stared as the red-faced Green Bone dragged at the terrified Abukei boy like a grasping demon from a pit.

Bero bent, snatched the crumpled paper envelope, and ran for the door.

He forgot he'd locked it. For a second he pushed and pulled in stupid panic, before turning the bolt and pounding out of the room. The diners had heard the gunshot, and dozens of shocked faces were turned toward him. Bero had just enough presence of mind left to jam the gun into his pocket and point a finger back toward the restroom. "There's a jade thief in there!" he shouted.

Then he ran across the dining room floor, weaving between tables, the two small stones digging through the paper and against the palm of his tightly fisted left hand. People leapt away from him. Faces blurred past. Bero knocked over a chair, fell, picked himself up again, and kept running.

His face was burning. A sudden surge of heat and energy unlike anything he had ever felt before ripped through him like an electric current. He reached the wide, curving staircase that led to the second floor, where diners were getting up and peering over the balcony railing to see what the commotion was. Bero rushed up the stairs, clearing the entire expanse in a few bounds, his feet barely touching the floor. A gasp ran through the crowd. Bero's surprise burst into ecstasy. He threw his head back to laugh. This must be Lightness.

A film had been lifted from his eyes and ears. The scrape of chair legs, the crash of a plate, the taste of the air on his tongue—everything was razor sharp. Someone reached out to grab him, but he was so slow, and Bero was so fast. He swerved with ease and leapt off the surface of a table, scattering dishes and eliciting screams. There was a sliding screen door ahead of him that led out onto the patio overlooking the harbor. Without thinking, without pausing, he crashed through the barrier like a charging bull. The wooden latticework shattered, and Bero stumbled through the body-sized hole he had made with a mad shout of exultation. He felt no pain at all, only a wild, fierce invincibility.

This was the power of jade.

The night air blasted him, tingling against his skin. Below, the expanse of gleaming water beckoned irresistibly. Waves of delicious heat seemed to be coursing through Bero's veins. The ocean looked so cool, so refreshing. It would feel so good. He flew toward the patio railing.

Hands clamped onto his shoulders and pulled him to a hard stop. Bero was yanked back as if he'd reached the end of a chain and spun around to face Maik Tar.